ANCESTORS

Robyn Davidson

SIMON AND SCHUSTER
NEW YORK • LONDON • TORONTO • SYDNEY • TOKYO

For Margaret, and in memory
f Poppy, mother and Gill—
my family

Simon and Schuster
Simon & Schuster Building
Rockefeller Center
1230 Avenue of the Americas
New York, New York 10020

Manufactured in the United States of America

1   3   5   7   9   10   8   6   4   2

Library of Congress Cataloging in Publication Data

Davidson, Robyn.
Ancestors / Robyn Davidson.
p.   cm.
I. Title.
PR9619.3.D275A54   1989
823—dc20   89-21660
                                                    CIP

ISBN 0-671-68062-5

I am indebted to the many people who offered advice, spare bedrooms and friendship during the writing of *Ancestors*. My special thanks to: Doris, Julie and Duncan in England. Rick, Liza, Gini, Bob P., Lucia, Bob H. and Vicky in the States. Lindy, Jenny, Steve and Ranald in Australia. And to Frances Coady, my editor, who encouraged me so greatly.

"Journeys to relive your past?" was the Khan's question at this point, a question which could also have been formulated "Journeys to recover your future?"

Prologue

The Sunseeker creeps up from the south into the dead air and barbarous light of the tropics. On its way north it is a sluggish capillary carrying sustenance to vestigial organs but on its return it is the only reliable route to Elsewhere. It clatters along eight hundred miles of coastline; through banana plantations and ghost towns; beside gangmen leaning on shovels; past figures framed in yellow windows, stripped to their singlets, sitting in chairs, waiting out the long, hot nights alone, as the curlew hoot of the train fades into distances. At deserted sidings it stops, shunts, then slowly starts again until, with a wheeze of Sisyphean fatigue, it arrives at Binjigul, the end of the Southern Cross line.

This summer afternoon, it is only four hours late. Three carriage doors ker-lunk open, releasing a trickle of passengers. A few minutes later, a woman steps down and stands alone, clutching a kid-leather handbag tightly to her belly. There is something discordant about her which attracts the curiosity of her fellow travelers as they struggle past her with suitcases and waiting relatives. She appears not to care that her expensive silk dress is twisted and marked with grease, and her hair, so fashionably cut, sticks up at the back like crows' feathers. While their skin is baked a terracotta brown, hers is as white as a cave-dweller's. Strangest of all are her eyes—the same bright blue as the morning glories cascading down the walls of the station house—with their startling color emphasized by thick black brows and lashes. She stares vacantly ahead, then focuses her gaze with sudden intensity on a clock without hands in the waiting room; the signal box; the broken teeth of a picket fence, as if each of these objects elicits a tiny shock within her.

Prologue

She stands quite still observing the last of the passengers disperse. Beyond her, in the waiting room, a boat salesman runs tap water across his wrists and smiles in her direction. She fumbles in her bag for sunglasses, scowls and turns quickly away. He stares at her back for a moment, taps his temple with his forefinger, then ambles along the platform, past stacked cases of southbound fruit, to a station wagon which the woman watches until it melts into the wall of shimmer surrounding the town. Then she too sets off down the platform, her sandals making soft, sucking sounds on the viscid tar.

She hurries past a jerry-built progress of brick veneer concealing buildings mutilated by heat and forgetfulness. Layers of silvery light rise from corrugated iron roofs to congeal with air already clotted by the stench of frangipani and fermenting pineapples. The streets are deserted, but here and there, under awnings, or behind doorways protected by plastic fly strips, a few somnambulant figures and panting dogs observe her without interest. A child peeps from behind a rustic sign, erected by a Shire Council flush with last season's tourist dollars. It reads:

"Binjigul has long been famous for its Yeti or Abominable Snowman. Many sightings have been recorded, but as yet no photographs have been taken. He was last seen in 1978 by a respected Botanist who described the creature as being covered in long matted hair, and swinging through the rainforest on vines . . ."

The woman glances neither to right nor to left as she continues along the road, which thins into a narrow strip of bitumen winding through fields of sugar cane. In the distance, flimsy showers slant through patches of sunshine, turning to steam before touching the ground.

Her clothes are glued to her body and her face is the color of a plum by the time she turns on to a gravel track shaded by a canopy of trees. She flings herself onto the leaf mold, throws her sandals into the forest and fans herself with her skirt, looking from the road like an enormous butterfly. She rests for half an hour, but at the sound of a vehicle quickly hides herself behind bushes crouching there until the car is swallowed by dust. She walks on furtively. Where an unused track penetrates the wall of foliage she takes one last look up and down the road before darting through the opening.

The luminous green twilight of the jungle does nothing to soothe her agitation. She is easily startled by odd noises punctuating the

10

racket, and glances behind her from time to time, as if she thinks she is being followed. For long moments she remains motionless, frowning with concentration, her head craned forward as if to hear better. Then, shuddering off her hesitation, she continues to scramble up the escarpment, beating back the asphyxiating growth with a stick. At last, exhausted and gasping, she breaks through the thickets to a clearing.

The house is almost invisible beneath its burden of growth. Parasite figs strangle the stumps; bougainvillea interweaves with cedar fretwork; ferns fringe veranda rails; mosses cling to steps and banisters; buttresses of trees support sagging timbers and orchids burst out of the guttering. So complete is the symbiosis that it is difficult to tell whether house has sprouted jungle, or jungle has created house.

Standing in a trance at the unhinged gate, the woman calls, "Is anyone . . ." But there is no one watching as she carefully climbs the stairs, no one listening to the wood creak beneath her feet or waiting for her in the deep, vegetable gloom of the interior.

She shrinks back from the darkness of a hallway, her hands pressed to her lips, then, summoning her courage, tiptoes down the passage where a stranger would need a light. At the entrance to a high-ceilinged room, she slowly puts down her handbag. Through window slats, light comes pouring across the floor in strips which fracture around furniture, boxes and bundles of yellowing newspapers stacked in six-foot piles. Trailing her fingers over the fuzz of lichen covering the walls, she wades into the still silence of the room, skinks and geckos scattering before her like schools of little fish. From cupboards and boxes she begins gathering photographs, clippings, and letters, brittle with age. Phosphorescent fungi cling to some bound documents which crumble to dust in her hand. She tries to wind a wall clock, but it is rusted solid. In the bottom of a drawer lies a musical box which turns out a tender melody cracked with missing notes.

Singing softly, she climbs a narrow, almost vertical staircase. "You are my sunshine, my only sunshine, you keep me happy, when skies are gray." She reaches the landing, pushes against a heavy door and goes hurtling into a sunlit attic. Against the far wall stands a chest containing treasures of satin, appliquéd with silk roses; crêpe de chine, sparkling with crystals; lace threaded with silver, all folded in fine tissue and emanating a perfume of naphthalene and long ago. She throws off her own dress and, holding each of the ballgowns against

11

her body, swirls around the attic creating tornadoes of soft dust. She stops abruptly, her attention caught by the open window. Covering herself in full-length blue satin, she hastily closes the shutters against tendrils bullying their way under the sash, then picks up her discarded clothes and rushes down the stairs to the bathroom.

The spider's web which covers the mirror on the wall cabinet receives a vicious swipe and the face confronting her there mutters "Ugly, ugly!" Pale as a ghost, she runs through the rooms, feverishly hunting in cupboards and drawers until she finds a pair of large rusted scissors. Her reflection, distorted by the mottled glass, stares sternly back as she hacks at her hair until only black stubble remains. Using the butt of the scissors she smashes the mirror—the image of her now weeping face splitting and falling into her cupped hand. She collects the slivers in her cast-off dress, picks up her handbag from the hall and carries the bundle outside. Saving a lighter from her bag and a thin wad of money she then burns the bundle and buries the remains.

The ritual seems to calm her. She kneels beside the mound as if praying at a grave, then walks resolutely back into the house and begins to search for the few things she will need—a cooking pot, a kettle, some food preserved in glass jars, two kerosene lamps, crockery, and matches which she lays out on the long kitchen table to dry.

When she flings open the shutters, the largest room is drowned in light and invaded by bird song. She hums to herself as she sweeps dust from the floor, disposes of marsupial mice who have made their home in the stuffing of a chaise-longue, shakes out old quilts and makes a nest for herself on the floor. Having completed her chores, she takes a photograph of a child from the shelf, wanders aimlessly onto the veranda, and props her back against a post.

On this side of the house, the jungle has been kept at bay. A pattern of lost garden shows through the grass, like the skeleton of a half-decomposed beast. Fruit trees defy encroaching lantana. Nasturtiums and pumpkin vines clamber over mattresses of kikuyu, and clumps of Monstera deliciosa, betraying their domestic origins, have joined forces with the wild things.

She waits there for the sun to go down, for the breeze to bring her the sharp smell of the sea. The forest, darkening into dusk, folds down into ocean. A tree snake with eyes like water, slides along the railings and into a tangle of leaves. Hundreds of black fruit bats fly across a mango-colored sky, some circling above the garden, red light rimming *their wings, then falling, like burning ash, into the custard apple trees. Again, she knits her brows and leans out to face the rustling wall of vegetation. Her hand lifts to her throat. She hesitates, then runs to the steps, shouting, "I know you're there, damn you. Come out." But her voice is swallowed up by the evening roar of crickets and frogs. The stifling tropical night falls quickly on the house. She hugs her body as if chilled and hurries back into the darkness which fills the room.*

I see now that I am impatient with her, that earlier self. I want to reach out, tap her on the shoulder, say, "Hey, you, old misery guts, it's me, your guardian angel." But God's most pernicious law, the law of entropy, which condemns us to proceed through life in one direction while understanding it only in the opposite direction, forbids me.

The truth is I am haunted by her. I want to shout across the barrier, "Listen, you with the broken wings and the belly full of pain, out of every ending sprouts an infinity of beginnings. Have faith in me." But faith in the future is powerless against her visions of her past.

In the first, she is lost in a labyrinth of Manhattan streets. It is night, and snow suffocates the world.

In the second, she stands at the entrance to a darkened apartment. Through a far-off doorway, a wedge of light falls across a parquet floor. Something inimical to her lies behind that door. She has crossed the planet in order to escape it. She has fled all the way back to the beginning because there is nowhere left for her to go.

Yet still the visions suck her consciousness to them with the gravitational force of collapsing stars. All I can do is watch her rip and savage herself like a dog, and try to be patient.

1

Lucky Lucy

My name is Lucy Elizabeth Huntington McTavish. I entered this world seven years before my parents escaped it. My mother left via the dam in our horse paddock; my father's exit ticket was grief. One month separated the accident from the heart attack.

I have since been told that these parental departures ought to form the central tragedy of my life but they caused me little immediate pain that I can remember. I cried, of course, that was expected, but beneath the tears lurked a secret and guilty relief. If I thought of my parents at all after this initial display of emotion, they were two distant strangers who rapidly merged into the shadows of the past. The doors to my early childhood are so effectively locked that only two visions emerge from those shadows.

The first: My father is standing before me. His clothes are wet, and his hair is white. He is shaking and blubbering and trying to comfort me. Filled with revulsion, and appalled at my fraudulence, I turn away from him and fly, weeping, into the arms and large breasts of a woman I do not know.

The second: I am standing in a dimly lit kitchen. There is a dry, tickling smell of dust mingled with an ominous smell of burning scones. The kitchen opens onto a porch. I am very small, and I am watching the silhouette of my naked mother, turned away from me on the porch, playing the second movement of Brahms's Violin Concerto in D Major. She bends and curves her body, sawing away on the violin, while crickets and cicadas provide her orchestra. Beyond the porch, a plain of yellowy grass stretches away to infinity. My mother's thin, sagging body is gleaming with sweat. She is oblivious to my calling her. I pee on the linoleum floor.

My amnesia is selective. It retains emotions but discards events. Before their deaths, I felt myself to be a remarkable but undiscovered person. There are photographs indicating that my mother kept my crow-black hair cut short and sleek; my pointed ears hidden by waves; my gangling body swamped by cheap cotton dresses of the most disagreeable kind. In one of the pictures, a bow catches in a clump of hair and hangs, ridiculous, over my scowling face.

I had one feature that no amount of artistry could camouflage—my eyebrow. Like a bird in flight, drawn in thick black crayon by a six year old, its double curve added emphasis to my wraparound, Reckett's-blue eyes, and lent my face a queer intensity which defeated adults and caused dogs to growl when I stared at them. It was the only thing bequeathed me by my father for which I was profoundly grateful.

With the help of the social mileage which came from being an orphan, I felt I could at last face life and demand something of it. I was out of the ordinary. I could deflect punishment from myself by breaking into tears at the appropriate instant and watching my attacker fold like pastry. But best of all I was free. Chance had popped me out of the parental cocoon before my time. I rustled my fragile new wings and felt my spirit lift. There was no one to tell me what to do, no one to worry about my eyebrow and no one to love or be loved by. Lucky Lucy.

I cannot remember the sequence of events that led me to my Great Aunt Laura. That year, which should have lodged in my memory like a crystal in a rock, was shattered by the sheer size of events. Whenever I try to put the pieces together now, I find too many have been lost. I know that, at first, my maternal grandparents claimed me but when I broke Grandma's Victorian bone-china jaw with my cricket bat, they let me go. I remember listening in fascination to the wheezy laugh of a very old man with an enormous nose who let me stroke the gray tuft that grew off the tip and tried to cuddle me while I struggled and writhed. I recall fragments of a long train journey, which ended in sweltering heat, and the smell of my great aunt who sat beside me, cool, silent and still as a stone—a thin, papery odor of lavender and hidden money.

My arrival at Binjigul homestead confirmed my suspicion that she was a witch. Even Mrs. Rawlinson, who owned the village store, cowered before her. I entered the dingy shop in the wake of my great aunt's black crêpe dress. Mrs. Rawlinson, who had been drowsily fanning herself behind the counter, leapt to her feet, her head bobbing up and down like a pigeon. I stood behind Laura and peered into the gloom at sacks and cans, ropes and harnesses. Sticky brown paper, covered in decaying or dying flies, hung in helixes from the ceiling. A dirty kerosene fridge sat behind the counter, along which jars of penny lollies competed for space with boxes of screws, pieces of leather and out of date *Woman's Weekly* magazines. My aunt stood straight as a crowbar at the center of the room, her arm stretched rigid as she pointed to sacks of flour, rice and wheat.

"Highway robbery," she grumbled, as if she'd bitten into a green persimmon, and counted out pennies from a leather purse, shiny and soft from years of stingy fingering.

"It's the fright, Miss McTavish," apologized Mrs. Rawlinson, her head pecking away at invisible grain.

"Bilge, and the word is freight, frrrrrreight," said my aunt, glaring at the woman who withered with shame but did not alter the price.

"How about an iceblock for the child, poor little thing." With this stroke of inspiration, Mrs. Rawlinson turned pleading eyes at me, then scuttled toward the fridge.

"Absolutely *not*," snapped my aunt and rose to her full height. "Rots the teeth."

"Only a small gift," cooed Mrs. Rawlinson, her head ducking so fast now she could barely focus on her persecutor.

"Oh," said my aunt, faltering. Her face stretched into a tight humorless grin. "Well . . . I suppose it won't hurt just once . . . very kind of you." She watched hungrily as I sucked a two-square-inch cube of frozen raspberry cordial wrapped in a piece of greaseproof paper.

Three sets of eyes shifted and met again before my aunt hoisted the sacks onto her shoulder with a grunt, and strode outside. I could feel the shop settle back into its torpor, relieving itself of her unbearable vitality with a sigh.

Later, in the car, she said, "Stupid, you understand, inbred. And they reproduce like rrrabbits." She thumped the steering wheel with her claw, then suddenly leaned over and snatched my iceblock. She looked at me sideways, while her mouth worked away, then, somewhat reluctantly, handed it back.

"All the men on this side of the family are milksops like your father. And all the women are formidable. I take it that you are not going to turn out a milksop?"

Alas, my nose could not manage her patrician sneer, but I lifted my eyebrow, jutted my chin and fixed my eyes on some distant point. "Absolutely *not*," I retorted, whereupon she broke into a cackle, the lines on her face crinkling up and out to reveal a hidden habit of laughter. We bumped our way over dirt tracks and tunneled through warrens of green, until we reached her lair.

The house, once white, was a flaking gray, with roof and shutters of green. Perched high on capped wooden stilts it sprouted alamanda, quisqualis, bougainvillea and trumpet vine. On the southern side, two rainwater tanks were being devoured by beanstalks; on the northern side a tidal wave of jungle was poised ready to engulf the entire building.

Laura parked the car under a slab of corrugated iron and took the sacks and the suitcase, leaving me with my musical box, doll and cricket bat. These we hoisted up fifteen rickety steps, through a creaky gate, across a veranda and deposited next to two gum boots standing beside an open, brass-studded door. At one end of the veranda, a Brazilian cherry tree, shiny as holly and dotted with bright red fruit, spat out the largest, most battered black cat I had ever seen, its bell jingling as it landed.

"Steeeenie, Steenie, Steeeenie," sang my aunt. I dropped my musical box, tucked my doll under my arm, clutched my bat like a weapon with both hands and swapped stares with the monster. It gave me an arrogant appraisal, snaked itself around Laura's legs, turned, shuddered its tail contemptuously at me, and stalked back to its tree.

"Steenie, you frightful old bastard, don't be such a snob," cried Laura, but it was obvious that she approved of his behavior. Later, while she sat in her squatter's chair, with Steenie rattling away in her lap, she described how she had cut out his testicles herself, using chloroform and scalpel.

"Poor old bloke," she crooned, "didn't forgive me for weeks, did you?" I did not like to ask what testicles were, but it was easy to imagine Laura, her tongue poked out in concentration and her knife glinting in the candlelight, hunched over the kitchen table, performing unspeakable acts.

The doors were never shut unless there was a cyclone. We walked straight into the dim hallway, and she proceeded to guide me through rooms in which lingered generations of whispers and lifetimes of sorrows.

"This?" she said, as doll and I sat demurely on an oddly shaped seat of studded leather. "This, my dear, is a cockfighting chair brought over from Scotland by your great great grand uncle, and you sit on it like this." She ousted me, then demonstrated by sitting on the chair backwards, one arm leaning on the curved wood, the other flailing at the air as she cheered an imaginary battle.

"Or was it great great great? I'll have to look up the tree."

I followed her vacant gaze upward. "Tree?" I asked.

"Family tree."

I decided not to press the point. The image of a Huntington McTavish oak somewhere in Scotland, full of goblins and mysteries, remained with me years after I found out what she meant. I nodded sagely, and we continued our stock-taking of cut crystal, silver, mahogany, cedar, diaries, Persian carpets, letters from Byron, letters to Shelley, cabinets full of seventeenth-century porcelain, four-poster beds, inlaid desks with hidden drawers, wardrobes with unreachable shelves, paintings of ancestors gloomy in gilt frames and, most alluring of all, locked boxes of secrets.

All these objects were enchanted and Laura, weaving stories around them like spells, could bring to life the lost worlds trapped inside them. So advanced were her occult skills that sometimes it seemed as though the objects had been conjured into being by her words, like the time Great Aunt Laura's father's cousin, that is, my great grandfather's daughter (or is it great great), performed a séance in the living room and a shower of pebbles fell from the ceiling.

"And here's one of them," whispered Laura, showing the whites of her eyes in a startling manner and producing a piece of polished agate from the folds of her skirt. "Ghosts," she added, unnecessarily. "Our family has always had a remarkable facility for contacting the spirit world."

Aware that I was perhaps too impressed by this story, she now changed the mood by seizing a whip and regaling me with the tale of my grandfather's single-handed defeat of the rabble during the great maritime strike of 1890. "What a man, what a time," she cried, slashing dangerously at the air above my ducking head.

"The whole of the labor organization in Sydney went on strike. The country was a frightful shambles. Louts and hooligans running through the streets throwing stones. Three thousand special constables were sworn in, plus mounted infantry and troopers from country areas. The wool had arrived by rail, but who was brave enough to drive through that mass of ruffians? Ah, but your grandfather mustered together all the prominent citizens and shouted to them, 'Come brave men, respond to your country's call.' So orf they went, driving the wool down Pitt Street to the wharves, your grandfather in his white kid gloves, shielding the drivers with nothing but his whip. The rabble went mad with rage, so your grandfather, being a magistrate, read the riot act. Immediately a great yell went up; the mounted troopers drew their swords and charged the crowd. Hundreds tried to escape, but were run down until they lay in struggling heaps in the gutter. Some sought shelter on a floating jetty, but your grandfather jumped his horse onto it, and they all dived into the shark-infested water."

I liked that story. It seemed to fit with the family crest on which a woman, who looked a little like me, carried a sword in one hand and a severed head in the other.

In the years that followed, Laura's tales of the ancestors instilled in me a sense that their distinctions had somehow percolated into us and that our connection with these legendary heroes gave us a natural and indestructible superiority to the "rabble." Sadly, the ancestors were far less generous with their material legacies. Family fortunes had been squandered, estates chopped up and dispersed among members of the clan and Huntington McTavish bank balances remained permanently in the red.

So intense was Laura's passion for hoarding, and so formidable her personality, that she had bullied various members of the family into sending her their heirlooms, "For safe keeping. To be stored in Binjigul homestead like a museum." She harangued and harassed the relatives, inflicting filthy letters, threats and, when really pressed, wheedlings so grossly out of character that few could refuse her. Gathering these treasures about her like a ferocious bower bird, she became not only custodian of our ancestors' sacred objects, but also the repository and interpreter of the stories contained in them. I see now that what she had hoped for in me was an heir to her distillations of the past, but I was to prove unfit for the role. If I had trouble remembering my own mother and father, how on earth could I be expected to remember this insect swarm of progenitors?

My fevered mind was already rebelling: ". . . commissary in chief of the Danish Army in 1798 and his son William married his cousin . . . daughter married a count . . . the second brother governor of the Danish possessions in the East Indies . . . first came to Australia five generations ago . . . pioneers . . ." as she buried me under a landslide of generations.

During my time with Laura I would often be assailed by a vision of the pink map of Australia, on which she sat, like a tiny light, a firefly, on the northeast corner, throwing net after net of Huntingtons, McTavishes, Fortesques, McArthur-Sunderwells and God knows who else across the country, until they formed a dense and impenetrable web clinging thinly to the soil, distorting the shape beneath. When I realized that this web began with my first relations, Adam and Eve, and that it would ramify and interconnect forever so that I could not escape being related to everyone in the world, an unbearable sensation of being both infinitely large and infinitely insignificant would seize me and I would have to run and run, oblivious to leeches and stinging gympie trees, until the vision and the panic had been burned away.

The burden of history was to have other strange effects on me, but they would not become manifest until puberty.

"You, young Lucy, have aristocratic blood in your veins. Do not forget this," said Laura, as we climbed over boxes of junk, wound through a labyrinth of hallways, around corners and past attic stairs to reach, at last, my own room. It contained a dressing table, a wardrobe, a stack of newspapers (Laura was incapable of discarding anything), and one enormous naked mattress. The cream weatherboard walls were pocked with worm holes. She took a gray army blanket and a damp crumpled sheet from the cupboard and made up a haphazard bed.

And then she did something so astounding that I could only gawp like a hauled-in mullet. She tugged off the black crêpe dress to reveal long hairy shanks, salmon-pink outsize satin bloomers, and then, flip, flap, two old breasts like dessicated paw-paws. "Ah," she sighed, "that's better." Flinging open the french windows she marched away along the veranda. I was still the color of a Brazilian cherry when she returned, dressed in her everyday clothes—men's trousers held up with rope, a sheathed knife on her hip, boots, a collarless man's shirt and a floppy felt hat.

"Come along child, don't stand there like a gorilla, it's time to see the garden of delights."

Everything grew there. Peanuts, strawberries, cabbages, loquats, guavas, custard apples, bananas, paw-paws, climber beans thriving on the tall tank-stand, mandarins, mangoes and macadamia nuts. There were even two coffee trees, heavy with beans, which she insisted on roasting each year, even though mangrove mud tasted better.

All afternoon my induction continued. "Not like that, like this. Pick this length of bean, not that. You pull out kikuyu thus." How clumsily, yet willingly, I plunged into my new role of witch's assistant, and how addicted I soon became to the fragrance of soil, smoke, gardenias and compost. I was beginning to understand that Great Aunt Laura had no wish to clip my pretty wings or stifle this new, intoxicating freedom and I was grateful to whatever force had set me down safely into this exotic life with a sorceress as guardian.

"You see," said Laura, as she placed her right boot on the spade and pushed, "your ancestors were heroes. They took this land and they gave it a . . . hhmph . . . shape." She heaved up the wet clod and turned it, revealing earthworms like wiggling fingers. I looked up to where the peak of Mount Misery disappeared into clouds and imagined a giant ancestor slapping bits onto the mountain as if he were building sandcastles. Was the razorback ridge, with the two valleys sloping either side, where he had put his bottom?

"Wherever they traveled," continued Laura, "they created prosperity out of nothing, culture out of nature." She shoved in the spade. "Values," she said, then, "progress," and finally, "civilization." With each word, she thrust in the shovel as if hunting for its meaning. "They turned this country into a great inheritance, and you, young Lucy, must make yourself worthy of it." I pulled at the kikuyu with renewed vigor. "Your great grandfather took up land here when everyone said it was impossible." She stood leaning on the spade, wiping sweat from her eyebrows then, placing a thumb on one nostril, blew a dollop of snot out of the other.

"Phlegm," she announced haughtily, when she noted the look of profound disgust on my face, "is good fertilizer and don't be so prissy." She bent down to me, looking ferocious. "There were hostile blacks you know, good Lord yes . . . cannibals."

22

"Did the cannibals eat anyone?" I asked, shifting my glance to the darkness of the forest.

"No," crowed Laura, "he shot them all." She wheeled toward the forest using the shovel as a make-believe gun, and blasted phantom bullets into the leaves.

"Good Lord," I said.

"Precisely," said Laura. "Then when he'd built the house, he brought his beautiful wife Charlotte up from the south. She was frightfully well-bred of course, she'd never even seen the bush. A city woman like that mother of yours, but she had two children, and turned Binjigul into a paradise, and did she ever complain?" Laura glared at me meaningfully. "Absolutely *not*. No self-pity. No weakness. No wallowing in misery."

I left an appropriately polite pause before asking, "Why did they call it Mount Misery, then?" Laura paused, sniffed delicately, and feigned deafness.

We moved over to the mandarin tree. She handed me a fruit and when I bit into it, a fine spray of citric acid stung my nostrils and burned my lips before the sweet juice cooled them. Brown scale from the skin stayed on my sticky fingers. We plucked stink beetles from the leaves and ground them into the grass beneath. Their smell mingled with the tang of the tree.

"Most of the rest of the family took up land further west. Drove cattle thousands of miles through dust and fata morganas." Laura became expansive now, extending her arms to indicate the vastnesses in which they traveled. "And they met up with the other pioneers who had come from the west. Cross-fertilizing you might say, to produce the great landed families of Australia." I could see it all—a wide, shimmering, indefinite land, a dreamscape, with phantom creatures floating in it, elongated to giant size by the concave mirrors of heat mirage.

Through the analogy of gardening, Laura explained the importance of strong genes. There were sturdy, aristocratic plants, nature's superior stock, and there were the inferior weedy types, whose influence could be guarded against by careful cross-pollination and grafting. Forever after, when she accused me of being weedy, and dosed me with worm powder, I knew it was not the parasites she was eradicating but some more malign, congenital substance. Once after a dose, I took some toilet paper and a china bowl under the house to check my

23

own stools. I held my nose and peered closely but could see nothing unusual. Unluckily for me, Laura found the bowl. In the circumstances, it seemed easier to be accused of backsliding, than to have to explain that I was seeking my inheritance in shit.

In the peanut patch she muttered crossly as she pulled up rotting shells. She took it as a personal offense when something refused to grow as she wished. I did not know that in time, this would include me.

"Heeeeer, chookchookchookchook, buck buck buck-awwww," chortled my aunt, her elbows beating at her sides like broken wings. Then she folded her arms under her sagging bosom and brought out such a resounding shriek that idiot hens came tearing out of sheds and undergrowth, leaving feathers zigzagging to the ground. The yard, choked with vines, contained twenty yellow-eyed, black-feathered chooks, one elegant rooster, and a crazy bantam. We scattered seed, then she led me into the nest house. Blowflies droned meditatively. Dust motes hung in the yellowy air. Tenderly I took the eggs from under clucky birds and handed them to my aunt who smeared them with Keep-Egg, and placed them in a gunnysack hanging from her neck.

My scream stunned the blowflies, splattered eggs on feet, caused nesting straw to whirl and pullets to fly. Laura grabbed at her heart, and turned to face a snake the size of a boa. "Jesus Lord," she said, "the mongrel's back." My scream became silent, but my mouth remained open. She handed me the gunnysack, approached the reptile like a mongoose and grabbed it by the throat with both hands. She tugged, wrestled and grunted. The long muscle of snake wound up her arm, over her shoulder and around her waist. I raced for my cricket bat.

"Where are you going?" she gasped. "It's only the old carpet snake, he won't hurt you."

My eyebrow had almost split in two but knitted together when I realized that my aunt was not only not dying, but was grinning at me like a mad person.

"Come and touch him."

"What?"

"Touch him, he's lovely."

"Ahhh."

24

"Touch it, for God's sake, what sort of a child have I landed myself with, touch the damned thing."

I closed my eyes and reached. A cool ripple of silk met my fingers. "Isn't he magnificent," smiled my aunt, as the snake tried to crush the breath out of her.

"Aren't you going to kill it?" I ventured.

"What in the Lord's name would I do a thing like that for? Kill the beautiful wild things why should I? So he takes a few eggs, why shouldn't he take eggs? Kill him indeed, I shall drop him out bush and it will take him two weeks to get back." She cast me a devilish grin. "And then you can get rid of him." With that, she took the snake to the car and drove off, leaving me to tremble in peace, and place what remained of the eggs in a net hanging under the house.

At four o'clock Laura could always be found, legs up, in her squatter's chair, smoothing Steenie's repulsive coat and reading a seed catalog or newspaper, cover to cover. I never once saw her open a book. She would doze off, her chin dropping, her snores sending me to the other side of the house, filling me with an inexplicable rage. On that first afternoon, I watched her through gaps in the passionfruit vines.

She had dark hair, like mine, but hers was long, silvered and tied in a bun. Clean sallow skin folded down to her shirt. Her callused hands, heavy with bones when she worked, led a different life while she slept. Like delicate moths they twitched where they lay, or fluttered upwards to brush away a fly. Her eyebrows were normal, but her pale eyes were set in dark circles, as if the skin had been thumbed round with ashes.

During that first hectic summer, there were only three things we quarreled about. Food, clothes and shoes. Laura insisted that I wear lace-ups, despite the sweat which made them reek like dead goannas. As soon as I left her sight, I would take them off. Consequently, my dainty feet spread like slabs of steak.

"For God's sake, Lucille, you're going to be over six foot," she would say, as she threw another pair of lace-ups into the bin. Laura was wrong about a lot of things: I am five foot six, and I have big feet.

She disapproved of my dresses, and bought me trousers and shirts at the local store. I hated these at first, but grew to feel clumsy in skirts. If I eventually won over footwear, Laura came first with couture.

Besides, there was only one small mirror in her house and vanity cannot survive such deprivation. At least she let me dress up in her cast-off clothes—gorgeous creations from a past I could not imagine. Aunt Laura the belle of the ball? Aunt Laura in ribbons and silk? Aunt Laura dancing with *men*?

"I loathe cooking and I abhor housework," she growled as she macheted pumpkins and chokos angrily, and stirred saucepans on the wood-burning Aga.

A heavy silence brooded around the kitchen table, on which sat two steaming plates. It was broken at last by Laura. "Every bit," she scolded, "and you'll sit there till you finish the lot." Her culinary effort sat piled before me—one whole parboiled saltless choko with skin; two hunks of saltless parboiled pumpkin with skin; a mountain of saltless parboiled beans which squeaked on the tongue, and whose strings wrapped around the tonsils on their way down, and then, most terrible of all, a sludge of lumpy white sauce, streaked pink with blood and clotted with unpeeled parboiled lamb's brains.

"I can't," I pleaded, trailing a fork through the mess.

"Every bit."

I was to win this desperate war. My tactics were deadly. First, I threw up on the kitchen floor. Next, I began wearing my pink candle-wick dressing gown to the table each night and stuffing hot vegetables into its voluminous pockets when she wasn't watching. Finally, I simply outwaited her. For hours of child time, we would sit in silence at the table, listening to the ticktock of the wall clock until, in exasperation, she scraped the foul muck into the compost bucket, crying, "All right, damn it, starve."

In the end, and to our mutual relief, I ate like Laura. Fresh raw vegetables and fruit picked from the garden, slabs of damper covered in dripping or treacle, a fish roasted on the coals outside, a scrub-turkey blasted out of existence by Laura's double-barreled shotgun or, most delicious of all, a mud crab hauled from the mangrove swamps, boiled alive and served with vinegar.

The lamp guttered in the warm night air. Laura stood still in the hallway, outside my room, and let the breeze billow her dressing gown. I undressed, placed my doll by my pillow and climbed onto the mattress.

"We'll build up your health, that's what," she said, placing the lamp on the dresser next to the musical box.

Silence.

"What?" said Laura.

"Nothing," I murmured, visions of boiled chokos making me feel faint.

"Hmm. Now, a glass of water before bed and one first thing in the morning. Flushes out the kidneys." She remained silent as I gulped, gagged, and gulped again. "That's the ticket. That's a good strong girl." She reached out her hand, hesitated, then tentatively patted me on the arm.

I ached to say, "Laura I love you." But such confessions require the right conditions which never seem to arrive. During my years with her, I would often imagine the day of declaration, always changing the setting but sticking to the words, until, unsaid, they rotted away.

"Shall I say my prayers now?"

"Ha! Prayers!" she hooted. "Poor old bloody Jesus couldn't even look after himself so I don't know what good he'll do you." She softened a little and her voice was gentle when she asked, "What's the doll's name?"

"It used to be Carol, but I changed it to Nancy, like Mummy's." I hoped my hammed-up grief would impress her. Minutes passed.

"You'll be all right," she said, leaning closer. She reflected a moment. "It's the Jew in you I should think."

"Dew?"

"Yes, of course, she was Jewish your mother, surely you knew that. Or near enough. Nothing wrong with it, of course," she said, sniffing, "but he should never have married her. All that unhealthy violin playing and sickly food. Overprotective of you. No wonder you can't keep good food down, your constitution's weak. All those frightful doilies and books. Couldn't breathe I don't doubt . . ." But then she smiled at me—long horse teeth in a mesh of crinkles. "Well we're going to put it right, you'll see," and she rose with a creak of bed springs, let down a whoosh of moldy mosquito netting, made an awkward attempt at tucking me in, bade me sleep well and left, sucking light from the room.

"What a strange new life," I thought. Gone were my days of crispy sheets, little-girl curtains, stories at night, electric light. Gone the tedium of grandparents' stoops, yes please and no thankyou, ribbons and frocks, seen-but-not-heard.

So many mysteries to ponder, there in the dark—family trees, testicles, aristocrats, milksops. Perhaps my life would have turned out differently if Laura had owned a dictionary, or if I'd been courageous enough to demand explanations. As it was, dew-tainted confusions swirled around in my head until it ached. There was something terribly wrong with me, but the old witch was going to put it right. Thank goodness.

And if, sometimes, in the heat of those interminable nights, I was possessed by the belief that when my leg slipped down the side of the bed to cool it would be grabbed by something hideous beneath; or that the dead ancestors who dwelt out there in the dark took shape in moonlight and wet leaves; or if the flickering of a lantern in the hall and the scratching of possums on the roof caused my heart to beat like an eagle in a tiny cage; or if, occasionally, tears leaked into my pillow, so that I longed for that irascible old cat to take pity on me and crawl into my arms, I never let on to Laura.

2
Gentle Jesus

Even during those peaceful weeks when the Stanislav boys were kept at home with their sisters to work the farm, and the attendance at Binjigul State School dropped to ten, Mr. Meikle could use up to two boxes of chalk a day.

I stood alone at the front of the classroom in an aspic of stale lunchbox smells and cigarette fumes. On the left, through a wall of windows, I could see the horse paddock, the big kids' toilet and the basketball field, covered in three feet of seeding paspalum grass which the breeze rolled into oily swirls. Behind me was a picture of the Queen and the school's only door, opening onto a veranda. In front of me—eight long desks with eight long seats, four on each side of the room, and divided down the middle by an empty aisle. There were six inkwells and six indentations for pencils along each desk top. Thirty-eight eyes and twenty faces were turned in my direction. Renée L'Estrange's right eye looked west, the other east, and her line of sight crossed somewhere over her nose.

I had won my fight that morning with Laura, even managing to keep down a whole dish of lumpy porridge in my effort to score points.

"But it will get all dirty and torn," she said, wavering.

"No it won't, Laura, please can I?"

It was a pale green nylon dress bubbled with sprigs of white lilies— my very best. A bow tied at the back, and pintucks ruffled the front. It was a little tight under the arms, and perhaps a fraction too short, but I left the house confident that at least I was dressed the part for the most important day of my life.

Their stares crawled all over me, like leeches. As always, I felt too big. I folded my arms over the empty front of my bursting dress, focused my eyebrow on the floor, and endeavored to shrink.

Mr. Meikle sat at the table, his eyes fixed in bewilderment on some part of the sky. The clouds, bunched into thunderheads, were accusing him of something. He picked up his second stick of chalk and chewed it, rabbit fashion, into more white paste then leapt up, rushed past me to the window and spat a golly of chalk-guano onto the rainwater tank. From the butt of his Ardath he lit another, let it droop from his powdery lips and commenced to pace the room, arms dangling from the cane braced behind his neck, smoke winding into his blackened nostrils and stick of chalk held ready for further mastication.

Flies buzzed near the ceiling, moving through angles as if bumping into invisible walls. Pupils shifted in their seats; Meikle paced; I stood hunched like a vulture. My gaze slid to the two wire-mesh trays sitting on his table, next to the crumpled Ardath packets and spelling books. One tray was for "in" chewing gum—dozens of pellets of P.K. looking like little white shells. The other tray held "out" chewing gum. As the day closed in on him and the fresh batch had either gone the way of the chewed chalk or been dumped into the "out" tray, Mr. Meikle would sort shakily through the sticky gray lumps, like an addict picking over butts. Laura had warned me that Max Meikle was the nervous type.

"So," he said, facing the class and pointing his cane at me. "Observe half-wits, and tell me why we should be so pleased to have Lucy McTavish in our midst." The half-wits remained dumb.

"You. Jesus Peterson. Delve deep into your gray matter and see what you can come up with." Jesus Peterson, thirteenth child of Bjorn Peterson, and the only one to receive the benefits of a formal education, could find nothing.

Mr. Meikle's eyes narrowed as they hunted for other prey. Children slid lower in their seats. Mr. Meikle smiled.

"Wally," he said affectionately as he pointed his stick at a chicken-chested child in the second row. "Stand up, Wally, and share with us your genius."

Crazy Wally had ears like hibiscus blooms that pulsed at the side of his head and betrayed him by attracting attention to his otherwise insignificant presence. At that moment I felt no pity. If the limelight could be shed on some other unfortunate, that was all right by me.

"I dunno," faltered Wally.

"You don't know?" said an incredulous Mr. Meikle. He reached across a desk, grabbed Wally's enormous flapper and squeezed.

"Ow," whimpered Wally.

"Think, idiot, think," shouted Mr. Meikle, spraying Wally's face with chalk paste.

"Sh- sh- she's pretty?" squeaked Wally. Half-wit laughter rocked the room as Wally was prized, ear first, like a clinging bivalve, from his desk.

"No," roared Meikle, "wrong again. She is clean. Say 'clean.'"

"C- c- c- clean," sobbed Wally and wrapped both spindly arms over his head.

Exhibit A and exhibit B stood trembling beside each other. "Observe the difference," continued Mr. Meikle. "Lucy is clean and tidy. Lucy, at the age of eight, can write her own name." (The evidence of this was on the blackboard behind me.) "And next to her we have Wally Gajic, whose shorts are torn, who is afflicted with ringworm and nits, who is covered, as always, in scabs and bruises, and who, at the age of ten, cannot do his multiplication tables."

With that, he wheeled toward the boy and demanded to know what twelve times twelve came to.

Crazy Wally closed his eyes. Blood drained from his ears to his brain where intricate calculations were taking place. "A hundred and forty-four?" he said, eyes flying open, tears draining off his chin. I admit, I had mixed feelings. My better self exulted in his victory and wanted to kiss his sweet misshapen face. But my dark self required that he continue to be persecuted. If Meikle were to turn his attention back to me, I would die. Besides, I knew instinctively that to be associated in any way with Wally would not increase my social standing one bit. Also, he stank.

Mr. Meikle seemed equally ambivalent. Muscles worked in his jaw and he looked as if he might weep. But he controlled himself, took up another piece of chalk, and told us to sit down.

I slid into my seat next to Jesus Peterson who had hit puberty the year before. He alone sprouted disgusting curls of hair from trunklike thighs. Blackheads the size of bull-ants dotted his greasy face, and his voice was a deep, slow bass, which cracked occasionally into contralto. His favorite entertainment during class was catching blowies and sticking them on the points of his compass needle. Once impaled, they buzzed willingly, while he pulled their legs off one by one. When not occupied with torturing insects the compass needle was used to jab fellow students who had aroused his displeasure—usually me. He was also extremely deft at tying reef knots in the long paspalum grass so that the rest of us, when playing "tig" at big-lunch, or running to escape a bully, would trip and fall.

At ten-thirty, Narelle Oakley rang the bell for little-lunch. I followed the others under the schoolhouse, and took up my bottle of tepid, government-provided milk. I retched and, trying to make myself as inconspicuous as possible, walked backwards to the cement gutter where I poured it out.

"I'm gunna tell on you." It was Beverley Ferguson, one of the big kids who was not only clean but dressed to kill. Four rope petticoats and two net ones flounced out her cotton dress; pubescent breasts poked at the darts of her perfectly fitting bodice and her liver was suffering permanent damage underneath a plastic belt. She also had a powerful skill which I eventually learned to copy, by practicing in Laura's bathroom mirror, but lacked the gall to use. She could crumple her chin in such a mesmerizingly coquettish manner that boys would bash up anyone she nominated. My eyebrow, it seemed, had met its match.

"See if I care," said I, caring desperately.

"Teacher's pet," she hissed. "Think y'self smart, doncha? You've got tickets on y'self anyway so." I was stumped for a reply. How could I compete with her verbal skills, her practiced malice, her petticoats, her chin-power. She stood, hip thrust out, lips pulled in at the corners. Foolishly, I used my trump card.

"I'm an orphan," I said, expecting her to wither, adult style, before me. But Beverley Ferguson didn't even flinch. Her eyelids drooped lower.

"You'd better watch out, Lucille McTavish, or I'll get a gang and bash you up after school."

She left me standing like a sheep, conscious of various eyes upon me. Hands behind back, I sauntered over to the wall and inspected it closely. I wanted to go to the toilet but dared not, under the circumstances.

Big-lunch proved no better. "Up your arse with a bottle of Sars," sang Jesus. "Up your bum with a bottle of rum," cried Floyd Stanislav. "Up your tit with a bottle of shit," screeched Beverley Ferguson and when I tripped in the paspalum, a group gathered to point and sneer. Determined not to cry, I got my slate pencil and escaped under the school to sharpen it on the cement. But the gang followed me. A couple of the boys tried to lift my dress, chanting "Aw-ful Or-phan!" Unable to hide my wobbling chin, I limped up to the veranda and spent the rest of the hour alone. For many years I was tormented by a nightmare in which I was innocently sharpening my slate pencil, while a group gathered around me, laughing. In the dream, I would look down and see that I was completely naked.

After the trials of the playground, the schoolroom felt like a sanctuary. A drowsy afternoon stretched ahead. We had been divided into two groups—boys on one side of the room, girls on the other. Mr. Meikle was teaching sewing to us, and basket weaving to them. I was having trouble with running stitch—the second grader's introduction to sample work. How I envied the older girls their square pieces of poplin, covered in colored lines of increasingly difficult stitches. How did that Narelle Oakley keep hers so clean? My sample cloth was already smudged and damp with the sweat of clumsiness. Her copybook was perfect too and it didn't seem right. She was ugly and her family lived in a one-room shack with cardboard windows. They probably didn't even know what an aristocrat *was*. I tried to take my mind off my rapidly filling bowels by going over the earlier events of that afternoon.

From my solitary corner I had watched the others come in from biglunch covered in grass stains and grazes; Jesus had been working overtime on the paspalum. Crazy Wally had disappeared but no one seemed to care, including Mr. Meikle who informed us, as soon as we sat down, that we were going to do some mental arithmetic.

"If there are twenty pupils in the school," he began, "and there are eight grades . . ."—twenty heads nodded in understanding—"what then is the average number of students per class?"

Silence filled the room as twenty heads searched for an answer on the ceiling, the walls, the desks, out of windows or on the soles of feet. It came whispering down the rows and, in its wake, the braver pupils raised their hands. Pulled by those flailing arms bodies strained upward out of desks. "Please, sir! I know, sir! Ask me, sir!"

Meikle spun to face us. He ignored the arms (some of the craftier students always raised their hands, whether they knew the answer or not, ninety percent sure that he would pass over them), and ended his perusal at two teenage girls, huddled together at the end of the grade-one form.

"Françoise and Renée L'Estrange," he beamed, "if there are twenty pupils in eight grades, how many half-wits are there per grade?"

"I dunno," said Françoise.

"T- t- t- taipan snake," said Renée and Mr. Meikle in unison. Renée's eyes had swiveled so that instead of crossing over her nose, they now tried to roll into her ears.

"Why do you come here?" whispered Mr. Meikle to himself, as he sank into his chair and allowed his head to rest in his hand. The clock ticked.

"You see," he said, lifting his long-suffering face toward us, "in the real world, that is, in places other than Binjigul, the answer would be an average of two and a half half-wits per class. However," and here he paused for emphasis, "in Binjigul, the physical laws which govern the rest of the universe do not apply. Here there are more than two and a half half-wits per class, isn't that so?" Twenty heads nodded in agreement, but when it appeared that this was perhaps not the response the teacher was after, some heads swung in the negative. Others remained still, waiting for further clues.

Nothing I could do would pacify the anger in my bowels, which were threatening to explode if I ignored the rumblings. "Please, sir," I whispered, and rose tentatively to my feet. Mr. Meikle was praising Narelle's herringbone stitch, and did not hear me. "Please, sir," I said louder, trying to ignore the stares I was attracting, "may I be excused?"

"I hate Narelle Oakley," I thought, as I raced for the closest lavatory.

I could be seen from the windows, so I forced myself to stop running. But oh, what agony my pride cost me. My mind wrestled with a wayward sphincter. Hands clenched and unclenched with the effort. My jaw locked and sockets popped with the strain. Acting nonchalant, I waltzed into the big kids' toilet then, bursting open the inside door, ripping down my bloomers, and shaking with relief, I flung myself onto the smooth wooden seat.

And fell, bottom first, through the hole.

This could not happen to Lucy McTavish. It might conceivably happen to Narelle Oakley, or Wally Gajic, but it could not happen to me. Like a beetle on its back, I waved my arms and legs in the air.

"Gentle Jesus meek and mild . . ." I heard myself say, hoping for a miracle of levitation. But Jesus and I had given up on each other lately, and no angels appeared to pull me out. Laura was right.

I eased myself up like a ginger-beer cork and surveyed the damage. Not only had my pristine bottom landed in the maggoty sludge, but so had the hem of my very best dress. The former I could scrape clean with the pages of *Woman's Weekly* hanging from a hook on the wall, but not my dress. I suddenly felt very alone in the world. For the first time since I'd arrived at Binjigul I yearned for my mummy.

Hot tears of anguish spurted forth as my face puckered into a howl of agony. I knew she must be up there somewhere, watching me, why wouldn't she help, why had she left me all alone, why didn't she *save* me. My knickers around my ankles, I stood and sobbed. But the roof of the toilet did not open. No one would or could save me, that was the unavoidable truth. I was a loner, an outcast, in a world full of feces.

Hiccuping, I walked under the school to the taps and washed, tucked my skirt into my bloomers and, salvaging what remained of my will, steeled myself against the inevitable and leapt my first existential chasm.

If only I could have held on to my newfound atheism, nurtured it, let it take root in the midden of my subconscious, shaping it to form one solid, homogeneous lump. Instead, a malicious Fate, arriving a little late, organized an epiphany. I stood at the base of the stairs, like a criminal about to ascend the gallows, and felt a mystical detachment flood through me. Never had the world seemed so bright and clear, as if a layer had fallen from my eyes revealing a cleaner light. Each paint flake curling beneath my hand on the banister sent tingles up my arm. The air was translucent, and every dancing dust mote proclaimed a religious existence—its meaning beyond me, but its presence giving me the courage to smile dementedly in the shadow of the noose. Too late in life I learned of the existence of endorphins—chemicals let loose in the brain by shock or terror; at the time it felt like God.

No one noticed me slink in. I slipped into my seat, bowed my head, slanted my eyes right and left, so far so good, and applied my trembling hands to the needle. Only ten minutes to go.

"Phew, what's that pong?" whispered a girl at the opposite end of the row. But no one pinned the pong on me, and by the time Laura came to collect me, I knew I was safe.

So powerful was my amnesia, that by the time we reached the house I had obliterated the whole event.

"What's for tea?" I chirruped, bouncing up and down in glee, fluttering my skirts around the kitchen like rejuvenated wings.

"What's that stain on your dress?"

"Gentle Jesus meek and . . . nothing," I said, eyebrow pushing up into hairline. "What stain?"

But I could never pull the wool over Laura's eyes.

"Let me see," she said, sniffing curiously into the breeze.

"Leave me alone," I growled, and directed my eyebrow at her.

"Now, Lucy . . ."

"No," I shouted.

"Lucy, dear . . ." Laura hesitated, aware that she had stumbled onto something very important. She smiled crookedly and bit the inside of her lip.

"I hate you," I screamed.

"Lucy, I only . . ." But her words were lost on me as I fled out of the house and into the drizzling jungle.

While my relationship with Laura plummeted, my education soared. Binjigul State School taught me a great deal and I shall always be grateful. Sadly, none of it was academic. If I could never bear to mangle insects, at least I learned to block Jesus's jabs with my coloring book and to counter his compass with a lead pencil plunged into his flank. If I never became a fully fledged member of the bullies' gang, at least my mouth was foul enough to earn their grudging respect. I even dreamed up a dirty version of "Mary Mac, dressed in black, silver buttons down her back"—which I amended to "crack"—"she likes coffee, she likes tea, she likes sitting on a blackfella's knee." If I could never quite shake off Wally, who hung around me like a wounded dog, I learned to taunt him publicly as the others did. And I managed to avoid being bashed up after school.

Try as I might to be wicked, I remained Mr. Meikle's pet. I would have had to fake ignorance of spelling and multiplication, to read "The Dying Nightingale" with pauses and gaps, my finger trailing along the lines, to finally put him off, and my pride would not allow me to stoop so low. Besides, I read "The Dying Nightingale" with such heart-wrenching emotion that some of the students cried and Meikle proclaimed that I had talent.

Then there was Narelle to consider. I just couldn't stomach her. She had cow shit between her toes, smelled of curdled milk and left threepenny drops of urine on her seat when she asked to be excused. How then could she be as bright as me? She would do artistic things with her maps, like coloring in little cliffs around the left-hand edges of Australia, so that it looked as if it were standing out of the paper, and once she even drew a whale off the east coast. It was no good my pointing out that whaling took place off the *west* coast, Mr. Meikle remained pathetically impressed.

I don't remember why I was allowed into the gang to bash her up after school. She stood in the muddy laneway, cringing and bleating. I thrilled with guilty pleasure when I pinched her pudgy arm and saw a red welt appear. Others threw her in the muck. But afterwards, as I stood bragging with my peers, eating Mrs. Rawlinson's iceblocks paid for by the pennies I had pinched from Laura's purse, and wondering what "cunt" meant, I began to feel ill. I could see Floyd's foot swinging in slow motion into Narelle's sobbing body. I felt it as a thud in my own stomach. And that pinch made my arm burn in sympathy. I slunk home alone, throwing up and begging silently for Narelle and God to forgive me. Even as a bully I was a failure, so I suppose it was only natural that on the day the Stanislav boys punched Mr. Meikle to the ground and then hoisted Wally up the flagpole I should be the one to bring him down.

"You can't pull the wool over my eyes," said Laura that morning, "you've been filching money from me again you frightful child I won't stand for it I've told you a thousand times not to use so much toilet paper do you think I'm made of . . ."

"Dumb cunt," I retorted, pleased and a little frightened when Laura turned away from me. What was this word anyway that it could render even Laura speechless? Abracadabra and Open Sesame were feeble in comparison. I felt a familiar regret, wanted to clasp my arms around her baggy old trousers and tell her I was sorry, tell her about sticks and stones breaking bones, but it was never so simple between Laura and me, and the adage had just been proved untrue. I went instead to saddle my horse.

The only time Laura and I ever hugged was when she had given Prince to me two years before. I had flown into her arms radiant with gratitude, but she had gone funny, and trembled, so I stroked my pony's warm chest instead. I would have been quite content to stroke him forever, like the rooster I dressed in doll's clothes and carted around in the pram, but Laura had other ideas. "Well of course you've got to ride him, you strange child, what do you think he's *for*."

"Bravo," she shouted from the gate, as I bumped around on Prince's back, welded to the saddle by pride and terror, thinking a lot about death but determined to smile. "That's it, break him into a canter, go on, don't be a weakling." Her arm waved in an encouraging circle above her head.

"All right," I thought, "this time I'll show you I'm not a milksop, this time you'll see that I'm not dewish like my mother." I grabbed the pommel, closed my eyes, dug in my heels, and allowed my steed to carry me forth into ecstasy.

By the time Prince pulled up at the gate, I was dizzy and breathless with joy. At last I had done something which would move Laura to praise.

"Did you see that? Did you see what I did? I galloped him, Laura! Oh, he's the most wonderful horse in the whole world. I love you, Prince, you're the best best horse . . . ."

"Not a gallop," she interrupted tersely. "That was a canter, and you're all over his back like a sack of potatoes when I was your age I was galloping bareback and your grandmother could buck-jump side-saddle. Gallop indeed, you have to hold him with your knees, no daylight between the knees and the saddle now orf you go again and this time grip on with your knees and don't flap your elbows around like a chook, he isn't Pegasus hold the reins more firmly. What are you looking at me like that for, if you've got a horse you've got to learn to treat him properly poor old bloke. Good Lord child I give you a pony and all you can do is scowl with that frightful eyebrow now orf you go, that's it, break him into a trot, up in the stirrups up down up down . . ." I turned Prince around and took him to the other end of the paddock where I could cry and say "dumb cunt," whether to myself or to Laura I wasn't sure.

Weeks later, Laura went so far as to say I had a "good seat," but by then I was set against her. Besides, she ruined the compliment by adding that when I rode off to school she was reminded of a centaur. I did not know what a centaur was but I knew an insult when I heard one, even when it was dished out with one of her wishy-washy grins, designed to make me feel as if I had been the one to hurt her.

Laura may have been penny-pinching but when it came to horse-flesh, she did not stint. Prince was a fine pony, well-trained and patient and, naturally, the best one at school. With a horse like that, and a wilderness to ride around in, who needed friends?

The morning of Mr. Meikle's demise was not heralded by any ill omens. Everything was just as it had always been. We stood in front of the flag in two crooked lines, hands on hearts, mumbling something about the Queen. Mr. Meikle said "Stand at ease" and we parted our feet and held our hands obediently behind our backs, while he dished out his usual abuse and Brian Rachett shot rubber bands at the children behind him. Then Chopin's Military Polonaise played scratchily from the gramophone on the veranda, and we marched, a gaggle of tattered goslings, into the schoolroom. Mr. Meikle felt secure in his authority, if nothing else. Although he was tormented by fear of the School Inspector, and other, more subterranean terrors, the notion that his pupils might one day rebel had never entered his mind.

The Stanislavs arrived late and as usual Meikle sprayed jets of liquid chalk around the room as he flayed them with his cane. Apoplectic with fury, he could not stop himself in time, and the cane came thwacking down across Robert's face. It was as if a wand had been waved, turning everyone to stone. Some children were half out of seats, others had their hands cupped across their mouths. The assailant's cane remained fixed in midair. Only the drips of blood hitting the floor broke the vibrant silence.

Meikle had reached the still eye of his cyclonic life and, when it passed, he was at the mercy of a reverse fury in which a debris of Stanislavs, whirling through the wind of whipped-up hysteria, smashed him against the wall and broke him into pieces.

Screams, sobs and shouts of "t- t- t- taipan snake" ricocheted around the walls. Children were circling, bunching, clinging and fleeing like leaves tossed into the storm. And in the midst of the fracas, Wally, his great startled eyes popping out of his pale face, went to help Mr. Meikle, who lay in a shuddering heap beneath the blackboard. The last thing I remember, as I fled to the horse paddock, was seeing Mr. Meikle, his hands covering his face, stumbling toward his house while Wally dangled half-mast from the flagpole.

I must have waited ten minutes, struggling with my conscience, begging it to shut up and let me go home. "The only way to deal with a cowardly nature," it said, as I galloped to the flagpole, "is to leap into life without thinking." Horrified at my bravery, I hauled the human flag down. He was dazed, uncomprehending. He stared into my eyes as if he were a long way away. "Come on, Wally, please. Get up behind me, please, Wally," and I shook his little rag of a body.

Perhaps it was this incident more than any other which would later turn me into a human magnet attracting the emotional cripples of the world and would lead to the belief that I could save humanity. Or, perhaps, a fatal combination of genetics and experience gave me my odd psychic shape—aggressive rabbit, jelly with a backbone. Or perhaps a fluke of atavism had caused the most bellicose of my ancestors to pour their DNA into this vessel of the future, there to be polluted with dew, producing a hopelessly oscillating dogmatist. However you look at it, nature and nurture joined forces that day, creating in the raw substance of my psyche a sense of omnipotence from which I would never fully recover.

We sped bareback along the secret paths that only Wally, the jungle boy, knew. He clung to my back and shouted instructions into the stinging rain. My heart was bursting. I envisaged a new Bible, in which there were gold-edged paintings of me on horseback, decked out in Joan of Arc armor, a half dead but tearfully grateful Jesus straddled behind me. I would be facing the painter smiling and proud, perhaps looking off a little into the distance, while God loomed out of the roiling clouds, beaming beatifically in my direction. But for the time being, Wally would have to do.

We rode into the folds of Mount Misery, where no one ever came because the rainforest was impenetrable. At dusk we arrived at a decaying railway tunnel—a leftover from the days when the cedar-getters had abandoned their visions of wealth to the suffocations of the wilderness. The rain came down in thick warm sheets, the leeches inched like black fingers through the mud, and inside the tunnel a colony of upside-down fruit bats carpeted the walls in velvet. Wally's hideout.

"Cripes," I whispered reverently, "this is where you live?"

"Kinda," said Wally, beacons lighting up at the side of his head.

Wally Gajic, Lucy McTavish, exhibit A and exhibit B, faced each other. "Cripes," I said again, because I felt the earth shudder under my feet. Something was yelling at me to get out of there, to abandon Wally to the fruit bats, to leave this tangential life path and get back on the main road. If I turned around now, I could be a normal person, and if I did not, some terrible shift in the prescribed pattern of things would alter the course of my destiny irrevocably. But when the clamor of warning bells ceased and the rush of the winds of Fate had died down, I looked at this harmless little half-wit and couldn't imagine how he could frighten anyone, least of all me. I told him to sit down while I bathed his cuts, dried his hair with an old rag, then wrapped him in a stiff and putrid blanket.

"Wally," I said, "you stink."

Wally hung his head in misery.

"And you have got nits, I bet."

Wally began to cry.

"It's all right, I'm going to come tomorrow and bring you some soap and things."

Wally looked up at me and said, "I love you."

There is a little empty hole in some humans, to which the words "I love you" form the plug. Once pulled, a never-satisfied yearning begins to seep into the otherwise adequate personality, and poisons it.

It was dark when I returned home. Laura came out with a lantern. "What in the Lord's name have you been doing I've been worried sick what happened at that bloody school you didn't strike him did you? Good Lord, Lucy, look at you. What's the matter . . . why are you crying?"

The next day Laura sent me to bed with a fever, and the day after that my first period came. I had only just turned eleven. It was all very predictable: I thought I was dying and Laura assured me I was not. She sat beside me, and after several false starts began to explain.

"You see man, that is, man plus woman, equals child," and she smiled triumphantly.

"Yes, yes I know, but what's this blood?"

She tried again. "You know how you get all upset when the rooster chases the chooks and gets on their backs, and you think he's being cruel to them, well he's not actually. I mean to say, it's true they don't seem to like it much," and she paused, musing. "No I shouldn't think they like it at all, imagine if you were a bitch with all those odious dogs after you . . ."

"Laura, what are you talking about?"

"Well, the point is, you see, that the rooster has a penis which he inserts into the chooks and he shoots some sperm into them and bingo, chickens."

"Penis?" I said. "You mean like boys . . . have, you know . . ."

"Precisely." Here Laura began to fidget and appear quite interested in something that was happening on the veranda.

"You mean," I said, as the truth began to crystallize, "that boys do what *roosters* do?"

"Quite."

"But . . ."

"And the blood is your entry into womanhood. It means that if you do what the chooks do, you could become, have a . . . chicken, if you see what I mean."

I developed pneumonia. A doctor was sent for. Pills were prescribed.

It seems impossible to me now that my innocence could have survived all those years at school, swearing and telling bad jokes; that I had lived with animals and watched them copulating, without making the necessary conceptual leap. I had been masturbating for as long as I could remember and lately, while I lay on my stomach puffing away, I imagined being held by a Prince Charming. And often, when I sat on the toilet, I would picture a man kneeling before me, in velvet pantaloons, begging for my hand in marriage. All of this, yet it took the henhouse to bring these disparate bits of knowledge into one horrendous understanding—when you married, your husband chased you, jumped on your back and bingo—chickens.

Perhaps it was the shock that was responsible for a crack appearing in the wall separating this world from the other, or maybe my ability to see ghosts had been waiting in my biochemistry for the signal of menstruation. Whatever the cause, my arrival at adulthood was heralded by high fevers and accompanied by an ancestral shade.

"Great Grandmother Charlotte has very dark eyes," I whispered hoarsely to Laura as she dripped more kerosene onto the rag around my throat. The hand hesitated, then continued pouring.

"We don't have a daguerreotype of her so how could you know that? Were you dreaming?"

"Not dreaming. I saw her at the door. She looked grumpy."

Some time later I heard Laura scolding the doctor in the hallway. "Don't tell me the fever's down you quack, she's delirious you think I can't tell when someone's delirious I'll have you struck orf if you don't do something you horrid little man."

During my convalescence, a rumor had spread that Mr. Meikle left

42

town in a white canvas coat which bound his arms in front of him, but Laura refused to verify it. Mr. van Senden, the replacement teacher, was tall, soft and creamy. He never shouted, yet his smooth, elegant vowels and slow smile could stun the Stanislavs and cause my viscera to solidify with fear. He had taken to visiting the house and sucking up to Laura, even letting her win at chess. In jealous silence I would listen as she, gullible as ever, referred to him as a "nice young man" or told me we were "lucky to have him."

I observed them from my blind in the passionfruit vines. Mr. van Senden smiled his oily smile at the liquid he twirled in his glass; Laura's hand hovered above the board, fingers wriggling. "I just hope you can drum some sense into the girl, she's as wild as wild I can't do a thing with her."

"Well she's willful, like you, and intelligent. But I do agree she needs disciplining."

"What do you mean, discipline, she gets plenty of discipline I don't believe in breaking a child's spirit." Laura pursed her lips and fixed him with her rheumy old eyes.

He tilted his head back and laughed softly. "I only mean within the realms of her education."

Laura's feathers settled down and she moved her queen. "She never plays with other children. All afternoon, dressing up and playing pretend games, talking to herself or that blasted rooster. God knows what she dreams up. Tells the most frightful lies about ghosts and it's no good me chastising her she just flounces orf. Hides and swings about in trees and says she's being chased by wicked soldiers now where does she get that from I ask you? I saw her the other day, crying her heart out over a dead chicken, and building it a grave with petals and shells, is this normal behavior I ask you? She won't even eat the chooks I kill, let alone pluck them. It isn't *healthy*."

Mr. van Senden considered. "Difficult, yes, I do see your point. It must be a very lonely life for her, but on the other hand it's given her a vivid imagination."

"Well I don't know about lonely. She's afraid of nothing, I've seen to that. She's a natural athlete have you seen what she can do on that horse, she can ride like the devil and she knows more about the rainforest than I do, she and that urchin Gajic—she runs wild with that simpleton. I may not be able to give her much . . ."

43

"Nonsense, you give her a great deal. You mustn't worry about her so much . . ." Laura harrumphed and stirred in her seat.

"Have you ever thought of sending her south to school? Expensive, of course, but there's a limit to what I can teach her here. Binjigul's not what you'd call an intellectual environment."

"Pah. Book learning. I know what they'd do down there, they'd turn her into a bluestocking, all mousy with bifocals and reading frightful romances and sitting with her knees together. I won't have her turned into a marriageable doormat. She has to be inde*pen*dent." Laura thumped her thigh for emphasis.

Having planted this deadly seed in my innocent old aunt's senile mind, my enemy fertilized it with an ingratiating smile, and moved another piece. "To be independent these days, girls need a good education."

Laura's hand swooped like a falcon. "Checkmate," she cried, chortled happily and in a momentary fit of generosity, poured more sherry from the crystal decanter.

Boarding school. Dull, heavy words, good for chanting in funeral processions. I tied Prince's reins to a pandanus palm and lay in the baking sand. Never before had I felt so in love with my home. The beach, marked only by the small claws of terns, stretched wild and windswept for hundreds of miles; the rainforest—secret, funereal and sinister to those who didn't know it—was a labyrinth protecting the sclerophyll forests on the western slopes of Mount Misery, where bark hung dead in shreds, wallabies thumped over crackling leaves, red-bellied black snakes coiled fat and drowsy beside shimmering rocks, and you could wander in splendid isolation as light and free as the eucalypt-scented breeze. The spirit of these places welcomed me. I could feel it watching from the trees, the waves, the rock pools, the warm blue air, the swarms of stars. Always watching as if it, too, were lonely, as if it had lost something and was eternally awaiting its return. Yet it vanished, this phantom, when I was with someone else. I could not share my pantheism with anyone, not even Wally.

I lay in the sand and felt the presence all around me, wanted to embrace it, swallow it, carry it with me wherever I went. I could not bear to leave it. No, I would not be wrenched away from here. This was where I belonged, this was the heart of the world. If I lost this, my child's instinct knew that I would lose part of myself. I decided to be good.

When I first brought Laura orchids, she was suspicious. When I swept the kitchen floor without being asked, she was mystified. When I put on a concert in her honor and invited some neighbors, I noticed with a pang that her chin trembled. I charged the guests a penny entrance fee; mimed Gracie Fields singing "I'm a char and I'm proud of it too, and that's that" on the wind-up gramophone, and ordered Wally and Narelle to dress up for a one-act play in which I was aroused from my slumbers by the kiss of Prince Wally while Narelle beat at us with her wand. For the finale, I dressed myself in white flowing robes and performed tricks on Prince's back while he galloped around the house. On the first round, I was sitting backwards. On the second, I was standing. On the third I was touching the ground on either side of his pounding hooves and leaping into the saddle. The guests sat on the front steps cheering while Laura clutched at her heart.

Sometimes I brought Narelle home with me after school to prove I wasn't the lonely type. But when I took her under the jacaranda tree, sat her down on the purple carpet of flowers and instructed her in the rules of my favorite game (the doll was to be deposited in the jungle in "swaddler's clothes," then she and I were to dress up in many layers of ancient crêpe and set off through the imaginary snow while the temperature reached 110 and the humidity shot past a hundred, to save the baby from the wicked soldiers who would be chasing us) Narelle could only say, "It's too hot, can I arx your aunt for a glass of cordial?"

"It's ask, ask, not arx."

"Arx," said Narelle. Nor could I explain to her the obsessive passion that had gone into the construction of my fifty secret animal graves. She wanted to play houses and eat. I humored her, but could not wait for her to leave.

Eventually my talent as a pretender permeated every part of my life, pulled the wool over Laura's eyes and gave Mr. van Senden the credit. It troubled me terribly that I could remember nothing whatsoever of my parents, so I compensated by making up lives for them. My mother became a famous violinist, lost at sea; my father, a war hero with one leg. Often, I could not remember whether my fabrications were true or not, so clearly had I imagined them. Once I slipped up and said his leg had been taken by a shark.

"I thought you said it was blown off in the war," said Narelle, her eyes slitting with suspicion.

"Yeah, well, I mean a shark took it off *during* the war, cripes, Narelle, can't you remember anything I tell you?"

Every now and then a little fear would claw at the back of my mind, but I shoved it away with all the others, and convinced myself that nothing peculiar was happening. My amnesia provided many empty canvases on which to paint. But this habit of distorting the past became more frightening as the past crept closer to the present, and the fake history lodged itself in my psyche like a parasite. Real events, imagined events, real feelings, concocted feelings, who could tell what was true any more, and did it matter? Didn't everyone borrow pieces of this and that, throw a patchwork of lies over a small core of essential self? Why then, the panic?

3

The Summoning

Lucy sat cross-legged on her nest of tatty quilts, poring feverishly over stacks of timeworn letters. The hem of her blue satin dress was ripped and stained with mud. A fuzz of black formed a faint bridge between her eyebrows, and her face, smeared with dirt, was crowned by spikes of butchered hair, sticking out at odd angles. She smelled strongly of wood-smoke and sweat.

From time to time, she stopped reading, rubbed her eyes, gnawed at the thin black lines of her fingernails, then took up one of the many faded photographs which she had arranged beside her. One, in particular, drew her attention constantly—a pretty woman smiling down with adoration at a newborn baby. She stared intently at the picture and wiped it carefully with the side of her grimy hand, as if the warmth of her skin might bring to life the mother and child captured there, like genies in a lamp.

The silk rose which dangled from the waist of her dress shed another petal when she stood up and stretched like a cat. Bones cracked delicately in her back. She stared down at her carefully cataloged bits of refuse, like someone puzzling over pieces of an incomplete jigsaw, yawned, scratched beneath her breasts, then strolled outside and started off down a faint path which led to the sea.

From the lush frondescence along the shore, a patch of blue in the wide white sweep of sand showed where she had discarded her clothes. The line of her tracks pointed toward a black dot bobbing up and down in the waves. Later, as she ambled along at the water's edge, mimicking the piping call of oystercatchers, the dreamy, distracted expression on her face sharpened into fear when she noticed some footprints by the rocks. Like a hunted creature, she crouched low and ran back to her dress, threw it on and scrambled back to the house. She was oblivious to the red welt which had formed where her arm grazed the leaf of a gympie tree.

Inside, with the shutters closed, calm returned. But the somber light in the room seemed to depress her. She folded up in her corner, cradled her belly, and began rocking on her haunches as if she were in pain. She stretched out on the floor like an invalid, tears coursing down to her ears. She waited for the pain to pass, then returned wearily to her puzzle of papers.

Often, during the weeks she had been there, she had left the house and plunged into the wave of jungle. Once protected by its glassy, underwater light, she would stop to listen to the cacophony of birdcalls, then continue on with a serene expression and a buoyancy in her step. Yet whichever direction she took, she would eventually be stopped short by a fence fragmenting an open space, or by a Coke can, or a piece of plastic, or a muddy scar left by a timbergetter's tractor, and her momentary lift of spirit would turn into dread. Once, she heard distant laughter, and fled to the attic, holding the ballgowns to herself like talismans.

Most of the time she sat surrounded by scraps of paper, mumbling incoherently, rocking back and forth, her hands tucked into the warmth between her legs. Her days were undifferentiated. She curled up in her nest whenever exhaustion demanded and lived on fruit picked from the garden, rusty cans of food found in a cupboard, things preserved in glass jars. She ate only in response to pangs of hunger and her blue dress often slipped off the bundle of bones inside it.

One night she saw what might have been a lantern flickering in the hall and hastened toward it. But it was only moonlight moving through wet leaves. She banged at the wall angrily with her fists then, as if a sudden understanding had come to her, leaned her back against the mottled shadows on the wood, and muttered, "Rotten old hag . . . of course . . . silly not to have . . ." Throwing a fringed silk shawl around her shoulders she hurried out into the night.

The cemetery lay on the outskirts of town. Like a felon on the run, she picked her way across fields, stumbling along the sides of roads and cursing under her breath at barking dogs. Squeaking open the picket gate which protected the district's dead, she went straight to an overgrown grave, so small that it might have belonged to a child.

Gently, she pulled weeds away from a leaning wooden cross, and a peculiar little smile—sad and tender—softened her face. She remained gazing at the mound for a while, then, with enormous resolution, got to her feet and began searching around the cemetery, peering at tombstones, until she stopped by a larger one, and eased herself onto the fat granite slab.

A big moon bleached the night; wind whipped at her damp dress; crackles of distant lightning switched Mount Misery on and off against a backdrop of silver thunderheads. She began to laugh derisively and scold herself: "B-grade horror movie . . . inner turmoil reflected in the elements . . ." When she stubbed her toe on the slab of granite, she cursed herself for a fraud and a fool.

By the time she got back to the house, she was so angry she did not notice that something was different. When she understood what it was, muscles in her back began to twitch under the skin, as if fingers were drumming gently up and down her spine. The clock was ticking. She stood in front of it with her hands pressed to the sides of her face. Rusty cogs were turning, the pendulum swung and when the minute hand jumped she let out an involuntary shout. For the next half hour, she kept returning to it, gazing at it as if hypnotized by its slow, soothing tick, tock, then, in a kind of frenzy, she would race to the other room, dive under her quilts and pull them up to her eyes which were wide with fright.

When the clock struck three, she bounded out of her nest and began hurling bits of paper around the room, savagely ripping letters and flinging them into the air, stamping on photographs and grinding them into the floor with her heel. She threw herself at the walls, banging her head, bellowing, "Come out, you bastards, I know you're there, you cowards." She stood in the center of the room, howling and cursing until, exhausted by her outburst, she folded to her knees, dropped her head into her hands, and allowed her threats to subside into sobs.

"Steeenie, Steenie, Steeeenie." Lucy looked up, and caught a glimpse of a trousered leg disappearing behind the french windows.

4
Crazy Wally

I had my first experience of double standards when I tried to tell Laura about my inherited capacity for seeing the incorporeal beings who prowled around the house. I thought she would be pleased at this display of Huntington-McTavishism, but instead she threatened to wash my mouth out with soap and water. I stopped insisting that I had seen at least half a dozen specters and, more importantly, that they had seen me.

Usually they came when I was ill, so that I was in no fit state to ask probing questions or understand their gibberish, and all I received from them was an emanation of sadness or anger. There was one nice round woman, I remember, in a long dress and apron, who used to shrug her shoulders and roll her eyes at me as if to say, "Strange, isn't it?" Then she would wave her hand at me from the doorway of my bedroom, in silent valediction, before melting away. Once, however, my bedside was visited by a more malign character. He had side-whiskers and blue eyes just like mine. Leaning down he whispered, "I know something you don't know. I know what happened at the dam in the horse paddock." But before he could continue, another grim-grinning wraith appeared, reading a book. Her presence behind him so touched him with terror that he disappeared with a pop, followed quickly by the victoriously snarling Charlotte.

"Laura, how did Mummy die?"

Laura was spattered in black ooze, and her arm was down a crab hole. "Ugh. Blasted animal."

"Laura?"

Her arm emerged holding a stick, a fat green muddie clinging stupidly to the end. She held it in front of its two back legs and turned it over.

"Blast, wouldn't you know, a damned female." Disgusted, she threw it back into its hole, its great claws clacking with fury.

"She drowned, I've told you a thousand times."

"Yes, but how did she drown?"

"Probably a cramp," said Laura, absentmindedly swatting at the cloud of fierce black mosquitoes. "They get very cold those dams, you know."

"Why didn't he save her?"

"Who, your father?" Laura snorted and was about to launch into another tirade about the genetic flaws on the male side of the McTavishes, but I interrupted her.

"He was all wet, so he must have been there."

"Well then, he must have tried to resuscitate her, mustn't he."

Both of us remained silent for a time.

"Why did you tell Mr. van Senden that he killed her then?"

"Good Lord, Lucy, are you trying to have me thrown in jail? Where on earth did you get that from?" Laura forced out a horrified laugh but her cheeks were splotched with red. Then she turned serious on me. "Nobody knows what happened, and you've just got to live with it. Both of your parents were fools, which has given you a handicap. I try to toughen you up. I know you think I'm hard but the world won't do you any favors, you've got to grow a thick skin . . ."

"I am tough," I said, fighting back tears, "I'm as tough as you."

"Yes, but it's only on the outside, you're all flummery in the middle, just like your ridiculous mother."

I never felt the same about swimming after that, as if the inherited dew-flummery would consign me to the transparent greenness of the ocean floor, there to sway around with the weeds. Even bathtime became an ordeal and sometimes I would have to go to the toilet during meals to vomit, so overwhelming was the vision of my mother, fish swimming into her hair and crabs nibbling at her toes. Laura worried about my health and made me drink iron compound in milk.

I gave up washing Wally. Luckily, I suppose, he had come to enjoy being clean. Thanks to Mr. Meikle's excellent sample-work instruction, I had been able to pass on my knowledge of the needle to Wally, who assiduously patched his clothes—mostly my castoffs. He was now scrupulously scrubbed and nit-pickingly tidy. He even went so far as to fold the blanket after each use, so that the corners met exactly. It was as irritating as the reverence with which he treated our three books—*Grimm's Fairy Tales, Marvels of the Universe* and *Customs of the World*. I had found them moldering in the attic, and brought them to the hideout.

Wally's lips moved as his finger plowed across a page headed "The New Science that Would Control the Future and Create a Nobler Race," subheaded "The Great End of Eugenics is Fine Germ Cells for Fine People."

"What?" I demanded.

" 'Is love ... an ... enemy of ... eugenics or a f- ... friend and if ...' "

"Give me that," I said. " 'Is love an enemy of eugenics or a friend, and if it is to be a friend we must search out and destroy those agents such as Priapus and Dionysus and ... Bacchus, which are apt to pervert it and make it useless for the eugenic cause.' Simple," I said, crisp and efficient.

"Who are Priapus Dionysus and Batchus?" asked Wally, as I tied a silk scarf around his speckled ribs and hoisted it up over his nipples.

"Now you do me," I said, lifting my arms and covering my ignorance.

But Wally's brain cogs had not stopped grinding. He flicked the pages back to the chapter headed "The Mystery of Sex and its Purpose in Life," subheaded "Man the Innovator and the Liberal; Woman the Maintainer and the Conservative." I sighed pointedly and rolled my eyes, knowing that this chapter, despite the promising title, was disappointing. Lots of information about zygotes and gametes, but no hard facts about how it was done.

Wally closed the book carefully, smoothed it down with his hands, placed it lovingly back on its box and tied on my scarf. Naked but for our shawls, we lay on the blanket and proceeded with "the game."

"If sex is a very ancient attribute found among insignificant species," recited Wally, "may we not find that the true course of evolution, hmmm, has been, is, and must be to control, narrow down, and even substantially obliterate ... ahh ..."

Such philosophical considerations, though tantalizing, were soon swamped by the thrill of untying, nibbling, sucking and kissing. Ever democratic with each other, we took turns in the doing and being done to. Thanks to Snow White and the Sleeping Beauty, I already preferred the passive role, but as Wally seemed to prefer it too, it didn't strike me, at the time, as anything to fret about. Besides, in matters other than sexual, I was definitely on top.

"Saaahhh . . . justice to the scientific truth and on no account to let it be soiled and dishonored, by the passions and prejudices of men and women, least of all by the most disastrous and abominable of pa- pa-passions, sex-antagonism . . ."

"Wally," I yelled, "I told you to keep that thing down." His witchetty grub of an erection dutifully wilted.

"I never arx it to," he said, sorrowful. "It just does it." The thought of that horrible piece of flesh being poked, rooster-style, into some hole or other (I thought I only had two) made my skin tighten with loathing, but in other ways, Wally was a considerate lover and each time the offending thing prodded me in the stomach, I generously forgave him.

I did not fully understand why I should be so terrified that an adult would discover our game and send us both to prison, until the night Laura interrupted my masturbation, and caustically informed me that I could be heard all over the house. The searing, unimaginable shame did not stop my now silent and secret onanism, but it did make me aware of my vile ugliness, which festered and grew in the dark. I began worrying late into the night about how much damage I was causing my genitalia, and whether my future husband would be able to tell.

Although our detailed knowledge of the physical universe and its scientific principles stopped in 1932, the year our books were published, Wally and I felt ourselves to be two geniuses, struggling to enlighten an ignorant world. We were hungry for meaty intellectual debate and thirsty for intoxicating metaphysical discussion. Binjigul starved us of both.

Wally was too shy to come with me, so I had to scour the countryside alone, searching for someone who could further my knowledge of eugenics, or who understood that "entitative" meant "real."

There was Mrs. Deathridge, who always poked her head through a crack in her door, and said, "What's it to you?" She wore her hair in rags, and no one could remember a time when they'd seen her without blotches of pink calamine lotion on her face. And Mr. Docherty the butcher—the happiest man I've ever known, who would laugh uproariously at me as he hacked away at offal, up to his elbows in blood.

"Well, girlie, you've got some pretty hairy questions there (wham) but if you ask me you're not going to find the (wham) answers in books but (wham) in the satisfaction of a job well done. Now why don't you take this leg o' lamb up to Miss McTavish for me with my compliments."

The most likely candidate was Edith Rachett, Brian's mum. The Rachetts were our nearest neighbors and they owned a pig farm. "Is that so?" she would say in the kitchen, as I warmed to my topics. "Well I never," or, "Who would have thought?" and so on. Visiting her had the added benefit of being fed fairy cakes—a conspiracy Laura would have been enraged to discover.

"Infinity never ends, Mrs. Rachett."

"But everything has to end somewhere, doesn't it?"

"Not infinity."

"I suppose infinity's another word for God, then."

"But what if there's no God?"

"I wouldn't let Mr. Rachett hear you say that, dear, he might stop you coming here." Mrs. Rachett looked around guiltily, even though she knew that Rachett senior and Rachett junior would not be home till nightfall. "And you do like coming here, don't you?" She gave me another fairy cake and a wistful, almost pleading smile.

"Oh, yes. You're the most intelligent person in Binjigul." Her face went all misty, as if I'd said something which hurt her.

The Rachetts visited Laura once a fortnight to pay their respects. On the surface, they were a well-matched couple. He looked remarkably like a pig; she like a sheep. He had a little pink squashed-up nose and was encircled by freckly pink rolls of fat. She had tightly crinkled blonde hair, watery, nondescript eyes, and two front teeth which stabbed her lower lip even when her mouth was closed. Mrs. Rachett told me, privately, during one of our discussions about germ cells, that the reason for her sheepishness was that, as a child, she had followed the jackaroos around when they were castrating the young rams on her father's desert property, and eaten the testicles like oysters.

As usual, they had tea with Laura on the veranda and ate fairy cakes topped with pink icing and hundreds and thousands. Edith sat primly forward on her chair, as if apologizing for taking up so much space, her hands working at a handkerchief. She smelled of soap, starch and warm ovens. Harry sat sprawled out, pipe in mouth, legs apart, the top of his fly undone so that the porky folds had somewhere to spill. The radio was on.

". . . the more certain it becomes that another global war would return what remained of mankind to the Dark Ages; the more evident it is that such a war can be initiated only by insanity or by blundering accident. Protection against war therefore involves two elements. The first element is complete readiness on the part of the free world, the nonaggressive world. It must, not from choice but from necessity, maintain such a degree of defensive and counterattacking power as will deter aggression . . ."

"Manure," said Harry, sucking wisely at his pipe. "Pig manure's the best, no doubt about it. Chook manure's good too, but pig's is better."

". . . Great Britain has, by a creative modern policy, converted colonies into independent nations, founded upon parliamentary sovereignty and enriched by the rule of law, while the Soviet Union has been busy converting independent nations into colonies under the rule not of law, but of the tank and the bomb."

"Russian swine," muttered Laura.

"I don't think we have any of those, do we, dear? Not Russian pigs? Ours are English pigs, aren't they, dear?" Laura and Mr. Rachett did not seem to notice that Edith had spoken.

"For the truth is that the Communist Powers, while practicing aggressive imperialism on the grand scale and with astonishing success, have in non-Communist and free countries succeeded in making peaceful Imperialism disreputable . . ."

"Marvelous speaker, Menzies. Marvelous statesman," pronounced Laura.

"Yes, marvelous, isn't he, dear. Knows what he's talking about that Menzies."

Harry remained oblivious to his wife's presence. "The Common Market's a bit of a worry though."

"Utter bilge. Great Britain would never sell us down the river, Mr. Rachett."

"Still she's a bit of a worry, the Common Market, only saying the other day, if they was to enter the Common Market, I'd have to sell to the Japs or the Chinese and I wouldn't do it, I was only killing 'em not so long ago."

"Not the Chinese," I found myself saying, but no one took any notice.

". . . to induce admiration for Russian applied science but also to strike fear into the hearts and induce minds to yield to the spread of Communist doctrines and practice. It is hard for me to understand those who would seek to abolish nuclear and thermonuclear weapons as the first step to disarmament and peace . . ."

"Now if us farmers have to walk off, because of the Common Market, who'll be here to stop the Commies when they invade from the north, eh? That's what I'd like to put to some o' them galahs in parliament. The Chinese want our land all right, they'd just come and take it, millions of 'em, like rabbits."

Edith perked up at the word "rabbits."

"We used to have bunny bashes out on the property when I was a girl, drive them up against the rabbit fence and club thousands of them at a time and have a picnic after under the coolibahs."

"Pig manure. Better than chook manure. Grow anything with pig manure."

"What delicious cakes, Mrs. Rachett," said Laura, glowering at me, because my sighs of exasperation were becoming noticeable.

When a horde of relatives visited one year to celebrate Laura's aunt Hilda Huntington's ninety-fifth birthday, I had hoped that I might be enriched by my first contact with denizens of the outside world. Laura grumbled for weeks before they came about how much money she would have to spend on the old coot. Nevertheless, she set me and Wally to polishing the silver for the dining room table which had not been used in living memory. It was all terribly grand and I was itching with excitement. Muddies the color of fire trucks sat poised in plates, as if ready to attack. Hibiscus blooms wilted in dishes. Blowies drowned in the mango and cream.

Hilda Huntington wore a high Victorian collar, walked with a cane, and carried a brass trumpet which she occasionally held to her ear. Even Laura was slightly subdued in her presence. The milksops spent most of their time on the veranda, discussing drought relief, how to deal with shearers and natives, and tucking into Laura's sherry. The ladies slyly picked up china and read underneath. At lunchtime, Wally was banished to the kitchen, and I had to sit next to cousin Beatrice whose false teeth whistled and clacked like the Sunseeker heading south.

"But my dear, it was simply ghastly. Quite beastly."

"Said I'd hang the blighter if he went on strike."

"What?" shouted Hilda, aiming her ear trumpet.

"Wouldn't work in an iron lung shearers these days, spoiled y' see."

"Now, my dear, I've been meaning to ask you for ever such a lorng time. Is it true that the Prince of Wales visited you on Gang-Gang and you offered him a boiled egg for tea?"

"What?" Hilda swung her trumpet around to the other end of the table.

"I did not give him a boiled egg," said Laura, incensed, "I didn't give him anything."

"Terribly amusing, my dear."

At last the ordeal was over, and Laura announced that they should all come and see the garden.

"What?"

"Silly old coot."

"What?" Hilda pointed her trumpet at Laura, who shouted into it, "I said you can't come without boots."

I was left at the table with Hilda who pushed the wreckage of crab aside with her trumpet, and glared at me.

"I suppose you expect me to give you something."

"No."

"I suppose you're waiting for me to die, like the rest of them, so you can get your horrid little hands on my money."

"I am not."

"Well I won't die, and you won't get a penny out of me."

There was no doubt about it, Wally and I were surrounded by fools. Who, at school for instance, could name the planets in the system, or stare at the glittering vault and know that the red ones were hot, but the blue ones hotter; that solar prominences leapt to heights of seventy thousand miles; that snow was made of exquisite crystals, each of a different shape. Who would know as we did that at the North Pole, lights hung in the sky like curtains; that in the deepest oceans, there were monstrous fish which lit up in the dark; that savages were literally degraded and lived an existence which was scarcely to be called human; that the Kaffir races degenerated at puberty, and became senile in their thirties or that the golden rule of health was to breathe through the nose because mouth breathers contracted consumption. Wally and I agreed that even Mr. van Senden was ignorant of such things. All he could talk about was sums and something called "literature."

Like two nineteenth-century naturalists, Wally and I knew our Arcadia intimately, knew what foods to eat and how to pin dead butterflies to boards. We took on the project of constructing a taxonomy for the plants along Humbolt Creek, our newly named dribble of gully which ran beside the tunnel. Laura Weed, Cut-throat Vine and Lily Gajicae were printed neatly in ink, beneath decaying leaves. Our only fight erupted over the naming of the latter. Naturally, I insisted that the flower should be named after me, but Wally pointed out that Lily McTavishae sounded silly and although I secretly agreed with him I punished him for several days.

Thanks to the treasures of knowledge available to us from the science tomes, the Brothers Grimm and the Australian education system, we knew that we existed in an outpost of civilization, at the periphery of the Entitative World, whose center was England. Dutifully, our imaginations created the forests of medieval Europe in our mystical terrain.

Such was paradise before the fall.

The fruit of the tree of knowledge has a bitter, acrid taste. Perhaps it was my own fault—my contrary nature brought ruin upon itself by always reaching for lemons like Wally. He had no mother, but was boastful of his father—a Yugoslav who belonged to a very exclusive club called "The Ustashia." He was, Wally assured me proudly, an anti-Tito fascist. I knew that fascists were beautifully uniformed soldiers, who had tried to conquer the world, so I assumed that an anti-Tito fascist was the Yugoslavian equivalent of a general. Yet, for all the swaggering praise he lavished on his dad, Wally had never allowed me to visit his house. When I insisted that I go home with him, his ears lit up and he went quiet. It didn't seem fair that Wally should have secrets from me so once, when I gave him the usual double-back home, instead of leaving him a mile from his house, I tethered Prince and followed.

If his dad were a general, he had certainly fallen on hard times. The house was a shack of corrugated iron flanked by a rickety tankstand and a chimney, from which smoke merged with blue haze, the hot pungency of gum leaves and the drone of bushflies. Outside, an old bath squatted beside an open fire pit. Hidden in the ranks of trees which closed around the shack, I watched Wally walk into the clearing and call. A man emerged from the hut, holding a bottle in his hand. Wally stopped. The man pushed himself away from the doorway and staggered toward the boy.

"Where you been, you fuckin' runt?"

Wally said nothing and remained still. The bell-birds had gone silent.

"Won't talk to Daddy, eh? Don't like Daddy, eh?" He stood swaying in front of his son. Wally stared at the ground.

The man took another long pull from his bottle, and then, without warning, hit Wally across the head, knocking him to the ground. "Get up, you fuckin' runt. Get in house, fuck you, or I fuckin' chop you. Get. Get."

With each yell, he kicked at the boy, who moved along the ground like a fallen fledgling. I put my hands over my face and doubled over to protect the hole which had formed in my chest. I tried to get up, to run, but my legs, too, had turned to flummery. All the way home, I tried to cry, but no tears would come.

I told no one what I had seen but I took to biffing anyone who called him Crazy Wally. I brought him more food than he could possibly eat, anointed his cuts with goanna salve and tried to soothe the deeper wound in him by staring soulfully into his eyes, until he turned away, embarrassed and ashamed.

I understood, at last, the ugliness which had disfigured his face the day we stole Laura's shotgun. Having studied the photographs of Aborigines in *Customs of the World,* we were adept at painting our naked bodies with mud and decorating them with feathers. We carried our spears as we prowled through the undergrowth, but so far had not made one single kill. This suited me fine. The joy of hunting lay, for me, in stalking—concentrating every sense, cell and fiber in the body on one single elusive object. But Wally wanted blood.

"Shh," I said, pointing to a mangy feral cat who glared at us from the other side of the creek. The gun exploded, blasting the cat to smithereens but not quite killing it. We raced across to the twitching pulp; I started to whimper and looked for something with which to complete the murder. Wally took up a rock and bashed the body until it was nothing but a flat piece of bloodied fur.

When he saw that I had seen the look on his face, he turned as white as a kitchen cup, before howling like an animal and running away to bury himself under the blanket in the bat tunnel. I found him hiding there but could not console him because I was afraid of what I had seen.

Fear was in season that year. A damp fear began to ooze from the walls of the house the day I noticed that Laura held on to the banister as she climbed the stairs. She had barely spoken to me lately, had been neglecting the garden and depositing the carpet snake farther and farther into the bush. When the fruit bats came to steal our mangoes, she no longer took to them with her .22, and tame possums left their fruity shit all over the veranda. I tried to help her with the work, but she scolded that I was useless and selfish and she wished I'd never come to Binjigul. But then she would look sad, and mumble something about her will, and how I would be taken care of no matter what happened. Once I caught her gazing out at the jungle, a weary and abstracted expression on her face.

"What are you staring at?" she snapped. She creaked down into the squatter's chair and pretended to read. Wishing to ease her sorrow by elevating her thoughts to a higher plane, I quoted from *Marvels of the Universe,* the section entitled "The Universal Fact of Death that Exists in the Service of Life." I was rewarded with silence. I continued with excerpts from "The Living Were Not Born to Die, but to Beget Better Life." She lowered the seed catalog and glared at me over the top.

"I said buzz orf, can't you give an old woman some peace."

A little uncertain now, I pressed on with, " 'Those who, looking only on the material surface of reality, and thus profoundly ignorant, would infer from the bodily disintegration which we call death, that nothing beyond remains, have yet to pass through science and knowledge, to wisdom, which knows, as Socrates said . . .' "

"Ho," she cried, throwing the seed catalog aside and grabbing the sides of her chair, "better life? You? Well let me tell you this disintegrated old spinster's got a spark of life to her yet, enough to give you a good walloping you morbid little ingrate you'll be the death of me."

"You'll be the death of her," whispered the ancestor with eyes like mine, invading a dream.

5
Little Murders

As Wally and I abandoned the garden of childhood, Laura began preparing for death. The following year, that is the year when in the Entitative World, Jackie Kennedy's dress was stained by her husband's blood—out on the periphery, in the limbo of Binjigul's jungles, another murder would be committed in which I would be implicated. From then on, all my actions would have about them a quality of desertion, or escape into the unknown.

Laura had promised that we would go to the New Year's Eve dance at the School of Arts in Tamboola, a small town fifteen miles away, where I would be attending secondary school. The steamy, enervating heat of December did nothing to exhaust my excitement. Very few inhabitants of Binjigul had ever seen the bright lights of Tamboola. Its main street was covered in tarmac and stoplights blinked at the crossroads. Wally, whom I had not visited for over a fortnight, had certainly never traveled so far from home.

I had promised to bring him cake and presents on Christmas day, but when the time came, I found any number of excuses to defer the visit. Poor Wally had no one in the world to share Christmas with except me, but he really did have colossal ears and besides, he was only a child, whereas I was mature for my years, and, as everyone said, pretty and talented. I had been finding "the game" not only boring lately, but repugnant as well. It wasn't that I didn't love Wally, of course I did, but he wasn't tall, dark and handsome like Mr. van Senden. I was soon to be taking my first step toward the center of the Entitative World (which I imagined as a beautiful woman, waiting for me with open arms and a smile of welcome) and it had to be said that

Wally could never belong there. On the last day of the old year I rode to the tunnel, laden down with leftover food and elaborate excuses, determined to camouflage my betrayal of him.

It was deserted. What a morbid little ingrate he was. With great relief, I left the parcel at the mouth of the tunnel and galloped off. It wasn't until I was halfway home that I realized the blanket was missing and wondered why he had drawn the mud map of Mount Misery with the arrow pointing to the top. If he had wanted to tell me he had gone up to that almost inaccessible cave we had once visited, why not write the message down and leave it in the tree trunk, as we always did?

I tried to ease the uncomfortable, niggling sensation by concentrating on important things. Would Laura let me wear lipstick? And the silk rose on the dropped waist of the dress, should I take it off? It didn't match the ugly court shoes Laura had ordered from the catalog. Thank goodness the dress was long. It was one of Laura's precious ones which belonged in the chest in the attic—dresses of starlight, moonshine and sunbeams. It didn't look like anything I'd seen in a magazine but it fitted almost perfectly. Its soft blue folds swirled around my ankles when I danced along the veranda. If only I had a mirror. What about jewels—treasures kept locked in a box—jet, and amber and pearls? And my hair, oh God, my hair. How did one construct a beehive or a french pleat? The *Woman's Weekly* gave no instructions. My anxiety about Wally melted under such feverish considerations.

Grappling with my hydrophobia, I took a deeper bath than usual, scrubbed at my feet and sparsely tufted armpits with a nailbrush, sandpapered my elbows with a washer, twisted it at the corners and poked it into my ears, and wondered if Snow White had to go through such humiliating rituals or if the grime simply refused to cling to her perfection.

"Good Lord, Lucy," cried Laura, as I swished, triumphant and bashful, into the kitchen. "What have you done to your hair? You look like an animal peeping through the jungle. And take orf that unspeakable lipstick this instant."

The final puncture to my defiance was the information that I looked like a black cockatoo. Grumbling and sour, I brushed out my hair and wiped off the red lipstick, leaving a fetching blur of pink.

Mindful of creases and snarled tresses, I sat rigid in the cabin of the

utility truck, and refused to roll down my window. The fallout from the argument still hung in the air. A full moon dulled the stars and one crooked headlight startled wallabies at the side of the road. Laura cleared her throat.

"You look very lovely." The words had been stuck in her craw. She reached into her handbag and pulled out a string of pearls. "If you hadn't been so cussed I would have given them to you earlier."

I placed the tiny moons around my neck, felt my eyes prickle with gratitude and long-suppressed love, and worried about tearstains and red noses.

Tamboola School of Arts was an unpainted, weatherboard hall tilting to starboard on stilts. The sounds of a tinny piano, a violin, and spoons clacking on a musician's thigh swelled orchestrally and curled through the dripping treetops festooned with Chinese lanterns. Balloons dotted square windows of light like confetti; streamers hung damp and limp from the porch where men lounged drinking punch from glass cups. I sailed past them, slicing through their stares with my bow, entered the brilliance of the hall, and went down like the *Titanic* in an ocean of short dresses and lipstick, rope petticoats and legs, pointed shoes and beehives. I was held under by the weight of eyes staring at me—a pariah in a twenties dress with a tattered silk rose, her chin crumpling in dismay.

"Lucy, my dear girl"—Mr. van Senden smiled conspiratorially at Laura and took my elbow—"you're going to be a very glamorous young woman." He held me up when I skidded on the Pops-strewn floor, and led me out for the Gypsie Tap. One slide, two slide, one two three slide. I silently gave thanks to Mr. Meikle for teaching us ballroom dancing under the school. Back slide, back slide, back two three slide. Mr. van Senden held me just right, gentle but firm, the way a good rider controls the reins. Beauty had uncovered the beast.

"G'day," said a pimply youth in an outsized suit. "Wanna lean up agenst me frame for a struggle?" It was the midnight dance, and I'd just seen Mr. van Senden choose Laura. The acid, wrenching pain of rejection went so deep that I gave the boy a cavalier nod. He danced as if he were driving a tractor. So vigorous was the pumping of his arm, and so vicelike his farmer's grip, I could not keep my eyes on my treacherous, never-to-be-forgiven aunt. We battled around the dance floor until the stroke of midnight, at which point my partner poked his tongue down my throat to my tonsils. I kept my eyes open as he

mauled away, and rolled them around until I could see my teacher. Yes, he was watching, and he looked gratifyingly peeved. I closed my eyes and tried to enter the spirit of the thing. It was difficult to breathe, and I was beginning to worry that I might choke, thereby showing up my woeful inexperience in an embarrassing way. I gasped for air when he let me go, but managed to control my retching and remain standing. Laura and Mr. van Senden prized my protesting partner from me, then we all linked arms and sang "Auld Lang Syne."

I had expected Laura to be furious with me but her silence on the drive home was of the worried, ominous sort. I could not imagine why. It was obvious that Mr. van Senden was in love with me and that after I'd completed secondary school, he would ask me to marry him and take me to live in the Entitative World.

Smiling dreamily up at the moon, which rolled brazenly through pillows of cloud, I let the wind batter my face and wondered when I should start calling Mr. van Senden by his first name. Even the police car parked at the front of the house at one o'clock in the morning did nothing to pin down my fluttering happiness.

Everything about the three men betrayed a deep embarrassment. Laura seemed to be treating them with her usual lofty disdain, but kept turning to look at me where I sat draped over the squatter's chair. I caught the words "few questions . . . gone bush . . . in the chest . . . the Gajic shack." "Gajic?" My stomach leapt upwards. I threw Steenie out of my arms and stood up as the four figures of the Apocalypse moved, slow motion, toward me.

"Do you know where Wally is?" said Laura, haughtiness belying the quaver in her voice.

"No."

"You see, she doesn't know anything. Anyway, how could you possibly know it was Wally. It could have been anybody he's just a boy he couldn't knife his father I've never heard anything so preposterous."

"He did it all right." The policeman fixed his stare on me. "You're wrong if you think you can protect him, miss. We saw the stuff you left for him up there. If he left you a message . . ."

"No."

"If he can murder his own father like that, miss, he's dangerous to other people."

"No."

"For pity's sake leave the child alone can't you see she's upset I won't have it I simply won't have it."

"He didn't do it, he didn't, he didn't . . ."

"Lucy, dear . . ."

By the time Laura brought me hot chocolate in bed, my mind had cleared enough to know what to do. I would not have time to get to the hidden cave before dawn, so I would have to go tomorrow night, on foot. I would leave a note for Laura saying I had gone to look for him, just in case I didn't get back in time to fool her. I plotted, schemed and planned until I dropped, like a rock, into sleep.

All the next day, Laura watched me out of the side of her eyes and occasionally asked me if I was all right. I wanted to go and bury myself in her arms, tell her everything, ask for her help, but Wally's life was at stake, and I had to deceive her. If they sent him to prison he would die like the nightingale in the story which made everyone at school cry.

When I heard snores from Laura's bedroom, I crept quietly out, picked up the package I had secreted under the house, containing food, a raincoat, salt for leeches, matches, kerosene, two magazines, paper and a pencil, all of which I tied up in a blanket with rope and strapped onto my back. There was no time for a saddle. I whistled softly for Prince, leapt onto his back and wheeled him away. But instead of taking the direct route to Mount Misery, I went in another direction. My efforts to soothe my pony failed—he knew me too well. I dismounted, tied him up and ran my hands over him comfortingly. He rubbed his head on my shirt as if to apologize for his terror. Then I climbed up a liana vine, up into the deeper darkness of the canopy. If I could stay above the ground for a while, the police would not discover my tracks.

Pain. The taste of copper in my mouth. Blisters forming already on my hands. I don't know how long I roped myself through the forest, from vine to hanging vine, groping, reaching out in the blackness, too frantic to be afraid. At last, I thought myself far enough away to step down onto the litter. The journey to the foot of the mountain seemed infinite, zigzagging along creeks, stepping from rock to rock, falling, sliding, feeling clothes and skin ripped by wait-a-while vines. Dread of what was behind me and in front of me, can't go any further, must go on, limbs trembling, how would I ever get back, snakes, can't see ahead, is Wally alive? Did he really do it? Maybe he's gone mad, maybe he'll kill me too, you know Wally couldn't do it, yes he could

65

you saw what he did to the cat. You're helping a murderer you'll be sent to prison, maybe Wally's dead and this would never have happened if . . . it's all your fault God will punish you for this, oh God please help me get up this mountain, and on and on until I reached the overgrown cave.

Nothing. Darkness. Not even the ashes of a fire.

I called for a long time and built a fire as a signal. The flames flickered on the paintings around the walls—strange spooky things—hands and animals and curious designs. I looked for tracks, but with only a fire torch it was difficult to see. I left the bundle and wrote a note.

"I love you. Everything's going to be o.k. I won't rat on you I promise. No matter what they do to me." It didn't seem enough to express what I felt, so I added "Merry Christmas and a Happy New Year," followed by another "I love you," underlined. It would be two decades before I could speak those words again.

By the time I got back it was almost dawn. My heart sank when I saw the light in the kitchen. I must compose myself, be ready to lie. I rubbed Prince down with a cloth, buried my head in his steamy shoulder, kissed him, thanked him, wiped my own face with the rag, then with what remained of my strength, climbed the stairs, calling, "Laura, don't worry. I'm safe. I couldn't find him though. I called and called and looked everywhere so he must have gone a long way away."

I was interrupted by Laura's screech of horror. She stood in the doorway to the kitchen with her hands up in the air, her face twisted, staring at me, wild-eyed. I looked down, saw the clusters of fat, black leeches, the long dribbles of blood, and fainted.

Mr. van Senden sat beside me on the bed. Laura hovered at the door. I stared at the ceiling.

"Lucy you must tell us everything you know. It's for Wally's own good. There are extenuating circumstances. He'll be sent to a home where he can be looked after. If you have any idea where he is, you must tell us, you must."

I glanced across at the dressing table which seemed to be moving toward the bed. The floor was heaving up and down like the deck of a ship. I fixed my eyes back on the ceiling.

"He won't survive out there. You wouldn't want to feel responsible for another death would you?" Now the ceiling began to undulate. "Lucy, listen to me, trust me, we only want what is best for you and Wally." Mr. van Senden put his soft warm hand on my forehead. I began to cry again.

"Poor little girl," he murmured and lifted me into his arms. "There there, tell us now, where is he?"

"No," I shouted, "leave me alone," but I did not squirm or struggle for fear that he would let me go.

After groups of police trackers and local farmers had spent a month scouring the wilder slopes of Mount Misery, it was agreed that Crazy Wally was dead. The funeral was a dismal affair attended by very few people. Laura wore black. I dropped a spray of Lily Gajicae onto the small empty box before the first clod of earth thudded on top.

Soon after that, I found myself staring through veins of rain which laced the window of the Sunseeker, watching Mr. van Senden put his hand on Laura's shoulder, as they stood, disconsolately, on the platform. Two parallel lines of water ran down her stern, unmoving face. I was heading south, to a prison called Saint Jude's Church of England School for Girls. As the train pulled out, I turned toward the front, and felt nothing.

6

An Uninvited Guest

When the shrieking virago in ripped blue satin took a flying leap at the ghost who had scuttled off down the veranda in fright, she went sailing through thin air and landed, cat-fashion, on elbows and knees, face to face with Steenie, who arched his back and hissed at her. She hissed back, rolled over, and inspected herself for splinters.

"Death hasn't changed you much," she grumbled, pulling a piece of veranda board out of her mound of Venus, and glaring up at the wraith, who, though still fading in and out a little, looked distinctly alarmed. The old ghost cleared her voice of static and demanded, querulously, what on earth she was doing here and whether she had gone completely barmy. At these words, Lucy began rolling around on the floor guffawing with such spectacular abandon that Steenie sought refuge between his owner's transparent legs and the old lady pursed her lips more tightly and backed away. But Lucy leapt to her feet and pointed a finger threateningly in the shade's face.

"Don't you dare go." The specter drew herself in like a poked sea-anemone, but did as she was told. Lucy lowered her finger, then stalked around the crone like a prosecuting attorney. "You know damn well why I'm here. I've been haunted all my life and this time I'm going to lay you fuckers."

"Lucille McTavish you've turned into an utter guttersnipe I won't have such language I simply won't have it." At Lucy's sharp intake of breath, Laura paused, shot her grand niece an uncertain look, and continued, in a more mollifying, if incredulous, tone. "Good Lord, child, you'd forgotten your own name."

"Yes. And a lot of other things which is why I'm here."

The sun came up and Laura, who was now solid enough to cast a shadow, slid her back down the warming wood, stretched herself out in the dazzling light and soaked up the hot, luxurious air of that perfect morning like a lizard. Lucy did the same. Together they gazed out at the languid blue haze that shrouded Mount Misery and listened to the buzz and thrum of countless tiny wings and rustlings, syncopated by secret calls from behind the wall of jungle.

"The trouble is, what you do remember, you remember wrongly." Laura said this cautiously, as if she expected her niece to turn rabid at any moment, but as Lucy only sat there attacking her filthy fingernails, Laura went on.

"For a start it was you who was the cold fish, not me. When you were very little, and I used to visit you on Gang-Gang, you'd hop into bed with me every morning and brush my hair. And you'd say, 'Never mind the geckos, they only eat the piders and the fies.' " Laura took on an uncharacteristically simpering look which was as convincing as a smile on a death-adder. "Then, when I finally rescued you, you wouldn't let me touch you. You'd frozen up. All the way up here on the train, you'd get that flinty look if I even tried to stroke your hair. I was scared stiff of you."

"I was seven years old, for God's sake."

"Ho, there you go, typical, I tell you the truth and you get angry. Well don't get all high-falutin' with me. I'm dead and I know a lot more than you do."

Lucy shot her a suspicious look and said, "Like what?" But as Laura only clamped her lips together and folded her arms tightly over her bosom, her grand niece got up and began to pace the veranda with her hands behind her back.

"How nice to see that your passion for winning has not been affected by transubstantiation. It's all you've come back for, isn't it, to criticize me all over again. I was either sickly or Jewish, or cowardly or . . . As for stroking my hair, what a laugh. You gave that stinking cat more affection than you ever gave me." She stood in front of Laura belligerently, her refurbished eyebrow doing its stuff.

The old woman's eyes were watery but she fastened them onto Lucy's like claws. "I've never criticized you in my life and what have you got that getup on for and fancy hacking off that lovely hair you look like a black cockatoo. When did you last wash? You smell like a compost heap and what's this Jewishness nonsense I may have said that I thought the old man was a Jew what's so terrible about that? I've got nothing against Jews." Laura sniffed and lifted her nose, causing Lucy to laugh softly.

"What an ungrateful and selfish girl you are, yes, go on laugh, but I've come back to help you and let me tell you it's damned painful entering earthly time. And what do you do with a child who storms around the house saying she hates you?"

"But I didn't hate you, Laura." Lucy, it seemed, was battling against tears and she brought her words out with difficulty. "But no matter what I did I always knew there was something in me you despised."

"Despised? Good Lord," Laura said softly. "I simply don't understand you."

Lucy sat back down beside her and dropped her chin to her chest. "Neither do I," she said at last lifting her head to smile ruefully at her great aunt. The two women stared at each other for a moment, then, spontaneously, began to chuckle. The chuckle grew into a laugh which cracked the invisible wall between them. Lucy grabbed Laura's knotted, freckly hand and squeezed.

"You want to know what it's like?" asked Laura, looking mischievous, even girlish.

"What?"

"Coming back."

"Certainly."

"It's like having an enormous shit, only you're the shit."

Lucy doubled over, hooting. Laura looked pleased with herself and was blushing slightly. But when they'd stopped giggling, she became very interested in her own toes and Lucy, smiling doubtfully at a kestrel hanging in the sky, gave her aunt's hand one last squeeze and let it go.

"It was painful for me too," she said quietly, but Laura only frowned and fiddled with Steenie's ears.

"It was my mother in me you hated, wasn't it?"

Laura, reacting as she had always done to the slightest criticism, retorted quickly, "What a preposterous thing to say."

"Why did you hate her?" asked Lucy, unexpectedly insisting, so that Laura, caught off guard, looked away guiltily.

"Were you jealous of her? I know you had a special attachment to my father despite all the insults you hurled at him."

"I was never jealous, never." Laura thumped the floor for em-

phasis. "But I bought him Gang-Gang after the war, and I defended him against the family he was like a son to me and then he up and married that ridiculous woman."

"Why was she ridiculous, what did she do?"

Laura's face was tight and bitter. "She was weak. A silly city woman full of silly city ideas—totally inappropriate for that sort of life. He should have married someone of his own . . ."

"Class," said Lucy hotly, and might have flung accusations at her aunt had a cold wind not slithered along her skin, raising it into gooseflesh. The temperature was dropping rapidly and static was interfering with Laura's voice. Lucy crouched down with her arms protecting her head, while the shutters shook and pots rattled on the stove. A man's hand clenched the side of the french windows and gradually a stout body in a three-piece suit formed at the end of it. The new ghost grimaced with some difficulty in Lucy's direction, then scowled horribly at Laura.

"Oh do bugger orf you horrid little man," she shouted, "what right have you got poking that great honker around my house."

"Right? Right?" thundered the old man. "I hear you slandering my daughter and you talk about right. It was that no-goodkin nephew of yours . . ."

"How dare you," cried Laura, standing up to face him. The insults flew back and forth like grenades until Lucy, grabbing at what remained of her hair, screamed at them to shut up.

It was as if the two ghosts had forgotten she was there, and they huddled together nonplussed and intimidated. The old man smiled ingratiatingly at Lucy and muttered, "Now look what you've done, you old battleaxe, you've upset the poor child."

He had an enormous nose with a little gray tuft growing off the tip. There were little gray beards growing out of his ears, too, and a ring of gray hair flanking a shiny bald scalp. He had eyes like Einstein. Lucy was peering at him closely with her head to one side. When she stretched out her hand and patted him on his dome, he tucked his head into his shoulders like a turtle.

"Prickles," mused Lucy. "I used to cut prickles off that. And stroke the tip of your schnoz. And I remember an unhealthy smell and that cadaverous old woman, and sitting on your lap listening to church music on the radio and I remember you singing to me and that wheezy laugh."

"That's it, that's me, your dear old grandad." The old fellow let out a wheezy laugh and cast an uneasy sideways glance at Laura, who sneered, folded her arms and moved away, leaving him to deal with his insane granddaughter as best he could.

As soon as Laura was out of earshot, the old man leaned conspiratorially toward Lucy and whispered, "Don't listen to her. Couldn't lie straight in bed that one, like all her family. You listen to your old grandfather, he'll tell you a story or two." Before Lucy could say anything, he had brushed past her, stationed himself in front of the squatter's chair, sighted Laura up along the length of his splendid double-barreled nose, dusted the canvas off with a crisp white handkerchief, and gingerly sat down. "The first thing you'll want to know," he said, as he folded his handkerchief neatly and placed it in the pocket of his dapper English wool suit, "is why my name is Oliver Meade." Lucy opened her mouth to speak but the old man plowed on. "Because my mother thought Oliver Meade would stand me in better stead than Mordecai Weber. She was a very smart woman."

By the time the sky had turned a luscious mango color, and the fruit bats were gorging in the trees, Laura was snoring intermittently from the chaise-longue inside and Lucy was yawning convulsively with boredom and fatigue. She had run out of excuses for interrupting the old man's soliloquy. She had, during the day, pretended to pee at least forty times, complained of headaches and hunger or used her aching back as an excuse for taking walks around the house.

On one such expedition she had found a gift on the back porch. She circled around the tin plate, containing stale, but edible, Kentucky Fried Chicken and jungle berries, as if it were an unexploded bomb. Eventually she sniffed the chicken and proceeded to devour the lot. Every day after that, she would find the plate which might contain a blackened rabbit carcass, a cockatoo feather, an orchid, mushrooms, candlenuts, or more Kentucky Fried. She came to accept these gifts with as little questioning as she might the arrival of the bats at sundown. Besides, if Laura and Olly were possible, then so were offerings on the back porch.

Olly's parents had emigrated from London where they had both been tailors. They had changed their names and their faith immediately upon entering Australia, but stuck to their profession. They saved enough to send their eldest boy, Mordecai Olly, to grammar school. His mother sewed him seven new suits and, determined not to let her down, he had studied industriously and become the manager of a haberdashery manufacturing firm. He had married the beautiful Emma, whose profound fear of sex was compensated for by her talents as a cook. Only she could prepare food bland enough to placate his angry ulcer, or soothe the gout which made him so pernickety and difficult to live with.

After the second child, his wife had a hysterectomy for psychological reasons. Although she was second generation Australian, and had never traveled out of this northern state, she referred to England as "home" and cooked roast dinners on Sundays in blistering heat; boiled the sheets on Mondays and starched her petticoats on Tuesdays. She believed in the debilitating effects of drafts and on her side table was a staggering array of pills. So cautious was she of the bacteria waiting to waylay her as she hobbled to the backyard dunny that she took to using a bedroom commode, which it was Oliver's duty to empty and clean each morning.

"Oo, yes," interrupted Lucy, who'd been trying to get a word in for some time. "I remember that sweet, putrid stench. I can see her now, propped up on a pillow, her greasy gray hair spread out. Do you remember how I broke her jaw with my cricket bat?" Olly flinched, drew breath, and continued.

Their first child, a son, died. The second child, Lucy's mother, became the treasure of their lives and the vessel of all their hopes. She could sing, dance, act, play piano and violin, had a nice, respectable job as a secretary and, best of all, had her mother's Gentile eyes and a sweet dot of a nose which turned up rather than down. She was frail as a flower, good, sweet and obedient. A perfect daughter. Then she met Lucy's brute of a father.

At the mention of her mother, Lucy, who was seemingly lost in her own thoughts and indifferent to his story, perked up and crawled closer to her grandfather's knee.

"Cruel, cruel," muttered the old man and trumpeted into his handkerchief.

"Bilge," said Laura, standing in the doorway and sucking in her cheeks so that the lantern glow from beneath made her face look more skull-like than ever. "My nephew was too soft-hearted to be cruel. That was his trouble. She ran rings around him and if anyone was cruel, it was you and that batty wife of yours."

"Liar. You've lied about all your family and your great aristocratic

73

lineage. A nastier bunch of ruffians never graced the earth. He did her in that's the truth, and you know it. You've been filling the girl's head with lies ever . . ."

Olly had the last words of his sentence blown out of him, as Laura sprang like a jumping spider. A violent struggle ensued, he florid-faced, she pale, and Lucy too dazed to intervene.

"Did her in?" she said, faintly.

The old man, wheezing and puffing as he struggled, managed to say, "Did you know, ugh, that your blue blood heritage, ah, began with a convict and that this woman's grandmother was, oof, an Indian or that . . ."

Suddenly Lucy began heaving with great belly laughs which caused the ghosts to disengage and stand around looking uncertain and flustered.

"You don't know any more than I do, do you?" she said, wiping tears away from her face. "You've no idea what really happened at the dam in the horse paddock." It was clear, from the ghosts' abashed expressions, that either they did not know or were unable to tell.

When her laughter had subsided, Lucy sank back, defeated, into the squatter's chair. Olly did his best to raise her hopes.

"But maybe what we can tell you will dislodge your own memories from the muddy bottom of the past."

"Go to hell," said Lucy, wearily, and headed for her nest.

Olly poked his tongue at her receding back and whispered to Laura, "Where does she think we are?"

7

Angel Drive

When the tall iron gates of Saint Jude's Church of England School for Girls clanged shut for the very last time, signaling that my four-year stretch inside was over, crippled pigeons rose from the hoops of barbed wire which scalloped the top of the wall. Nuns, proud of their success at transmogrifying another batch of girls into marriage fodder, moved, like bustling magpies, back into the secluded grounds. I was almost seventeen.

On my body I bore the ritual markings of an expensive and exclusive initiation into womanhood. Thanks to a diet of sugar and starch, my once perfect teeth were packed with amalgam and my buttocks were traced with the silvery snail trails of stretchmarks. My powerful eyebrow had been tamed into two femininely impotent arches. Far from being a bluestocking, I was more the rubber step-ins and sheer denier type.

I knew how to sit with my legs together and slightly to one side, how to ask for *charcuterie* in French and how to cut my slices of Tip Top into thin strips before applying the margarine. I knew vaguely about the kings and queens of England and that only laborers and Catholics voted for the Labour Party. Although ignorant of its meaning, I knew that the word Communism signified evil. I had read the abridged version of *Hamlet,* in which no mention was made of an "enseamèd bed," thus extending my reading list from three books to four. I had learned the importance of putting a Modess pad on in the privacy of a toilet, of sprinkling talc on the bathwater to prevent unseemly reflections and that it was unladylike to excel at sports because no one would marry someone with bulging calf muscles. All this I knew, and yet, somehow, I felt unprepared for the future.

What my teachers had not been able to fully extinguish in me was an instinctive loathing for authority. It remained as a cold, hard anger in my chest knocking against my ribs, demanding to be let out. I had even been labeled a "disruptive influence" and was almost expelled the day I helped the nuns decorate the hall for the senior girls' end of year dance—supposedly their first contact with members of the opposite sex—by secretly filling all the balloons with hydrogen sulphide made in the chemistry lab. When the cocky's sons let down the fishing net from the ceiling at ten o'clock for the traditional balloon-bursting finale, a giant fart oozed from windows and doorways, carrying gagging humans with it. Reaching out its foul tendrils to the hessian walls which had been constructed around the hall, it pole-axed the nuns who, in order to ensure that no monkey business occurred, stood guarding the various exits. Luckily, my neck and my future were saved by my drama teacher, who said I was an orphan with talent. My one great gift, that of pretending to be someone else, had grown in those four years, like the overdeveloped arms of a legless man.

Thus groomed, plucked, waxed, shaved, corseted, amalgamed, stretched, overweight, monosyllabically shy and longing to be anyone but Lucy McTavish—in short, educated—I now faced the Entitative World at last, certain that the beautiful woman with the open arms would take one look at me and turn her nose up in disgust.

Unable to bear the embarrassment of my school friends and their well-dressed mothers meeting Laura, I had told her to pick me up at five. From my lonely post outside the school gates, I watched her drive up the hill, hunched over the wheel and grinding the gears, oblivious to the furious honking of other cars.

I had seen her only once during my boarding school years. That meeting had made us both so miserable that we tacitly agreed I would spend future holidays with the families of my school friends. I had not told her that my school friends sometimes refused to have me, so that I often stayed penned alone in the schoolyard, with only the pigeons to witness my single-hander plays in which a very beautiful and tragic woman (me) would lose her lover (an empty teachest) and, in the final scene, wring her hands at the sky, passionately bewailing the meaninglessness of creation and the cruelty of life. The head nun had been a secret audience to one of these plays and had called me into her office to tell me that the dancing in the play was very good indeed and perhaps I might convince my aunt to provide ballet lessons. She turned her gaze contemplatively toward the ceiling and paused for a moment before pointing out that the universe was not meaningless because God was in it, then asking me if I were disturbed about something and if so might I not find blessed release through a life of devotion to Him.

The hideousness of my transformation was reflected back at me from Laura's eyes.

"Good Lord," she said, after a moment of shocked silence, "look at you," and she tried to smile. I blushed and flashed my amalgam at her.

"You look very well, Aunt Laura," I said in my new elocution voice.

"Well I'm not," she retorted, "and what's this 'aunt' business? You've never called me that in your life, what's the matter with you."

It was a bad beginning to a worse evening.

We sat in uncomfortable silence over celebratory chops and peas at the Gresham Hotel—a hangout for visiting rural gentry. Lonely, leathery men in moleskins, R.M. Williams boots and broad felt hats tucked into mountains of beef. I thought bitterly of all my fellow graduates of Saint Jude's who, at this very moment, would be eating filet mignons in restaurants which revolved around the tops of office blocks. What was my education for, if I were not going to be able to show it off in the right places?

"The Fortesques are willing to have you out on their cattle station as governess, you know. It's a marvelous property, ten million acres, and you'll meet the right sort of person."

"Oh," I said. All evening, I had been winding up the courage to tell Laura of my plans. "You see, Laura, I've got a kind of scholarship, to go to an art school. Only it's eight dollars a week and I think I'd need about another four to live because I'll be moving into a flat with a girlfriend and . . . studying acting and dance . . ." My courage wound down under her horrified glare.

"Four dollars a week as if I'm not broke already from that damned school of yours and what do you want to be an actress for you'll never be any good at it. Nothing but heartbreak and poverty I won't hear of it I simply won't."

The knocking in my chest was getting louder. I swallowed another mouthful of peas.

"And don't look at me like that. I've done nothing but worry over you for years and what do I get at the end of it but your scowling ingratitude . . ."

It was no good, vegetables could not pacify the raging beast caged in my ribs. It wanted blood. I stood up, knocked the plate from the table, sending peas flying around the room like bird-shot. "Well I don't need you, you horrible old crow," I yelled. "You never thought I was good at anything. I'll do it on my own. I don't need anybody." Aware of my startled audience, I flared my nostrils, flexed my spine and made a grand exit from the room.

Propelled by the adrenaline my burst of honesty had given me, I strode through the streets, feeling grown-up, free and morally supe-rior. It lasted until I realized, at the second corner, that I didn't know where I was, or how to survive in a strange city with no money. Guilt and remorse crept in, followed by a hefty dose of self-pity. Another block, and I thought how sorry everyone would be if I hurled myself into the river. Two streets more I toyed with the idea of going back to Laura and falling on my knees before her. She would, of course, be weeping with love and begging for forgiveness in this scenario. But no, it was always resentment and anger between us, better to start a new life, Lauraless. I hailed my very first taxi and gave the driver the address of a school friend. He stared at me in the mirror, and I prayed that she would be home.

Aware that the oddness of my arrival would need to be justified by melodrama, I embroidered a portrait of my wicked old aunt with baroque weeping. My friend Julia and her mother kept glancing at each other, and Dr. Broun tactfully left the room. Of course I was invited to stay, the taxi was paid for, the sheets were crisp and the curtains were floral. Julia came in to say good night. "Shit, Lucy," (Julia was very worldly) "this flat's going to cost a bomb, Mum can't pay for your half as well, you know."

"I said I'd get a job, Julia, tomorrow. Only I haven't got a dress."

"Tsk. Well you can wear something of mine, I s'pose."

I entered the Entitative World via the Golden Delicioso Pineapple Cannery which lay, like a suppurating wound, on the outer skin of this ugly provincial city, and for which, as fate would have it, so much of Binjigul's primary produce was destined. I wore a green and purple stretch dress, which made Julia look like a film star and made me look like a white marshmallow tightly bound with Christmas decorations.

Even now, if I need to vomit for any reason, all I need do is stand within fifteen feet of an open can of Golden Delicioso pineapple. I blushed and hung my head when the migrant women teased me; I felt sick when the foreman admonished me for being too slow at cutting out the black bits; the sweet reek and the cuts and peelings on my hands caused Julia to hold her nose and demand I find other employment. At the end of a month, I felt the wad of money in my paypacket with something approaching joy, and handed in my notice. I had enough to pay my rent and to buy some material which Mrs. Broun promised to sew into a frock.

How I envied Julia her nylon panties, her makeup, her mother, her ability to talk to boys. I tried to copy her erotic titter but from me it sounded like a colony of fruit bats. Far from feeling jealous, I worshiped her for all the attributes I so thoroughly lacked. I repaid her kindnesses by ironing her frocks and washing her knickers. I was even tongue-tied with Mrs. Broun and when she pinned the dress on me I blushed horribly. What hope, then, did I have of holding down a conversation with the second-year medical students who visited the flat with alcohol, pissed in the goldfish bowl and threw up in the bath? Next to Julia, who tossed her head and flirted, I was a social calamity.

"Lucy," she said one morning, as I squeezed into one of her dresses and gazed, tearfully, into the mirror. "You need to lose weight. And really, I don't know how you think you're going to get on with blokes, you never *say* anything. They all think you're stuck-up."

I sniffed.

"Tsk. Look, I'll get some diet pills. All those cakes and chocolates you eat, it's a wonder you aren't a mass of acne."

The pills did wonders for my figure but damaged my working life considerably. At night, I lay awake; by day, I could scarcely keep my eyes open. I was now selling lottery tickets at a newsstand. Sometimes I would go to the toilet, pass out on the pedestal and have to be woken by the boss who thought there was something seriously wrong with me. I took to drinking Nescafé and never eating anything until five in the morning, when I eventually went to sleep. Thin and neurasthenic as I had become, the pills did nothing to alleviate my verbal inadequacy.

Julia had fallen in love with a medical student and was doing things in the room next to mine at night. The noise exacerbated my insomnia and caused me to glow red in the dark.

"Shit, Lucy, do you have to prowl around all night, it's really creepy. Wayne reckons you need a psychiatrist." I couldn't bear it when Julia was angry with me. She was my best, my only friend. She cared about me enough to lock me in the toilet until I'd worked up the courage to insert a tampon. I was in there for six hours. She had instructed me in the arts of beauty which knows no pain. Both of us spent a great deal of time now with sticky tape attached to our faces, because, as her beauty book said, "Every time you smile, frown, look puzzled, or show any emotion on your face, you are creating the ground work for WRINKLES. Wear sticky tape as often as you can, and you will begin to train yourself into keeping those damaging expressions off your face." Julia had become so adept at banishing wrinkles, that I could only tell if she were angry with me by the pitch of her voice. As for me, my eternal weeping caused the sticky tape to hang off my face like soggy eucalyptus bark, and Julia to shake her head and sigh a lot. I knew she had not given up on me when she not only lent me a long black dress to wear to the Med. ball but organized a partner for me.

With nervously unreliable fingers, I applied the blue eye shadow to my lids, the brown to the hollows above them, the white under my eyebrows. I glued half a dozen mink eyelashes to the outside bottom lid and drew a black almond with eyeliner, adding little wings at the sides, like Cleopatra. Dollops of black mascara followed, then black eyebrow pencil to extend my ruthlessly plucked eyebrow. The pancake makeup was as thick as plaster and the lipstick left wrinkled red worms on the coffee cup. Rubber step-ins prevented any unsightly wobbles of flesh from my already caved-in shanks and a strapless bra pushed my breasts up like balloons and cut a deep welt into my back. As I had given up eating, enough money had been saved for a visit to a hairdresser. Rigid with lacquer, a bunch of curls sat on top of my head and two starched ringlets sprang fetchingly in front of my ears. Next came the slinky dress, and last of all, the false fingernails.

Similarly trussed, sprayed and ringleted, Julia said I looked "fab."

"Now just remember, don't stand around dumb, you've got to be animated. Doesn't matter what you say, just laugh and stuff, okay?"

Brian "Balltearer" Simpson arrived in a borrowed tuxedo but instead of a black bow tie, he sported a large flappy one on which was a naked hula dancer. He wasn't even a medical student, but Julia had hinted that beggars could not be choosers. I tried not to stare at the rampant sun cancers that were trying to take over his nose, and to concentrate on his surfie physique.

"Hi," I said animatedly, and laughed.

He stared at my bulging mammaries and asked, "What are those for, darling, to keep you afloat?"

"Ha ha, yes," I answered, but could think of nothing with which to extend the conversation so I said "ha, ha," again. Brian handed me a glass full of Bacardi, colored by a few drops of Coke. Desperate to break the grip of my shyness, I swallowed it in one gulp.

Wayne and Julia sat in the front of the car, Brian and I in the back. Wayne and Brian reminisced about football pissups. Julia asked me if I thought that slut Janet was going all the way. "Ha ha," I said, "I don't know. Ha ha." So far, so good.

I danced with many medical students that night and had my photograph taken leaning blearily on Balltearer's arm. The music was so loud, and the alcohol so free-flowing, that I could not have spoken even if I'd wanted to. But all Brian seemed to require was a string of "Is that right's" and "oh really's" as he talked about the quality of pipelines at Alexandra Headlands and how Midge Farrelly had outclassed the wogs in Hawaii. I draped myself against my various partners and smiled woozily at the spinning walls, unable to decide whether the double vision was caused by alcohol or unglued eyelashes. I threw up a few times in the Ladies, and ripped Julia's dress on the door as I crawled out, but nothing mattered. I danced. I was tongue-kissed under beer-soaked tables. I was a success.

I held Brian's arm as we staggered down the pavement. Giggling helplessly, I took off Julia's high heels which were too small and had created vast blisters.

"I s'pose a fuck'd be out of the question," he said, plunging his arm down the front of my dress.

"Ha, ha," I said and tripped in the gutter. Brian hailed a taxi. As we grappled in the backseat, he mentioned something about a pain in the balls. I was animated, but somewhere in the back of my mind, muffled by Bacardi fumes, a quarrel was taking place—something about sluts and going all the way. Balltearer tried to pinch my unyielding rubber bottom as he pushed me up the stairs. I could not place the key in the lock; it seemed very funny at the time.

Once inside, the grappling continued. Brian called on Jesus Christ to help him undo my bra. I felt it snap apart with a twang, releasing a burden of breast. He was breathing heavily. Was I doing all right, I wondered. I heard the sound of a zip.

"Here," said Balltearer, "stroke it."

I looked down at what had been placed in my hand and screamed. The size of the thing—where on earth would it fit? The last thing I remember before I fainted dead away was sliding past four false fingernails which dangled off the front of Brian Balltearer Simpson's tuxedo.

He never came back and word spread through the medical fraternity that I was a "pricktease." In the six months which followed, I took to making up plays in my head, in which a beautiful and misunderstood woman kills herself and all the people who have ever known her realize how blind they have been. They enter a deep and anguished mourning, marked by long conversations in which they all agree that the woman was the most interesting person they had ever known. But at the very nadir of my misery, who should arrive on my doorstep but Mr. van Senden, bearing a letter from Laura. He smiled around at the laminex and brick veneer before hugging me. "Well well, little Lucy, I knew you'd turn out ravishing."

A lobster blush constricted my throat and traveled up to fizzle the roots of my hair. I didn't even have any makeup on! Mercifully, Julia came out and helped the conversation along. Harry van Senden reminisced about the bad old days in Binjigul when he had dandled me on his knee. I did not remember any dandling but wasn't about to say so. Memories are never true after all. For my part, I couldn't help thinking that Harry had shrunk. Julia was deeply impressed, not least by his colossal age. Harry was now thirty-one. I thought she might disapprove because he was only a teacher, but on her way to bed she gave me a lascivious wink. My blush, which had been hiding in my ears, decided to travel. "A grooling evening" was how I described it in the locked pink and gold diary I kept under the bed.

Harry resumed his teaching role with me. He brought jazz records which I hated, and books which I refused to read. When he inquired gently as to whether I had a boyfriend and if so, was I on the pill, all the blood in my body rushed to my head, almost exploding it. Most embarrassing of all were the questions about my parents which I could not answer, and about Wally, which I would not answer. But, intellectual that he was, he was too dumb to notice that I was violently in love with him. Plagues of unfulfilled sexual fantasies decimated my days and nights like locusts. Now, when I sat on the toilet, it was Harry's voice I imagined saying "Marry me." I no longer needed the diet pills, desire prevented me from eating or sleeping. Waves of heat rose from my body as he sat next to me, reading incomprehensible sonnets, but Harry remained impervious.

It wasn't until the day of the picnic that I finally broke through to his baser instincts. Julia, Wayne, Harry and I had driven to the country with a crate full of Barossa Pearl wine. I knew that Harry did not think much of my friends, in fact he referred to them as "dickheads," but he came along for my sake. Julia had given me some tactical tips, so during the long drive home, I put my head in his lap and pretended to sleep.

Cozily, I nestled my head in his warm crotch, and felt something soft stirring against my left ear. Harry cleared his throat and his hand dropped gingerly onto my arm. I made murmuring noises and squirmed my head a little more. The lump in Harry's trousers pushed comfortably at my receptive ear. He took his arm away and I heard him swallow noisily. Harry's honor was no match for Barossa Pearl and hormones. Three weeks later, under a lime green candlewick cover, we were doing what Julia, Wayne and chooks did.

Such was the intensity of my unplugged lust that the night I offered up my maidenhead went by without a hitch. I don't remember any pain, in fact, I don't remember much at all, except thinking how uncomfortable and overrated the experience was. But oh, how different the dawning. I was painfully aware that my hair must be ruffled and there were probably mascara smudges all over my face. Luckily, I woke first, and did my best to repair the damage so that I would be acceptable to my love. Something was tickling my legs. I lifted the covers tentatively, and found little black house ants crawling over the blood on the sheets. I crushed them brutally, careful not to disturb Harry, and prayed that he would not look down there at the sticky mess. What a thoroughly unromantic business. How could he love me if he saw me like this? When he did wake, he seemed moody and uncommunicative even though he cradled me like a father. My nose was being squashed sideways by his sternum as he rocked me back and forth. This intimacy, despite what had occurred only a few hours earlier, made me rigid with embarrassment and I had to resist an urge to struggle loose and run.

Harry did not contact me for a week, but when he did, he seemed to have made up his mind about something.

For four months, the pink and gold diary recorded that I was "blissfully happy." Even diaries can lie, but at least I was happier than before. Deep, permanent happiness, the kind that other people had, was just not part of my chemistry and I figured that this was as much as I could expect. Harry pampered me and took me out to eat filet mignons. Under the warmth of his growing love, and increasing possessiveness, my old butterfly self was beginning to emerge again. I clowned and acted and made him laugh. I put on funny voices and strange hats. I twirled an umbrella and walked along the wrought-iron railing of the patio, twenty feet above the ground. I dazzled him with my colorful wings, so that poor Harry failed to notice the ugly insect at the heart of his butterfly.

I kicked myself for being so petty as to notice the brownish stains on his underpants and the faint ruff of dandruff which dusted his black polo-neck skivvie. I wanted him to wear suits or football shorts like everyone else. Harry was not as socially acceptable as I had once thought. Wayne confided to Julia that he thought my love a "poofter-wanker," and even Julia was now proclaiming him a bit "dullsville." I defended him, of course, and insisted that it did not matter that he played Aussie rules instead of Rugby League, but I could only, for so long, hide the information that he voted for the D.L.P. which wasn't as bad as voting for the A.L.P. but nevertheless suggested pinko tendencies. The truth came out one night when Harry, made bold by Bacardi, started a political argument with some of the dickheads. I died with shame and Julia muttered something unkind about Commies and Micks.

Lately, when he pushed his books at me, the knocking in my chest would start up and a pout of resistance would mar my otherwise adoring countenance. At first, in an effort to please him, I had struggled through ten pages of *Being and Nothingness,* but spent so long with a dictionary open beside me, that I eventually threw both books at the wall with a roar of rage. Sometimes, as I lay with my head on his shoulder at night, suppressing gargantuan yawns and listening to him lecture on literature, I felt a faint rustle of annoyance when he put a finger under my chin and tilted my head toward his because he sensed that my attention was wandering, or that I might be going to sleep.

Worst of all, when he came to my narrow bed, all damp and wrinkled from the shower, I felt like a patient about to be examined by a doctor. The fact that I didn't have the required orgasms worried him terribly. He took to rubbing ever more energetically at my already gravel-rashed genitals. I lay, wincing, with my legs apart, appalled at my frigidity.

The next night, as I lay with my nose puckered, I decided to save face and genitals by moaning heavily as described in Julia's sex manual. Harry moaned also. "Oh God," I said. "In, in, in," said Harry. "Ahhhh," I sighed. "Jesus," puffed Harry. And then it was all over. He flung himself onto his back, teeth phosphorescent, penis detumescent in the moonlight—a smiling, victorious man. I looked at him and said, "wow," in a throaty voice. Harry said, "I told you it would just happen."

Perhaps it was the pressure of this constant lying which turned my distaste into an overwhelming desire to escape. My once tropical longings had cooled into a frosty rejection. Perhaps Wayne was right, and I needed a shrink. Here I was with everything a girl could hope for—the love of a professional man, prospects of marriage and travel, children no doubt, why then did I feel the walls closing in, why did I endlessly fantasize about leaving one morning, dressed in a monk's robe, my hair chopped off like a boy's, with no money or possessions and throwing myself into the freedoms and fortunes of the open road. What explanation could there be, other than that I was mad?

I had a good job as a library assistant but, owing to the destructive power of love and diet pills, I seldom went to work and when I did, my acting skills were stretched to their limit by having to walk with a convincing limp, or having to speak with a perennially blocked nose. Anorexic and prone to falling asleep while answering the telephone, I found it easy, at first, to convince my employers of my shockingly feeble constitution. I complained variously of flu, hay fever, back strain, liver problems, kidney ailments, nervous disorders, migraines, twisted ankles and that-time-of-the-month disease.

"I'b sorry I'b late, Bister Hobkids, I've got the flu agaid, but I did't wad to take adother day off I dow how busy we are." I had arrived two hours late and Mr. Hopkins sat nervously fiddling with his spectacles.

"Miss McTavish, I'm I'm I'm"—Mr. Hopkins was a most timorous man and I knew that even looking at, let alone addressing, me demanded enormous courage on his part. I smiled warmly and tried to help him out.

"You're busy? Wel dod't worry, Bister Hobkids, I'll get idto the reshelvig straightaway." I wheeled my trolley to the one hundreds, limping. No sooner had I settled on my seat with a book in my hand and nodded off to sleep, than I felt his presence hovering at the end of the stack. I leapt up, shelved the book and turned to him brightly. He clutched the gray steel bookcase, took a big breath and said, all in a rush, "I have to terminate your employment."

"Terbidate?"

"You used up all your sick pay weeks ago, and you shelved several English Literature books under the six hundreds last week. Your mind doesn't seem to be on your job." Sweat had broken out on his forehead and he seemed close to tears.

"Oh, Mister Hopkins," I said desperately, "I'll do better I promise I will." Such was the shock of being fired that I quite forgot my flu, but Mr. Hopkins, for reasons of his own, suggested kindly that I go home to bed, and not bother coming in again. For the first few moments, as I stepped back out into the stunning sunshine the more pleasant aspects of leaving this dusty morgue forever made me light-headed. But the fleeting sense of relief was soon crushed.

I plucked aimlessly at the tufts of my lime green candlewick bedspread. I wanted to say something, but when my lips moved, nothing came out. Harry van Senden, the older man of my dreams and depository of years of toilet-trained sexual fantasy, upon hearing the news of my unemployed state, had just asked me to marry him. His eyes were fixed on some faraway point and behind his intelligently furrowed brow his imagination raced.

"We could travel, you know, all over Australia. You're special, Lucy. You're not like these dickheads you hang around with. When we're married I'll be able to show you things, teach you things, introduce you to a larger world."

How I yearned to roam that larger world, to witness the Aurora Borealis, the Leaning Tower of Pisa, the Pyramids—but a hundred

Binjiguls were not what I had in mind. It seemed churlish and ungrateful to say so.

"And old Laura would like it, knowing you were being looked after."

"You haven't told her we're together though, have you?" Harry looked at me sharply, displaying the guilty grimace of a cradle snatcher, though who snatched whom was open to debate.

I had picked a three-inch patch of bedspread bald. In order to cover my profound ambivalence to his proposal, I offered myself up for love. Later, when his satisfied snores grated on my insomnia, I prowled the flat with bowed legs, in a welter of conflicting emotions. There was something cold and wicked in me which shut out love—a frigidity of the soul. I betrayed people. First Wally, then Laura and now Harry. Probably my parents as well if only I could remember. I was a failure at everything. I did not fit anywhere.

Why did my gorge rise when I thought of life with Harry? He was good and kind and I owed him everything. He had even introduced me to a director at the local repertory theater who had given me my first part as a talking wall. I never understood what the play was about but I delivered my only line with such gusto that everyone agreed it was just the beginning. There were rep. theaters all over the country, even in Tamboola.

During that long night's vigil in front of the blank television screen, my desperation was boundless. Everything I touched seemed to turn to shit—the coprous touch. I imagined holding a pistol at my temple and pulling the trigger to blast this perverse head of mine all over the world. Curiously, this act of violence made me feel much better, so then I imagined swimming out to sea on a dark night, until I was too tired to return to shore. That made me feel better still. I would sink below the surface, swallowed forever by a blackness of ocean. No need to struggle and fail any more, everyone would miss me terribly and understand, at last, how deeply I had suffered. The relief was only temporary, however, because death would prevent me from enjoying the flattery.

Listlessly I picked up Harry's newspaper and tried to read, but the words trembled on the page like little black ants. "Actresses." The little black ants began to bunch themselves into recognizable phrases. "Actresses who respond to strict discipline required. Excellent pay. 176 Ocean View Heights . . ."

I stood up, sat down, stood up again and laughed out loud. Ripping the advertisement out with a flourish and holding it next to my hammering heart I strode around the flat, made more coffee and shivered in wonderment at the plan taking root in me. Could I? Dare I? My second self, my guardian angel, stepped forward and took control.

My note to Harry said, "You are too good for me. Try to forget me. Be happy." The note to Julia said, "Jules, here is the five dollars I owe you, thanks for everything, heading south." My note to Laura said, "I've just landed a fabulous acting job. Will write soon. Much love, Lucy."

I threw my sleeping bag onto the floor of the cabin, fingered the thirty dollars in my pocket and swung myself onto the high seat, smiling at the navy-singleted man behind the wheel of the Fridgemobile road-train. He started at my shoes and slowly worked his way up to my eyes. His grin was gap-toothed as he handed me a greasy pillow.

"Righto, kid, no questions asked, your job's to keep me awake and to watch out for the fuzz."

"You bet," I said.

Oh, the unmatchable, delicious vertigo of a spirit unleashed. I had taken the correct fork in the road of life: I had done something right. The sticky past was vibrating to a blur in the rearview mirror, the future lay unsullied through the windshield. I could erase all the flaws and mistakes and make myself up. Not one regret, not one fear nagged at my delight. All had been obliterated by this one supreme act of inspired folly.

"What do I call youze, then?" he shouted above the drumroll of cylinders.

"Huh? Oh, ah, Julia. Jules Hunter."

"Righto, Jewels, hang on to your hat, kid, we'll chuck her into angel drive." My new friend swallowed six pills with a swig of whiskey, followed by black coffee from a thermos, put the truck into neutral, tucked his legs up on the seat and sent us hurtling down a long, winding hill, laughing maniacally.

"Oh," I ventured, tentatively.

"No worries, kid, we'll get you to the big smoke, no wuckin' furries." And then he started to sing.

"Bring me my spear of burning gold, bring me my arrows of desire, bring me my something, da da dee dee daa . . ."

"Bring me my chariot of fire," I bellowed.

Eight hours later, we'd exhausted our repertoires and high spirits. Les was having trouble with his eyelids and my punch in the ribs technique was losing its effect. I was worried.

"Les, we've got to stop."

"Like I said, one wife in the Cape, one down south, keep 'em both happy no wuckens," and he shook his head like a wet dog.

"Les, I have to go to the toilet."

"What again? Struth, you must have a Japanese bladder, girl."

Les jogged around the truck, beer gut bobbing, while I crouched behind a bush pretending to pee. The exercise seemed to do him some good and we drove for another four hours.

The white line flicked like a strobe light, splitting the road into halves which seemed to be curling up around my ears. I floated down into the furrow.

"This isn't your track," said a voice.

"Wally? Wally, where are you?" But to the right of me stretched a dark plain, dry and crackling. On the left lay a cemetery. "You're in the wrong dream," said a voice, but now it sounded like a woman I knew but couldn't remember. Now a naked black woman, decorated in ocher and feathers, beckoned me to the cemetery, saying, in a strange tongue, "This track doesn't belong to you. I'll sing you to sleep or I'll sing you to death." The grass plain had turned to a lake. Like brown muscles the swirling water closed over me. I'll just hide underwater, I thought, then they won't be able to find me. But the soldiers would not go away and I was drowning. I struggled for the surface but it was such a long way up. I broke through the muddy eddies, just as the truck crashed into the cliff.

Luckily, we had been crawling up the mountain, not swooping down it. Les agreed that maybe he did need to snooze for a while after all. He set six alarm clocks, pulled out some blankets and fell asleep right in the middle of making a lunge for me. He landed, snoring, in my lap, one hand on his fly.

And so it was that, borne in a chariot of fire, and having witnessed my gladiator's sword sleeping in his hand, I set all my bridges aflame, crossed an enchanted harbor, and entered Sin City at dawn, proving that there is more than one way to leave a life behind.

8

The Little Existentialist

Crystalline towers jutted from rims of sandstone which plunged down into the mouths of breakers breathing spume. Bridges as delicate as fish skeletons disappeared into the haze of the northern shore, and quarreling blossoms of lorikeets burst from the branches of coral trees into iridescent air. The sun rose and a rainbow formed over my city of gold, my New Jerusalem.

I leaned against the sea wall a little longer, the breeze rubbing against me like a cat as I breathed in the harsh, salt smell, and listened to a music as beguiling as the sound of a forest—the rhythmic boom of rollers, the clink of anchor chains, the tender cries of terns as they lifted into the gathering light and the sleepy, mechanical grinding of streets.

All around the park were groups of people with long hair strumming guitars and inhaling so strenuously on their cigarettes that the veins in their necks stood out. I sat as close to one party as shyness would allow, mimicking their odd ritual, sucking on my Drum tobacco like a professional. They noticed me, smiled and nodded and one of them held up two fingers in a V. I wandered off, dizzy and disappointed, wondering if, perhaps, the V sign was some kind of insult. I had seen these types giving that sign to policemen on television, so they were probably Communists. This rejection of them did not ease my anger with myself for being a coward. I had abandoned my former self; had blazed a trail all the way from Binjigul to the metropolis, but where was the different, dynamic me who could stride up to strangers and impress them with my wit and intelligence? I had the looks, all I needed now was the personality.

Rather than give way to these gloomy thoughts, I decided it was time to embark on my career as a famous actress. I took out my much fingered newspaper cutting, and rang the number. The man on the other end of the line told me to come straightaway, which could only mean that he liked the sound of my voice and my excellent presentation. He did not even ask if I had any experience. I swung into the public lavatories to wash and change for the interview.

Unwilling to appear like a country bumpkin, I had neglected to ask for directions. By midday, my blistered and bleeding feet had lost their way twice and been misdirected once. Sweat waterlogged the pancake makeup; my hands were red and swollen from heaving a suitcase and sleeping bag through the city and out to the suburbs. I hailed a taxi, wondering anxiously how much of my thirty dollars would be eaten up by such extravagance, but if the audition went as I expected, I would soon enough be riding in limousines.

The office was disappointingly small and rather grubby. Photographs of women in black lace bras pouted down from the walls at a grizzle-haired man whose attention was buried in *Being and Nothingness*.

"Great book, isn't it," I said, trying to remember what I had read in the first ten pages. The man swept an unemotional gaze up and down my body, as if I were a short-horn being judged in the Tamboola Show. A sudden smile cracked open his rocky face.

"Ralph," he said, extending his hand.

"Jewels," I answered, extending mine.

"You a little Existentialist, are you?"

"Not necessarily," I said, "I'm an actress."

The smile broadened. "Okay, turn around will you, Jewels, uh huh, bend over, yeah, turn right round, yeah. Okay sweetie, not bad, now let's see your titties."

I laughed carelessly and asked him to repeat what he had said.

"Titties, boobies, little pink rosebuds, come on, sweetie, haven't got all day."

"There must be some mistake," I said faintly. "You advertised for actresses."

"Want to move straight in with the big girls, eh? Big money, big girls. Have to have some pretty pictures first, don't we, darling. Come on now, dress off or piss off."

There was a buzzing sound in my ears and everything seemed to have slowed down. It was impossible that anything bad was happening, so there was no need to feel frightened. This was probably what all movie stars had to do at first. If only I could stop tripping over as I tugged off my rubber step-ins. City people knew how to take their clothes off with panache, without blushing. I tried to straighten my vulture hunch and to control my arms which kept wrapping around my body, inadequately obscuring the rosebuds and triangle of black which Ralph referred to as my "beaver."

Despite the hot lights of the studio, I shivered as I curled my body around a papier-mâché palm tree and dangled a bunch of plastic grapes in front of my open mouth.

Click. "Come on baby, think sexy thoughts."

Click. "I said *sexy* thoughts."

Click. "Forget your grandmother, imagine your boyfriend's cock, all drippy and juicy."

Somehow, the image of Harry van Senden's penis did nothing to remove the stony grimace from my face, or to control the wobbling of my chin.

Ralph came out from behind the camera, with one hand on his hip, the other clapped to his forehead.

"Haven't done this before, huh?"

"Well, not exactly this sort of thing, I mean, I thought, you know, if I could just have a really small part at first . . ."

Ralph considered for a moment. He looked at me in a kindly sort of way. "Your old pal Sartre once said, 'We only become what we are by the radical and deep seated refusal of that which others have made of us.' " He paused, letting the gravity of his words sink in. "I'm talking about the liberation of women here. Take yourself, for instance." He allowed me a moment to take myself. "Now I'll just bet that where you come from, they're a bit, ah, prudish, would that be right?" I did not need to answer.

"Okay, 'nuff said. Listen I've got sheilas putting themselves through Uni. doing this stuff. And remember, man is free. The coward makes himself cowardly. The hero makes himself heroic. Your pal said that, so what do you reckon, sweetie, you want to do this or not?"

I wanted to say no, but pride forced a weak little yes from my lips. Ralph poured me a stiff gin, chucked me under the chin, and turned down the lights.

"Okay, your face is a problem, so we'll forget the face. A nice tasteful picture, don't even have to look at me, just open your legs a bit, come onnn baby, trust me, trust me, now a dab of pussy juice there to catch the light . . ."

The pussy juice, a Vaseline-like substance applied from a bottle to my "beaver," which Ralph was endeavoring to split, terminated my modeling career. I snapped my legs together like nutcrackers and, numbed by gin and shame, threw on my clothes and fled. Ralph followed me up the street waving something. "Hey, sweetie." He caught up with me, laughing, stuffed five dollars and a pair of rubber step-ins into my hand and said, "If you'll take my advice you'll give up philosophy and go marry an accountant."

Luckily, there was a huge park not far away. In a quiet clump of friendly trees, I flung my possessions then my body on the grass, and wept. Every time I thought the tears had dried up, I would see myself clinging to a palm tree eating grapes, and the stinging disgrace would release another bout of howling.

"Failure, idiot, hayseed, hick, fool, moron, baby, unsophisticate," I sobbed. But, as any victim of a histrionic nature will tell you, there is a point at which one realizes that all the flooding in the world does not alter the facts. A girl has to go on, one step at a time, left foot, right foot, the Arthur Murray dance strategy of life. I dried my eyes, imagined what I might have done to that creep Ralph if I'd had Laura's shotgun, and went to the kiosk in search of chocolates and cigarettes.

I nestled down in my sleeping bag to enjoy the sunset, then counted the stars hanging like fireflies from the branches, before drifting on to the quiet sea of sleep. I was dreaming that I was saddling my horse, and when I heard the words: "What do you think you're up to?" I thought it was Laura.

"You bloody hippies, I ought to turn you in for vag. Pack up and get out of here before I call the police." The park warden looked like Nessus silhouetted against the trees.

How different the streets looked at two a.m. Where there had been iron lace and Afghan hounds, now there were locked doors, alley cats and armies of big, self-confident cockroaches. I built myself a poisonous little fire, there in the alleyway, zipped the sleeping bag up to my neck, wedged myself between a rickety fence and a garbage bin, and tried, again, to sleep. The fire managed to keep the metallic rustling of cockies out of my dreams, but was powerless against Evil Incarnate who, every time I closed my eyes, took on the form of my whispering ancestor with the sidewhiskers. Rather than let him gouge out my eyes, I forced myself to wake into an overcast morning and an equally bleak state of mind. Life, it seemed, was nothing but preparation for an exam I was destined to fail.

I hauled my belongings back to the park, hid them in tall grass then walked to the city. I signed on at the dole office and asked an estate agent if she had anything cheap to rent. She drove me to a subsiding fibro cottage. I paid her a week's rent in advance, and a small deposit for gas and electricity, which left me with just under ten dollars on which to live until the dole check came through in two weeks' time. I walked back to the park then caught a taxi which delivered me and my luggage to 44 Leadbelly Street.

The driver, smiling lasciviously, asked if he could come in. I smiled deferentially and said, "Um no." Still smiling lasciviously, he said, "So maybe next time." Still smiling deferentially, I said, "Um, yes," and retreated into the safety of my new home like a peeled snail finding its shell.

The cottage consisted of four rooms, rather like the ones used in psychology tests. There was not a ninety degree angle anywhere. The walls were dung-colored fibro, papered in fly excreta. A stained mattress reeked of cat piss. An antique sewing machine leaned into a corner. There was a broken gas heater, a gas stove, an ancient Dresden-Meyer piano with missing teeth, two dangling light bulbs, neither of which worked, and seventeen feral cats, who watched me from various holes in the walls with green, suspicious eyes. The cottage was also the hub of the city's cockroach colony. "Gosh I can do a lot with this place," I thought gleefully and set about doing just that.

Youth, believing itself invincible, imagines it can take on the world without getting scarred. Youth is very stupid. Yet it is often accompanied by an innocence so palpable that even the most hardened exploiters falter before it. Proof of this was that during my months in Leadbelly Street I was threatened by many mighty swords, but never actually run through. Unwelcome penises became a kind of leitmotif in my life. There was the taxi driver's penis, for example, which he took from his trousers and gently laid on the piano keys. I had invited him in for a cup of tea because he seemed so lonely. There was the penis which belonged to the gentleman flasher in my street. He always asked very politely whether it could be of service to me, to which I replied, equally politely, that it could not. Sometimes, a penis of unknown origin would poke through a hole in the back fence and I often considered building a fish-trap for it. I began to wonder whether I emanated some chemical which attracted them. Even Bas Manson, the poet I found asleep on my front porch one evening, could not resist telling me the story of his penis, although he did not offer to expose it until the following night.

Looking back, I feel a wistful desire to protect this young woman's innocence. I see her turning a mattress, whistling to herself, swatting cockroaches and sweeping floors with a branch of grevillea, stealing milk from porches at six a.m. and begging in restaurants for leftovers. She crouches by her candle, scribbles frenetically in her little pink diary, seduces cats from their corners with fish scraps from Mrs. Pasquali's shop, discovers treasures in the refuse of others—three-legged chairs, cups without handles, bottles to hold roses stolen from the gardens of the rich. I see her rummaging through dumps with the translucent look of the divinely ignorant, or stretching out on her mattress of cat piss and other people's dirt, thinking that the world was hers, and could not hurt her.

I see her walking ten, twenty, thirty miles a day, under lamplights, through alleys, along harbor walls, always looking, listening, comparing and wondering; pausing to watch a fully dressed sailor standing in a doorway, fucking a fully dressed prostitute, who is mindlessly munching on a meat pie with peas under the lid; observing a woman douche herself over a drinking fountain at four a.m. I see that there is neither disgust nor fear nor pity nor judgment on her watching face, only a starving curiosity. She survived because she loved life, not because she feared death, and I want her back, I want her to move in with me, so that she might remind me how it feels.

Mrs. Pasquali's enormously fat arms jiggled as she banged the sizzling fat out of a cage of chips. It was as if, during her years of slavery to the vats, grease had osmosed through her skin, bloating her into yellowish blubber. Her peasant generosity was the size of her bulk. She thumped one last time and turned a vast portion of chips onto paper.

"No good you eata the chips alla the time. A young girl like you, no good how you live, ah?" Mama had been looking out for me ever since I told her, proudly, that I lived on three dollars a week. She would tap on my window from time to time, to see if I were all right, or bring little parcels of home-cooked food. Once, she chased the gentleman flasher with a carving knife, threatening to cut his "cazzo" off. I struggled to repay her by giving her little things I had found in garbage cans, but this only increased her generosity.

"It's no good, ah? Lebanese men, they watcha your house. Maybe coonsa too." I looked up at the photos on the wall—one of a tomb-stone Mama's money had bought back in Italy. It was a large slab of polished granite with a crack chiseled in it, and plaster casts of her father's hands, ripping the crack apart. Her conversation continued along its usual lines. How her son Nick was getting on at dentistry school. How the Lebanese who shared this suburb with the Italians were worse than pigs; how the coons from the neighboring suburb caused so much trouble, interspersed with details of Papa's splenec-tomy. Luckily, Mama had enough spleen for both of them.

I liked Mrs. Pasquali a great deal, and did not, for the moment, dwell too much on her racial theories. Besides, I was not devoid of them myself.

I had wandered into the Aboriginal suburb one night and felt a prickling of unease. It was as if all the eyes watching me through broken windows and dilapidated doors were full of hate. I tried to control the hastening of my footsteps. "What are they angry at me for? It wasn't my fault I was born into a superior race, any more than it was their fault that they were born into an inferior one. Survival of the fittest. So what right did they have to make me feel that I couldn't walk on a street where they happened to live. It was a free country and it belonged to everybody."

One of the cruising police cars had pulled up beside me. There was something about the eyes of those policemen, the anger with which they told me to piss off out of there, and the growling of their Alsatian dogs, which frightened me more than the eyes of the people who inhabited the derelict houses. It was the first area of the city which had defeated my courage and the experience remained in my memory like an uncomfortable itch. It made me feel guilty and I hadn't even done anything wrong.

Bas Manson looked so harmless, tragic and Wally-like, curled up against my front door in the fetal position with his hands clasping an empty flagon of Invalid Port to his chest, that I brought him inside without a moment's hesitation. He lived in an old two-tone Holden station wagon, but there were moments when even he needed comfort and security in which to rest his free spirit. His nose, which had an uncanny ability to sniff out the suckers who would take in strays, had directed him straight to me. He rocked back and forth, warming his hands on the cup, quiet tears rolling down a face which might have been beautiful had it not been malnourished from birth, and had its features not been rearranged in countless brawls.

Bas spoke to me as an equal, as if I would understand the sufferings in his life. In the flattering light of this acceptance of me as a suitable receptacle for his trust and confidence, I was transformed into a woman of the world, capable of taking all its burdens on my shoulders, able to soothe away all pain.

"Oh, yes," I said, my voice throaty and mellow with maturity, "I know."

"I was fourteen when they sent me to reform school. My mother was a drunk and my father was a psychopath. I still wet the bed. I'd do anything to hide the sheets but they always found out. I got whipped and beaten up and laughed at. So one night, I tied a rubber band around my penis. It swelled up like a balloon, you know?"

"Oh, you poor thing. I know. I know."

"But even in jail they couldn't break me. I never let them win, I've got scars on my back, you know? Here, look."

Tentatively, and with something approaching worship, I touched the bubbly marks across his puny back. But suddenly, my new friend became feverishly excited. He leapt to his feet and began pacing the floor where I knelt, gazing up.

"Don't you understand? I don't want pity. It's of no use to me. Losing is purely a state of mind. If they say, 'Scrub out this cell with a toothbrush, cunt,' you do the best job you can, and then you say, 'Is this all right, or shall I do it again?' 'Yeah, prick, do it again,' so you do it again, you know? And you do it and do it, and you whistle as you do it, you know? They can't beat you unless you let them."

"That's *it*," I cried, standing up and pacing around the room behind him. "You're absolutely *right*."

"So I started going through the dictionary, you know? Every day, ten new words and I started writing poetry."

97

"Gosh, that's fantastic."

"You like poetry?" Bas had stopped pacing, and was looking as if he'd just opened a mussel and found a pearl.

"Like poetry?" I said ferreting around in my mind for any shreds of those hateful verses about daffodils drummed into me at school, "I *love* poetry."

"You're wonderful," said Bas, seizing my shoulders and smiling toothlessly into my face. "You're fresh, you're young, you're wonderful." He dashed out to the Holden, and came back with books. " 'You do not doooo, you do not doo any more black shooo, in which I have lived like a foot for thirty years, barely daring to breathe or achoooo, Daddy, I have had to kill yoooo.' It's a love poem really. That cooing sound, like a dove, you know?"

This time I did know. The words of the poems made me expand, filled me with a sorrowing joy, as if something I had longed to express had finally found a voice. By the time the first light poked through the clothes hanging from the curtain rails, I knew much of Sylvia Plath and Ted Hughes off by heart, and I was hopelessly infatuated, whether with Bas or poetry, I was not sure.

I gave him my bed to sleep in while I curled up beside the piano, and when I woke him with tea at midday, he proclaimed his undying love for me.

Before I'd had time to recover from the shock, he had swung me around the room and, with contagious enthusiasm, begun to imagine how we would fix up the house once we were married, what we would plant in the garden, how many babies we would have. Babies? It was all so sudden. But he was so much what I wanted to be that the whirlwind romance sucked me up and dumped me, gasping, on the bed.

Luckily, our chances of having babies were severely hampered by the fact that Bas's baby-maker refused to obey his commands. Whether this was due to rubber bands, or some other secret affliction, I did not know and dared not ask.

"Damn, damn," he spat, moving agitatedly around the room, candlelight playing on his scars, one hand punching into the other palm.

"It doesn't matter, honestly Bas, I don't mind." Not only did I not mind, I was relieved. Bat-tunnel activities with Wally had obviously left permanent scars. He climbed back into bed, said nothing, and flinched when my leg happened to brush against his. Slowly, the understanding that it was my fault crept over my flesh and into my chest. I was so frigid, uninteresting and ugly, that I couldn't even raise an erection on the man I loved. Tentatively, I reached out to touch him. "Get off," he growled, and rolled away from me.

The next day, and every day thereafter, no mention was made of our nocturnal failures and the marriage plans continued unaffected. It was as if the daytime couple, so happy and full of love, had no connection whatsoever with the nighttime couple, who lay on separate sides of the bed, one wondering if there were a school you could go to to learn how to make love, the other grinding molars in accompaniment to his dreams.

It was not long before the problems of the night began corroding our days. Bas might disappear for twenty-four hours without warning or explanation but when I questioned him obliquely as to what kind of life he led away from Leadbelly Street, he intimated that I was suffocating him. This tactic always chastened me, but did not kill my curiosity.

"Been somewhere nice?" I asked, smiling brightly and chopping carrots.

"Lucy, you're as beautiful as sunshine and domesticity does not suit you."

"But we've got to eat," I pointed out, feeling oddly wounded, and trying to get back the knife, which he held, just out of reach.

"Nature provides for all her free spirits." Bas looked at me tolerantly and handed back the knife. I felt something rankle inside, like a spanner in the works. I did not object to his having a free spirit but why did he never cook for me or shop or take any responsibility for the cats or wash up?

"Well she hasn't done much to help me find an acting job," I muttered, afraid at my own daring. I continued chopping while Bas leaned against the doorway. He laughed suddenly and came over to kiss my neck.

"You don't need to do art, Lucy, you *are* art."

I was flattered, of course. But just being art was not all that fulfilling, I wanted to do it too.

That week, I scrimped enough to be able to buy poster paints and a brush, which I hid under the piano. For the first time in our friendship, I found that I was anxious for Bas to leave. At last he went, saying in a surly voice that he didn't know when he'd be back. I smiled and said

"Fine," which only seemed to sour him further, a piece of behavior which, had I studied it, might have helped me understand something about the nature of power, but there was no time for that, because I could hear the wings of the angel of inspiration beating high overhead, and the answering twitters of my own creativity. I waved cheerfully as he drove away, locked the door, retrieved my materials from under the piano, and sat in front of a wall, waiting for that hovering creature to land on me.

I waited for a very long time. It wasn't that I couldn't *see* the landscape I wanted to paint, but when I put the brush to the wall, the autumn trees, the little thatched cottage, all vanished, and what remained were ugly green and brown streaks.

I wandered up to the Pasqualis' shop, demoralized, and wondering if a bullet passing through a brain would cause death before it caused pain. There, waiting for me on a shelf behind the counter, was Inspiration in the form of a chocolate box covered with the very scene I had been imagining. If I bought the chocolates, I would be penniless for the rest of the week, but what was more important, life or art? With Bas's aphorism—There is no work of art that is without shortcuts—in mind, I scurried home and applied my attention, again, to the wall.

Six hours later, I stepped back from my creation and experienced that incomparable moment of perfect stillness a true artist feels when she has given her all. My mural was not a faithful copy of the landscape on the box, but the bridge looked like a bridge, and the blobs of color in the water could, with a generous amount of imagination, remind one of lilies. It was such a wonderful painting that I could barely believe Lucy McTavish was its author. I hid the chocolates and burned the box.

But when I came back to review my work, I saw that not only was it vile, but even when I cheated I could do nothing but fail.

There was no time for further castigation, because Bas might return and see my monstrous lack of talent displayed all over the living room. I tried to wash the wall clean with soap and water, but the ghost of my incompetence remained. In panic and rage I grabbed the cans of paint and began to throw their contents at the offending wall.

"Take that, you fake." A streak of bright, dribbling red.

"And that, you cheat, you stupid cow." Lines of blue, like stab marks, then furious squiggles of white. I took up the brush like a weapon, and added jabs of black. And so on, until the whole horrible

100

lie had been covered with snarling, swirling, seething paint. I had emptied myself out. I no longer cared that I had no explanation ready for the violence on the wall. At least Bas would never know that I'd tried to be an artist and failed.

When he came in I was in a deep, exhausted sleep. He was in a daze, and after handing me two white pills and a flagon of Invalid Port, he sat on the floor of the bedroom, and proceeded to take apart a rusting alarm clock, piece by tiny piece. The tink tink of minuscule pieces of metal being lined up on the floor had an effect on me similar to chalk screeching on a blackboard.

"What are these pills?"

"Mandrax." He giggled and continued fiddling. I felt a scream rise in my throat, but suppressed it by swallowing the pills.

"Why are you taking the clock apart?"

"So I can put it together again."

"But why?"

"Because, just because."

"Can you make it work?"

"No."

"Then why are you doing it?"

"Because it's there."

I knew if I did not leave I'd become violent, so I went to the kitchen and tried to make tea. For some reason, I could not aim the water straight into the pot. Every now and then a knee would refuse to support me. I lurched into the bedroom and swept away the innards of the clock, whereupon I found that my veils of shyness had lifted, exposing the person I had always wanted to be. I do not recall precisely what was said, but I know we had a soaring conversation about Poetry and Life, after which I pulled us both off the bedroom floor and, colliding with various doorways and walls, stumbled toward the alcohol in the kitchen. One of the walls we bumped into was spattered with paint.

"Fuck," said Bas.

I didn't say anything. He repeated himself, and let go of my arm in order to peer closely at the abomination.

"The spontaneity of it," he breathed, "the hostility and ferocity, and these strong passages of black and white, forcing the eye to move from vortex to vortex of intensity." He turned to stare at me with his mouth open and new respect in his eyes.

I took a long, lingering look at the wall. Eventually I said, "Yeah. The vortexes were the hardest bits."

Later, the pills and the alcohol knocked me into sleep; I woke to the sound of vomiting.

"Listen and listen carefully. I've shot up too much smack, heroin, understand? Stay awake and look after me."

"Ambulance," I gasped, and tried to get up but he gripped my arm hard.

"You don't move. You don't do anything. If you call a doctor they'll put me back in the nick." Surges of panic struggled just beneath the heavy weight of the drug, and I pulled away.

"If you call a doctor, I'll kill you."

My body was begging for sleep. I watched him walk toward the door, saw his legs buckle sideways and his body collapse to the ground, but could not move.

Late the next morning, when he brought me a cup of tea in bed, his face was ashen and eerie and his hands trembled. Overcome by guilt that I had not even stayed awake during his ordeal, I threw my arms around him and begged to know how he was. He smiled at me as if I were mad, said he was fine and peeled my arms away from his neck.

Our life went on as before, only now there were two taboo topics that belonged to the night and disappeared without trace each morning.

"If you bring forth what is within you, what you bring forth will save you. If you do not bring forth what is within you, what you do not bring forth will destroy you." Bas was referring to my doubts about ever becoming an actress. For all his faith in my future, he had offered no suggestions as to how it might come about. It seemed to me that his words could equally well apply to the schizophrenic existence we were leading. The charade was gnawing at me, and if I could feel it so strongly, how could he ignore it?

"You don't doubt that I love you, do you?" His face was beseeching.

"No, of course not . . ."

"Don't I make you happy?"

"Yes, it's just that . . ."

"Well, that's all that matters. Right now is what matters. Not yesterday, not a minute ago, but right now. And you can always choose what right now is like, you know? You choose to be happy or unhappy and that means that no one and nothing can hurt you." At the word "hurt," I felt my chin begin to tremble.

"But I don't feel very happy. I feel as if there's something wrong with me, all the time, like there's something I know I have to do, but every time I get close to finding out what it is, I get scared and run away, and then the whole business of coming back to it has to start again, over and over. Why am I like this? I wish I was someone else. I don't know why you love me, there's nothing in there to love."

Bas put his arm around my heaving shoulders, but when I drew away and looked into his face, it was growing blank, as if it were disappearing into a snowstorm. "But it's okay," I said, straightening, and smiling bravely through tears. "You're absolutely right, I was just feeling a bit, I don't know, depressed or something. Hey, I'm over it now. I was just being silly." It was the first time I had shown anyone this part of myself and, of course, he found it distasteful. I had to compensate, and quickly, before he disappeared forever. I acted the part that I knew he liked—coy girl, flatterer, cajoling young thing. When he started singing at me, "She's got everything she needs, she's an artist, she don't look back," I knew he'd returned. We planned a picnic at dawn.

It was a long time since I'd been outside in the blessed, healing landscape. While the billy sang and bubbled on the fire, our laughter traveled down the valley to disappear into an expanse of forests and paperbark swamp. Dew lay fragile as glass cobwebs; blue woodsmoke chimneyed up through flowering wattle, and fairy wrens, sweet busy things, handfuls of feathers and bone, flittered through the bushes like quick slivers of glass, reflecting the sky.

"I've never shown it to anyone before. You're the first. It's my secret place," said Bas, ripping off his clothes and darting among the tea trees, his white bottom flashing like a rabbit's. I wanted to fold him into my belly and keep him there forever.

We set off down the track that led up from the darkness, the valley and the mist. By the time we reached the sandy bend of the creek, where the water spread into swamps, the sun had risen. We slid into the cold stream and swam for half a mile until Bas swerved to the bank, beckoning me to follow. A hundred black swans were sailing toward us. He crouched down and began to call them. Soon the whole valley was echoing with organ pipes and musical bells.

Afterwards, as we lay on the bank, letting the sun dig deep into our bones, I knew I had discovered how to live in the moment. In just three weeks, my mentor had given me this gift. I turned toward him and tickled his birdlike ribs with some grass. I wanted to express my great joy and gratitude. "This is the happiest day of my life," I blurted awkwardly, and immediately regretted it. He did not move, or open his eyes, but a small smile played about his mouth.

On the journey home, he was ecstatic about our future together. Such plans we made—sailboats, exotic places, a farm, children. When I woke the next morning, he had gone. The note said, "White bee you buzz in my soul. Remember, losing's just a state of mind."

Would I answer the door, or wouldn't I, that was the question. Was it important to answer doors? What was the thing that could make me either stand up and move toward the front door or decide not to answer it? Filled with a dull curiosity, I sat and waited.

I had tried, at first, to resume my pre-Bas existence. But the aloneness had turned to loneliness, then panic, then this gray empty waiting.

I had not stirred from the house for a long time. It was not important. I sat in a corner, searching for the forces that would make me choose to act. I watched, dispassionately, the slowly dessicating wattle, or the hairs sprouting from my grimy shins. Something might eventually convince me that it was important to shave those legs, but until it did, I would wait. Sometimes a voice would tell me that of course it was important, but immediately a second voice would disagree. And the ghosts were back, skulking around in my sleep, waiting for me in the dark corners of rooms, whispering secrets in my ear which I could not remember when I woke up.

Only two necessities—relieving my bowels and, occasionally, eating—had caused me to move at all. The need to pee had not. Sometimes it was comforting to just sit and let it run out on the floor. Warm.

A pounding noise penetrated my consciousness, and without thinking, I stood up and went to the door.

"O Dio mio." Mrs. Pasquali was, for once in her life, lost for further words. I, too, felt no compunction to speak, so we stared at each other for some time.

104

"Whatsa matter, you sick? Look a you girl, no good, ah? You come with me. You no fright a Mama."

During this one-sided conversation, I had been backing into the gloom of the house, cowering before the windmills of Mama's fat, gesticulating arms.

"I worry you no come so long time, me and Papa, no one see, ah?" She glanced around the squalid room, shaking her head in disbelief, but by now I was back in my corner, quivering like a laboratory animal. Lesser folk may have thought the situation beyond them at this point, and called for reinforcements, but not the redoubtable Mrs. Pasquali. She knelt her great puffing bulk in front of me, pulled my hands away from my face, and gave it a resounding slap. Convulsive sobs were released. She lifted me up, shouldered me out of the front door, along the street and into her shop. As we swept through to a Mediterranean-blue back room, Papa was ordered to call a doctor. I was stripped of my clothes and washed all over by Mama who muttered in broken English and Italian all the while, and took no nonsense.

"What you do. Life's a not so bad you want to mess it up. Where's your mama, ah? You write a nice letter tomorrow, tell her you come home." I curled around her ample bottom, took one of her warm plump hands, and hid my face in the folds of her dress. "I'm so sorry, I'm so sorry, I'm so sorry."

The doctor prescribed antidepressants and Valium. I heard them murmuring something about a psychiatrist before I fell into a velvet blackness that lasted until Mama woke me the next evening with home-cooked food and writing paper.

By the third day I was well enough to soak up the sun in the patch of green cement at the back of their shop, totter around replacing goods on shelves and wonder what should come after "Dear Laura." One thing I knew was that I did not want to be a mad person. I had seen enough victims of psychiatry on the 72 bus, sitting in the two front seats of the top deck, talking fascinating nonsense to themselves, objects of ridicule or avoidance. Acting was definitely out. If I could not walk down the street and look people in the eye, how would I ever stand on a stage and deliver?

Some people, when they reach the bottom of their own personal pit, find nothing but quicksand. When I discovered that mine was lined with good solid rock, firm enough to jump off and begin the long climb up, I knew that I had Laura to thank. But what could I say to her? I did not have the words to express what I felt, and why worry her further by telling her the truth. Her anxiety for me was so suffocating that lying to her had become an art form. I had run away from all that, and could not go back.

Dear Laura,

   I just wanted to tell you that I am really happy and city life is really exciting. (Contemplative pause.) Please don't worry about me I am really okay. (Angry pause in which I see that I have used too many reallys.) Please give Prince and Steenie a pat for me. Will write soon. Don't work too hard.

Love,
Lucy

Mrs. Pasquali knelt in front of a small statue of the Virgin Mary, murmuring in Italian and crossing her chest. She sensed me watching her, held up her hand, and finished her prayers, before heaving herself up from her knees. With new resolve, I told her I was going to find a job and a place to live. She threw up her hands and said it was too soon. I insisted. She demurred. I pressed the point. She gave up and told me that her son Nick lived with young people from the university, and he'd found them through a noticeboard, and why didn't I go with Papa to have a look. I went alone.

By the time I reached the university, I was faint and nauseous, and could make no sense of the hundreds of notices which fluttered about in the breeze.

"TUBA PLAYERS AND MACROBIOTICISTS NEED NOT APPLY." I was fairly certain that I wasn't a macrobioticist, so I homed in dizzily on the Day-Glo letters. "Will you wash up and do the shopping when it's your turn without complaining of prior political commitments? If so, ring . . ."

"Hello?"

"Darling, get off my ear will you."

"Oh, but the . . ."

"Who do you want to speak to?"

"The notice about the room, I was wondering if . . ."

"Hey, George, it's for you."

A voice in the background yelled, "Turn that thing down, will you."

"Yes?" George was a woman.

"The room for rent, could I come and see it?"

"Sure I'll be home all day. What's your name?"

"Lucy, ah, Hunter."

"What's the R stand for?"

"Oh, nothing."

"Lucy Nothing Hunter. I like it." The voice laughed, a warm foghorn sound, then said, "See you later, then. Bye."

Wings of hope sprouted on my shoulders and lifted me gracefully out of the pit. Dressing for the interview took an hour, during which time I managed to convince the Pasqualis that everything was settled and that I would take a taxi to my new home. I did not want Papa cramping my style.

My stomach was turning over like a butter churn and I noticed, with dismay, that nervous sweat had left bird-wing patches under the arms of my pink crêpe dress. I closed my eyes and sank down into the backseat, so that when we arrived, I thought for a moment that the driver had made a mistake. This was no house, this was a mansion surrounded by two acres of overgrown garden undulating down to the ocean. I checked the address, took a heave of oxygen, crunched my way down a weed-infested gravel driveway, banged on the massive front door, and waited.

And banged and waited and pounded. Nothing. Betrayed. Yelping like a run-over dog and with black eyeliner streaming down my face, I threw myself against the door, fell into the surprised arms of Georgia Delancey, knocked her to the floor, and locked her in a passionate, if clumsy, embrace.

9
Henry Dudgeon

Olly coughed, stooped over his granddaughter, where she lay twitching in her sleep, then tiptoed quickly away, holding his hands up in front of his chest like a possum. Lucy continued her twitching. He scratched his shiny scalp, said, "Drat it," softly, then pushed tetchily at her with his shoe and hurriedly sat down when she stirred.

"Is that you?" She sat up groggily and slowly focused a blank blue stare on her grandfather who demanded to know, rather gruffly, who she thought he was. Tears welled up in her eyes. She brushed them away impatiently and said, in a dry, matter-of-fact voice, "My husband."

"Puh. Love is it. Burns you out in the end. Mind you, more difficult for you because half of you's Huntington McTavish." After a short, reflective pause, Olly's tone changed and his face became grim. "Incapable of real love, the whole bang lot of them, starting with poor old Henry Dudgeon. Never admit it, of course, not that Huntington crowd." Here he let out a scornful wheeze. "Thoroughbreds my foot."

"Henry Dudgeon?"

"Little English runt he was."

At the word "runt" Laura materialized at the door, bearing a lamp. "You think it matters a damn what you tell her? Tell her your blithering stories." She bared her horse teeth nastily at the old man who, at the sight of this persecuting apparition, had tucked his head down into his collar and slipped behind Lucy. "I might tell her a few of my own," she added, then blew out the lantern with a decisive puff. Without thinking, they all shuffled closer together.

"Go on, do your worst," whispered Laura.

"What are you whispering for?" whispered Olly.

"Oh, for heaven's sake," said Lucy in a voice loud enough to make the ghosts jump. She relit the lamp and the three of them sheltered inside the dome of light, turning their backs on the black night. Presently, Steenie sidled in through the open doors as if he were a piece cut out of the enveloping darkness and given life by infernal forces. He leapt into Laura's lap and fixed Olly with glittering green eyes. The old man cleared his throat, shoved a pillow behind his back, and said, "Your great great great great great grandfather was a little English runt who stole a rancid shoulder of mutton . . ."

Henry Dudgeon lay rotting quietly below decks. Around the prison hulk, in the brown eddies of the Thames, floated the more fortunate victims of the disease, sewed up in sacks. The screams, oaths and moans which had so offended him at first now seemed far away and unimportant. The fever grabbed at his muscles and shook them; pustules bubbled under his skin and broke to the surface; his soul wafted in and out of his body, sometimes hovering above the filth, sometimes drifting into a dream where fantastic animals peered through grotesque foliage and the black face of the devil uttered incantations over him.

Just as Henry was about to die, he understood that this was what he had always wanted. He felt himself rising into a sky of purer blue than he had ever seen. There was an instant of rapture, before the fever reached its peak and passed, allowing his soul back into his body with a thump, leaving him scarred for life of which he would have to endure another ten years. Even death had tricked him.

At the end of that decade, which was attached like a coda to the main movement of his existence, Henry would be one of a convict gang building a road along pathways trodden only by savages. Some of these wild men had gabbled about an ancestral track that linked their sacred places, but there were no shrines in the interminable scrub, only an occasional animal carved on a headland overlooking the sea, or a cave decorated with meaningless symbols. The road crept mindlessly forward into oblivion, leaving names, places, fences and huts in its wake. Henry often thought that if it were possible to stand in the trackless waste waiting for the road to appear and give it *meaning, the order of settlement would appear as the reign of chaos. But by then Henry's thoughts were those of a madman.*

Before his second death, when the devil with the black face speared him through the heart, he just had time to remember his prophetic dream. The convicts were buried in an unmarked mass grave beside the track; the savages were hunted down, shot, and left to bloat in the forgotten furrows of a land of submerged dreams.

There were delays in getting under sail. While the carpenters tarried over securing the hatches with grilles and padlocks, studding the bulkheads with nails and placing prongs of iron in the barricades dividing the ship's company from the abominable cargo during their voyage into the classless society of the future, down in the pestilential hold some of the prisoners wrote letters to their loved ones, while others, like Henry, gave way to listless dread. He wanted to pull a blanket of dreams over his eyes and sleep forever, but Black Caesar, the Negro to whom he was handcuffed, had other ideas. There were female prisoners coming on board, and men were clustered around cracks in the hatches like blowflies around dung.

It was only a glimpse, but it was enough. When he saw the blazing red hair, the demure blue skirts and the furry eyebrow which clung like a bat to the broad forehead of Mary Watling, all the bitterness which had accumulated in Henry's heart turned into love.

He could tell by the way she hung her head and wept that she was not like the others. All around her whores flung curses back at the men who shouted their depravity from holes riddling the ship. He ached for her purity. Wanted to bury her head in his chest like a lamb and finger those bright curls.

Such was the power of this love that the netherworld for which they were bound appeared an Eden where he and his Mary could live happily forever. Even the squalid ship became a Noah's ark, as squealing pigs and clacking geese were loaded aboard, two by two, sow for pig, goose for gander, Mary for Henry. It was several days before he found out her name from the doctor.

Their strange and unlikely friendship began the first day at sea. As Henry scrubbed the deck, Doctor Sharp leaned on the rail and stared disconsolately out at the rain, toward that place on the horizon where old England sank beneath ashen mountains of water. "Oh, did they

love as well as I do," he moaned, "they would have stayed the ships
another day." Clasping a locket around his neck and manfully holding back tears, he turned his doleful gaze upon the pockmarked
creature at his feet, to whom he found himself confiding that he'd had
no time for a final farewell to his wife—his beloved Mary. When
Henry shook his head slowly in commiseration, the doctor, on an
impulse, opened the locket to show the poor devil the perfection of his
wife's dear face.

"That there could be such beauty on earth," breathed Henry,
though he thought her a plain wench, compared with his own Mary.
Mary Sharp and Mary Watling. One a dream in a locket; the other
locked up in a dream.

Henry used his icon as protection against despair. Red hair would
fall like a flame, burning away the smell of bilgewater, vomit and
quicklime, the singing of the three Negroes, the praying of the Jews,
the secret tinkering of counterfeiters fashioning coins from belt
buckles, the wafts of piano music from the Captain's cabin, and the
slithering of another corpse into that lonely ocean. Even the sight that
met them at Capetown was licked clean by the flames of Mary's hair,
and Henry was not afraid.

All around that harbor of hell lay torture wheels on poles, and
on each wheel the remains of a man lay strapped, hands cut off
and impaled on a stick. Crows, like bits of black rag, rose and
rustled; vultures waited on the ground. A hush fell over the convicts
as they strained to peep through the holes. Someone was whim-
pering but down came the flame, stopping the stench, and Henry's
trembling.

But the break-ins, which began as soon as the ship rolled on deep
ocean swells, tormented him beyond bearing. Despite the heaving of
ship and passengers, sailors and marines, drawn by the scent of
women, crawled through gaps, slipped between bars and slunk under
hatches. Some of the more shameless whores, deciding among themselves that prostitution was more profitable than rape, were found
sitting up in sailors' beds drinking rum. What anguish it caused him to
think of his Mary being defiled. How he relished the screams of the
guilty men being lashed, and the tears of a loud-mouthed whore
gagged and flogged with a rope.

What gratitude he felt toward the good doctor, when he learned
that the noble man considered Mary Watling a model convict, and

111

made it his business to look after her. Once, Henry had seen her on deck, handing the doctor some nightcaps she had sewn.

The ship was alive with dreams. He could sense them snaking their way around bodies, lifted gently on the sighs of sleeping men, drifting up through the hatches, crossing barriers, choosing victims. In his own dreams, Mary appeared to him dressed all in white and let her long red hair brush softly against his skin. Yet one night she was naked, and around her waist hung a skirt of multicolored penises, flayed and dried. That same night, the doctor dreamed of his wife, sitting by the fire in her nightcap, weeping. But when he tried to give comfort, her mouth opened wider and wider, until it became a great, gaping maw into which he was falling. Henry suspected that his dreams might be shared with the doctor, but was only certain of it the day he heard the poor man whispering "Mary Watling," as he gazed distractedly out to sea.

This realization so terrified Henry that he seized his friend and shook him. "It's Mary Sharp you love, not Mary Watling." But the doctor turned to him full of fury, hurled him to the deck, and ordered him on irons.

By the time the ships rolled into Port Jackson, Henry felt as if he had made the whole journey underwater. He was swollen and pulpy with unshed tears. Still he clung to the vision of Mary, despite the inexplicable cruelties of the doctor, and the debilitating fear of a recurring nightmare. When the first beams of daylight filtered into the hold, scattering dreams before them, he could not grab its tail. It taunted him from the shadows of his sleep.

They rowed toward the small white beach, oars dipping through emerald water glittering under the brassy light. But what seemed lush and inviting from the ships became a cruel and mocking beauty as they approached. A surreal world greeted them where blossoming trees burst into showers of birds and the grass was as brittle as spun glass. There was a blackness behind the landscape, like the backing on a bright mirror. Untidy bark hung shredded from dismal trees, the leaves turned down against the force of that poisonously blue sky. Nothing was quite the shape or texture it should have been, as if an imp had been at work in Eden. Along the headlands, straight columns of smoke rose into the still heat.

The initial quiet that had fallen over the company broke. People moved into action like a flock of startled pigeons, as if noise and bustle might dispel the somber mood of this haunted place. There were tents to erect, fires to be built, cashes to be rowed ashore. And as the work progressed, a mild hysteria was rising. Convicts, no matter how ill, laughed, or wriggled their toes in the sand like children, while others sang, until the aguardiente was distributed at dusk, and the first curious natives arrived to peek, point, rattle their spears, confer, disappear and return.

Henry was selected to go with Captain Philip's party to approach them. He felt heartened by this, and wondered if his luck was changing. But when the Captain ordered him to take his trousers down, in order to prove to the natives that white men were indeed men, the air coagulated round him and the whole world fell silent. He turned slowly to see everyone watching, waiting. Slowly, he untied the string in his trousers and felt them drop to his feet. In the eternity it took for them to fall, Henry had enough time to understand everything. Mary, his Mary, was standing next to the doctor, whose arm was around her shoulders, his hand close to her breast.

Henry saw mouths open slowly, and a slow roar of laughter surrounded him like a wall. The natives were pointing at his penis and laughing. The doctor and Mary were laughing and something inside Henry's chest tore apart.

That night, during the drunken reverie, he stole into Mary's tent and raped her brutally, ousting Doctor Sharp's seed and planting the Huntington family tree. While he was receiving his five hundred lashes the following day, moving in and out of consciousness, he saw his own flesh flicked to the ground by the cat-o'-nine-tails; felt his own blood and urine fill his boots and remembered his nightmare. He was a red rose bush, bending over Mary's sleeping body. One of his blooms had been cut off, leaving a thick ugly stem crowded with thorns. Mary opened her eyes, and started to scream, but he plunged the prickly stem down her throat . . .

"No, no, you liar," shouted Lucy, "that's my dream. I was lying there, trying to scream, my mouth opening wider and wider, while he pushed the stem right down into my stomach, and then the stem turned into his hairy arm. It was me in the dream, not Mary." Lucy was sobbing and shaking her grandfather, while Laura tried to pull her away.

"I told you not to tell her that story, you garrulous old coot."

10
Georgia

Georgia pushed a cracked yellow cup half full of whiskey toward me. The enormous table was cluttered with crammed ashtrays, coffee mugs sprouting penicillin, crumpled green apples under a nimbus of fruit flies, papers, books, paint, carpenter's tools, wooden frames, bunches of waratah, rolls of canvas and neat, powdery patches of bird droppings.

We sat dwarfed by what, Georgia informed me, was once a ball-room. A sea breeze blew wattle fumes and a whirring racket of cicada song through the tall glass doors with missing panes, that led on to the garden. Behind us gaped a fireplace large enough to swallow a truck. A few ratty armchairs, the stump of a tree, six feet in diameter, and several filing cabinets were the only recognizable pieces of furniture. The other objects defied taxonomy. Frenzied constructions of poles, funnels and waves painted every color imaginable leapt out of the walls. High above the fireplace a vast canvas was covered in nothing but black, white and gray lines. My eyes roamed the room, looking for something I might safely comment upon. By the door, a board held written notes pinned between photographs. From its center a picture of a handsome, brooding man with a starred cap placed rakishly across his brow stared over our heads. Someone had disfigured that passionate, holy face by drawing in an enigmatic wink and bunches of bananas.

"Who's that?" I asked, as a conversation opener. Georgia looked a little taken aback.

"It's Guevara," she said.

"Oh yes, of course," I nodded, unwilling to display further ignorance by asking "Guevara who?"

She cupped her face in her hand, leaned her elbow on the table and regarded me with long green eyes, the kind that can leave smoking holes in the back of your head. I lowered my own, pulling the blinds over the windows of my soul. I did not want her to see how sparsely it was furnished.

Georgia was in her early thirties, practically middle-aged, and when she smiled, fans spread out from the edges of her eyes down to the middle of her cheeks. I knew she was smiling at me now and the thought that her kindness masked pity sent a hot flush across my tear-stained face. I gulped whiskey.

"Hey," she said and took my other hand, "what's happening in there?" I looked up from under my brows, saw her eyes flick tactfully away from my bright pink fingernails, retracted my hand and wished fervently that I were as far away as possible from this mortifying humiliation.

Everything about me was wrong. Her hair was long, strawberry blonde and straight; mine was waved and sprayed. Her generous breasts bounced freely under a dark T-shirt; my puny ones were imprisoned in whalebone and perished elastic. Instead of beige high heels, she wore sandals made out of leather and car tires. Her face was free of makeup; mine lay buried under it. Her body smelled of mush-rooms and jungle litter; mine smelled of stale stockings and Miss Balmain perfume. Where they showed through the jeans, her legs displayed a covering of soft golden fur; mine were like wood rasps. There was no escape, so I took a shuddering breath, topped up the whiskey, sucked on my tobacco and launched into a highly embel-lished rendition of my life story. The need to impress her and my determination to live in this unearthly house provided the necessary adrenaline.

I had never acted so well. Hands cut through the air, characters fell over me like costumes and alien voices issued from my mouth like séance spirits. I was so excited by my own explosion of talent that I ignored the little chant within—"Liar, liar." I sensed that Georgia did not really believe my yarns, but at the same time did not despise me for spinning them. On the contrary, her encouraging squeals and that laugh—raucous, throaty, and infectious—spurred me on to greater heights of elaboration. Performers are so very dependent on the re-sponse of their audience.

Right in the middle of the Leadbelly Street chapter, as I laid my taxi driver's penis on the piano keys of the table, I realized that I had hardly lied at all. I had only added a few artistic flourishes here and there. While I had been doing all these things, they had seemed mean, small and clumsy. Now, in the fertile atmosphere of Georgie's appreciation, they expanded into the realms of the mythical. My painfully tedious life had become epic, dramatic, poignant. Maybe that's what Bas had meant when he said there was no need for me to "do" art.

"You didn't get conned by Bas Manson did you?" Georgia raised her eyes to heaven. "He's an emotional pygmy and he takes it out on any gullible female he can find." She laughed again, sympathetically, but to my ears, the word gullible was synonymous with stupid and although I did not know what "patronize" meant, I certainly understood when I was being patronized. My soaring self-confidence fell like a shot duck. Here I was in a teeming, infinitely interpretable city where one could be lost and anonymous, where one could safely make oneself up and Georgia had recognized the first name I mentioned.

The room was now softened with the whiskey-colored light of late afternoon. She leaned back in her chair, stretched like a cat and yawned so deeply I could see her uvula. I tried hard not to stare at the hair which hung from her armpit like sphagnum moss but I was riveted. Not only was she not ashamed of the growth, she flaunted it. This struck me as challenging, even faintly frightening. But on reflection, I realized I wasn't frightened of the hair, but for Georgia, because such a taunting signal could surely only bring vengeance. But vengeance from whom? And for what? New and difficult thoughts.

"Okay, Little Lucy, the rent's eight bucks a week, the kitty's five and your room has a view. Want to see it?"

I followed her up a graceful sweep of staircase, along a corridor smelling of lost wealth and beeswax, past six heavy oak doors, the last of which she opened with a flourish. On the opposite side of the room, the view of gray-green scrub running bluer and smokier toward a jumble of red roofs and a jagged city skyline was framed by the iron lace of a balcony. The sea was a strip of ultramarine ending at a crumbling ledge of apricot sandstone. A slow heartbeat of waves thumped on a shoreline obscured by two acres of garden.

"Oh," I said, and beamed at Georgia.

"Oh," said a strangely distorted version of Georgia's voice. A pink and gray galah stood in the doorway, bobbing its head up and down, glaring at me with ratlike eyes. It flew up to sit on Georgia's shoulder.

"Hello, darling," she said and scratched the little thing behind its crest.

"How cute," I simpered, but when it flew, like a winged reptile, into my hair, I shrieked.

"Don't panic," she laughed, "it's only men she bites."

"Why doesn't she like men?"

Georgia widened her eyes and stretched her mouth into a silly grin. "Are you kidding?" she said, turned and went downstairs.

"What's up, darling?" said the galah as I rummaged through my suitcase for something to wear. My jeans were pressed and stiff as boards, thanks to Mrs. Pasquali, and were so tight they looked as if I had jumped into them from the top of a five-story building. Having experimented with several floral shirts, none of which looked right, I rolled the jeans into a ball and shoved them under the mattress, hoping for natural-looking creases. I ripped off my fingernails while Darling echoed my cries of pain. I dislodged the bird, ruffled my hair to make it look slept-in, shoveled away makeup and threw a shirt over my now braless chest. When I jumped up and down to test the wobble, it felt unnatural.

"Herro? Herro?" said the parrot, its beak full of my sandal which it was attempting to murder by thrashing it about on the floor, then rolling onto its back and kicking at it with ridiculous legs.

How could I work up the courage to go downstairs? The effects of the whiskey had worn off. The front door slammed a dozen times and the record player was blasting out many decibels. I could not stay here all evening with this brain-damaged bird. I had to do something. I sat on the mattress, nervously twisting the quilt. Darling waved her claw in my direction, bobbed her head up and down and crawled up my leg.

"Come on, darling," she said, when she reached my shoulder.

"Okay," I said, and went down.

At the door of the ballroom where a red lamp cast an eldritch light over bodies draped in various poses on the floor, I hesitated. One of the horizontal bodies wore a cap just like the man in the poster, only without the star. Someone in a black satin cape was dancing alone facing one of the "things" protruding from a wall. On the stump of the tree were various bottles of alcohol, two large pipes, a plate of unappetizing-looking dried mushrooms, a hookah and some dried flowers that looked like brown paper roses. No one paid me the

117

slightest attention. Out on the patio two women were playing with a life-size chess set, picking up the carved wooden statues as if they were made of air, and in the floodlit garden, a woman in a pink tutu floated across a tightrope strung between a big yellow moon and a scribbly gum. I could see Georgia in the kitchen, bouncing to the music as she stirred a large pot on the stove. Every now and then she took a long drag from a cigarette.

"Hi," I said, sidling in, grateful that the rosy glow camouflaged my blush. She didn't hear me so I tapped her on the shoulder causing her to smile absentmindedly and hand me the cigarette. I held it for her. She looked at me quizzically.

"Haven't you tried it?"

"Tried what?"

"Pot. Dope." Having understood that I was in a state of some confusion, she demonstrated.

"Oh," I said, "right." I leaned back against the sink, one foot crossed carelessly in front of the other, and puffed, and bounced. "I'm smoking marijuana," I said to myself over and over, waiting for the finger of God that must surely poke through the ceiling at any moment.

"Some performers are going to give us a show in the garden later on."

"Oh," I said, "right."

"And if I were you I wouldn't eat any of those wood roses, they're really fucking poisonous."

"Oh," I said, "right," then added with a knowing toss of the head, "fucking poisonous." Still God's finger did not appear.

After five minutes of hanging around the sink watching Darling rummage through the litter on the table, I realized, with a mixture of relief and dejection, that the drug was having no effect. What I really needed was enough alcohol and Mandrax to help me enter the ballroom. But the door seemed a long way away and I had forgotten the reason why I did not want to go into that room because my attention was caught by the mold on an orange. It was like living phosphorescence, all silver and green. I had never noticed before how movingly beautiful the mold on oranges was. But I was trying to think about that other room through the weirdly shaped door that shone so soft, velvety and RED and I found myself drifting into the heart of a ruby.

The people inside were strange and wonderful; the alcohol in the bottles tasted like liquid diamonds and when I saw the wall I was astonished because I had never seen anything as astounding as the object which hung on that wall. I stood next to the man in the black satin cape who was also peering at the planes, curves and colors of the thing. He turned to me and said, "Archie's paintings are incredible, aren't they," and I said, "Oh yes, they're just absolutely incredible." He nodded his head and we understood each other perfectly and for a long time we stood together and understood the paintings saying "wow look at this," or "incredible" or "amazing" and that was when Georgia touched me on the shoulder and told me that the performers were ready and I said, "what performers," and she said, "the performers in the garden." I wondered why the pot hadn't worked on me as we floated arm in arm down the patio stairs. She giggled and told me I was stoned as a parrot and I giggled too because maybe I was and if so I liked it, and I couldn't stop laughing until we reached a group of four women who looked at me doubtfully while I stood before them swaying, smiling and holding out a bottle of liquid diamonds as an offering of abject veneration because they were incredible and I was just Little Lucy from Binjigul.

Georgia introduced me first to Ruby who had long, dark curls, a rather angry face and a body like a young tree. Belying the intensity was an ethereal nervous quality, as if a little frightened creature scuttered around in the lair of her body, hurting her. There was something spooky about Ruby, something not quite healthy.

"But everyone calls her Hydraulic. She can lift anything." The others tittered and what might have been the faint beginnings of a smile threatened to alter the downward slopes of Hydraulic's face. Further introductions were interrupted by the woman in pink tutu and gym boots.

"Listen," she said, as she shifted her weight to one leg, drew herself up and poked at the air with her index finger, "what I was saying was that the family, I mean the crucial place of women's oppression is not functionally determined by capitalist needs alone."

I nodded vigorously, but pretended I was only scratching my head when Hydraulic interrupted with, "Yeah, and what I was saying was that I reckon we ought to be committed to a nonreflexive but materialist theory of gender ideology, I mean it's obvious . . ."

And so the two Titans clashed. For all I understood of their words they might have been agreeing with each other but their bodies—hips shifting, fingers puncturing the air—suggested the opposite. As always, I was getting caught up in the underneath of things—hearing a wordless language so loudly that I could barely concentrate on what was being said. The spoken words were like an oil slick over the deep and disturbed waters of the real drama which was all about power.

I tried to rid myself of the subterranean din and to make a list of the words which bounced off intellects like sparks from shields. Ontological, ahistorical, Engels, chauvinist, dialectical materialism. So much to store away for later perusal, but my mind was furry, refusing to focus, and I was terrified that someone might ask my opinion and why was I always two steps behind everyone else and why was I so stupid and what would happen when Georgia found out I was a fake? In the ballroom I had not been required to use many words but here the opposite was true and life consisted of a chain of rooms, each one demanding something different of me and I never knew what was required, only that I did not have it.

"Look, Hydraulic, the point is that what we need is an historical analysis that will steer between the Scylla of reductionism and the Charybdis of empiricism, wouldn't you agree with that?"

The company fell silent. Hydraulic sagged in defeat. The audience made small shuffling or sniffing movements. I thought to myself, "What's a Charybdis of empiricism?" and heard everyone else thinking, "What's a Charybdis of empiricism?"

"What's a Charybdis of empiricism for fuck's sake?" said Georgia, snickering irreverently. Now there were different movements and signals indicating relief that Georgia had let them off the hook, followed by resentment that she had pointed up their cowardice, ending with an unspoken agreement that one day they would like to take her down a peg or two.

Later, when I had looked up "empirical" in the dictionary and found that it meant "guided by mere experience, without knowledge of principles ... charlatan ..." I realized with dismay that I was all washed up in Charybdis, and Scylla was a long way away.

"All over this city, right now, women are being raped and bashed and they've never heard of a Charybdis ..." Georgia was interrupted by someone announcing that the show should begin.

120

Oil lamps flickered. Scarlet bottlebrush dipped down all around us like the velvet curtains of a theater. Everyone was shushing everyone else when blue flames burst from the darkness of the trees followed by a man waving wands which he blew into sheets of fire. A juggler emerged from the left, and along the rope dividing the patch of light like a horizon the pink fairy made her dainty way. While we clapped and cheered a man and a woman, knotted together, spun cartwheels around the circle.

My chest began to ache. Agitated by the applause which belonged to it by right, my soul was beating its wings against the bars of my body. If only these people could have seen me swinging through a forest, standing up on the back of my galloping horse, causing Laura angina pains by balancing on the veranda rails. I saw myself a hundred feet in the air, spotlights following me as I serenely sailed through space, risking death in order to give my life meaning, borne aloft on the adoration of an infinite audience.

But no one was looking at me.

Afterwards the party turned into a stamping, sweating sideshow of assorted freaks. I slipped into it like a stray fish into its school, danced, leapt, shook, collapsed, drank, smoked and danced again. There were several sticky moments. A big, burly character with frizzy hair said he'd just come back from a place called "The Nam" and I asked him if he'd had a good time. There was Georgia's ex-husband chasing women around with a loaded syringe of pethidine. (He had long white hair and he donated his old surgical implements for use in our kitchen.) I tried to help my friend with the satin cloak who was throwing up in the corridor, but he was beyond it. When I opened one of the many doors in the house there was a naked threesome rolling around on the floor. I was saved by the doorbell.

By now I believed myself immune from further shocks, but how could I have predicted what awaited me at the door. Three of them—real live Aborigines. I remembered the prickling I had felt up and down my spine when I walked through their suburb and here was a real live one saying, "Hey, baby, hold this," as he handed me a bottle before crashing like a felled tree at my feet. The other two picked him up and put him on Georgia's bed before going down to the party with me following behind, my lips ever so slightly compressed. When I told Georgia that there was an Aborigine drunk and asleep on her bed, there must have been something in my expression which she did not like because she looked at me in a way that made me blush. Everyone I'd ever known had used words like boong or coon or Abo even though they had never met one, and they had cracked jokes like, "Why are Abos called boongs? Because that's the sound they make when you hit them with the roo bar." I wanted to creep away into a corner because I had never thought about it before and I was ashamed. Then the sneer vanished from Georgia's face and she said, "Come on, let's fix him up or he'll piss in my bed."

Billy Byrd was a large, comatose man. It was not easy getting his trousers and boots off and rolling him onto the floor. Georgia put a pillow under his head and tucked a blanket around him. He came to for a moment, made some gurgling sounds and opened glazed eyes which leaked tears all over his face. Georgia wiped them away with her palms. I started to cry and just for a moment thought, "I am a good person because I am crying over this poor Aborigine." But the thought had a nasty flavor and I intuited that Georgia would disapprove. So I banished it and used my second sight to "look through the deeds of men."

No. Surely I must be wrong. Georgia was sitting cross-legged beside him and the upper half of her body had collapsed back on the bed. She took in a great heave of air and said, "Christ."

"How well do you know him?" I tried to keep the incredulous tone out of my voice, and failed. She sat up, looked at me with that grin, threw her head back and laughed.

"You mean do I sleep with him? A couple of times I did, yeah, but it's not like that. He's a friend. Understand?"

My face betrayed me again. She looked away and closed her eyes before turning back to me.

"He's one of the nicest men I've ever known. There's not a shred of nastiness in him except what he unleashes against himself. There aren't many basically decent people in the world and he's one of them and if you were half the person he is you'd be very lucky. He's drinking himself to death and this stinking society rips people apart and robs them of their potential and the sooner you understand that and decide to do something about it the sooner you'll be a useful person."

She got up, tousled my hair, as if that might compensate for the verbal slap she'd just delivered, and walked out.

122

I did not feel capable of negotiating any more rooms that night. Whichever one I entered, I opened my mouth only in order to change feet. I wanted to sleep but when I closed my eyes, the room spun and I had to race for the bathroom. In the colorful remains of half-digested chicken cacciatore and red wine, a man's face, covered in pockmarks, grinned up at me from the toilet bowl. I slammed the lid on him and went downstairs where I danced until there was no one left awake at the party except the burly man with the frizzy hair who had just come back from The Nam. He asked me to take my shirt off and dance on the table for him. When I looked appalled, he said I was too well brought up and middle class, so I took off my shirt and began to dance, clumsily and self-consciously at first then, as the music poured into my body, with increasing abandon. I felt proud being so free and sophisticated then brave enough to open my eyes and smile at the burly man who, to my horror, was sound asleep.

Georgia was leaning in the doorway shaking her head. "Sucker," she said.

I woke late and decided immediately that I would spend the rest of my life in bed. There was one seven-square-foot patch of safety in the entire world, and I was in it. I sank sluggishly back into sleep. Georgia came in at three p.m. with Darling, who hopped on the bed, flipped onto her back and crawled under the bedclothes along the side of my left leg.

"She's taken a real shine to you," said Georgia, as I tried surreptitiously to kick the creature away from my feet. In my misery, I knew that Georgia had brought Darling up so I'd have a friend my own size. "Little Lucy" indeed. "Useful person, sucker," how those words still stung.

"You know," she began, and stopped.

"What?" I said, tragic but brave.

"Oh, nothing. Anyway, I've brought you up some books to read. If you're going to spend your life in bed, you may as well use the time."

I looked at them balefully. *Madame Bovary. The Second Sex. The Vivisector. The Golden Notebook. The Idiot.* I did not miss the message in the last title. I had no intention of reading them anyway. I already knew the kind of musty pap that nuns tried to force-feed you, or the incomprehensible rubbish that old boyfriends said would improve your mind. No, sir, not for me. Books were the weapons of the enemy.

"Thanks," I said, in a small, long-suffering voice. I kept my eyes lowered and wished she would go away. When she did leave, I felt abandoned. Surely she could see that I wanted her to stay?

By five p.m. I was so bored, I began to read. By eight p.m. I was in a fever of excitement and asking Georgia if she owned a dictionary. In an offhand way she said I could take anything I wanted from the library that lined the walls of her bedroom.

"Hang on," she said, grabbing my sleeve, "give me a hand with the washing up, I'm sick of cleaning up other people's muck." Her face was stern but there was a little secret smile flittering around it. I set to with gusto because the sooner it was done, the sooner I could set out on my voyages of discovery. Why hadn't anyone told me about books before? Reading them was like coming home. They contained worlds I had always longed for and characters whom I could love and emulate in the privacy of my own room.

Thus were the small paper doors of the world opened for me. I feasted on fiction, devoured dictionaries, got drunk on literature. It never occurred to me to remember the names of the authors. I simply entered their worlds selfishly, as if they had always existed, independent of their creators, waiting just for me. And when Georgia thought my absorption in those worlds had become unhealthily prolonged she would bring tea to my room and, to relieve my eyes, would spend an hour reading to me or discussing what I had learned.

I suffered the autodidact's biggest problem—where to begin. Knowledge did not start at one point and proceed in a linear fashion, it went round in circles. To understand A, one first had to understand B, but in order to understand B, one had to have a working knowledge of C, and so on. My net of knowledge was so frail that most of what I read fell through holes. Why hadn't I had an education like other people? I was a victim of society, the family, men. I was angry—I was catching on.

"Georgia, where do you find things out from, I mean apart from dictionaries?"

"What do you want to know?"

"I don't know, like, anything."

"Well, I suppose an encyclopedia's a good start. There's one in my room you can use."

In one week, I had got as far as the end of the Ab's. But then I calculated that I would be quite old before I'd gone through all the volumes and while I would be terrifically knowledgeable about everything beginning with A, I would know absolutely nothing about that which began with Z. And would knowing that an Abalone was a mollusk otherwise known as a sea-ear help me score points in a conversation with Hydraulic?

Knowledge was also shifty. It kept splitting up into opinions and each one sounded right until I heard a contradictory one. My thirst for understanding took me from group to group, but I could never work out why it was that all the people in one group adhered to one set of ideas, while all the people in another group adhered to a slightly different set of ideas. And if a new person with different ideas entered a group that person would, soon enough, begin to conform to the ideas of the group. Did people stick with the ideas of one group because they believed in them, or did they simply come to believe them by being with the group? And why was it that I always felt uncomfortable with any group, no matter what its ideas, because I sensed that I was being coerced into accepting its ideas wholesale.

Then there was the problem of a little knowledge being a dangerous thing. One night Hydraulic brought around one of seven television sets she had lifted. When we all fell upon her and called her a genius, she said, "Ah, it's nothing, all property is theft." For some reason, she then turned to me abruptly and asked if I'd like to go to the pub with her. I was so flattered and confused by the invitation that I went crimson and before I'd thought about it, I told her that I couldn't because I was feeling a bit bucolic. Lucky for me, Hydraulic never laughed at anything. In fact, nobody laughed, because Georgia was glowering at them all, but she could not prevent amused glances being exchanged. When I found out what bucolic meant, I wouldn't come down for three days.

I entered a deep depression when I finally realized that no matter how willfully I tackled the problems of educating myself, I would never catch up. It might have been easier if I had had the courage to ask questions, but how, in all seriousness, could one interrupt a conversation which contained phrases like "Scylla of reductionism," and ask please what socialism was. I didn't even know what democracy was, or how a parliament worked or what a union did, and you just could not admit things like that in public. *Das Kapital* was no help at all.

However, I had come to understand the power of silence. If you kept your trap shut and your brow intelligently furrowed, people assumed that you knew what they were talking about, especially if you could translate glances, sighs, gestures and pauses well enough to know when they required a nod or a shake of the head. Sometimes they assumed that you were having deep, even judgmental, thoughts. My gift for mimicry came in handy as well. I may not have fully understood what a Marxist was, but I certainly looked like one and only I knew the true depth of my fraudulence. Even the man in the Che Guevara cap who visited one day could not have guessed what poor revolutionary material I made. He suggested that if we were serious about the revolution, we would be able to shoot our reactionary parents. I just didn't think I'd be able to shoot Laura no matter how politically incorrect she was. Then he said that some white person should commit suicide as an act of solidarity with the black struggle. Why was he looking at me like that? Georgia told him to piss off. He accused her of being a fascist property owner. She suggested he jump off a building as an act of solidarity with the human struggle. Georgia was so enviably fearless.

It was a tough six months entering the bosom of that family, whose core was Georgia, Hydraulic, Archie and Frank, the anarchist photographer who developed film all day in the basement. But the house was also a resting place for traveling poets, poofters, performers, philosophers, painters, dope peddlers, playwrights and political journalists who gave minimal rent or paid their way by dedicating works of art to the already burgeoning collection. People like the Pasqualis were noticeable by their absence, except where they entered discussions under the heading "proletariat." Every second week, Georgia's ten-year-old daughter Annie came to torment us. And there were animals. Georgia's magnetism attracted them from all over the city. Stray dogs yelped at the fence, guinea pigs found sanctuary in the grounds, smelly tomcats yowled at her window and I yowled from my room whenever my unhappiness became intolerable. Georgia mothered us all.

By the end of the adoption period, I had become "Little Luce," the household mascot whom everyone adored and worried over. There were a lot of suitably left-wing men entering my bed and me at night. (As I found it difficult to give my soul to the revolution I thought I could make up for it by donating my body.) And my silences had become eloquent.

11
Hubris

I peeked into Archie's room, hoping there would be a transformation, but nothing had changed. For three days he had been sitting on his single mattress, staring at sheets of cardboard. The only indication that time had passed was that the level in the tequila bottle had fallen. Light from the bay windows drenched once-white walls smeared with variegated blobs of oil paint. The floor was strewn with duffel bags, boxes, and piles of clothes from which paintbrushes poked like sea-urchin quills. Spattered postcards of the great masters were pinned haphazardly to the legs of a trestle table on which stood many cans of paint and a cassette recorder pressed all over with multicolored finger-prints.

"Have you moved at all since yesterday? You'll get piles if you sit there any longer."

"Shh. I feel nirvana coming on. Any day now repressed semen will send alpha waves up my backbone to flood my brain and I'll paint something so . . ." His face contorted with the effort of finding the correct superlative. "Anyway, I've got piles." He smiled at me wickedly, tweaked his eyebrows up and down and asked if I'd like to see them.

"God, you're the most disgusting person I've ever met," I said, plonking down beside him and slapping him on the back of the head. He shook his head as if deeply worried.

"Sometimes I think my arsehole is trying to take over. It's frustrated because it can't express itself properly. Jealous of my mouth. It has an important function, yet everyone despises it. What sort of life is that for an organ? No wonder it pokes its tongue out at the world."

"Stop," I said.

He leaned toward me, his eyes shifting furtively from left to right, and whispered conspiratorially. "I'm scared of my own arsehole. I think it's trying to take over. That's why I feed it the right food and say nice things about it in public, but just between you and me, I don't think it's got a lot going for it." He sat up and said in a loud voice, "Yessir, ignoring your arsehole is like cutting off your finger to spite your nose."

"Please, Archie, I want to talk to you, it's serious."

"Serious? You think you've got serious? I can't even paint." He threw himself into my lap and pretended to weep hysterically. "Why can't I paint any more, Little Luce? I'm a butcher. My work's all . . . sensation. There's no . . . substance."

Naturally, Archie's crisis was a topic of endless debate among the rest of us. All he seemed able to manage was frenzied sketching—the most recent of which was a series of me practicing double somersaults on Annie's trampoline. For hours he would watch, covering reams of paper, but when I looked at them, the drawings were nothing but tangled webs of line. They had passed through order into chaos. No one knew what it was that had scrambled his imagination, but we all agreed it was driving him crazier, and making him even more intolerable to live with than he had been before.

He would behave perfectly normally one minute, then start thumping a wall the next. Images assailed him and filled him with manic energy, but by the time he had raced to his room, the images had been replaced by fresh ones. Consequently he hadn't put brush to canvas for months, and each of his new obsessions was more disagreeable than the last. At night I could hear him pacing his room, twelve steps up, twelve back. Sometimes it continued until dawn, when I went in and forcibly put him to bed. Lately he had cropped his hair, given up all hallucinogenic substances, and taken to eating nothing but brown rice and vegetables. Only the alcohol and the creative block remained constant in his life.

He looked up at me suddenly, his face clenched and suspicious. "Have you been eating like I told you?"

"Yes, yes," I lied impatiently. At first we had resisted his attempts to change our diets and the more he pestered us, the more we baked cheesecakes and waved raw meat under his quivering nostrils. But he wore us down by insisting that he check everyone's stools in the toilet bowl before we flushed them away. So offensive and infuriating was the sound of Archie hammering on the toilet door that we caved in, ate our brown rice, hid our cheesecakes and lied.

"You're lying," he said, "I'll have to check you-know-what."

"Oh, will you stop," I said, flaring up. "Can't you ever be serious? Everything's falling apart in this house and it's ever since Jack came."

Archie sat back and regarded me coolly. "So she's in love, that's all right, isn't it?"

"Of course it's all right," I snapped. "But she's hardly happy, is she? I mean, when do we ever see her these days, she's either cross all the time or she's in there with Jack, waking everyone up with the fighting or the sex. I don't know which is worse. She's even neglecting Darling. If that's love . . ."

Archie was laughing softly. "But that is, exactly, love," he said, "an agreement between two adults to behave like children and give each other as hard a time as possible. Makes the world go round. Anyway, he's a nice bloke."

It was no good even trying to talk to Archie. He was dyslexic when it came to the underneath of things. Besides, it was difficult to explain my resentment of Jack. When he was around, everyone became serious and thoughtful. They leaned forward slightly when he spoke and were less careless with their own opinions. He was a brilliant, committed intellectual who never uttered words like "fucking," "amazing" or "incredible," and his excruciating civility toward me was worse than being ignored. Since he had arrived, the shape and pattern of our household had changed drastically and Georgia refused to see it.

It had begun innocuously enough. She came up to my room as usual for a late-night gossip. This was an institution providing both of us with the safest, warmest, most enjoyable hour or two of the day, in which world events, my week's reading list, the behavior of friends, my manifold inadequacies and imminent suicide, her problems with her ex-husband, daughter, work, mortgage, were all dissected and analyzed, prodded and laughed at with equal irreverence. They were harmonious conversations, even when we disagreed, because we used the language of the underneath of things as shorthand. After she had gone to bed, I always felt a deep satisfaction, as if I had expressed myself and been understood, perfectly. The talk would go on for hours sometimes, until it petered out in comfortable silences and a good night hug.

This particular evening, it was as if Georgia's batteries had been charged. Her eyes were shiny, and her grin wrinkles abnormally deep.

"Uh, oh," I said, as she landed on my bed, "who is it this time?"

"Clever clever, but it so happens that I am not interested in him that way, it's just nice to have an intelligent conversation with a man and be understood. Needless to say, he is not Australian."

"So, who is he?" I asked, wondering why a small part of me was not feeling at all pleased.

"I was in the staff room today and they were all maundering on as usual when this new chap, Jack Schrader, a Pom who's taking over from Harvey Dale thank God, the lecherous old spider, if I'd had to listen to another dissertation on temperature tolerance in frogs I would have killed. You know what that rotten old fraud does, by the way? He catches frogs, pops them in a beaker, boils them and notes the temperature at which they kark. He calls this Biology. Isn't it odd that these people are only comfortable studying life when it's dead? Anyway, Jack was saying very little and the same old conversation starts up. I'm sure they do it just to goad me. It was about dungflies this time."

"Dungflies," I said, putting my book over my face. Georgia pulled it away.

"The mating behavior of dungflies is very interesting. Female lands on dung. Male mounts her. Other males try to mount her. He elbows them off. Whichever male mounts her last, his genes will be the ones she accepts. So this idiot describes how the male grabs the female and subdues her. And out it all comes—subdue, dominate, grab, exploit and of course I try to ignore it but then I can't. 'Don't you think,' I said, 'that these are rather loaded words for scientists to use when describing the behavior of animals?' Off they go. And that woman, honestly, one of these days I'll throttle her, the only other woman in the room and she just sits there like a little wart and stares at her hands. I pull in my horns, of course, and try to talk reasonably. 'In Western metaphysical systems,' I say, 'pairings like black and white, male and female are presented as balanced when in fact they operate as covert hierarchies so that we can't imagine difference without domination and subordination.' " She took a breath.

"Anyway, in the middle of all this, Jack says, 'I think Georgia's quite right. It's a way of enshrining social discriminations.' They shut up like clams, Lucy. God, I wanted to kiss him. I've been fighting for years on my own trying to instill some sense of wonder and curiosity into those poor bloody students . . ."

How many times had I covered this battleground with her. I had been to the noisome department, sensed the tacit persecution of her because she proclaimed loudly that scientists could not plead immunity from social concerns. They were frightened of her and they controlled her by belittling her work. Her Ph.D. was grinding to a halt under the weight of it but she was not the type to compromise or to sweeten her approach, and this only compounded the problem.

So now she had someone else with whom to commiserate. Good. But why were my antennae twitching and why could I feel a small snake coiling in my chest? Why was Georgie so pathetically grateful for a few sentences tossed her way like scraps? It wasn't like her to be so starry-eyed as not to question motives.

So uncanny was my perspicacity that I disliked him already, knew that he would dislike me and that he would soon move in with Georgie. For her sake, I would do my best to welcome him into the house and charm him. If he infantilized me as the others did, if I posed, therefore, no threat to him, the shifts of balance that his entry would necessarily cause could be controlled. No one need be jostled out of position and things would settle down again into the big happy family it had always been. At all costs, this first family of mine must hold together and no Jack Whatsisface was going to jeopardize that.

My best-laid plans were ruined when he visited the following night. For one thing he was very attractive, in that heavy-lidded, sleepily arrogant, highly articulate and utterly self-assured way. There was a lazy half-smile on his face, which only went away when he was deep in highbrow conversation. When stressing a point he never sat forward, but lolled back in his chair. He never hurried his speech, or giggled, and he paused thoughtfully before answering a question. He had far too many perfect Oxbridge teeth, and a habit of slowly running his beautiful hands through a straight shock of black hair, which fell back adorably across his intelligent brow. I hated him.

He engaged Archie in a discussion about art and Archie transmogrified into a serious person. He charmed Hydraulic by telling her how lesbian seagulls rubbed cloacas together, built nests and raised young. Hydraulic almost smiled and the wild thing inside her body lay

132

down and purred. Even Frank, the shadowy photographer, hung around the kitchen for an hour to listen, before evaporating into the basement.

Georgia remained unusually silent during the evening, sending him little shy glances, which he pretended not to notice. I could hear her insides melting under her pretense at cool and it made me want to cry. Only the week before, she had talked eloquently and movingly about the debilitating effect of heterosexual love on women, how it diminished them, weakened them, threw them back into ancient patterns of behavior.

"You're very quiet, Lucy." There was a not quite insolent smile on Jack's face and the others stopped talking to look at me. As everyone knows, this is the cruelest thing one can say to a shy person trying to be invisible in a group—like sticking them up a pole and pointing at them. I sat on top of the pole, holding down the blush, willing a little saliva back into my mouth.

"Oh, am I? I'm just a little tired." I faked a small yawn.

"Tired? Little Lucy, you sleep sixteen hours a day," said Archie, chuckling.

"Leave her alone." Hydraulic placed a sisterly arm around my shoulders. "She's doing all right."

I glanced at Georgia for help, but when she caught my eyes, she stared back down at her whiskey and I was alone. "Actually," I said, as casually as I could, "I think I'll hit the sack. Got a big day tomorrow." I returned Hydraulic's squeeze, said "Good night all," and began climbing the stairs. Jack had wanted to get rid of me but what really hurt was Georgia's collusion. She wanted everyone to go to bed so that they could proceed with their courtship ritual. Like dungflies.

After that, whenever Jack was there, I fell into an autism deeper than the Marianas Trench.

Archie was right about my capacity for sleep. It was my one great talent. When I woke, usually at around ten, my many failures loomed over my bed like gargoyles. I would pull the covers over my head, and let myself subside into a warm ooze of fantasies, or dream-clogged sleep. The fantasies were always variations on a theme. By some magic means, I would be transformed into a small, ineffably beautiful redhead who could speak fifteen languages, paint, sing, write poems, toss off theses, play piano, guitar, sax, drums and harmonica, who had unbitten fingernails, never felt shy or awkward, wasn't frigid and who was the sort of person who rose joyously at six a.m. And she could wither Jack Schrader with a glance.

These soporific states could only last for so many hours. Eventually I would have to face a world bled of all luster, an empty house and a blank television screen. I needed coffee strong as sump oil and a shot of whiskey to lift myself into a frame of mind where I could contemplate dressing and going to work at the art school down the street. Usually I would miss the first modeling session, thus raising the ire of the class teacher who would probably never book such an unreliable model again. My addiction to sleep meant that I lived many fathoms below the poverty line.

Jack moved in within a fortnight of Georgia telling me his name. The first sign that the subterranean shifts I had predicted were affecting the household appeared when Darling began to spend all her time destroying my room instead of Georgia's. I had come to admire the bird's intelligence and courage; her hatred of Jack Schrader was as bitter as mine, but, noble beast that she was, she expressed it by flying into his face and screeching. This was her undoing. I would hear the quick trit-tritting of her claws on my floor at seven in the morning, a few minutes after she had given up hurling herself at Georgia's door.

"Hello, Darling," she would say, as she hopped onto the covers and tickled my ear. If I refused to acknowledge her, she would give it a brutal tweak.

"Oh, go away," I'd say.

"Oh, go away," she'd repeat delightedly before crawling under the sheets. There was a conspicuous sadness in the little creature these days. When I woke properly at ten, she would be sitting on my pillow, ruffled and disconsolate.

"Never mind, Darling," I would say, scratching the repulsive gooseflesh under her feathers, and she would close her eyes and sway.

The piles of greasy washing-up grew and it became my responsibility to bully everyone into doing their share. And when sick or lost creatures followed the pull of Georgia's animal magnetism to our door, it was I who had to feed, doctor and console, just as I had to doctor, feed and console Archie, Hydraulic, Frank and all the other beautiful, broken people taking refuge in the house.

On the night the tops blew off Frank's fifty bottles of homebrew beer causing the big burly man who'd returned from the Nam, who was groping his way toward the toilet in pitch darkness, to smash up Archie's paintings looking for the Vietcong before raging down to Frank's room to tear him to pieces, it was I who had to pull him off and soothe him because Frank was too dumb to understand what was happening and Archie was huddled uselessly in the kitchen in his dressing gown and Georgia was curled into a tight ball with Jack Schrader willfully oblivious to the bedlam.

I understood the depth of Jack's contempt for me when I returned home alone after one of the most inspiring events of my life. A group of street performers had come to stay with us, and so overtly worshipful was I of our gaudy, theatrical guests, so hungrily did I watch them rehearse in our back garden, and so shamelessly did I copy their every gesture, that they invited me to participate in one of their performances. I was to walk on my hands and deliver political pamphlets with my feet to the audience who would undoubtedly be lining the streets of the city. As a finale, I was to catch three black papier-mâché bombs which my partner would be juggling nervously, and toss them into the crowd.

That morning, I forced myself to rise early. With immense effort, I swung my legs to the floor, tried to focus my recalcitrant eyes and tottered toward the landing. I gripped the door, shielded my eyes against the glare and lunged for the rickety chair. I had got myself past the gargoyles at the crack of nine a.m. The world was a very different place at this hour. The temperature was still in the eighties and I could hear a desultory bird twitter. The sky was more delicately cobalt than the febrile blue-black which usually greeted me. I almost dozed off in the chair, lulled by the measured beat of surf on the rocks, but another surge of willpower got me to the bathroom.

I chose the watermelon-pink satin pajamas, a fifty-cent bargain from the thrift shop, ballet slippers and an army surplus jacket. With a sprig of fresh jasmine in my hair and a smudge of kohl around my eyes, I flung open Archie's door, dived onto his bed, tickled him mercilessly and accused him of being addicted to sleep. Then I set out with my bombs ticking excitedly in their box.

We set up on the busiest corner. A few shoppers stared at us, as if we'd emerged from the sewers, before shuffling on. When I distributed my political leaflets, a group of older women said they wouldn't use them for toilet paper. At the end of the performance, an office worker leaned out of a fourth-floor window to urinate on us. So incensed was our juggler that he threw all his bombs up at the window, yelling, "Come down from your bourgeois complacency."

"Ya father shoulda slipped out and split yez on the lino, ya Commie poofter," came the reply. It was not quite the reception I had anticipated, but I had done my hand-walking well, and the dizzying exaltation did not leave me until I arrived home to find Jack, sitting alone under the lemon tree, reading Noam Chomsky.

I took tea out to him and smiled in what I hoped was a haughty and superior way. I might have said "Great book isn't it?" but words refused to form. He looked up, said thank you, then added: "I see you've got your uniform on." I pretended not to understand the insult. Everyone dressed up except Jack, who always looked like an office worker. I was too stung by the little cruelty to leave so I sat sipping tea, a stunned sheep awaiting slaughter.

He closed his book with the gesture of a priest closing a Bible, leaned back and said, "You're very young, but . . . it seems to me it's time you stopped treating politics like a party. It's time you started thinking for yourself. You can't expect people to look after you and mother you all the time . . . everyone's worried sick about you, the scrapes you get into . . . The only thing you seem interested in is acrobatics which may look very pretty but is hardly a useful occupation . . . And these depressions of yours, if you engaged with the world more and didn't concentrate on your own problems so much . . . None of us can afford such self-indulgence . . . And you'd be happier."

That night, the gargoyles used thumbscrews. It was so unjust. He talked about despair as if one could turn it on and off at will. God knows I tried to make up for those periods of gloom by making everyone—even Hydraulic—laugh.

Whenever the horrors hit hard, Georgia knew. She would come to my room, cuddle me, tell me I was wonderful, and I would sniffle and say things like "Why does it have to be so hard," or "I wish I was like you," and she would laugh at me until I laughed, and then I'd feel better and go to sleep. But that night she did not come. My soft weeping got a little louder. Still no Georgia. What was she doing? She knew I was hurting, that I needed her. She was downstairs fucking Jack, that's what. My weeping gave way to sobs then howls of pain. Tremendous pain. Surely she must be able to hear them from her bedroom, damn her. Damn him. I heard her footsteps on the stairs. When she came to the door I looked up, as if surprised, then hiccuped and flung my face down on the pillow.

"I'm sorry, I didn't mean to disturb you, go away now, I'm okay," and my heart broke all over the bed.

"Lucy, you've got to stop this, you know."

"What?" I sniffed and lifted my head a fraction.

"You've got to pull yourself together."

"I can't," I said and threw my face back down on the pillow. She patted my bottom.

"Lucy, I'm tired. I've been at that stinking university all day. Billy Byrd pissed in my bed. I can't pay to have the roof fixed. I may have to sell the house. Clive rang and threatened me about Annie. Jack's here and we're trying to sleep. And if you don't pull that pretty head of yours out of your navel I swear I'm going to scream."

I sat bolt upright. Georgia's head was resting in her hand, so I could not see her face. She looked up, relented, put her arms around me, dropped her forehead onto mine and said, "Listen, little darling, you're just going to have to accept the fact that you're not dashingly and attractively mad, you're just neurotic like the rest of us and you must stop feeling sorry for yourself because it gets awfully boring and underneath it all you're as tough as a boot and I love you very much but now I'm going to bed."

I think I hated Georgia then.

"You know Hydraulic's really close to the edge."

"She's always close to the edge," said Archie, sitting motionless in the bath I had run for him and staring at the walls he had covered in paint years ago. In my opinion, the mural—cabbage tree palms, screeching parrots and flat white sails against a background of intense blue—was the loveliest thing he had done.

"No, I mean worse than usual," I insisted.

"Oh yeah?" Archie seemed uninterested.

"The other day she attacked a taxi driver because she thought his packet of peanuts was a knife he was about to kill us with. Sometimes I think that shrink of hers isn't doing any good at all."

"Oh bother," said Archie, "I was thinking of going to him myself. He might knock my creative block off. Hey, maybe he could come and live here and do bulk psychiatry." Archie paused. "You'd have to fuck him of course."

"If you don't stop, I'll . . ."

"Well you fuck everyone else. Think of us. Selfish you see, that's your problem. And what about Hydraulic. She even loves you. We could have furnished the whole house with Hydraulic's talents but no you have to be picky picky."

"Stop," I growled, shaking him.

"Hey do you really think sitting is bad for piles? I know it's bad for my varicose vein. Do you think women are repulsed by my varicose vein? Is that why you won't make love to me, because of my varicose vein? Tell me the truth. You won't hurt me I promise. Or is it my piles? God I should never have told you."

"You know why you can't paint?" I said coldly. "It's because you can't feel." With that, I closed the door firmly behind me. When I crept guiltily into his room an hour later, he was in the fetal position facing the wall and pretending to be asleep.

The truth was, that for all the practice I was getting, I did not seem to be improving at sex. This tepidity of response was a source of unending heartache. There was, after all, a sexual revolution taking place. Women were liberated at last from the shackles of pregnancy and therefore it was up to them to disburden themselves of centuries of ingrained prudery. But my prudery was so deep it refused to budge and the pill only seemed to cement it. All I could do was fake well, keep practicing and hope for a miracle of dislodgement. Left to my own devices, I could orgasm in thirty seconds flat, but with a partner, hours of grueling foreplay only pushed me further away from the erotic abyss. I loathed my body, hated the stares which bored through it as I swung down the street, despised the men who were so easily fooled. There was certainly no dearth of them.

Although I laughed just as harshly and bitterly as everyone else at the notion that all women needed was a good fuck, I spent a large amount of my time certain that all I needed was a good fuck. The secret grew even weightier when I understood that no other woman had ever suffered in this way. The snorting and whinnying of un-bridled passion emanating from Georgia's room was proof enough of my deplorable inadequacy. Once, a linguistics lecturer, who had taken to doing striptease and who could make her breasts rotate in opposite directions so that the nipple tassles looked like little electric fans, had announced to the company around our kitchen table that she'd had crabs in the eyebrows. She was a libertarian socialist. When I asked how she'd got them there, everyone laughed at me fondly. I tried to imagine doing that act which led to the gaining of crabs in the eyebrows and it made me gag. How do they manage it, I thought. How could they possibly enjoy it?

And Hydraulic did love me. I knew for sure the night of the pool cue incident. Of course I loved her too, as I did all my family, with a blind devotion. But not like that. The idea of doing anything sexual with her was out of the question. Women would probably know when you were faking. At least with men I had some idea of what to do and there was never any expectation of loving. Sex and love, my instinct told me, would be a fatal combination—the weft and warp of a new cocoon—the ultimate wing-crippler.

The pool cue incident was the finale to a day in the country. A group of us had stopped off on the way home at a pub, which had four pool tables, a lovely beer garden, and several taciturn farmers who sat at the bar, exuding a silent but palpable dislike of poofters, Commies and blacks. Our small company contained representatives of all three. The stored-up charge of dislike and mistrust between the groups was so intense that I felt duty bound to provide a current of communication. After all, I had known country people like these all my life. They were kind and phlegmatic. When they spoke, they squatted on their haunches and looked at the ground or, if forced to stand because a lady was present, shuffled their feet and twisted their battered Stetsons. They were competent, reliable and knew about livestock and weather. In the early days, their wives might have baked me fairy cakes and lamingtons. They were my people.

I sat on a bar stool next to one of them and said, "G'day."

There was no reply.

"Reckon you must've got a spot of rain lately."

The man acknowledged me by turning away slightly and concentrating on his beer.

"Shoot," said Archie, in a loud southern drawl, "ah been run ouda towns where ah wouldn' have stayed if you'd paid me."

Billy Byrd smiled, but his eyes flickered nervously. Hydraulic's voice went down an octave. She swaggered, jutted her pelvis, tipped

139

back in a chair and hooked her thumbs in her pockets. I could never figure out why, in her revolt against male oppression, she emulated the least attractive aspects of enemy behavior.

"Pricks."

I grimaced threateningly in her direction and tried again. "Just come down from the 'dilla. Pretty dry up that way. Missed out on the rains by the look of things." But my country cousins could not be wooed. I understood, with sadness, that having left their world there was no way back, and if their wives were to bake me cakes these days, they would probably add sheep dip to the batter.

By nine p.m. I was so drunk that I was playing magnificent pool. Balls click-clicked into pockets as if pulled on elastic. When one of the locals purposely bumped Hydraulic, just as she was lining up the eight ball, she swung on him, her jaw squaring belligerently, her pool cue poised in midair, her nose in line with his navel. "Watch it, arsehole."

The poor man was rendered momentarily speechless, but eventually he remembered a suitable retort from his past repertoire. "Cunt," he said.

That magic word again. A word so powerful it could turn Hydraulic into a banshee. She stepped back, lifted her left arm, stiffened her right arm and poked the tip of her pool cue into his chest.

"En garde," she shouted, leaping onto the table and dancing out of the way of the arms of the fuming publican.

What I remember of the return journey was having to stop occasionally by the side of the road, to vomit violently, and on all fours, while Hydraulic held my forehead. And I remember her cradling me to her in the backseat saying, "There there, little Lou," while I tried to think up excuses for struggling free.

Often I would sit in my room, tightening my resolve. I would imagine myself sitting down next to her and being simple, frank and open.

"Hydraulic," I would say to Darling in a no-nonsense voice, "you're a very nice person but I don't find you attractive." One day, when I knew she was downstairs by herself, I repeated the sentence over and over.

"Hydraulic," I said, when I sat next to her at the kitchen table, "you're a very nice person . . ." Unfortunately, the rest of the sentence refused to come out. She looked soulfully into my eyes.

"Ah, aren't you sweet. So are you." She gave me a hug and looked hurt and puzzled when I broke loose and announced in a grumpy voice that I was going to prepare dinner. From then on I avoided her, which hurt her feelings so badly that the friendship ended along with the problem.

There were other endings. Household gods and goddesses were beginning to look all too human. It was not that I loved them any less, but I had absorbed their many gifts and now I needed a new Pantheon. Like a leech, I waited for a fresh host.

I watched the traveling performers come and go as if they were rare and exotic birds. When they stayed with us, they not only tolerated my presence, but taught me their tricks; when they left I would haunt the waterfront for a week, consoling myself with fantasies of a day when I might fly south with them. Secretly, in the back garden, I strengthened my wings. I climbed ropes, dangled from the top branches of trees, and practiced spirals, double back flips and jack-knifes on Annie's trampoline. It was there that I discovered my soul's most comfortable position—as close to the angels as possible. Only when I was looking down on the world was the weight of its judgment taken away; only when I leapt high, higher, into the air, was I blessed with celestial lightness.

Meanwhile my feverish search for enjoyable sex had cooled off, which only seemed to make my onanism more ardent. The trouble was that every man I met, I could place. They held no mystery, no hidden depths. Even jugglers and clowns, once divested of their costumes, were disappointingly predictable. The celibate life suited me now that my list of conquests had gone from A to X and might have continued to include Yolande and Zara, but Love, in the form of a small man with clever eyes, a flamboyant bad taste in clothes and a mysterious bulge in his trousers, raised its serpentine head and hissed in my ear.

When I heard that an illegal gambling club was opening, I put on my watermelon-pink satin pajamas and set forth, unknowingly, for nemesis.

12
Temporal Triangles

The windows of the third floor were blacked out and the door, which looked as if it had come off a bank vault, bore the words "Professional Chiropractors' Association" printed in gold lettering beneath a shuttered slit. I caught a quick glimpse of eye before the bolts trundled back and the door creaked open, revealing a mesomorphic man with ears like lettuces and something resembling a nose folding into his left cheek. Muscles struggled like trapped pythons under the taut fabric of his shirt. His other eye turned up and out, as if trying to see into the stygian darkness behind his shoulder.

The doorman beckoned me, Lon Chaney style, to the far end of a large room, where a perfect triangle of yellow light framed a tableau vivant. Five men sat smoking heavily and comparing fat, platinum watches around a semicircular baize table. As my eyes adjusted to the greenish gloom, I could see that the walls were covered with chartreuse and gold wallpaper the texture of navel lint. There were three plastic chandeliers, mauve velveteen drapes, gold tassels and a deep-pile burgundy carpet. Royal routine flushes, measuring two feet by four feet, spread out in fans around the walls. I reeled biliously for an instant, and followed.

"Not bad. Yes, a nice piece, Nick. Two thousand, you say?" said a dapper little man in a three-piece suit. He spoke with an upper-class English accent and turned the Rolex over in his manicured fingers, before returning it to his neighbor—an obese Greek, whose bald scalp glistened as richly as his diamond rings.

At the center of the tableau sat The Boss, resplendent in mauve suit, black lace shirt and canary-yellow tie, an outfit which did little to dilute the intelligent criminality of his face. It was a cheeky face, the kind that drives policemen and overly romantic young women wild. He tipped insolently back in his mock Regency chair and shuffled cards to form riffles, fans and blurred flower shapes which collapsed back into his magnetic hands. His eyes jittered over my pink satin pajamas then fixed on my own.

"G'day, ah, Lucy, in' it? Well siddown, Lucy, and tell us what you reckon about the daycore. Done it meself. Had a bit of a disagreement with the interior decorator." He chuckled; his friends smiled on cue. "But he didn't have much luck."

"Oh," I said breezily, "it's very impressive." I gazed around the room, making small appreciative gestures with my head.

"Impressive see? What'd I tell youze. She's got class. And that's what my establishment's gunna have. Class. And she talks nice, don't ya, Lucy." The boss looked around for confirmation of this fact and got it.

"Real nice voice. Yeah. Got an eye for the visual tastes, too. Larry, mix the kid a drink. Brandy Alexander. Nah. Give 'er a Black Russian." The boss took out a three-inch wad of fifty-dollar bills fresh from the mint and ostentatiously peeled off four of them. "Here, get yerself some flash clothes, kid. Somethin' that'll complement the daycore. Now siddown here, beside me, that's it, you smoke dope or what?"

Four hours later, I stumbled back into the ordinary world, like Alice leaving the rabbit hole. I zigzagged down the street in the wrong direction, clutching more cash than I had ever held in my life and a pack of beautiful Kem Number One cards. I had discovered that I had an innate knack with those cards. They were as slippery, smooth and seductive as the crim who had just taught me how to deal stud poker; how to flick the things like wings across the baize, while whisking chips away with the left hand; how to spread the cards in front of me in a flat fan and fiddle with the chips, stacking them deftly into piles while calling "ace bets," or "up two," or "three of a kind wins." There are some games which transcend themselves: chess is one, pool is another, but five-card stud is the most transcendent of all, especially when played in a smoky room under a triangle of light with birds so ostentatiously feathered they made actors look like sparrows. The Silver Slipper was a stage set, and I was the leading lady.

I waited impatiently for Georgia to return that evening, pacing the empty house in a delirium of excitement, banishing gargoyles with an easy flick of my cardsharp's hands. I heard the door bang, and leapt down the stairs three at a time.

"Guess what, you'll never guess, we're rich, we can fix the roof." I waved the money under her rigid face and pretended not to know what was written all over it—another fight with Jack.

Georgia and Jack had been together nine months and the alliance was on the point of disintegration. At first I had resented the way Georgia devoted all her energy to salvaging it, but when the first romantic gloss had worn off the love affair, to reveal the pits and crannies of incompatibility, a curious reversal had developed in our friendship. I was now the emotional support, the wise, world-hardened one, who had not only lost all inarticulateness with Jack, but could now openly voice my contempt for him. I was a tiny pinprick to his monstrous self-importance, a go-between, a dumping ground for anger and a corner of the triangle. Jack and I were comfortable enough in our dislike of each other to get on quite well, and this amusing, abrasive bond between worthy opponents was compelling enough to keep us hooked, even without the hidden frisson.

Georgia tried to join in my enthusiasm for the Silver Slipper, but her body and her smile remained reluctant. I sat in the ballroom and felt my happiness dilute.

"Okay. What happened?" She heard the impatience in my voice and tried to laugh the tightness off her face.

"Nothing. Same old nonsense. Come on, show me the cards."

"Georgia," I said, folding my arms over my chest. "Sit."

She looked at me sheepishly for a moment, sighed and sat. She stared ahead blankly, lips contracted, elbows on knees, shoulders slumped, the closest to crying she ever came. I prepared myself for an account of the latest battle, knowing that if I agreed that he was a beast, she would defend his point of view, and that if I took his side, she would tell me I did not understand her. What she wanted to hear was that it was not ending, that he loved her in the same way that she loved him.

"We had a fight in the pub," she began. "About Annie. Honestly, Lucy, he's such a creep, he just ignores her. All she wants is a scrap of recognition every now and then, but when she comes anywhere near him, you can see him zip up like a sleeping bag."

"Yes, I know."

144

"So I said, 'Look, I have a daughter, you can't just pretend she doesn't exist.' And, of course, he answers that it wouldn't be fair of him to form an attachment to her, which is just another way of saying that he's intending to leave, that I'm not important enough to him. And I say, 'But Jack, we live together, I just want you to be friendly to Annie when you're there, I'm not asking you to be her father.' And it builds into another poisonous fight . . ." Georgia banged the side of her head with her fists.

"Well, he is a beast. I don't know why you don't give him an ultimatum, either accept Annie or leave, if you really think it's damaging to her."

Georgia gave me a wry look. "You really hate him, don't you? Well, why shouldn't you. But maybe he's right, perhaps he shouldn't concern himself with my child when he's got one of his own to worry about." Jack's child was conveniently in England and for all the anxiety his son caused him, he took no responsibility for him at all.

"Maybe," I agreed, and waited.

"Well, Christ, you just imagine if it was the other way around, if his boy was here." Georgia hooted and her eyes were brilliant with resentment. "Just imagine what an unnatural abomination of a woman I would be if I ignored him." I wanted to say to her, "You let him get away with everything. Big, tough, uncompromising Georgie who everyone's scared of, you buckle under to him, you give up your intelligence for him, and he punishes Annie because he's frightened of any form of commitment. He's threatened by my friendship with you and he's a moral coward." Instead, I did what she wanted.

"It'll be all right, Georgie. I won't pretend I like him, or that I think he's good for you, but he does love you in his way."

"Do you really think so?" she turned bemused, pleading eyes at me.

"Sure," I said, hating myself for my duplicity. Jack was leaving, and we all knew it, even Archie.

We continued discussing it for an hour, laughing ourselves sick at the frailties, the inadequacies, the weaknesses of men, and at our own mysterious collusion, until the banging of the front door startled us into silence. Georgia shot up out of her seat, tense and hunched. She appeared combative, but I knew she was feeble under the bravado, and that she was gearing herself up for a confrontation she felt bound to lose. She lit a cigarette as Jack paused at the foot of the stairs.

He raised an eyebrow, smiled his insultingly laconic smile, ambled into the room and eased himself into an armchair. The air curdled with tension. He lit a cigarette, relaxed back in the chair and regarded first me, and then Georgia.

"So, have I been found guilty, or do I get a chance to defend myself?" He directed his challenge at me. I let out a little snort and smiled mockingly back at him.

"Don't shovel it off onto Lucy, Jack. She's got nothing to do with it."

Jack smiled sarcastically. "But your little sister doesn't approve of me, Georgia, hadn't you noticed?"

Georgia was white-faced, and I knew that my role was now to deflect his anger with her onto myself. I put my head on one side and mimicked his look.

"It's not that I disapprove, Jack, it's simply that I know you're a fraud."

"Ah the deeply perceptive Little Luce who's seen it all before. Do you know how ridiculous you look, like a bantam protecting its egg."

"And you look, as always, like a peacock," I said, laughing at him, as he went to the kitchen and began making a lot of noise with kettle and cups. I raised my eyebrow at Georgia, meaning, "Do you want me to stay?" She frowned, fiddled and shook her head, no.

"No tea for me, thanks," I said sweetly into the kitchen door, before retreating upstairs, my viscera pumping adrenaline and my role played out to perfection.

Annie was playing in her room which was opposite mine. I went in and chatted with her, but when the sounds of shouted abuse came hurtling up the stairwell, and I saw the dead look in her eyes, something snapped in me. There was an unspoken law in the house that when Jack and Georgia were fighting we all pretended we were deaf. But I was tired of watching people creep into corners and of seeing Annie close up like a baby clam. I tore down to the kitchen and yelled at both of them to shut up. I grabbed Georgia by the front of her shirt and shook her. I took a swipe at Jack's knee with my leg. My rage stunned them into silence. I had broken the rules.

Predictably, my outburst gave their affair a new lease on life. The triangle had been flattened, the couple was reunited and I was the odd woman out. They lapsed back into their own secretive universe, their special language of looks and gestures from which I was excluded. With me, Georgia was unconvincingly lighthearted but I knew that

146

beneath her façade, desperation hummed along at the same high pitch. Our conversations became studies in avoidance. When she chatted about every subject except Jack, she was as cautious and light as a dragonfly.

In many ways, it was a relief. But every now and then, I felt a reckless urge to break the conspiracy. We were in the kitchen, cooking together, when I interrupted her prattle.

"Darling is sick." She paused, disconcerted by the accusation in my voice, aware that I was really saying, "*I know what you're doing and I'm tired of the game.*"

"Oh really, I hadn't noticed." Meaning, "*I need this thing to work too much and it requires everything I've got and I can't cope with anything else.*"

"If you ask me she's got a broken heart." Meaning, "*You're betraying everyone else in your life for Jack.*"

Georgia laughed. "Nonsense, Darling hasn't got a heart to break." Meaning, "*You're a woman, you must understand, our friendship is strong enough to be put on hold for a while.*" She poked a finger into my ribs, trying to tease me into laughter, silently begging me not to say any more, but when I didn't respond, her face hardened and she turned away.

"I'm more worried about Annie quite frankly." Meaning, "*If I had any spare energy, I would have to devote it to Annie, not to you,*" a statement which also indicated a consideration for the important things in life, greater than my own.

"Well," I said, disliking the petulance in my voice, "I suppose I'll have to take her to the vet then."

"Yes, I suppose you will." Meaning, "*The more you demand of me, the less I'll give.*" For a minute or two, we both clattered and banged around with saucepans and cutlery, acutely aware of each other's anger. She then put down her dishes and looked at me with a sad little smile. "*Don't abandon me*" was the message—an appeal I could not resist.

We felt easier with each other after that, but my visceral dislike of Jack was made more potent for being bottled up—a gradual fermenting. I would catch him watching me slyly, and the lubricity in those looks made me feel soiled.

I began to distance myself from the murky emotional whirlpools in the house. A group of theater people from all over the country had taken over a warehouse down by the docks. I now spent most of my spare time there, helping them out, copying their lines, on and off stage, and aching to belong to their world.

When Georgie announced a surprise picnic for my birthday, I went out of a sense of duty rather than pleasure. She unveiled a three-tiered extravaganza of cake, covered in rainbow icing, ribbons, penny lollies and a cluster of sparklers ready to be lit. We all piled into the ute, Georgia, Annie, Jack, Archie, Hydraulic, myself and Darling and sped north to the vast national parks which fringed the city like a nest protecting a cuckoo. Annie and I leaned on the cabin letting the wind flap our cheeks and stream our hair straight back. It was so rare to see her laughing and happy, but when I cautiously slipped my arm around her, I felt her little body shrink and stiffen. No one liked Annie much. She didn't do the endearing things children are supposed to do and had a knack for making adults feel awkward. We teased Georgia that her daughter would become a policewoman.

When we arrived at our spot, and turned off the engine and the music, the bush sent its hush into all of us. We spoke very quietly, as if in a cathedral. Annie went ahead, carrying a basket.

"Here, let me . . ."

"I can do it," she said, pulling her arm away, puffing and struggling down the rocks. Her surly doggedness filled me with admiration and anger. Part of me wanted to pick her up and squeeze her, the other part wanted to strike her.

But I wasn't about to let a ten-year-old ruin my day. It took me a minute or two to block out the presence of the others, and to become fully receptive to the surroundings. My thoughts, unharnessed, roamed freely through the wilderness. I loved its misshapenness, its secret softnesses, its freakish shapes, its bold curves of stone, like protruding bones, as I might love the body of a lover, or a mother. I understood its language—the creaking of crows, the thin piping of a kestrel way overhead, the snap and thump of a startled wallaby, the protesting chatter of a Jacky Winter. I read its signs—here, the scratches of possums scarring the smooth skin of a gum and, further on, the dragmarks and sharp scrapings of an iguana. In the under-growth, a native robin displayed his chest like a tiny welcoming flame.

My possessive love of natural bushland was seen as an endearing eccentricity by my friends. "People must have access to it Lucy. It's there for everyone to enjoy." I would nod my head glumly, utterly incapable of feeling democratic about it. Whenever I saw a colony of prickly pear, or the burrows of rabbits, or the glint of human junk, or heard the roar of a distant speedboat, I felt bruised inside, as if my own body were being invaded.

What my friends could not know was that beneath my pantheistic delight, an old, dull pain lay in ambush. How had Wally died? A fall? Starvation? A snake? Perhaps a knife? And Laura? Was she too old to do battle with the carpet snake? Was anyone looking out for her? Yet no sooner had I thought of them than a black veil fell over my memories of home. They constituted a past which belonged to somebody else.

By now, I had completely obliterated the presence of my friends. The midday sun scorched my shoulders and puckered my face into a squint. I followed a small creek, running cold and glassy over hot rock. Scraggly gums cast a parsimonious shade; tea trees dipped into transparent pools. I skipped from shade spot to shade spot, enjoying the prickling of sticks and dry litter under my feet, the tickle of sweat on my back, the scratch of rough undergrowth on my shins.

The secretiveness of the bush ended dramatically at an escarpment—a rim of stone, like the curve of a rampart, a mile long. Water fell sheer into more gray-green scrub, then fed out into the dazzling ocean. Blue on blue, space and more space, a piercing brilliance. I wanted to open my arms and shout into the emptiness, or go down on my knees and rub my cheek reverently on smooth stone. "As long as I can have this," I thought, "I can survive anything."

"Come on, wild child, you'd better lead us down."

I turned around to see that everyone was smiling at me, as if I were a little bit touched. Georgia rubbed the muscles in my shoulders. "You're so funny in the bush, you completely transform. I can never understand why you choose to live in the city."

"She's mad. Did you see the way she attacked that prickly pear back there, like she'd gone feral or something."

"Puritanism," said Jack.

I led them through rainbow mist to the foot of the waterfall—a deep green pool shot through with yellow rays penetrating right to the sandy bottom. Ferns draped over crannies in the chill rock wall and a hundred yards farther on, the stream crossed a thin strip of glittering white sand, before emptying into the sea. We ate, struck out into the ocean, salted ourselves on the sand like hams, plunged into the cold pool and let the waterfall drum and thunder on our heads. In the soporific haze of midafternoon, our little party broke up into its constituents. Georgia and Jack, who had barely spoken to each other all day, went off by themselves. Archie, morose and withdrawn, sat inert on the beach, transfixed by the waves, drinking steadily, pretending to sketch, ripping out bits of paper and bunching them angrily in his fist. Annie squatted in the shade, playing with pebbles, sticks and a small doll. I somnambulated for a while, then lay down, lulled by the drone of bushflies and hypnotized by the sweeps and turns of a solitary sea eagle.

By the time I realized Hydraulic was heading toward me, it was too late to get up and run. I beamed at her welcomingly. "I haven't had a yarn with you for ages," she said accusingly, handing me four blue meanies, picked from the fecund cowpats of my home state.

"No thanks, they don't seem to be doing much for me lately."

"Oh, come on," admonished Hydraulic, "let yourself go for once."

Unwilling to admit that I suffered from that most socially unacceptable disease of all—paranoia—I took the mushrooms, masticated slowly and felt trapped. Hydraulic wandered off in one direction, I, in another.

The bush had changed mood, was withdrawn, melancholic. I felt as if I were intruding. Even Darling, who circled above my head or landed on my shoulder, could not dispel an odd sense of foreboding. I had often felt this ambivalence in the bush, as if it were suddenly suspicious of me, but usually I could soothe away the unease by sitting very still, and watching it come alive around me. I placed myself in a clearing and waited. The psilocybin was beginning to take effect. Tree trunks writhed and I thought something moved just behind my shoulder. Everything else was very still. Darling sat in a tree as if stuffed.

The goanna was at least four feet long, glowing with iridescent colors, flicking its bright blue tongue and staring straight into my eyes from six feet away. It came toward me, swinging its ponderous, monstrous claws out to the side, until its tongue-tip touched my feet. The world stopped. I don't know how long we remained locked in intense interspecies communication. When it ambled away, Darling ruffled her feathers, I took a breath, spirals of hot air teased at leaves, things moved. I was receiving a powerful message in the pit of my stomach and on the back of my neck, to run. I shivered, and whistled the bird down to my shoulder.

The sun was obscured by boulders and I stumbled clumsily along a dry gully, first one way, then another, blundering over rocks as if hounded, feeling the power of the bush to consign me to oblivion. When I caught a glimpse of ocean through the trees, like a twinkling beacon, I hurried toward it, appalled at my disorientation. All I needed to do was descend then walk north along the beach. I lunged forward, oblivious to the little cuts and stings, but when the dense foliage gave way and I saw the void, my legs went limp. Navy-blue water stretched away from the precipice to infinity. Carved on a flat patch of pitted sandstone was a shark twenty feet long, and inside the shark, another small fish. I sank to my haunches, overwhelmed by a feeling of utter insignificance. How had I ever imagined myself welcome in this place? It held more mysteries than I was capable of understanding, laws which I could not help but break, messages which I could never decipher, as if an arcane knowledge seeped from its roots into the brittle brightness. I did not, could never, truly belong.

By the time I reached the beach, even Jack was a welcome sight. I flung myself beside him panting.

"What on earth's the matter? I can hear your heart thumping from over here." He placed his hand carefully on my shoulder. He was wearing his sly half-smile. The image of a small bird flittering and dancing before the eyes of a snake came into my mind. His hand rested, heavy as a stone, then moved slowly down toward my breast. There was a glint of victory in his eyes and he struggled to cover it up.

"Georgia won't be back," he whispered, and it was enough to break the spell. There was a loud thrumming in my ears that I had always associated with fear, but what I felt was a white-hot rage. I reached across to his genitals and twisted as hard as I could, hearing my own voice, like a death rattle, saying, "If you ever touch me again, I'll kill you." I left him writhing in the sand.

No one noticed my agitation when I arrived back at the pool. Georgia was white as a ghost, and Hydraulic had tears of blood sparkling at the corners of her eyes.

"My God," I said, "you're crying blood." They stared at me as if I were mad, then began talking at once.

"Where's Annie, have you got her?"

"I'm not crying. I thought she was okay and then she just wasn't there. I'm sure she followed Archie up to the car."

Something turned hard in my chest. I took Georgia by the shoulders. "Stop panicking, she's ten and she knows enough to stay in one place and yell. You go back and get Jack, then the three of you fan out and start climbing. I'm going to race up to the car to see if she's with Archie. I'll meet you there, and if we haven't found her, we'll decide what to do then. Just stay calm and stay within cooee of each other."

The wretched drug was still playing tricks—bark swaying in freak twists of air turned into Annie's skirt disappearing through the trees.

"Please don't let her be lost, so many places for her to fall, she won't know what to do, another hour until dark." I broke into the clearing where the car was parked, its trunk open, and for a moment, wondered why Archie was slumped by the rear wheel, a hammer beside him, holding a bright red flower. The flower was his own hand—a pulp of tiny crushed bones. The air vibrated around me and the throbbing in my chest was unbearable. I knelt beside him, thinking he was dead, but he was only stunned and unable to speak. I closed my eyes, blanking out everything but my own heartbeat. Something made me look back to where the dark mass of trees rose up against the glow of twilight. Annie stood motionless as if she had stood there forever— watching, judging, old.

13
Elizabeth Likorish

When the fevers of four a.m. struck, Lucy was at her most frenzied. The two ghosts waited in trepidation for the chimes of the wall
clock, knowing that she would either wake in a rage, abuse them
horribly and fling herself about the room until her bony body, already
rattled loose by nightmares, burned up the little stamina it still
retained—or, worse still, explode into tears, doubling over to protect
her stomach as if a volcanic grief were about to form a crater there.
Eventually, she would collapse onto her back, cover her face with her
arm, and lie as still as rock, immured inside herself, beyond hope of
rescue.

It was during this witching hour that the ghosts would tell their
stories, every night, until dawn light burned the stars away. Immediately upon hearing the first fragile bird call, Lucy would rise
from her quilts with a shudder of relief, apologize to the ghosts for
whatever excesses she had unleashed against them and patter
lightly outside to watch gluey nets of dew evaporating under the
sudden sun. She would pick fruit from the garden, check to see what
gastronomic gifts had been left in the tin plate on the back veranda,
nibble on a Brazilian cherry and sometimes change mood so dramatically that she would crack with laughter, tease her relatives fondly,
and hug them. It was this unpredictability in her which so confounded
them.

After the rosebush dream the two old ghosts had, for a short time,
put away their reciprocal enmity in an effort to deal with the uncon-
trollable Lucy, but that salutary effect did not last. Now, their own
war was a cold one, and in an effort to ingratiate themselves with

153

Lucy, each would take her aside and attempt to claim her at the other's expense.

Olly, full of scorn for the indolence and hypocrisy of Laura's family to whom he referred, scathingly, as the Scabrous Squattocracy, would potter around the veranda in his highly polished slippers, muttering his displeasure to himself, but always where Lucy might overhear. Laura's tactics were rather more devious. "Woman to woman," she might begin, or, "As women, we . . ." or "Us women."

The house itself was returning, imperceptibly, to its former splendor. First carpets began to glow, rich red and blue. Next, dust disappeared from walls. Soon the workings of the wall clock shone with oil and the plaintive melody of the musical box was no longer syncopated by missing notes. Yet from outside, everything looked the same. Vines wove a cerement around the house, which hatched its spells in safety and seclusion.

"You want to hear a good tautology?" Laura wore her vulpine expression.

"What?" said Lucy, resigning herself to another attack on her grandfather.

"Weak man." Laura cackled at her own joke and shot evil glances at Olly, who was out of earshot. He looked up, full of suspicion.

"All that moral rectitude," she continued bitingly, "let me tell you how he treated his poor barmy wife."

"Laura, really I . . ."

"Ho. It's all right for him to tell his poisonous stories but not me. It's back to being all my fault I suppose." Lucy dropped her head and held her hands up in the air indicating surrender. Laura nestled back on her chair like a broody hen.

"Right you are, then, I'll have to go right back to give you the full picture so make yourself comfortable child get yourself some cushions and I'll have one while you're about it. You never think of me, I notice, of my comfort." By now Lucy was impervious to these small criticisms, and she patted the old lady on the head as she went past to grab six pillows and fling them into the pool of lamplight in the corner. Laura cleared her craw and began.

"Your maternal great grandmother was plain as a lavatory seat and had the constitution of a Clydesdale . . ."

*   *   *

The first trait saved her from being picked as a "servant" to one of the crew during the voyage from an English poorhouse to Sydney; the second, from succumbing to the various diseases which plagued the ship. She was sixteen years old, uneducated, hard-working and a God-fearing Protestant. She'd set out on the journey convinced that she could wrestle with life and squeeze something decent out of it. Like everyone those days she had wanted to go to America, but the assisted passage for women was an offer she could not refuse.

When poor Elizabeth Likorish realized the truth, it was too late to turn back. Women were packed two to a bed, and punished frightfully for the slightest misdemeanor. She saw one of her fellow emigrants, a pregnant woman, hung by the waist from the rigging until she died. But all that was nothing compared with what awaited the women at the wharf.

There were a thousand men at least, eagerly anticipating the landing of females. As soon as the boat reached the shore, the men rushed forward howling like dingoes and the half-dozen constables were splattered underfoot. An avenue opened through the rabble and as each female passed along it, little girl or old woman, she was jeered at and insulted in the most brutal language imaginable, or she was wrenched from her companions and almost raped on the spot. It was a degradation of the most macabre kind. The chins and knees of even the toughest prostitutes trembled, and the more the women wept the more the brutes laughed at them.

Elizabeth Likorish experienced a momentary weakening of spirit, and for the first time in her life fainted dead away. As fate would have it, she fell straight into the gingery arms of Paddy McAvaddy, who carried her out of the crowd without a word, and took her to the Blackboy Hotel. Such was the trauma of that landing, that she would always associate his red shirt, thick moleskin trousers and high, watertight boots with something religious, like the blue robes of Christ.

When she recovered sufficiently he asked her to stand still while he inspected her conformation. He hoicked up her skirts and felt her calf muscles; he measured the width of her hips by spanning his hands across her rump; he prodded the bones of her back; weighed the heaviness of her breasts; looked in her mouth and felt around her teeth. With that done he asked her to be his wife. So dazed was she by the events of the day that she nodded her head like a docile cow.

As soon as the business of the wedding was over, he got about the even more peremptory business of impregnating her.

"Bingo just like that." Laura snapped her fingers. "That's Catholics for you."

He was not a bad man at heart but he'd never known love and he did not expect to. Elizabeth set about teaching him. At first, she used the placid sweetness of her disposition, which only caused him to retreat further into moroseness. He barely spoke to her and when he did it was to grunt orders. Even in their lovemaking he displayed a curious need to avoid contact with her. He would lie on his back, hands behind his great bovine head, eyes closed, fencepost sticking out of his middle and growl, "Get on wid it woman, move." And she did.

Not too many days had passed before she tried a new and more effective tactic with him. Scathing criticisms and invective poured out of her. At first he countered these with a few solid backhanders but she waited until he was asleep, and opened his skull with the handle of his very own gold pick. As he was about to strike her in retaliation, she calmly said, "You have to sleep some time," and he never hit her again.

After they had sorted out these preliminary matrimonial troubles, he hoisted her onto the back of his wagon and together they joined the diaspora of people heading for the diggings. Gold fever infected everyone, uniting all under one great democratic law—to get rich quick. Broken aristocrats, bank clerks, butchers, Chinese, Californians and Scots swarmed out of shops, deserted ships, abandoned desks, betrayed loved ones to take up the dish and the swag. Tides of humanity, swayed by the moons of rumor, created towns which waxed and waned in a month, leaving scars on the pastoralist's land, creating panic in government circles.

Elizabeth would have liked to stay in the Blackboy Hotel forever. In the music hall, she clapped and hooted the comedians and encouraged the drovers to string out their ditties. The diggings were a long way from anything resembling cultured life. There were twenty thousand people, almost all men, living in row after row of tents, set by row after row of holes. Elizabeth had to threaten her husband with her besom before he would agree to build her a bark hut as big as this room. She sewed curtains and napkins from flour sacks, coaxed vegetables from rocks, placed buttons in bottles and set them to shine under the window, made lace from string, pomades from wild oranges, roses from paper. He allowed her to bully him into washing before meals, oiling his magnificent orange beard, cleaning his fingernails and listening to passages from the Bible. And he did not know until Emma, your grandmother, was born, that he was in love.

It was new to him, the pain he felt as he watched his wife adore her first-born. She would gaze into the girl's milky eyes and croon, or inspect every crevice in her perfect, tiny body, tenderly, wonderingly, and all he could think was, "What about me?" When the jealousy tore at him he would return to his hole and dig like a wombat, or visit the sly-grog seller and afterwards beat the dog, or find some unfortunate Chinaman to torment. Once, in a drunken rage, he had taken up the baby and threatened to drop her. His wife had calmly taken Emma away from him and then screamed until the whole compound arrived at their door, revolvers drawn, ready to save her. What they found was Paddy McAvaddy staggering around the hut, with his wife on his back, and a gold pick stuck in his sternum.

As for Elizabeth, she now had something which was capable of returning affection. She made a vow that this child would have the genteel life which she herself craved, but knew would always be denied her. She treated Emma like a princess—spoiled, coddled and protected her beyond all reason. The child was fed the best morsels of food, sewn pretty dresses, was never spanked and had her long lush hair brushed one hundred times a day. Emma reigned over the bark hut and over her mother's daytime heart.

But the nights were another matter. However bitterly Elizabeth berated her husband during the day, at night he became the object of her passion. In trying to get some response from the loglike body, she had stretched her own sexual imagination, and in the process had discovered all sorts of hidden cravings in herself, which both shocked her and caused her to giggle at inappropriate moments. She might be scrubbing linen on the washboard, or sweeping eucalyptus leaves from the hard white ground around the shack, when all of a sudden she would remember what she had done the night before, and her breasts would tighten and pucker of their own accord. She would lift her shoulders and smile to herself as if to say, "Strange, isn't it."

She was wise enough to know that these desires, coupled with her health and fecundity, would, in the end, bring about her ruin. She longed for quality, what she got was quantity. Every year a new baby would come and drag at her, until she came to despise all of them except her precious Emma.

She had a dream which both exulted and disturbed her. In it, she was standing at the bottom of a steep hill. A narrow dusty path led upwards and in front of her was a gleaming black stallion.

Lucy let out a small cry and clutched at her aunt's arm. "My dear niece," said Laura, "why is it so difficult for you to accept that the sap in family trees carries more than physical attributes to its leaves?"

"Because I've always treasured my dreams as something unique to me, something which sets me apart from the rest of humanity. Now you tell me that they connect me more deeply to others, and it gives me an uncertain sensation, like being lost and found at the same time."

"I had that dream just after I met him. The black stallion galloped up the hill and I ran behind it. The scene changed and a small girl child was sitting with him in a trotting rig. The black stallion was taking them up the hill on that treacherous path. I was down below watching them, and suddenly another rig came tearing down the path and crashed into them. The stallion was bent almost double, but he recovered himself and came hurtling down what had turned into a precipice, dragging the rig behind him. It seemed impossible that they wouldn't all be killed. I looked away and thought to myself, 'Not the stallion. Please don't let the stallion die.' Then, he and the child came up to me and the stallion was trotting along free, behind them. They were all unhurt but the little girl looked bewildered and frightened, so I said to her, 'Now wasn't that the most exciting thing you've ever done?' And her face lit up and she started chattering about how thrilling it had been, flying down the mountainside."

But here Lucy began to cry again and Laura, after much hesitation, put her arm around her shoulders and rocked her. "But the stallion did die," said Lucy, giving way to a sob or two.

"Nonsense," said Laura. "He's dead, not the stallion."

"Yes," said Lucy, in a small resigned voice. She smiled wanly, sniveled a little and begged her aunt to continue with her story.

When Emma was three, her father had a change of luck. He had been digging so furiously that he almost missed it—a nugget the size of his wife's Bible. He was all for staying on the goldfields and finding more but her imprecations became so terrible that he succumbed and agreed to take the family to the city where they bought a guest house. Things went smoothly for a while, but Paddy's restless spirit soon yearned for empty horizons. Elizabeth was pleased to see him go so that she could set about hiding Emma's humble origins under clouds of lace stuck with pink rosebuds. She instructed her daughter in the arts of cooking and needlework, admonished her to stay out of the sun and showed her how to soak her perfect white hands in her own urine. What she could not bring herself to teach her were the facts of life.

Each year, Emma's father arrived in time for the birth of a child and stayed around long enough for the sowing of the next. Emma found him uncouth. He did not respond to her imperiousness as the rest of the family did. She was even a little afraid of him, and the noises which issued from her mother's bedroom at night gave her gooseflesh. She did not know how the never-ending stream of brats made their way from the dome of her mother's belly, nor how they came there in the first place. Her curiosity was faintly stirred by the "marriage" night-dresses which her mother sewed for her, and which had an embroidered hole in a certain awkward spot. But when she inquired what these holes were for, her mother only replied, "ventilation."

Emma grew up resenting the energy her mother squandered on the milky-smelling, squabbling siblings, who got in the way of her dainty feet, and did not enhance her prestige at all, with their raggedy clothes and dirty faces. She lived inside the sugary bubble her mother had created and was incapable of believing that life might turn out to be sour.

The bubble burst the day the fourteenth child was born. Emma was seventeen years old. As usual, she had been sent away to stay with neighbors, and was having a lovely time playing cards, when their attention was drawn to the clacking of hooves on the pebbly ground outside and the noise of running footsteps. There was a violent banging on the door, and a voice shouting for her to come quickly. She was bundled unceremoniously into the buggy and she pouted all the way home.

Hearing the screams from the doorway she rushed to her mother's room, but when she saw the hideous sight—ugly, dark hair clotted with blood, the pallor and sweat on her mother's distorted face—and heard her dying words—"Never marry a . . . man"—she shrieked, fell straight back and remained unconscious for three days.

Her father took to the bottle. After two months, he left on his wanderings, swearing he would never return, a promise which gave Emma the strength to rise from her sickbed and set about running the guest house with something approaching happiness. She found she had quite a talent for it, since all it required was ordering her brothers and sisters about, while she queened it over the guests and served the most delicately boiled vegetables and the thinnest slices of rich roast beef in the area.

Her guest house gained a reputation for its gentility, and the middle classes, yearning to be proper Englishmen, flocked to it like ugly ducklings seeking metamorphosis. She made enough money to hire a nanny, which left her free to sit out under the trees, her skirts spread like dove's wings, tapping her foot a little so that the bells stitched onto her slippers called her many admirers to her feet. Twirling her pretty umbrella she would allow the first photographers to poke their protrusions at her from a respectable distance and would have been quite content to sit and be adored forever, but alas, her father came back.

He said wicked things to her, drank all the profits and fussed over the brats, calling them his "liddle leprechauns," as he bounced them on his foot and allowed them to crawl all over him like lice. His ill-bred ways embarrassed Emma in front of the guests.

She felt a great trepidation at going against her mother's dying wish. But what could she do? What, besides a man, could she marry? And how else could she slip out from under the weight of her father's dislike?

For the first time Emma truly missed her mother. She took to praying to her, wringing her hands and begging for assistance. So when the dapper young man with the unsightly nose and substantial bank account proposed to her under the wisteria bower, Emma mistook it for an omen.

It had been so beautiful, the wedding—tulle and frosted cakes, photographs and mirrors. Even her father had managed to remain sober and civil. She snuggled into the big new bed, feeling pleased with herself and safe. When Olly opened the door and came in, she was surprised and a little abashed.

"What is it," she asked, simpering sweetly. He fell to his knees beside the bed, grabbed her hand and told her that she was the most beautiful woman in the world. She tittered prettily but felt a vague unease. He began to kiss her hand, quite roughly, and when his kisses reached her elbow, she pulled her arm away, full of confusion. She sat up and said, "You may brush my hair if you'd like."

He was taken aback at this, but recovered himself and accepted the offer. She swished past him, sat on the stool in front of the dresser and handed him the Mason Pearson. She watched him in the mirror as he nuzzled her neck. It was as if ants were crawling under her nightdress. "Stop it," she scolded and stood up quickly. Then he saw the hole.

All that followed was confusion. She would always remember it in painful little flashes. He, thundering at her to take off that obscene garment. She, trembling and begging for her mother. He ripped her nightdress from her. And then, the terrible act itself. Not only did he do it, but he ordered her to move. The traits in one generation are often reversed in the next and although she submitted to him, in all her days she did not once move.

Her hatred of her husband was immediate and consummate. The trauma of the first birth aged her prematurely. Sourness set in. Her once aquiline nose turned to bone; a beauty spot on her chin bubbled into a bulbous pink mole; her back hunched; her fingers turned to hooks; her belly protruded; her legs buckled; her crowning glory turned a yellowy gray. But still he would not stop. Every night he forced himself upon her, and every night the hatred and disgust brewed inside her like acid. All manner of ailments invaded her body, transported on her wish for death, but were unable to do the job properly because she had inherited her mother's constitution.

After the death of her first child, and the arrival of the second, she tried to kill herself, but her animal health pulled her through the crisis. It was then your grandfather took a mistress, granting his wife a hysterectomy and a separate bed.

Olly's footsteps could be heard cracking along the veranda. He poked his head around the corner and demanded to know what they were talking about.

"Wouldn't you like to know," said Laura, and gave Lucy a cryptic wink.

"I know what you were saying. But a man has his needs. I only did it to save poor Emma from . . ."

"Bilge. You did it for yourself and what's more you tormented her with it you horrid little man. If it hadn't been for Lucy's mother you would have left her to rot in her bed."

"I saw the error of my ways, don't think I didn't. And I lived the *rest of my life with the shame of it. I loved my mistress, would have died for her and in the end I loved Emma, too, poor soul. And what about you, you lying old tyrant. What about you with your . . ." Olly smiled a malicious and taunting smile. From behind his back he suddenly thrust before them a large white feather. Laura paled. Indeed, she almost disappeared. There was a long silence. Unsteadily, she rose to her feet, her fingers bunching, and advanced toward Olly. But he was too quick for her, and darted behind the chaise-longue, holding the feather up at Laura like a cross before a vampire. He made faces at her and laughed wickedly, his wrinkles distorted with hatred.*

Laura moaned, "Oh, oh." Lucy cried, "What? What?" Olly waved his white feather. And a butcher bird, landing on the veranda railing, sang a morning song as sharp as glass, as sweet as sugar.

14

The Devil Makes an Appearance

I pirouetted coquettishly in front of the boss.

"Yeah, not bad," he said, tapping his chin with Spats' silver-capped cane.

"Yeah, not bad," echoed Spats and Larry.

"Whaddya mean," said the boss, turning to them, "she's beautiful, tell the kid she's beautiful."

"Beauuutiful," agreed Larry and instead of nodding his head up and down, began to swivel it from side to side. Spats whistled quietly through his teeth.

"Yeah," said the boss, satisfied.

Today he wore a purple three-piece suit with a green shirt and when I risked suggesting that the canary-yellow tie might be a bit much for opening night, a silence fell during which Larry and Spats glanced nervously at each other and the boss regarded me thoughtfully, causing my mouth to go very dry. He took the tie off without saying a word, replaced it with a nicely subdued pink one, and glared at the two men who seemed very interested in what was going on behind the blacked-out windows and on the lavishly decorated ceiling.

Despite this little moment of tension, I was as excited as a child on Christmas Eve. Dressing up had always been a vice of mine, and now I could indulge it to my heart's content. For this evening's performance, I had chosen a classy chiffon skirt, split to the thigh, black ankle strap high heels, a silk blouse which plunged dangerously front and back, and a black velvet band around my neck. My perfume struggled to overpower the boss's after-shave, and failed.

"I think I'll call ya Raven," he announced. "You know, like as in raven-haired beaudy." He grinned cheekily. "Lucy's a dill's name, doesn't do ya justice."

I gave a throaty laugh, placed one hand on my hip, extended the other, dropped the wrist and strutted back and forth.

"I like it," I said. "It has a certain, je ne sais quoi."

"Jer naissai quoi," said the boss, pleased. "Yeah."

I never did find out what his real name was. Sometimes it was Harley McDougal; at other times, Dougal McHarley. Once I saw him wear a gold tiepin on which were inscribed the words "John Brown." Many of his acquaintances called him Doug, but to me he remained "The Boss." His chameleon qualities would have been absolute, if it were not for the silver bracelet which never left his wrist. Ferocious dragons surrounded an opal and around those were inscribed the words "love" and "joy." All he ever told me about his history was that his parents had wanted him to be a violinist—remarkable pre-science on their part considering how well a violin case would go with their grown-up son.

The doorman's name was Al, which, because of the amount of scar tissue in and around his mouth, he pronounced "Ow." Ow spent most of his time sitting on a stool by the door, encased in a tuxedo, staring vacantly into space with his head slightly on one side, and his mouth open. "A bit punchy" was all the boss would say. It was obvious that Ow would die for the boss, but I did not know, until later, that in the underworld such devotion requires a certain reci-procity.

Larry, our chef, had learned his culinary skills during his many stays in the nick. He had decided to go straight, but could not resist the allure and hominess that the criminal world provided. He missed the life, he said, and was often tempted to don his work clothes (black trousers, black skivvie, black balaclava) and come out of retirement. The boss confided that Larry was the least talented, most accident-prone tealeaf around. Consequently fences had refused to touch his stuff and potential partners were always busy on other jobs.

All I knew about the Greek was that he owned a lot of the city and liked gambling it away. His skin was buttery and smooth; his fingers were pudgy, with fine black hair fringing the pulpy pads between his knuckles. When he took off his coat at the table, large breasts flopped under the silk of his shirt, which was always marked with sweat. His flat head, unable to sprout hair, produced bubbles of grease. What he lost on the swings of good looks, however, he made up for on the roundabout of wealth. A seemingly endless succession of studiously stupid blondes chucked him under the chin and glanced at his gold.

Nor did I ever find out what Spats did for a living, other than walk with a cane and entertain a lot of bank managers. One day he simply stopped coming to the club. No doubt he had been sucked into the black hole of "The Bay."

At the Silver Slipper I had, once again, been taken into the bosom of a family, no questions asked, and it was perhaps as much this sense of belonging and acceptance which bedazzled me, as the discovery of such a thrilling new world.

My coworkers came in at eight—all professional dealers and croupiers. I could tell the boss was nervous by the way he continually tugged his shirtsleeves down over his wrists, checked his Rolex, snapped out orders, and wetted a finger to slick down his eyebrows as he passed the cupid-bedizened mirror.

All the top gamblers, millionaires, shady socialites, bent lawyers, con men, Mr. Bigs and flash gangsters had been invited. Riffraff were turned away at the door. Pearls, diamonds, lamé and sequins glittered through the cloud of cigar smoke. It was a gala evening.

My job was to mingle with the guests, ply them with free drinks, help Larry in the kitchen, deal poker and converse mindlessly with those corpulent businessmen who, the boss knew, had brought thick wads of money to lose. I ran from kitchen to bar to poker game to blackjack table and back to kitchen, pausing only to drape myself vampishly by the roulette wheel and chat up some guests who looked as if they were about to leave with their winnings. On one such occasion, the ball landed on 13, and as it happened, a large pile of chips was riding on 13. "Thirty-one," cried the croupier and hastily respun the wheel. The boss employed only the best.

When I dealt poker, he played for the house, and it was here that he displayed his true genius. He could have been a brilliant psychiatrist, so well did he judge human behavior. But the boss was not out to heal the sick, only to exploit them. He knew just when to lose a hand in order to keep a mug punter at the table a little longer, hoping to win again. The mug punter invariably left the table empty-pocketed, while the boss shook his head in mock disappointment saying, "Better luck next time, mate."

By six a.m. I was ready to faint with fatigue. The small of my back felt as if it had been kicked, my feet squelched like overripe tomatoes in the high heels, the cards had begun to blur in front of me and I could no longer quickly calculate five percent of the pot. The boss set up a small table next to me, on which were arranged a tumbler, a bottle of whiskey, an array of purple hearts and a pot of black coffee.

"You're doin great, kid, gimme the nod if you need more pills."

By nine a.m. the last of the glitterati had gone home, leaving a wreckage of ground-in peach melba, and an acrid reek of smoke, booze and laundered money. While the rest of us collapsed in various attitudes of pain and exhaustion, the boss whistled cheerily and counted the takings.

I was to discover that he had a peculiar attitude to sleep. He often went a week without closing his eyes, keeping himself awake on artificial stimulants, and when exhaustion threatened to engulf him, he would place an angina tablet under his tongue.

"You'll die young if you keep doing that," I said, when I knew him well enough to take such liberties. He laughed until the tears ran then endeavored to explain his philosophy of life.

"Live by violence, die by violence," he said, and the denizens of the underworld joined in his litany in mock solemnity, as if they were proud of a perverse morality which stated that all life was cheap, including their own. The boss had other, more sinister reasons for not wishing to sleep, but a month would pass before I discovered the secret of his twice three toes.

Meanwhile I attempted to explain my philosophy to him. I made clear why I was a socialist, and why he should be one also.

"Raven," he said, shaking his head sadly, "for an intelligent woman, you sure can talk a crock of shit. There's only mugs and smarties in this world, and you've gotta work out which one you're gunna be. If you had your way, the mugs'd run the joint, and I'd be outa work." This did not deter me. I knew that, given time, his essential goodness would win through. "It is never too late to be what you might have been," I said to myself.

I wanted to walk home, but he insisted on driving me, which meant that I had to wait until everyone had gone. While he fastened the many locks on the outside door, I groped my way toward his car through the brutal glare of midmorning. I reached out for the door handle, then felt myself hurled across the footpath and slammed up against a brick wall, with the twisted and bloodless face of the boss two inches from my own. "You don't never do that, understand," he screamed.

"What?" I screamed.

"You don't never open no door, or start no engine or nothin' until I've checked it, understand?" he screamed.

He let me go and I slid twelve inches down the wall. He regained control of himself by shrugging his shoulders back, flicking his head and pulling his shirtsleeves down.

"Nail bombs, see," he said in a reasonable voice. "You could get blown all over the fuckin' joint. Now wait here." He marched up to the car and without a flinch of hesitation, opened all the doors, turned the ignition key, came back to me and said, "Okay, kid, get in. Sorry if I scared ya."

The drive home did nothing to soothe my nerves.

"Um," I said, as we rounded a corner on two wheels.

"Ah," I managed, as we changed down and hurtled toward the yellow lights.

"Interesting driving," I croaked when we screeched to a halt in front of my door, leaving wobbly black streaks all along the street.

"Yeah, used to be a professional in me youth." At the time I thought he meant on the racetrack.

"Oh, no," I groaned when I discovered that I had left my keys inside the empty house.

"Oh, no," I stated firmly, when the boss offered to break and enter. He insisted that he put me up in a hotel in the city and nothing I could say would dissuade him. I didn't mind going to sleep in a hotel; I did mind getting back into his death machine.

It wasn't so much a seedy hotel as an empty one. It gave the impression that live human beings had never stayed there. The sheets, though crisp, smelled of dust. There was a moment of awkwardness as I pointedly said good night to the boss at the door, then he left me in peace. I ripped off my finery, pulled the curtains against the blaze of midday, and dived, gratefully, into unconsciousness.

Hours of sweet blackness must have passed before I became aware of bedsprings creaking. I sat up clutching blankets to my neck, mouth open ready to shout but the boss interrupted.

"It's okay, kid, it's only me."

"How did you get in?"

"Manager's a mate o' mine."

"Look I don't . . ."

"Shuddup will ya. I ain't gunna do nothin' to ya. Whaddya think I am?"

Silence.

"Kid," he said eventually.

"Yes, boss."

"You're okay."

"Thanks, boss."

"Ya got somethin' special about ya. Rekkernized it the minute ya stepped in."

"Thanks, boss."

Silence.

"I think I got the hots for ya."

Silence.

"But I respect ya too, so don't think I'm gunna take advantage or anything like that."

More silence.

"Now get some shuteye and I'll come and get ya later."

He went to the door, turned back to me and said, "One more thing."

"Yes?"

"If you was to sleep with anyone else, he wouldn't have much luck, understand?" He closed the door gently, as on the bedroom of a sleeping child.

In many ways the boss was old-fashioned in his dealings with women. Or perhaps he understood the heat-increasing properties of repression. A month of groping would pass before I discovered the nature of the bulge in his trousers.

He had driven me home, and after half an hour of our usual frenzied grappling, I had invited him in. Some sixth sense had prevented my telling even Georgia about my attachment to the boss and I was glad that I would not have to explain his presence in the house. Everyone was asleep.

The first part of his anatomy which caught my attention was not the bulge in his trousers, but the gap where his toes should have been. He sat on my chair, neatly placing his socks and shoes beside him, and unbuttoning his lurex shirt.

"Boss, what happened to the rest of your toes?"

He looked down and wiggled what was left of them.

"Bolt-cutters," he said, noncommittally. "But the bloke what done it didn't have much luck." I didn't have time to gasp with horror, because the next thing I noticed was what caused the bulge—a very professional, very loaded Colt .45.

I gasped with horror. "You're not bringing that thing into my bedroom and that's that."

"You wouldn't be tryin' ta stand over me would ya?"

"I don't care what you call it, I'm not having a gun in my room."

I folded my arms across my chest, indicating an impasse. He glowered at me a moment longer, then raised his eyebrows in a comic look of surprise and said, "You're unmannin' me fair dinkum." We agreed that just for tonight, his rod would stay on the chair, but henceforward would be left in the car.

I don't know why the boss loved women, but that night it was apparent to me that he did. He curled into me afterwards and placed his head on my belly—as soft and warm as a puppy.

In the dead of night, I was woken by an air-raid siren. "It's the bomb," I thought as I dived for cover under the table, but the siren was hidden somewhere inside the boss. A terrible wailing issued from his mouth, as if he was being slowly gutted. I jumped over to the bed, cracking my forehead on the table on the way, and clapped my hand over his mouth. His hand went to my throat and we flailed about among the crumpled bedclothes until the light went on and Georgia said, "What the hell's going on in here?" Then, "Ahhh" as she saw the blood on my forehead, the boss's hands around my throat and the gun on the chair.

We both lunged for it at the same time but Georgia got there first. Her eyes sticking out like champagne corks, lips pulled back into a doglike snarl and arms straight out in front of her holding a dangerously wobbling pistol, she said, "I've got the bastard covered, Luce, ring the police."

"Police?" gurgled the boss, coming out of his fit.

"No, no," I said, "it's not what you think."

We were all frozen in position, me sitting forward on the edge of the bed, my hands raised toward Georgia, palms out; Georgia holding the gun, looking in wonderment first at me, then at the boss, who lay twisted up in a corkscrew of sheets, one leg stuck up the wall and his head thrown back so that he was forced to gaze up the barrel of his very own pistol, upside down.

169

"Georgie, I can explain everything."

"Explain everything?" She swallowed noisily.

"He's a friend of mine, I mean he's my boss, I mean he was having a nightmare."

Georgia nodded slowly, inspected the gun in a dazed sort of way, and lowered herself into the chair. She sat motionless for a moment, staring straight ahead, then said, rather too calmly I thought, "I'm going back to bed now, Lucy, but I'd like to see you in the morning. If you wouldn't mind."

"Sure. You bet."

She stood up, placed the gun gingerly back on the chair, looked at me, looked at the boss, looked back at the gun, and left.

After she'd gone, the boss and I lay stiffly parallel to each other, the sheet pulled up to our chins.

"Well it wasn't my fault," I ventured at last.

"I feel like a fuckin' *mug*."

"Boss, that scream came straight out of hell."

He turned his head on the pillow. "How did you know that?" he asked, impressed.

"First of all I'm up in heaven, see, with angels flappin' around. Then this big booming voice says, 'Hey, shit-head, what are you doin' here?' I know I'm fuckin' gone, and I try to fly away but me wings won't work. The next thing I know I'm falling and the voice says, 'I'm the angel of death,' and I'm falling straight into hell and everything's flappin' and black and I know someone's waitin' there with bolt-cutters but that's not what scares the piss outa me, see, it's somethin' else. I know they got this small room down there and I have to sit in it, at a table, and they're gunna poison me with sugar, piles and piles of sugar that I gotta eat. I think that's when I scream."

"Gosh," I breathed after a while. "How often do you have it?"

"Whenever I go to sleep," said the boss, in a matter-of-fact tone. "I was gunna leave ya, see, but I must have dozed off or somethin.'"

We spent the rest of the night comparing devil dreams and reading from Carl Jung.

"Well, whaddya know, eh?" repeated the boss at intervals, or, "What'll they think of next," or, "All this time I thought a collective unconscious was when ya banged two heads together." I let him out quietly at six a.m.

At seven, I took a tray into Georgia's room. It contained freshly squeezed orange juice, strong brewed coffee, two exquisitely fried eggs, a rasher of curly bacon, wholemeal toast with vegemite, and flowers. "Wakey wakey," I said, and felt her eyes burn my back as I put the tray down on the chest of drawers and fiddled with the flowers because I wasn't quite ready to turn around.

"Before you say anything," I said, turning around, "the gun will never come into the house again, I promise."

"Neither—will—that—thug."

"He's not a thug, for heaven's sake." I laughed dismissively at such a preposterous notion and busied myself with the breakfast things. But Georgia grabbed my wrist, spilling orange juice on the blankets, and said, in a penetrating whisper, "What do you think you're doing? He's straight out of gangland, do you want to get yourself killed?"

At those words I saw, like a dream, the vision of a room. I was being compelled to open the door of that room, which led into a long labyrinth of other rooms. I wanted Georgia to come with me but knew that she could not. I felt terribly sad. There was a strong wind blowing and I had a powerful feeling of vertigo. When the vision dissolved, I watched her pick at the food in silence.

That period of my life is very hazy to me now, as if it has sunk into a smoky mirror. Was I with the boss six months or a year? Surely it could not have been longer. And yet, I feel him looking over my shoulder, pointing himself out in the glass, claiming years of my life. Facts contradict. Dates do not tally.

Like space, my memory contains an infinite amount of nothing, with here and there, a pinprick of light in the blackness. I try to weave a web between them in which I might catch myself, but the web is too frail.

There is another difficulty in stitching my story together. Life had frayed, even then, into fragments. There was Georgia's world, the Silver Slipper, the theater and there was the secret universe in the back garden where I practiced when no one was watching. Only there could I find temporary freedom from my own netherworld which lay beneath reality like a swamp. I would hastily paste over the cracks in my life only to fall through a gap and find myself back in that dark, watery realm, wondering if, this time, I'd be trapped in it forever. The ghosts belonging to that world crawled up through the cracks to invade my nightmares. In an effort to rid myself of their blight, I had followed a scorched earth policy regarding my own history. But no amount of burning could consume the shadows which chased me as I fled from world to world, destroying, forgetting, distorting the past, but never escaping its effects.

It was when I sensed that the fragmentation was beyond my control that I finally, and in secret, sought the services of a psychiatrist.

By the time I'd reached the venerable doctor's studded leather armchair, I understood why people in his profession were called "shrinks." I felt like a dwarf. To compensate for this uncomfortable state of affairs, I crossed my legs, tossed back my hair and thought of longish words with which to impress him.

"You see, doctor, I feel that my quest for synthesis only leads to further fragmentation. I consist of a multitude of contradictory selves which are often at war. To inhabit so many different worlds requires an exhausting degree of dissimulation. And these discrete worlds are themselves filled with ambivalences, so that as soon as I try to decode them, they disintegrate, do you see what I mean?"

I hoped he did because I certainly didn't.

"You mean, you feel you have contradictory selves, which you want to synthesize but feel you can't."

"Precisely. And I feel fraudulent all the time. There's my life at home, with my friend Georgia and all the others, and I love them, but they all want me to ... no, they think I'm like them, but I'm not. Sometimes I feel suffocated there, as if I'm now patronizing and being tolerant of them, while everyone pretends it's still the other way round, but then I feel guilty as if I've betrayed them or something."

"You feel guilty because there's been a role reversal in which you are now the parent and they the children."

"Gosh. Yes. That's it. And I don't know what I believe any more. Because everything contradicts everything else, every truth I mean. I doubt everything. It's much easier for me to be in opposition to something, than to join in and be positive about something, I mean, to be *for* something. So whenever I feel certain about something, there's this perverse desire to demolish that certainty, because it disallows other interpretations but that means I'm a fence sitter doesn't it, a dilettante, and I can't believe one thing, or be one thing, do you see? I become impotent."

"You mean you can't hold one set of beliefs and you feel impotent because of it."

"That's it. I watch these militant, radical men for example, sounding off and it's not that I disagree with what they're saying, it's that I look at them and can't help wondering if they beat their wives . . ."

The doctor permitted himself a small smile.

"But I feel awful about it because that's not what's important."

"What is important?"

"To change things. Obviously. The world is teetering at the edge, it's falling apart, everything's falling apart."

Why wasn't the doctor saying, "You mean everything's falling apart." Why was he looking at me like that, making me shrink still further. His eyes did not waver from my face.

So, that was it, he had divined my most hidden secret. In the same way that my fantasy of holding a pistol at my head made me feel better, so I sometimes wished for the bomb to drop and blow my stinking species to bits, clean out the planet with a great and terrible fire, and if I thought that, then presumably others thought it too, and there was some flaw in human beings which could never be altered, which would condemn us to an endless history of cruelty, torture, destruction, violence and pain and all that the sane people in the world could do was stick their fingers in dikes and wait for the tidal wave. But I did not want to admit this nihilism to myself, let alone to anyone else, and most certainly not to this parrot of a doctor.

Later he asked me about my childhood, but I felt that the fact that I could remember nothing of my first seven years, or that my father had murdered my mother by drowning her in a dam in the horse paddock, or that I had subsequently murdered Wally Gajic, my only friend, by betraying him on New Year's Eve, or that I sometimes had conversations with ghosts, was none of his business. Instead, I described what had happened to me on the day of the demo.

I had stood on the sidelines, feeling uncomfortable and ashamed of my physical cowardice. Once I had felt a sense of unity and purpose at such events, now the pulse of the crowd disturbed me. Nor could I join in the heightened emotion and mutual back slapping that went on afterwards, as we watched ourselves on TV. I felt like a priest who, having lost his faith, continues to go through the motions. Better to die with the finger in the dike I reasoned, but these were hardly occasions for joy.

That day, there were more police than demonstrators. There was a moment of stillness, then pandemonium. I saw the event in a series of freeze-frames. A man swung by the hair. A pregnant woman kicked down steps. Billy Byrd, staggering and bleeding. I dived into the crowd, grabbed his sleeve, and ran.

Billy was dazed by a hit on the head but would not hear of going to a hospital. He was laughing dangerously.

"Let's have some white man's magic," he said as we threw ourselves into his beat-up old van. He turned the radio on full blast. Bones vibrated inside my body, nerves coiled tight, ready to snap. I wanted to go home and pull blankets over my head. I wanted to turn the radio off and push Billy into the stream of traffic. I wanted to look after myself. Instead, I did as he instructed, and drove north into the bush.

After stumbling through undergrowth for half an hour, we arrived at a petroglyph overlooking the sea. The world flopped in the still heat. The rustle of trees and the distant thumping of water on shore only intensified the silence. I lifted my arms into the puffs of breeze, letting the sweat cool. Billy popped open another beer can. When at last he spoke, all the harshness had gone from his voice. "This is my mother's country. Used to hunt here when I was a kid. Big ceremonial ground back there." He flicked his finger west. "We were walking down there once, and we came across an old man blocking the path. 'Don't look at him,' she said, 'he's warning us not to go that way.'" Billy laughed. "I was scared, when I looked back, he'd disappeared."

"You mean a ghost? You see ghosts?"

"Of course." He fell silent again and I saw that he was quietly crying. "Before I went to university, I said to my uncle, 'Old man,' I said, 'you've got to teach me the law, otherwise it's all going to disappear.' And you know what, he said he wouldn't teach me because the right people weren't here to back him up, and rather than risk doing it wrong, he said he wouldn't tell me anything. He's the only one for that country, everyone else has gone. There's only one old lady who remembers the lingo. He wouldn't tell me anything, like I wasn't good enough to know."

"You mean," said the psychiatrist, as I struggled to control tears, "that you felt a sense of shame, or guilt." I hesitated.

174

"It's just that I understood then, I mean with my gut and not just my head, the enormity of what had been destroyed, not just family, not just something you can grieve over, but ... everything," I ended, feebly, because I could not voice what I had sensed. "And it wasn't guilt I felt, not exactly." I waited for the memory to crystallize.

"I felt ... loss."

I sat squirming under the doctor's passionless stare and sobbed, whether for myself, or for Billy, or for the world, I could not tell.

That night, I had one of my recurring dreams. I was alone, bodiless, omnipotent, flying through the blackness of space. Then I felt a tug, a surge of vertigo and a great fear. I was flying over a jungle, and my body was becoming heavier, slower, and I knew I must enter that place full of swamps and hidden pools where someone was waiting for me, pulling me down, drowning me. Next, I was in the old schoolhouse at Binjigul, and outside the window was a young and vigorous tree. From its branches hung blocks of stone, like building foundations, suspended by thick hessian ropes.

I woke up sweating, dizzy and sick, and decided to cancel any further appointments with the psychiatrist. Life went on as before, left foot, right foot.

15
Dead-Eye Ted

Sometimes a poker game would continue for thirty hours without a break, but usually the cards were stacked and the chips sorted by five a.m. As no one ever signaled that they were tired by yawning, or that they ached to go home by glancing at their Rolexes, the Silver Slipper seldom shut before ten.

Theoretically, I worked five nights a week, but as the nights sometimes spread into days, and as the boss often gave me extended time off, it would make more sense to say that I lived most of the time at the club, and the rest at the actors' warehouse where, with the help of speed, coffee and whiskey, I stayed awake until it was time to go back to work. My body now resembled a worn spindle, but my anorexia was not of the nervosa kind. Whenever the drugs wore off, I tucked into Larry's prison pavlova like a ravenous dog.

Finishing work at such early hours gave me an opportunity to experience that time of day previously denied me by the gargoyles— the cusp of burned-out nights and born-again mornings. I usually walked the streets for an hour or two before heading off in the direction of the theater, as a way of preparing myself for the next role change.

"What are ya?" said the boss, when I first announced to the assembled leftovers of a game of five-card stud that I was going for a long stroll. "What's wrong with a taxi?" He peeled a couple of twenties off the wedge of money he kept in his back pocket, but I shook my head and insisted that I *liked* walking. There were a few mutters of disbelief, which only caused the boss to swing round angrily and proclaim that if I wanted to walk I could fuckin' walk, and did anyone have any

objections. No one did. I became known, however, as "Rovin'
Raven," and, when the boss's back was turned, "Raven Mad." I
didn't mind.

My friends at the theater trusted me with the keys, but could not
work me out.

"What do you do here all alone?" they would ask.

"I think," I would answer, Garbo-like. I did not tell them that I also
studied whatever play they were doing, and performed the lead parts
alone on stage in the dead of night. If a part required crying, I threw
myself on the floor and sobbed; if it required anger, I became apoplectic with rage. I ached to be seen; would have died of shame if I had
been. Arrogance and inadequacy stalked hand in hand across my
inner landscape, and so powerful were these opposing opinions of my
ability that sometimes I could not act at all. When that happened, I
held the metaphorical pistol to my head, then went home to climb my
ropes, practice the splits and fly.

Once, in an effort to spot-weld the increasingly disparate segments
of my life together, I had brought the boss home to a party. He'd liked
the music and the clouds of smoke colored by rotating lights and film
clips projected onto the ceiling. But, compared to the outlandishly
costumed inhabitants of the house, the boss looked underdressed, and
he did not like being overshadowed. When we looked into a bare
white room, and watched a naked man covered in white makeup
sweeping a red balloon around with a broom in slow motion, the boss
was unimpressed. Archie's paintings only caused him to mutter,
"Fuckin' wankers. I could do this stuff."

When Frank and two haunted-looking women in black dresses
floated out of the fog taking photographs, the boss yelled, "Hey, what
are ya?" as he wheeled to escape their lenses. Attacking the air with
one hand, he hid his face with the other, while the women circled him
like snapping crows. They had trained themselves to be surprised by
nothing that life might present, but when the boss grabbed one of the
cameras and ripped out the film, I could see they were a little shaken. I
suggested that perhaps they should leave.

"Your friend is, like, deeply weird," said one of them, over her
shoulder.

Despite his lack of respect for the artistic milieu, the boss took it
upon himself to encourage me in my nonexistent career. "You're
beautiful enough to be a star fair dinkum. One of these days, I'll take

ya to Hollywood." Hollywood seemed a little ambitious, but a drama
school had opened and for a while I thought about trying to enroll.
When finally I mustered the courage to inquire, I'd missed the audi-
tions for the coming year, and would have to wait another twelve
months.

I was dejected that night at the club, and when I told the boss why, a
distant, calculating look came into his eyes, the kind of look a recently
dead fox might have. Shortly afterwards, I saw him cup a conspiratorial hand under Ow's elbow and whisper something in his ear. This
conferring in corners was referred to as "business talk," and I was
almost always excluded from it.

When the game folded very late, my usual routine was to buy the
morning papers from Bruce, the legless man on the corner who pulled
himself along in a kind of dogcart, bring them back, have a cup of tea
with the lads, then head off in the vague direction of the ocean. But
that morning, the boss called me over to a table in the corner, where
Ow, Larry, The Greek and Adelaide Paddy were sitting.

"Raven, I wanna talk to ya."

"Sure, boss." I took a big steaming mug of tea and a tomato
sandwich from Larry, and wondered why everyone looked more
villainish than usual. "Something must be up with the business," I
thought.

"Who is this, ah, Registrar?" began the boss.

"Yuh," said Ow, cracking his knuckles.

"Sca-da, puh," said the Greek, exploding a bunch of pudgy fingers
under his chin and pretending to spit with disgust on the floor at the
very idea that such a thing as a Registrar should be allowed to exist at
all. Adelaide Paddy opened a bottle of Bollinger and bit off the end of
a fat Havana.

"Who is he? Oh, I don't know. An old ham actor I think. Why?"
Glances passed around the table like proferred cigarettes.

"Don't be dumb, kid. I wanna know where he lives, see."

I became aware that my head was swiveling from side to side, like
those sideshow clowns waiting to devour Ping-Pong balls. I let out a
nervous laugh.

"You can't be serious."

"Sweet as a nut, kid," said the boss, smiling with affection. "What's
'is name? Where does he live? And has he got any kids?" They waited.

"Gee, fellas," I managed, "it's really nice of you and everything, and don't think I don't appreciate it, but it wouldn't really help me, in the long run, if you did anything to the Registrar. Like, break his arm or anything." No one else was laughing. The boss lolled back in his chair and looked at me for a second, delaying the argument which would force me to admit that when it came to dealing with the realities of life, I was a mug punter after all.

"Listen," he said.

"No."

"Well it's up to you, kid." The boss indicated that the conversation was over by taking up the champagne glass, extending his little finger, taking a delicate sip, placing the glass gently back down and popping an angina tablet under his tongue. He opened the paper with a crisp flick, and absorbed himself in the headlines which were all about police corruption.

"But boss it's a terrible thing to do I mean to threaten his children my God what were you thinking of as if I would want to be involved in something like that it's unthinkable. I know that you would never really hurt his children of course you wouldn't but even to threaten it you can't do that sort of thing to people . . ."

By the time I'd remonstrated with him to the point where he was shamefaced and apologetic, I was halfway to the ocean and he was still back in the club drinking Bollinger.

Live by violence, die by violence. Somehow, whenever he had said that, I had imagined him doing something innocuous like robbing a bank, or driving a fast getaway car. I had not pictured him using a bolt-cutter on the pinkies of little children. This little piggie went to market, chop, this little piggie stayed at home.

The club was situated in an old red-light district which was struggling toward respectability. Behind this area lay a wealthy suburb of elegant apartments, Moreton Bay figs, ocean views and regular garbage collection. At night, the rich suburb laced fingers with its neighbor, but denied all contact next morning. At dawn, I could just catch them in the act of disentangling. I had always thought it a privilege to be so intimate with the gutter life of the city. Like all the other nocturnal creatures I was a marginal and obscurely proud of it. That morning, it just made me sick.

I wandered the derelict streets, watching, with jaundiced eyes, a beaten army of tottering people yearning for the sun to come up so they could go to sleep. Thin cats slunk between broken boards, or

179

shook their paws fastidiously free of the human excreta which slicked the pavements. Gay boys and coprophagists, released from secret S and M parties, hid their costumes under greatcoats and caught lone taxis. Twelve-year-old runaways, children with chopped wrists, shot up smack in back streets. Leaning up against a wall, a striptease dancer, her swollen legs stuffed into gestapo boots, dropped a single pink ostrich plume from under her mac. A derro, his face corroded by a life of failure and meths, put his hand up the skimpy skirt of a heroin-dazed prostitute. She kicked him; he cursed her. "On the bottom of the heap of life," I thought miserably, as I wheeled away from the sleazy vision and headed toward the cleansing wind of the Pacific, "there are no sides to take."

Did the boss really break the arms of people he didn't like, I mused, as I strode along. Perhaps he broke the arms of people he did like. If that was the case, could it be said that the boss liked anyone? And if he didn't like anyone, then how could he love anyone, and if he didn't love me, then might it not be possible that one day, he might break my arm?

Or Annie's arm. The vision of Annie being bundled into the boot of a car so filled me with terror that I felt faint. It wasn't my own arm I was risking, it was the arms of all those who were near and dear to me. If I should break an underworld law, my attachment to my friends would be my most vulnerable point. By the time I reached the ocean, Georgia and Annie had been raped and mutilated many times over and Ow had paid a visit to Laura.

I sat on the headland and surveyed the great, scalloped sweep of beach and cliffs. A few microencephaloid lifesavers, with bodies like ice-cream cones and noses bubbled by a carcinogenic sun, hoicked their Speedos up over their buttocks and set out to sea in boats. A couple of dogs forgot about council catchers in a frenzy of seagull chasing and defecation. Sometimes, I ran along the path, then dived into the sea and struck out for the headland, but today the ocean was foaming and dangerous. Beautiful, yes, one of the most physically beautiful cities in the world but, as always, some perversity in me forced me to look at what lay beneath. Two hundred years ago, the beach would have been smooth and clean, not dimpled by footprints. The wild, primeval power of the place would not have been tamed by bitumen paths and parking lots. Where another might marvel at the prettiness of this man-made metropolis, I could see only the ugliness of the destruction it wrought. Instead of progress, I saw defeat. And here, on the cliff, ignored by the ice-cream-licking hordes who walked past on the cement footpath, was another petroglyph, littered with potato-chip packets and splashed with urine.

So blinded had I been by the excessive brightness of underworld life that I had failed to see the violence on which it depended. I admired the boss's scandalous disrespect for the legitimate world, the shameless delight he took in finding chinks to exploit like a rat finding cracks in a storehouse. It was a matter of pride for him to be able to beat any system of authority, no matter how trivial. Credit cards existed in order to be forged; traveler's checks in order to be cashed illegally; parking meters in order to be jammed and poker machines in order to be jimmied with small magnetic discs which caused them to vomit out their money. It was also a matter of pride to be able to give a couple of grand to a friend who needed it, or to dole out large sums to the wife and children of a mate who had been sent to the nick. I had believed that the victims of his fiddles and scams were institutions rather than individuals and because of that I had found his attitude toward the world seductive.

The night he took me to see *O! Calcutta!,* I was charmed by the dodge he had worked out. He had bought tickets to a whole row of seats on the assumption that the theater would be booked out, and nothing I could say about the quality of the show would dissuade him. I stood outside for half an hour in the rain, watching the boss, resplendent in a pink silk suit, front up to passersby, offering them tickets to the show at vastly inflated prices, only to be treated as if he were some roseate variety of skunk. A man of lower caliber might have been humiliated by the failure to sell even one ticket, but not the boss. He made a great deal of noise going into the theater, so that the whole audience had to pretend he wasn't there. He spread himself out along our empty row, like Kublai Khan. "Hey, Raven," he said, loud enough for people across the street to hear, "have these mugs got pineapples up their bums or what?"

It was precisely this anarchic streak in him which had reinforced my belief in his essential goodness. I was doomed, it seemed, to be attracted to misfits, to love the Walliness in people, and there was certainly enough of that in the boss to have blinded me to his short-

181

comings. But this was self-deceit on a grand scale. He was a thug who hurt people.

And how would I be able to tell if I broke a rule? The boss and I had been strolling through town one day, shopping, and I had seen Adelaide Paddy across the street. That very morning, we had shared a joke over a bottle of Bollinger in the kitchen of the Silver Slipper, and there he was in a pinstripe suit, looking for all the world like a top-flight executive.

"Hey, Paddy," I yelled, and waved energetically. Adelaide Paddy looked straight through me and the boss gripped the back of my neck so hard I yelped. He steered me down the street, then snarled in my ear, "Can't ya see he's on his way to work, ya dill. You don't rekker-nize no one see, till ya know they wanna be rekkernized." He refused to speak to me for the rest of the day, except to call me a "fuckin' dill," and to castigate me for possibly ruining Adelaide Paddy's cover.

I got up, turned my back on the ocean and caught a taxi to the boss's flat. Fear fluttered around in my stomach like a big, dark bat.

In the relaxed atmosphere of the penthouse, with its bile-yellow and green swirls of shag-pile, and one of the finest collections of heisted kitsch in the world, Ow's six-grunt vocabulary expanded by a few monosyllables. I lounged in an orange vinyl armchair, in my swimming togs, sipping a daiquiri and listening to the two men reminisce about the time they went to Las Vegas to blow a million.

"Yeah," said the boss, "and remember when we hired that loser to come and sing in the hotel room?"

"Yuh, duh huh," chuckled Ow.

"What a prick, Raven, fair dinkum. We threw food at 'im, made 'im stand on a table and sing, and he did it, woulda done anything for the dough."

"Duh huh, yuh."

"He was big-time too, world-famous, and he couldn't take his eyes off the wedge. Coulda made 'im piss in 'is pants if I'd wanted to."

"Duh duh duh huh, duh huh, yuh."

I stood up and went to the window. I knew why he was telling this story—it was a warning to me that he liked the way he was, and was tired of my moralizing because he would never be the Jean Genet of Australia. When I gave him one of Genet's books to read, all he had said was, "Deviant poof. Wasn't even a top-class villain. Crushed farts and petals. Jesus, Raven, I could write shit like this." I twizzled my drink and gazed down at the deserted swimming pool, boxed in by three other vertical villages, identical to the one we were in.

When Ow brushed past me, I felt my skin prickle with loathing. The boss had assured me that, after some initial misgivings, Ow had grown very fond of me but I could see no appreciable difference in his behavior. My fear of Ow was minor compared to that inspired by the clean-cut young cadaver who visited the club early one morning, and with whom the boss was having "business talks."

I had gone to buy the papers. Someone else was at the corner, exchanging pleasantries with the legless Bruce. I smiled to myself as I crossed the street, at how incongruous the man looked—a wealthy young grazier, perhaps, having a first fling in this cesspit part of the city, dazed at the depravity of it all.

"Morning, Bruce," I said cheerfully.

"Morning, young'un, fine day for it, eh?" This was our daily ritual, and I smiled as I took the papers and handed down the money. I kept my smile on for the young grazier as I turned to walk away, but when he caught my eye, the roots of my hair rose slowly on the back of my neck. I hurried back to the cozy domesticity inside the club—men with their ties loosened, their shoes off, their legs on chairs were sipping their morning tea and folding their newspapers correctly like family men all over the country. At first I had mistaken their careful perusal of the papers for a lively interest in world events. They argued about political corruption all right, but from a rather different perspective. They discussed who could be, had been, bought, who was doing the buying and how much, who had been caught and how it would be covered up. Crooked politicians, judges, solicitors, detectives and company directors were despised because they lacked an ethical code, but were seen as a necessary evil. All the rackets, scams, torts and crimes depended upon the greed and largesse of such men. Australia was, after all, where the cream of English crims came to retire; a nice climate in more ways than one.

Our peaceful breakfast was interrupted by a tap on the door. By now, I could tell a "dog" or a "pup"—detectives and their trainees— at fifty yards. I slid the catch across and who should be there but the grazier.

"Hey, boss, I think some creep from the street followed me. There's something weird about him." But when the boss saw who it was, he opened the door grinning.

"Ted, g'day mate, glad you could drop in." They shook hands warmly.

"Nice place you've got here," said Ted. "Pretty decorations," he added, looking at me.

"Ah, still a bit slow, ya know, gotta wait for the word to spread."

The truth was that the more established clubs were angry at the way an upstart like the boss had encroached upon their territory. When I commiserated with him, all he'd say was, "Don't worry, kid, I'm gunna be guv'nor and no one's gunna stop me." I knew that the other clubs were increasing the percentage they paid to the gaming squad and waiting for the boss to run out of capital. The night a man won over a hundred thousand dollars on the roulette table, the boss had been about as approachable as a baboon with rabies.

Ted was dressed in polished riding boots, pressed moleskins and a blue R.M. Williams shirt—the uniform of a successful landowner. But his hands were as soft as a baby's. His face was bland, and there was nothing remarkable or memorable about him except his eyes which were blue and as lifeless as stone. When he read my palm, and predicted, correctly, that I would travel far, I could not stop my arm from flinching. Later, the boss told me that he was a respectable businessman who also happened to be the best hit man in the Southern Hemisphere.

I turned away from the window feeling chilled, rubbing gooseflesh from my upper arms. Ow and the boss were wrapping something in a blanket.

"What are you doing?"

"Watch out the window, you'll see."

A couple of minutes later, they emerged from the building and strolled nonchalantly over to the pool. They laid the thing down on the Astroturf. The boss went to the other end of the pool, glanced around, and sat. Ow fiddled with whatever it was, then walked away and stationed himself, arms folded, at the other end of the pool, looking casually from left to right. I heard a muffled boom, saw the blanket rustle, and smoke curl out from under it. Ow strolled over and stamped all over the blanket.

I flew out to the lift well, then swooped like a Valkyrie toward them.

"What are you doing? Are you crazy? Anyone could see you, you lunatics. What if a child had come out? Why test a bomb in front of five hundred windows? You're insane."

"Shuddup before I clobber ya." The boss's face was not pretty and Ow was standing very close behind me.

That night I did not want to make love because there were cold, slimy things moving around inside my chest, but the boss did.

16
Nemesis

The club was running out of money and dust was collecting on the chandeliers. Larry, the only inmate of the Silver Slipper with whom I felt comfortable, had to go, taking his prison cuisine with him. We now served sandwiches to a different type of customer—men with visible scars who kept their little fingernails long so they could slip razorblades under them and carve up people's faces; men whose low-life repellent was enough to keep the high-fliers away. To cater for this new clientele, we dealt Manila rather than five-card stud. Top gamblers did not care for the game and went elsewhere. The boss grumbled that he'd have to go back to work, and when I asked him why he was doing so much conferring in corners with Dead-eye Ted, he said, "Mind y'r own fuckin' business." He stayed away quite often, leaving me to run the place with Ow, who one night let in two men, and a woman covered in bruises. They sat around a table by the bar and each of the men in turn poured abuse over her in a soft, almost loving, monotone.

It is quite true that when anger is of a certain intensity, one sees red. The air of the club had turned a kind of burgundy when I grabbed one of the men by the ear and told him to get out and never come back because if he did he wouldn't have much luck. When I marched Ow to the kitchen to vent my spleen on him, he said nothing but his eye spoke volumes. The boss, hearing what had happened, got the twisted-up look on his face, and instead of castigating Ow, raged at me for being a fool.

"You don't treat them pimps like that, they'll do anything. They'll dong ya with a monkey wrench quick as look at ya 'cause they got no brains, ya dill. Do ya wanna get yourself done over in a back alley? I've told ya a thousand times, don't try ta be a fuckin' hero."

"Boss, I can't cope. I don't want to work here any more."

The boss was shocked and it took him a moment to recover. "Hey, kid, you're just het up. You can't let me down now, I need ya. Take a few days off. Come in on Thursday, no ifs and buts. And make sure you dress up. You're startin' to let yourself go fair dinkum. Look at your neck, it's gone all scraggly on ya."

"My neck?" I touched it involuntarily.

"Yeah, might have to start callin' ya crow." He laughed, tweaked my nipple and went back to business.

The budding friendship with Ow died on the vine when the boss decided to send him to the police station with the dogs, instead of me. The other clubs had finally run out of patience. Money had been given to the gaming squad to break our door down and round up our hapless clientele. Of course the only two important people there, a businessman and a dog trainer, were left huddling in the kitchen. "Sorry about this, Dougie boy," said the D., after he'd demolished the door and shepherded his bleating flock to the paddy wagon downstairs. The boss smiled brightly.

"Woulda opened the fuckin' door if you'd knocked."

"So, who am I going to take of your people—this little lady work for you?"

"Na. She's a famous actress, mate, what are ya?"

"Is that right? Don't recognize the face."

"I'm a theater actress."

"Is that right, eh?" A slow smile opened his face. "Hey would you mind signing an autograph. My kids'd like it."

I signed "Raven Huntington" with a flourish and handed it back.

"Thanks. Would you mind signing anotherie, for the wife?"

"Be a pleasure," I said. An imperceptible nod from the boss sent Ow through the sledge-hammered hole with the star-struck detective. "I can't cope," I said, as my knees gave way. Luckily, the boss had a chair and a compliment waiting.

"You're a natural."

"I can't cope," I said to the psychiatrist. Going back to him after so long seemed like defeat.

Jack had left long ago and Georgia had still not recovered. Sometimes I would catch her sitting in her room with the curtains drawn, staring blankly ahead.

"Georgie, you must talk about it. You can't block everything out like this."

"Talk about what?" She looked genuinely puzzled. She had become more brisk and efficient than ever, but now there was a new coldness—a punishing quality. It was unbearable to watch her with Annie, and one day I could not restrain myself from commenting.

She was sitting in front of the child, looking directly at her. "Annie you can have a tantrum if you like, but it would be better if you told me what it was about so we could work it out together." Her voice was infuriatingly reasonable. Annie threw her doll at the wall. "That was a stupid thing to do."

Annie scowled.

"Very well, if you don't want to tell me that's your business." Georgia picked up the doll, which the child took and threw against the wall again, before running upstairs. I was furiously chopping onions when Georgia came into the kitchen.

"Well, what?" she said tersely.

"Why don't you just belt her?" I said before I could stop myself.

"Oh, good old progressive Lucy. How bloody helpful you are."

"I only mean that she wants some response. She doesn't know where she is with you, she'd rather you hit her physically than . . ."

"Torture her mentally. Well I don't believe in brutalizing children, and if that makes me a bad mother . . ."

"For Christ's sake, Georgia, you're not a bad mother, I don't know what it is with you, you take in every waif and stray but when it comes to Annie, you're all buttoned up."

"It's so easy for you, isn't it. You've never taken on a responsibility in your life. You run when anything gets tough, when anyone makes a demand on you. You get to be Auntie Mame without any of the hardship . . ."

"She's not my child," I yelled, then because I was still smarting from her quite truthful accusation, added, "You resent her because she was foisted on you when you were too young to know what you were doing. And what you secretly want is for her to go and live with that psycho husband of yours so you can get on with your life, and what's awful is not that, but that you won't admit it to yourself." Georgia's face was white and closed, but we were in too deep now to stop. "And you blame Annie for what happened with Jack."

"Go to hell," she said quietly, and left the room.

Two days later, she broke the silence by asking if I'd go to the vet with her. Darling was very sick. As we climbed into the car, I said I was sorry and she said, "Me too." I carried Darling tucked into my shirt, her little crested head poking out of my collar. "What's up?" she said in a croaky voice.

We waited at the clinic for over an hour, taking turns in telling the receptionist, politely, that this really was an emergency. The day before, Darling's health had been so prodigious she had eaten her way through a door. Now her eyes were closing and her breath coming in little gasps. I went again to the receptionist.

"Listen, lady, this bird is sick, and I want to see a vet right now, got it? Right now." She was about to remonstrate, when I spied a tiny man in a white coat, surrounded by half a dozen students who bent respectfully to catch his words. I begged him for help. Grateful for this opportunity to demonstrate his knowledge, he led us all into a small room, whereupon he strutted, lectured and held his free index finger in the air or poked it confidently at Darling who tried her best to bite it, but lacked the strength.

"I think she needs something quite quickly," I interrupted.

"Ya, ya," he said, dismissively, then continued. "You vill notice how zis bird looks sick. Zis is bad because ven ze bird starts showing signs of sickness, it is almost alvays too late."

"Excuse me, don't you think . . ."

"Chost a moment. You see, ze bird must pretend it is vell or it vill be picked on by ze crows unt ze hawks so effolution has made zis strange phenomenon, vich iss dat ze bird vill not display its symptoms. Probably zis bird has been sick for a lonk time."

He rolled her over clumsily in his hands. "Darling," gasped Darling, and tried to struggle.

"For God's sake do something," thundered Georgia, and I had to hold her back. The students stood dumbly watching the bird pant in the vet's hands.

"Ya," he said, a little discomposed now. "I vill give her now ze injection. You will zen notice how . . ." Darling opened her beak.

"Please," I pleaded, almost in tears. The vet scurried forward, then back, then scratched his head. One of the students let out a nervous laugh and bit his lip. Darling began to flutter horribly.

"My goodness," said the vet and began to pump her tiny breast with his fingers.

"Don't vorry," he added, smiling up at us. Darling lifted her crest, gave one last heroic, defiant, noble screech, and died. The silence was paralyzing.

"You see," managed the vet at last, blushing deeply, "zis proves my theory zat it is almost alvays too late."

"You've killed her," whispered Georgia, still staring at the heap of feathers. The students concentrated on the floor. The vet could think of nothing further to say and he, too, stared down at the pink and gray corpse whose head lolled over his thumb. He handed her back to me decisively.

"Don't vorry, zere vill be no charge at all."

In all the years I had known her, I had never seen Georgia cry. She lifted her head, splashed tears on the floor, and yowled at the ceiling. I wanted to laugh. I wanted to disembowel the vet and join Georgie yowling. Instead, I placed Darling tenderly back inside my shirt.

"Sorry," whispered one of the students, but stared back at the floor when the vet frowned at her disapprovingly. I put my arm around Georgia and led her away. Her bouts of weeping kept up for three days. I made her go to bed, cooked her food, took the television into her room, brought her new books, read to her and held her while she sobbed.

A fortnight later, I was at the club when I received a phone call from Archie, telling me Hydraulic was ill. It was four a.m. An ambulance was stationed on the opposite side of the street from our house under a flickering street lamp. Two ambulance men leaned against their van, smoking and drinking coffee. Against the opposite wall cowered Hydraulic, clutching a blanket. Georgia in a dressing gown and Archie in a hastily tied sarong stood helplessly in the middle of the street.

"She thinks we're part of the invasion."

"Invasion?"

"From space. There's an underground army but it's full of spies and counterspies and she has some essential information and she thinks we're trying to kill her for it."

"Oh God."

"See if you can talk to her, get her into the ambulance."

"Have you rung her doctor?"

"Doesn't answer."

I got to within six feet of her before she shrank away from me, her white hands clawing at bricks. The blanket fell, leaving her naked and shivering.

"Ruby. What's happening, Rube?" I used the soft singsong voice with which, in the past, I might have quietened my horse.

"You're one of them, I know you are."

"No, honestly, I'm not. You can trust me. I won't let them hurt you." I smiled and extended my hand slowly. After half an hour of this coaxing, she let me touch her. I stood there for a few more minutes, silently holding her hand.

"We'd better get into the ambulance, eh? Come on, I'll take you. Don't be frightened."

"They'll lock me up and torture me."

"You must trust me. I won't let them hurt you, I swear." We got into the ambulance, but when it started up she screamed and tried to get out, so that the ambulance men had to restrain her.

I waited with her in the casualty section of the hospital, not knowing what to say. She stank of fear. A nurse brought a pink potion. Hydraulic knew it was poison but she took it from me with resigned numbness, watching me over the lip of the glass. I could not hold her gaze. She was admitted to a psychiatric hospital, pumped full of Stelazine and Librium, and later, electricity.

"You had no choice, Lucy," said the psychiatrist, handing me a Kleenex. "She needed professional care."

"But she was right, don't you see. I *was* the enemy."

I quit the Silver Slipper and took a job as a waitress. But when it came to cutting the last few threads binding me to the boss, I found that I was too frightened. Even the warehouse, my haven of safety, was undergoing an upheaval. Grotowski had visited Australia. During secret workshops he had dropped bombs on my theatrical friends, the force of which had caused groups to break away from the original whole like icebergs from the Antarctic. Some actors had created their own small company and drifted south. Others had followed the great man back to Paris and a third collective had coalesced around the idea of creating a new kind of circus—an amalgam of traditional skills, theater, comedy and politics. I spent long nights with them feverishly drafting funding proposals, fantasizing costumes and acts but never daring to dream that I might one day be more than a stagehand.

I still practiced in the back garden, and could now do a triple somersault on the trampoline, balance motionless on one point of my ballet slippers until that tortured foot stood in a pool of sweat, and juggle three oranges while standing on a branch of scribbly gum. But was I, could I ever be, good enough to perform for someone other than Georgia?

The night Ow and the boss came by there was no one at home. They were very drunk. I was exhausted and I wanted, desperately, to be left alone. At dawn, I asked them to go. At eight o'clock I asked them to go. At nine o'clock Georgia's ex-husband arrived and when he came into the room it was like seeing The Redeemer himself. I burst into tears.

I remember the next few moments only as a blur—Georgia's husband bundled to the door. A knife hacking at the kitchen table, then placed just under my Adam's apple. The boss, laughing, his eyes very bright. Ow, like a dog let off a chain. For the next four hours, I gave the greatest performance of my life. I cracked jokes and played songs. I taunted them and flattered them just enough to save myself and whoever else might come to the door. When Ow placed one arm down the front of my dress and the other arm up my skirt, I let myself go limp; any struggle would have excited him. My mind raced wildly ahead as I foresaw all the possibilities and worked out ways of dealing with them. I sat on the boss's knee while the knife hacked at the table, or tickled my throat.

By the end of that four hours, Ow was dismissed and the boss hauled me up to bed, telling me fondly that I was a fuckin' dill. We slept. I woke in the dark, found his face and punched. His fist came down a dozen times then he left. My nose was not broken, but there were clots of black blood on the pillow. Two days later, a small parcel arrived for me. In it was a bracelet on which were inscribed the words "Love" and "Joy."

Archie took his withered hand and his paints to England. Frank disappeared from the basement. Cats no longer clamored to be let in. Georgia and I did a lot of silent drinking on my balcony and refused to answer telephones. Sometimes we talked in a listless, dilatory way about leaving, then we'd top up the gin and wait for the shadows of night to close us in. I continued to practice my backbends and flip-flops, but the boss's blows had tamed both my violent ambition to perform in public and the bravery of innocence. If I took risks now it would be with the full knowledge that I could be, probably would be, hurt.

Perhaps when I recall the day I flapped my way out of the ashes, I imbue it with a prophetic quality which was not there because I want to believe that those threepenny pieces of luck on which an existence turns can be glimpsed ahead of time. I can see myself in the kitchen, a cigarette (the last I will ever smoke) dangling from my lips, the detritus of late breakfast scattered across the table. There is a summery feeling of dampness under the old silk dressing gown; the smell of jasmine and burnt toast, and the lazy ticktock of waves. My hand reaches back to pick up the phone. As I place myself inside that earlier self I am certain I feel a presentiment that the indistinct frontiers of my future are about to take shape.

I watch myself put down the receiver, get up from the table, sit back down, put my head in my hands and battle with a sickening nervous-ness as Georgia reproaches me, "Oh, Lucy, really! You don't deserve your talents. You'll go if I have to drag you."

"All right, damn it, I'll go. But I'll make a complete fool of myself in front of everyone. He calls himself Daedalus. Have you ever heard anything so pretentious? His real name's probably Claude. He'll be a petty tyrant pontificating away about dedication to one's art." I mimicked a pontificating Frenchman then fled to the bathroom to prepare myself ever so carefully for the famous aerialist's class.

My only correct prediction concerning Daedalus was the accent. His modest manner together with the poise and grace of his move-ments inspired trust. He had cropped brown hair and eyebrows that met hesitantly in the middle. If we were to be judged on physical attributes alone, we might have been taken for brother and sister. His real name was Mikhail Miroshnichenko, he had taught at Châlons-sur-Marne but hoped to stay in Australia. A livid scar on his left shoulder explained the almost fatal ending of a stratospheric career.

The warm-up over, it was time to attempt the climb to the rigging waiting thirty feet up.

"The distance between the rung are measured for my arms so some of you will make difficulty in reaching. You approach the ladder sideway and then heel toe up and up."

There were five of us. An assistant waited on the platform while Daedalus fixed the mechanical around the waist of each fledgling in turn. Two could not complete the climb; two reached the platform but could not bring themselves to jump. Daedalus was kind to them all, telling them to rest and try again later. Then it was my turn.

Heel toe, heel toe, up the flimsy, swinging ladder. It was not the height that dizzied me but the thought of being seen to fail. "Don't look down," shouted Daedalus. I looked down at the tiny faces below and grinned. Encouragement from the ground, a smile from the assistant as he helped me on to the platform and held the trapeze, just out of my reach. I rubbed powdery stuff on my palms. It was absurdly easy, balancing there on the edge of the platform, one hand touching the side, the other reaching to receive the bar. But then a wrong feeling as I leaned out—too precarious. The net, which had looked so substantial from the earth, was nothing but a spider's web from up here. And the trapeze was much too heavy. I would have to hold it with one hand then grasp it with the other during the fall. I could not trust my strength; there was no intelligence in my body.

"You must spring up to take the trapeze," said the assistant.

"I can't move."

"Just go. Don't think about it."

"Go. Go," shouted Daedalus. I closed my eyes, felt my heart contract and blindly stepped off the platform. I think I yelled. I dropped into the net to the sound of whistles and applause. I stood before Daedalus unable to speak, then ascended the ladder once more.

"You must leap, not step, or you will hit your bum again," said the assistant. "Propel yourself into the swing. Don't hunch up. Don't hold the bar so tightly." Again I went; again I bruised myself by falling gracelessly into the net.

"Enough," said Daedalus. My arms hung like knotted rope; there were no bones in my legs. Nevertheless, I croaked out that I wanted to try again. He hesitated.

"Can the hands take more?" I curled my fingers so he would not see the blood, and nodded.

"You are sure?" I nodded again. Somehow, I climbed the ladder. I was back in the jungle, on a night long ago, fighting the darkness for Wally.

"Go," shouted the assistant in my ear.

"*Allez-y! Sautez!*" came a voice from somewhere far beneath. I launched myself into the void.

And so it was that Lucy McTavish, Jewels, Little Lou, Raven Huntington, the mangler of many a cocoon during the process of growth, discovered, through one exalted concentration of will, her real name, her ultimate form—Louise Hunter of the high trapeze, foe of gravity, friend of flying things, cynosure of upturned eyes. And as I gave myself up to the medium which was now my spiritual home, I declaimed to the ghosts of my past, "Look at me soar, watch me swoop, I have conquered the gravitational suck of your world. I can . . . fly."

17
Sharada/Charlotte

"The most awkward thing about being dead," said Olly, twirling the white feather between thumb and forefinger and studiously avoiding his granddaughter's gaze, "is that you can no longer alter your own past." Lucy examined the map of wrinkles on her grandfather's face as if it might direct her toward the truth of his life. Only a few hours before, she had detected the work of a saintly cartographer there, but in the harsh light of Laura's revelations, the web of tracks traced a route to hell. But this, too, was an illusion. Faces, lives, history were as infinitely interpretable as Rorschach blots.

"But even if you're alive, how can what happens now affect what has gone before?"

"Because each new idea reinterprets the past. All the things that have ever happened to you crowd around inside your skull, jostling for importance, some moving up front, others falling behind, combining and recombining with new events in unpredictable ways. So you see, what happens now cannot help but affect what happened then." He rolled his bottom lip over the top one, thought for a moment, then added in a quiet voice, "But only for the living."

His granddaughter was no longer listening to him. She was leaning out of the french windows calling for Laura who, at the sight of the white feather, had melted into daybreak and refused to come back at nightfall. It was almost the witching hour, and Lucy, pacing nervously back and forth between the veranda and the clock, muttered distractedly to herself about sticks and stones. But the chimes of four o'clock failed to summon her aunt and she slumped down in a chair, dejected.

"Yes, indeed," Olly went on, staring thoughtfully up at the ceiling, but shooting cagey glances at her, "I am dead and therefore impotent but you—you have the power to cast new light on my past as well as your own."

Keeping his eyes steadfastly on his granddaughter, the old ghost scuttled over to her and demanded to know whether Laura had told her anything about his daughter. When Lucy shook her head, he nodded to himself and sighed, a deep, lonely sigh. He eased himself down, flicked dust and cat hairs from his suit, and stared at the feather twirling in the pulpy bark of his hands.

"They never thought your mother was good enough, you know."

Lucy looked at him quickly, her interest revived.

"Proud and cruel all of them. And believe me, nothing much to be proud of. That's what got my goat about them. As for your aunt's grandfather—nasty piece of work he was." Olly squinted at the french windows to see if Laura was about to descend on him, but reassured by the empty blackness, he said in an ominous whisper, "Do you know how he really came by Binjigul?"

Robert McTavish was a mercenary hired by the government to wipe out a tribe of blacks and in exchange he was granted land and a seat in the Legislature. He was indeed an aristocrat but, being the fourth son, had to make his own resentful way in the world. His brutal arrogance, which had been something of an embarrassment in Scotland, was looked upon as an attribute here.

He gathered various hooligans together from the streets and prisons of Sydney, and trained them into a vigilante band. The Aborigines used the rain forest for protection, but their guerilla tactics were no match for the rifles and sanguinariness with which they were hunted. McTavish laid out poisoned baits and ambushed them when they came to the sea for food. Babies were split open on the sword; women were raped and tortured; men, castrated. On his belt he carried a tobacco pouch made from a scrotum, which he took off when he returned south to assure the authorities that the extermination of these last troublesome natives was proceeding as humanely as possible. The outcries of liberal disapproval at his tactics were barely heard amid the clamor of congratulation at his success. Even so, in polite circles he was not liked, and the settlers who had most reason to be grateful to him appeased their uneasy consciences by calling McTavish a queer devil and keeping their daughters away from him.

The Jirralangi who survived fled west and north to join with neighbors and from there, occasionally, made raids on the usurpers of their homeland. These petered out as the people were weakened by immigrant diseases for which their doctors could find no cure. Meanwhile, McTavish cut cedar, built Binjigul and later, blackbirded slaves from the Pacific Islands to plant his sugar cane. All he needed then was a wife.

He went to Bombay, to visit the Danish branch of his family who had shipping interests there. But instead of marrying his docile and willing cousin, he chose the daughter of a wealthy Hindu merchant because of her dowry, which was considerable, and the lust she aroused in him, which was overwhelming. Her coldness toward him only inflamed his desire. In the heat of Bombay nights, he tossed in his bed, dreaming of riding her into submission.

Perhaps his urge to dominance would not have been so keen had her skin not been the color of mother of pearl. On the voyage to Australia he crammed her into corsets and a blue crinoline but no matter how diligently he tutored her, her accent betrayed her origins. Nor was Sharada a willing pupil. Far from riding her into submission, he found himself thrown, again and again.

Both families were scandalized at the alliance, but as she was one of fourteen daughters, her father soon came to see the wisdom of the idea. Not so her husband's family who continued to pretend that she was British, and would not hear of her coming to either Denmark or Scotland. Her real name was Sharada, but from the moment she married her name became Charlotte.

Some transplanted species wilt; others thrive. As much as Sharada pretended to loathe this uncouth, uncivilized country, and although she demanded to be taken home the instant she arrived, the wildness of the place touched something hidden in her. When her husband bought her a grand house in the city and attempted to bury her in it, the hidden thing began knocking at her chest, demanding to be let out. At the most decorous dinners, where flies buzzed around the candelabra, and patronizing smiles masked the contempt on her guests' faces when she confused her v's with her w's, she would mutter under her breath, but loud enough for her husband's most important connections to hear, that the English were cow-eating goondas and the most *boring thing in the vorld was to sit at a table with such ignorant wermin. She took to eating with her fingers again and rustling her silk saris shamelessly in public.*

McTavish soon saw that his original plan to leave her in the city while he went north to keep an eye on his holdings would have to be altered. Not only was she an embarrassment to him, but he now believed her capable of anything—even of returning to India on her own. One morning, he glanced up from his papers and suggested casually that they might go on a picnic. Husband and wife smiled at each other from the opposite ends of the long table—he, plotting capture; she, escape. Each politely informed the other that a picnic was a capital idea. Both agreed that the weather was altogether too delightful to remain indoors.

When they had journeyed five miles, she feigned a full bladder and headed back to town along a little gully. But he chased her, tied her to the seat of the buggy with harness leather, and thus they set out for Binjigul. The servants and the dray-loads of possessions met up with them later.

At first she railed against her fate and uttered oaths that no respectable young woman should know. She threatened, wept and, finally, retreated into silence, vowing never to utter another word until her husband took her home. Consequently he did not hear her voice again until the day of her death.

Sharada took to eating cattle with a perverse and angry relish. She noticed that her feces began to smell of rotting meat and wondered if her soul might not also be emanating a foul and sulphurous odor. But these acts of defiance, originally intended to punish herself, soon had an astonishing effect on her. For the first time in her life she was tasting the sweetness of freedom. Having cast off moral codes like ropes, her thoughts were able to sail where they pleased. And the primordial landscape into which fate had cast her mirrored the inscrutable horizons of her own inner world. Fate, she knew, may be like an ocean, unpredictably calm or stormy, but the individual always remains in control of the rudder.

She marveled at how her body, which had been wrapped in cocoons of silk and weighted down with hoops of gold, grew more powerful by the day. It could stride along like a man, even aim a rifle and bring down a bustard. Nor did the heat annihilate her as it did the others. Under the billowing shalwar-kurta, her skin stayed as cool as cream.

Her two servants protected her from the less pleasant aspects of bush life. They washed her clothes in the sweet water of billabongs, pressed them with irons from the campfire, massaged her legs when she demanded and listened to her grumblings with tactful reserve. She would never admit to herself, much less to anyone else, that her spirit, if not her heart, was happier than it had ever been.

When they first saw Binjigul mountain it was a blue bump, a mosquito bite on the back of a low, lumpy range. Sharada laughed out loud. "A mountain he calls it, a mountain." As they came closer, the hills disappeared into more hills, lost themselves in convolutions, petered out in rifts and valleys and switched back on themselves until even the stars lay scattered around the sky in disorienting confusion. By the time the little party sat around the campfire on their last night the mountain that wasn't a mountain had merged into the black silhouette of the surrounding humps of hills and loomed beside them, obscuring a quarter of the sky. Sharada leaned across to her servant and whispered, "Vhat is Binjigul?"

This servant leaned across to the next servant and asked, "What is Binjigul?" The second servant leaned across to Sharada's husband and asked, "What is Binjigul?"

"It's a native word, something to do with bats." The answer was passed to Sharada along the same route.

"Now it is Mount Misery," she announced to her servant.

"Mount Misery," said the first.

"Mount Misery," said the second.

No matter how often or how vehemently McTavish insisted that it was Binjigul Mountain, the new name stuck to the hump as tenaciously as its gloomy morning mists.

Sharada thought of her long journey as a trial by fire from which she emerged as hard as tempered steel. She understood her husband well now, and knew that her silence was more poisonous to him than any words she could utter. Claiming the homestead as her own domain, she surrounded herself with her treasures, buried herself in books and froze him out. The jungle, too, was hers and each time he tried to shave it back she would stand before the little army of men bristling with axes, her arms folded, barring their way as effectively as a Mogul fort. Sharada had no desire to enter the rain forest herself but she held to the irrational conviction that its wildness would protect her spirit from domestication. She knew she would never leave Binji-

200

gul physically, but her imagination and the stories she read carried her, every day, as far away from there as it was possible to go.

After fathering two sons in as many years, McTavish could no longer bring himself to make love to her. It was like slithering into his own tomb. He took to visiting the Kanaka camp and fathering other children, without giving them the dubious benefit of his name.

Sharada's children grew up haphazardly, confused by a mother who ate with her fingers and seldom spoke, but whose mercurial nature was capable of suddenly bundling them to her and singing gibberish songs. She would tire of them quickly, and hand them back to the servants, or to the ambiguous care of their Aboriginal nanny.

This woman had been wet nurse to both the children from their first week of life. Sharada watched with profound disgust as the two-year-old whined for one black breast, while the one-year-old clawed hungrily at the other. She would never allow the wet nurse into the house, and kept her waiting at the end of the veranda. If, by chance, Sharada's pearly skin brushed against the velvety blackness of the wet nurse she would shudder and go to wash herself.

She took pitiless pleasure in seeing how much her offspring loathed each other as they competed for her sparse affections. Sometimes she would tease and torment one, while cuddling the other. But inevitably the situation would be reversed so that both the boys were in a constant state of anxiety as to the day-to-day condition of their mother's love. They grew up moody and prone to fits of tears. The timidity of his sons worried McTavish greatly—yet the more he beat them, the more they retreated from him, and hid behind their mother's gloating if temporary protection.

Sharada delighted in her husband's fear of her. She knew that her cold hatred defeated and haunted him, as if she were a product of his own conscience. She knew she was the only creature capable of making him cower, and that when he felt her eyes following him around sweat formed in the small of his back. He had tried everything he could think of to break her, but all his efforts only deepened her silence.

One morning he watched his wife's habitual flinching from the touch of the Aboriginal woman and, although he had seen this countless times before, a cunning smile twisted his mouth. That evening Sharada looked up from her book to see her husband dragging the wet nurse up the stairs, along the veranda past Sharada's chair, and into their bedroom, where he proceeded to rape her. Sharada followed them and coolly watched from the comfort of an armchair. Her Mona Lisa smile, the way she folded her hands primly in her lap so appalled him that he let out a cry and fled from the room, not noticing the flicker in his wife's glacial eyes when they looked into the fiery eyes of the young woman, like a flame reflected on ice.

The two women remained in the bedroom for a long time, without moving, without a sound passing between them. Then Sharada grabbed the wet nurse by the arm, flung her outside, ripped off the sheets, screamed for the servants and flung the bedclothes at them when they came running.

A little hole had been burned through Sharada's defenses. The looks the black woman now cast her mistress were like moths fluttering against the nape of Sharada's neck. There was something disdainful about the way the wet nurse watched her, then quickly dropped her eyes. As if she, a primitive, the equivalent of an untouchable, felt herself superior to Sharada. There was pity mixed in with the hatred and it made Sharada curious even as she burned with shame.

What did this savage have that could sustain her through such brutalization? Why did she always return to the homestead, a willing captive? Only once did Sharada see the startling white teeth of the wet nurse. She had been sitting on the veranda, staring out at the wall of jungle, singing a Hindi song to herself, and looked up to see the black woman grinning from ear to ear. But again, that quick, enigmatic downward glance, as if she were hiding something.

Sharada's curiosity grew into an obsession. She brought the young woman inside the house, gave her sweet things to eat and tea from fine cups, plied her with questions and bullied her for replies. But the woman would only drop her eyes, pretending that she did not understand, or shift awkwardly in the cockfighting chair and turn her head toward the door.

One day Sharada followed the wet nurse out of the house and along the path that led toward Mount Misery. The woman stopped, turned to stare at her, then continued on until she met up with a wizened hag who carried a large goanna slung across her back. They looked back at Sharada as if she were a trespasser then, ignoring her, continued until they reached a clearing where they built a fire and threw the goanna onto it. Sharada sat down in the shade, fifty yards away from them, feeling obscurely envious of their whispering and giggling.

202

When they had finished sharing out the cooked meat, they began painting each other with white ocher and fat.

The singing began—a mournful chanting which sent ripples across Sharada's stomach, and seemed to rise from the very ground on which they sat. Hours passed. The heat and infernal music began to make Sharada dizzy, and at last she could stand no more. She strode over and stared down at them coldly, demanding in a thin, peevish voice, "Vhy don't you leave, run avay. Vhy do you stay?"

The older woman looked down, embarrassed, but the wet nurse turned her eyes toward Mount Misery. At first, Sharada thought they would not speak and she began to feel foolish, standing before them, her face quivering with emotion. But then the wet nurse pointed with her lips to the folded ranges and said, "Pinjikurlu, woman place. Look apter 'im." Then added, with a kind of defiance, "Some old people mob tsing you whitepella . . ." but here, the older woman touched her companion to silence her. They waited uncomfortably for Sharada to go.

Sharada, who came from a culture which understood the efficacy of spells, looked up to the brooding mass and shuddered. She turned, hurried back along the path intending to go home. But the moment she emerged into the sunlight and stood before the house her fear of what awaited her there was greater than her fear of the forest. She doubled back to the clearing and hid herself near the women.

Smoke from their fire coiled into the air like a rope. They stifled the coals with their feet, then came toward her and crossed the little creek behind her. They moved like powerful cats, their large horny feet padding noiselessly along the litter. The forest ignored their passing. They began to laugh and chatter, the noise ringing out like bird calls, receding now, down the weaving path, into the sudden dark, past the house where McTavish would be waiting for his wife's coldness to engulf him. But Sharada could no longer feel either vengefulness or rage, only the shame and humiliation of the abandoned. She imagined the women not pausing even to glance at the house where they labored at the senseless tasks the white people gave them, but returning to the light of their own fires, wrapped up in a warmth of belonging which excluded her, their eyes full of impenetrable understandings, self-contained, aloof and pitying, for they knew that Sharada and all her kind were lost in oblivion with no hope of being found.

18
Circus Caelestis

A man in top hat, tails, and striped bloomers entered a thick column of dusty sunlight which transected the interior of the warehouse. He stopped, glanced to the ground twenty feet below him, then continued to skip through the air, balancing a long pole. In another luminous shaft, a one-woman band, suspended upside down, crashed at her cymbals and blew in her harmonica. Where the light fell in a patchwork on the floor, groups of oddly dressed people, oblivious to these aerial improbabilities, worked like ants dismantling vast wings of red and yellow plastic.

I unbuckled the mechanical from my waist and wiped sweat from my face and neck. I had just completed a lengthy workout for the benefit of a television camera.

"If you could all sit behind me in a group . . . no, keep sewing, it looks good." We bustled behind the interviewer who slicked down his hair, straightened his tie and, gathering his features into a serious expression, faced the camera.

"Tonight we will be speaking to members of the newly formed 'Circus Caelestis,' a circus with, as one of its members put it, 'brains, imagination and a social conscience.' "

"Yuk, who said that?" whispered Bella, digging me in the ribs.

" . . . impassioned by a collective vision, seventeen young people, nine women and eight men, have done what everyone said was impossible . . ."

Andrea and Dolly did most of the talking, telling him that we paid ourselves forty dollars a week and worked sixteen hours a day every day, practicing our circus skills, creating and rehearsing the acts, making the tent, constructing the bleachers, sewing the costumes, each learning to be a carpenter, cook, musician, mechanic, truck driver, performer and comedian. Our esthetic derived from new circus, new Vaudeville and avant-garde theater and dance. Only two of our company came from circus backgrounds. Steve, Bella and several others were actors and directors who had set up the Warehouse Theater two years before. Duncan had been studying mathematics. Jenny was a choreographer. Renaldo, Murray, Julie and Steph were street performers. Andrea spoke five languages including Latin.

When the crew had packed up and gone home, nobody felt like resuming work. Instead we lounged around drinking tea, a little stunned that our year-long dream was now a reality.

Circus Caelestis was at once my convent and my celebration of freedom. Inside its circle I generated energy from an internal fire lit by Daedalus. I looked across at him leaning into the door frame, a little apart from the rest of us, and wondered, again, why he refused to join our troupe.

He had said nothing when I descended from my first, vertiginous flight, but only inspected my bleeding hands as a doctor might, then sent me out of the warehouse. With the others he had smiled, said "*Extra*," or patted them on the shoulder. He had not even looked at me. I had wanted my tears to keep flowing so that he would understand how much my victory meant to me and I was so proud of the stigmata on my open palms that I would not wash them. Twenty minutes passed before he called me back inside.

I smiled hesitantly as I entered, expecting him to tell me I was wonderful, the way Georgia did. But the gentle Frenchman had disappeared and in his place, a demonic *doppelgänger* sat astride a chair, arms folded, head tilted back, everything about him displaying a challenging contempt. "You have some physical ability but this mean nothing. *Zéro. Comprenez?* The courage to work, to develop, this I think you do not have."

I stood before him and felt a sudden, explosive anger. "What a pig you are," I said to myself.

"You are weak. You cry like a baby."

I straightened my back and jutted my chin at him. "I'm not crying."

"You lie to me about your hands."

"They were all right, I tell you."

"But yes," he scoffed, "all right, if you had first idea how to hold the trapeze. You grip it like an ape."

Words rose from my aching solar plexus and burst between my teeth. "And you're a PIG."

That was the beginning of our long struggle—six months of rope burns, blisters and bruises. Of days beginning in blackness at five and ending in blackness at nine. There was no respite from his "timing, timing, timing," which pounded through me like blood-flow even in dreams.

He started me on the web, building muscle and resistance to pain. Nothing could protect my arm from the remorseless gouging of rope and when my body refused to accept any more punishment, or my brain the weight of concentration, he would bully and insult me until I tried again. When I felt energy flash through me and got things right, he would only say, in a sarcastic voice, "See what you can do when you *really* try." I lived in a vapor of exhaustion which distilled into pure hatred of my tormentor. I fought him, ran away from him, returned to him, hated him anew, and when I went to Georgia with tales of his wickedness, she would only cock her head on one side and say, "I suppose you'd better give up then."

Sometimes I heard them laughing together in the kitchen. "I'll show them," I whispered into the dark, grinding my teeth with fury before crash-landing into sleep.

As usual, Georgia had understood in a week what it took me six months to work out. With the instinct of a master, Daedalus knew that to strengthen my will, he would have to ignite the fuel that had been collecting inside me for years—a dangerously flammable rage. Finally, when I understood his dedication, and no longer needed anger to sharpen the edge of my talent, he became my trusted friend— sweet, broken Misha.

A week after the filming, we were all gathered around Georgia's television set like a flock of quarreling parrots. The one-minute clip was more than a disappointment, it was an outrage. A whole day wasted. In desultory silence, the others wandered off to their respective perches, leaving Misha, Georgia and me enveloped in the intimacy of night.

"You know what speed the body make in the quadruple?" His

question was rhetorical and Georgia and I continued to gaze down at our feet.

"But, Mish, it was eight years ago and I can't see why it stops you doing other things. You're still a fine acrobat. And we need you. *I* need you."

He rarely spoke about himself, and getting his history out of him had been as easy as uprooting a tree. Orphaned by the war, he had ended up in France, and been passed from family to family until, at the age of fifteen, he had joined a circus.

Now, for the first time, he was divulging details of the accident. He and his catcher, Dominique, had been practicing the quadruple somersault on the trapeze—an almost impossible feat which had never, at that time, been performed in public. Dominique had miscalculated by a fragment of a second. Misha's shoulder smashed into his partner's head, killing him. His guilt had been crusted over and it was partly this that made him a little remote from the rest of us. No doubt his sense of isolation was intensified because he was older, because he was foreign, and because, having been formed by the hierarchy of traditional circus, he found it difficult to adjust to collective decision making. But I sensed there was more to his resistance, and that Georgia knew what it was.

When at last he left, she said, "You're his own desire to fly made manifest. He's terribly proud of you."

I shifted about in my chair, longing to know what he said about me but pretending that such matters were of no significance. "He's never said one good thing about me, about my work."

Georgia lapsed into silence.

"So what *does* he say?" I asked eventually.

Her small smile did not escape my notice.

"He says it's the things you aren't conscious of that make you a true artist. The tilting of the head, the grace with which you enter the rings, a special kind of smile, the joy and charisma you transmit when you're flying, they all add up to a personal style. He could teach you technique, but he could never have taught you that beauty."

My heart gave several thuds of pleasure against my ribs. "Well, why does he never say that to me?"

"Because, like any Pygmalion, he's terrified of the moment his wunderkind doesn't need him any more."

"You mean to tell me that he won't join us because at some point I'll discard him? That's ridiculous."

"But don't you think it might be important for him to find an identity in the ring beyond 'spotting' for you?"

I digested this information for a long time then said, "Georgia what would I ever do without you?"

"Start thinking for yourself probably."

I reached out for her hand, and smiled.

Not long after this conversation, I was in the warehouse with Misha, having just presented him with an act I had designed all by myself.

"I didn't ask you whether it was too dangerous, dammit, I asked you if it was possible." I flung the paper and pencil to the floor and fixed him with such a challenging look that he unconsciously fingered his scar and got up to walk behind me. At last he mumbled, "It has never been done but it can be possible, yes, maybe."

"I knew it," I shouted, leaping out of my chair and kissing him loudly on his forehead. Turning to the others who were hammering at bleachers, I shouted, "Mikhail Miroshnichenko is a frog prince." I gripped him by the upper arms. "You can see what I'm going for, can't you? Dreamlike, poetic—all lightness and grace, then the tension and expectation, then wham . . ." So contagious was my enthusiasm that Misha was now exhibiting symptoms. He paced around me in circles, flinging his arms about, and the others dropped their tools to come and listen.

"You would have to make somersault at front, one somersault, or you will come feet first . . ."

"Of course. I see. So the tempo is, L seat at the back, one two and three, releasing just before the vertical?"

"But it is too crazy. You will fight against the speed. It will feel strange and frightening and you will let go always too late . . ."

"Yes, I'm sure I will, so we had better start practicing straightaway. Now the rigging, four king poles and the apron set up . . . Why are you all laughing at me."

Later, after a difficult and discouraging practice session, I planted the seed I had been carrying for days.

"You know Mish I've been thinking. This circus lacks one very important element: sophistication in the humor. What we really need is someone who . . ."

Like the moon, Misha had only displayed one half of himself to the light. When he turned we were all stunned with admiration. His shadow self was a creature doomed to failure, to be made a fool of and yet, with indomitable pluck, to persist. If we were the body of the circus, Misha's wistful, long-suffering clown was its soul.

"It is the romantic myth that grounded fliers become clown," Misha said. "Grounded fliers never become clown."

"Clownzzz," I corrected him, and applied the last touches of rouge to my face.

Tonight we were about to taste the final ingredient—an audience—and the pitch of excitement in the dressing rooms was exquisitely intolerable. Excavating a red plastic nose from the makeup box, I placed the elastic around the back of his head and twanged the nose onto his forehead.

"Misha, dear, you've all the right ingredients—sensitivity, pessimism and somewhere deep inside you, just a soupçon of spite. Think of it this way. You're a born clown who was, for many years, a born flier."

I jumped up from the dressing table and inspected myself in the long mirror. Red lips, darkened eyes, black hair short as a boy's, a simple, opal-blue leotard cut to reveal one powerful shoulder and arm. I liked what I saw there. Not the flimsiness of a butterfly, but the strength and grace of a bird.

"Fabulous, aren't I," I cried, whirling in front of the mirror.

Just then, Bella came in, fighting with the long back zip of her tuxedo. "Help me, somebody, it's stuck." At once, gaudy silk hats, sequined jackets, striped bloomers with bells, all fell to the floor as we went to her assistance. In the midst of this babble of laughter and rodomontade came Dolly's call from outside: "Fifteen minutes."

"Where's my nose? My nose," yelled Mikhail, flinging the contents of the makeup box all over the floor. I twanged it again then we tumbled out of the dressing room, clutched each other one last time and filed into the dimness backstage.

I paused at the tent flap for a moment to watch these monks and nuns, my sisters and brothers. Their expressions were solemn now, the faces of old souls. They had retreated inside themselves. On the left, Steve walking on his hands; on the right, Jenny softly leaping onto her partner's shoulders. Renaldo and Andrea checking each other's stilts; Misha laying out costumes on the trestle and Bella tying herself in knots. Dull light caught on their glitter as if angel dust had been puffed over them. I thought, "They will never again be as beautiful to me as they are at this moment." Then I, too, began to stretch and warm my muscles.

Darkness. The audience rustling its sheets. An overpowering feeling of unreality. A drumroll from Dolly. Deep breaths, lights, then we burst into the white glare for the Charivari, blasting notes from our instruments and cavorting around the ring.

". . . Circus Caelestis, written, produced, directed, owned and built by Circus Caelestis." A boom of applause. Joy swift as cocaine in the bloodstream.

I danced my way to the band area where I took a thirty-second breather before bounding back. Up onto Dolly's shoulder I sprang, then Jenny, with a fine economy of effort, leapt onto mine. All seven held it, counted, then dropped like rubber balls to somersault around the ring once before taking our places in the band. The sweat was already pouring down me in runnels as I picked up the sax and blew it out, hearing nothing now but the swish of blood in my head. We were functioning like the cells of one body—our timing, perfection.

The lights dimmed. A sweet, dreamy waltz heralded Mikhail. He came out on a bicycle with wobbly wheels, blowing pearly bubbles which trembled in the air, reflecting multicolored arrows of light. He was enchanted by them; wanted to feel them in his hands, possess them. A collective "ahh" of sympathy went up as the bubbles burst, breaking his innocent heart. He spied a spotlight on the floor and, forgetting the bubbles, took a mop and bucket from the handlebars and began to wash the light away. It moved. Misha followed it and tried again. Again the spotlight eluded him. He turned to the audience as if to say, "I am only trying to please, why are you laughing?"

The laughter broke into warning shouts as two twelve-foot-high policemen appeared behind him. Misha turned again to the audience with a baffled look. "Behind you," yelled the children. He turned and opened his arms in fright. For a moment he cowered then, remembering that he had done nothing wrong, began to mime his innocence. But the more he explained, the greater his culpability. He spilled water on their trousers which he groveled to clean, but in doing so, trod on his mop which leapt up, hitting the wooden shins of his persecutors.

From beneath his elongated coat, one of the policemen pulled an enormous truncheon and brandished it at Misha, who dropped his bucket and ran.

Misha's clown covered the changing of props, gave the rest of us badly needed breathers, released the tension after dangerous acts and, most importantly, provided the counterbalance. Where we succeeded so effortlessly, poor Misha could only bungle. He longed to be like us; to be loved and respected by us. When Nick bounded from a teeterboard, turned a back somersault and landed, without a tremor, on Dolly's shoulders, Misha wanted to try too. They rolled their eyes and laughed behind their hands, but Misha would not be dissuaded. He spat on his palms, lined her up, took an almighty backward leap, missed her shoulders and fell. And no one in the audience had the smallest inkling that he risked breaking his bones in that perfectly executed fall.

My solo act on the web came toward the end of the second half, which gave me forty-five minutes to prepare my body and gather my concentration. I wore a hot pink leotard padded front and back by dyed chook feathers. A pink ostrich feather crest was bound tightly to my head. I skipped into the ring, tossed back my feathers and, dragging the spotlight with me, began piking up the web, while Bella played appropriately unearthly music on the didgeridoo. I slipped my wrist through the loop; Misha twirled the rope, and I spun into a bright pink blur.

Nothing had prepared me for what I felt then—a *coup de foudre*. The roar of the crowd created a bursting sensation in my chest. I flung out my arm, greedily making more room in my rib cage for the adoration which poured into my intoxicated heart. I would give them more, much more.

I went to the roman rings, slid my legs through, and with the help of Misha's rope, soared up and back, higher and higher, feathers flying like tresses, and every muscle in my face and body communicating to the people below, "I am a creature of the air. I am liberated from the earth and all things heavy. I am bliss."

"And now, ladies and gentlemen, you are about to witness a feat unique in all the world. Louise Hunter, our silly galah, will leave the roman rings entirely, turn a somersault in midair, and without the benefit of a safety net, catch the rope for her descent. Watch, ladies and gentlemen, her vengeance on gravity . . ."

Higher and higher, whizzing through the air, waiting for that hundredth of a second, and knowing that the tiniest miscalculation would mean a body bag of shattered bones. A distant thunder of drums. Now! I make my fly-away off the rings. I turn in the air. My eyes cross to focus the flash of vertical white line speeding toward me.

I miss the rope.

My own bellow was swallowed by the gasp from the bleachers as I plummeted down and across to land, spread-eagled, in Velcro. The lights went out and amidst the laughing and cheering, Jenny and Misha quickly pulled me off. His body trembled as we embraced.

"*Superbe*," was his first compliment to me.

The hour and a half seemed to have passed in a matter of seconds. When the lights went up and we all went out to love and be loved by our audience, I stumbled and had to be held up by the others because there, sitting like Kublai Khan in an empty row of seats was "the boss" who stood up as I took my bows, shouting "Bravo" and then, to the people who turned to stare at him, "What are ya, ya mugs? Stand up for the kid, can't ya tell a star when ya see one?"

I never saw or heard of him after that. Perhaps he has died by violence.

The peripatetic life began the following spring, curing the itching restlessness of my previous existence. Misha continued to teach me and as I pushed beyond barriers, I discovered reserves of power I never dreamed I possessed. The inner redhead of my fantasies, who had once parasitized all my courage, and confirmed repeatedly that I was not, could never be as good as she, had been bullied to the back row first by my teacher and then by my own will. Of course there were still drowned bodies in the stagnant pools of my psyche which were too deep, or too grotesque to allow to the surface, but when they threatened me with their malignity, I would work and work until they sank out of sight. Flying was an antidote to fear.

And if, from time to time, my inner redhead got the upper hand and convinced me I was a prune, there was always Georgia on the end of the line, telling me I was a plum. Or if shadowy ghosts appeared like demons in the tent, willing me to "cast" and fall, there was always Mikhail, holding the safety rope, guiding my flight from them.

Now that my years with the circus are over, I often dredge up their

residue and relish the captured fragments which, like Laura's possessions, hold lost eras locked inside them. In my reverie, all the images,
spread through time and space, merge to form one world, which
moves inside the larger world through long tunnels of road. And the
grass or sand or cement of so many different towns condense into one
patch of earth beneath the tent which accepts a new performer or
releases another as if magically transforming one of its eternal citizens, just as now that I have gone, another will be there in my place,
sucking in the timeless air as she sails between the silver trapezes.

Memories of that time seem to exist close to the surface of my mind
and can be triggered by the most fleeting sensations. I might smell a
freshly washed baby, and find myself spirited backstage, breathing in
the clean sweet smell of sweat as my friends and I flock to the dressing
rooms. Or I might touch some textured surface and instantly, the
peeling colors of Bella's truck will appear beneath my hand, as I turn
the corner and duck beneath the awning where we so often sat,
gossiped and sewed and I enter the truck to witness her child being
born.

If I imagine my life as a complicated topography of hidden valleys
and broken rocks—a turbulent place in which it is easy to lose one's
way, those years rise up like a long plateau above the surrounding
rubble, its outline sharp enough to use as a reference point as I
navigate my way through the lost realms of my past.

Yes, the memories are easily accessible, but if I try to hold on to the
sensation of happiness associated with those old moments, it proves
as elusive as Misha's spotlight, as ephemeral as bubbles.

19
Misha

I do not remember when Misha and I became lovers. We simply drew together during that first year on the road, like a right hand automatically coming to rest in the palm of the left.

I had thought that someone with a history like his would harbor rage, but his goodness remained incorruptible and his gentleness implacable. When I slammed doors, shook him by the shoulders, behaved badly, he always forgave and, worst of all, referred fondly to my temper—the most shameful flaw in my character—as "artistic temperament." "What rubbish," I would shout, shaking him by the shoulders. "I just want to know whether you're alive or dead in there. It's a wonder you don't break out in boils."

Although I could never rouse him to anger, I did give him one great gift—the ability to be depressed. Before he met me, a doubt never sailed across the perennial blue of his equanimity. After me, he could sink into vaporous states of despair, wondering what the answers were to questions that everyone knows have no answers. It was as if my unhappiness traveled down the safety ropes like some foul excrescence of the soul, and contaminated Misha.

Along with this essence of misery, he also absorbed my ability to feel the prevenient breezes of the winds of change. It was he who opened the door of the truck one morning, craned his neck a little as if listening and said, "Something bad is going to happen."

I took no heed. Circus Caelestis was more successful than any of us had dared to hope. We traveled to festivals in Europe and the U.K. and received consistently good reviews. I loved my work with religious devotion. My soothsayer was not at home to repeat his warning

214

when the German filmmaker arrived to talk me into accepting a part in a coproduction called *The Burning Plains*. Predictably, I was to play a beautiful aerialist who becomes the object of a traveling musician's passionate obsession.

The film was jinxed from the beginning. The director and the lead actor threw tantrums at each other. Fresh Hitler jokes appeared on the walls of the portable latrines every night and law suits were threatened when some of the crew walked off the set. Once I found the producer in a Nissan hut banging his fists on a case of oven-temperature beer chanting, "The Burning *Pains,* the Burning *Pains.*"

Objects of passion are not required to say a great deal, but I was asked to pout incessantly and to perform my tricks under the baking lid of desert sky. When the heat turned my frustration to steam which scalded anyone who came within range, I, too, gained a reputation for being "difficult." Infernal as the twelve-week shoot had been, I rapidly discovered that it was only the First Circle of Hell.

As communication between the lead actor, the director, the writer and the producer disintegrated, the film company had to find something promotable. The something they found was me.

"Superwoman swoops to the silver screen," announced one magazine headline.

"High-flying career in the movies," said another.

To my astonishment, the film was a hit in the art houses of Europe and America. Overnight I became a darling of the film industry—interviewed, photographed and courted for my opinions. I was besieged by journalists to whom I refused to speak, film scripts which I refused to read, and fan mail which I endeavored to answer during the few precious hours I could be alone.

When the dust from this explosion of fame had settled, I lifted my head cautiously, and found that reality had been severely distorted. Friends pretended they'd never met me before, while in other circles, I became unaccountably popular. People whose names I could not remember declared themselves my closest buddies and when they ignored Mikhail in my presence, my desire to protect him from hurt made me more publicly animated while he withdrew even further.

One night, after a party, his pressurized discontent found a vent. As usual, I had chatted and entertained, commanding the center of attention and compensating for Misha's reserve. Later, as I drove us back to the hotel, I had tried to make him feel better by saying he was really the one my friends liked.

"You don't have any friends."

"What an absurd thing to say. We're surrounded by them. All the time."

"You think they care about you?" He snorted his contempt. "You are never in one place long enough to make real friends, or to see your old ones. You would not even go back to help Laura when she was ill, you were so busy chasing the tail."

There was a silence, during which Mikhail saw the expression on my face and hugged me so hard that we swerved all over the road. I wept for a long time, Misha said that he knew I could not have gone and that he was a shit for mentioning it, and after I agreed with him I felt a little better.

I returned to the sanctuary of my circus, feeling as if I'd survived a plane crash with nothing but the dubious compensation of money and notoriety, only to find that everyone was mad at me for betraying the collective vision and becoming a star.

Numb from the loss of Laura, and of a previous, less complicated existence, I tried to concentrate on my work and to place the pieces of my life into a familiar shape. But after each performance, as Misha and I sat comfortably beside each other, slapping cold cream on our faces, I would notice that the queer expression in his eyes had grown more intense, while the level in the vodka bottle had dropped alarmingly, and I knew without a word what it meant.

We were camped outside a large country town one night, by the base of a wooded hill, in a wide, grassy paddock. We had been up since sunrise, lugging equipment, hoisting the tent, checking the rigging and, as always, were addled with fatigue. I was returning with supplies in time for a meeting and must have been a half a mile away when, on a whim, I turned off the engine and the headlights. Through the silence came the distant pulse of the generator, loud then soft as it traveled on the invisible movements of the night. The world was all silver, pewter and glass. Moonlight frosted the trees and the clustering stars were cold and brittle as ice. The tent, touched by the wand of the Southern Cross, glowed with a supernatural light and the trucks gathered around its gothic shape resembled little houses crouched against the skirts of a church called up from the Dark Ages. It was a fairy place, a child's place.

216

I felt an odd sensation, as if I were stranded in a phantom region between two worlds. The vision of the tent, eerie yet innocent, was linked in my memory with some other place I could not name. Then an old pain touched at my heart. I was riding to the bat tunnel on a New Year's Eve long ago, aware that I was betraying something larger and more complex than a friendship. Wally's hideout was the realm of innocence. The memory ambushed me because I knew what must happen at the meeting in the tent and not only was I powerless to prevent it, I was, in some metaphysical way, responsible for it.

"Why don't you put the light on, it's like a burial chamber in here." A single candle flickered in its cage, illuminating Misha's inert form on the fold-down bed. I sat next to him, smelling the alcohol fumes.

"You'd better get yourself ready for the meeting," I said, both of us knowing that this was a pretense. I rubbed his feet but kept my back turned to him.

"Misha," I began, clumsily, "it's only blind luck and a pretty face that's made me . . . it doesn't mean anything. Can't you just . . ."

"Go to the meeting, Louisa. They are waiting for you."

I loved the simplicity and spareness of my truck. It was like a ship, everything battened down, able to be folded away. Along one wall were my books and beside the small window opposite hung a bunch of everlasting daisies, picked from various roadsides and seasons. My practice trap was lashed to the ceiling above the dressing table containing Misha's makeup and mine. Opposite was the long glass in which, now, I saw us dimly reflected. Behind the door hung an ancient mask—Misha's gift to me—and an embroidered dressing gown—my gift to him. Our lives formed one life, defined by the shape and contents of the truck. I patted his ankle and left.

The others were warming themselves around a fire in the middle of the tent. Announcing that I was famished, I dropped beside Bella, kissed Spike, her little girl, and ladled out a huge portion of stew from the steaming pot. Someone handed me a chunk of nutty bread topped with a mound of butter and everyone understood that I was postponing the business of the evening with my mumbles of approval, and waiting for the right atmosphere in which to begin.

"Where's Misha?" said Nick at last because a silence had formed.

I licked each finger before answering, "He isn't feeling well." Now the silence held another meaning; everyone knew Misha had stayed away to make it easier for us and for himself. I rested my face in my hands and stared into the fire.

Boris began. "What are you going to do about him?"

"What am *I* going to do? I thought this was a bloody collective."

"Come on, Lou, don't put those cocky feathers up," said Dolly. "Whatever's eating him does have to do with you. We're not handing the responsibility . . ."

"Oh yes you are."

Bob interrupted. "It's pretty obvious, isn't it? The more successful you get, the more he corrodes. If you ask me he's punishing you."

"Well I'm not asking you. You weren't here when we made this circus and you didn't see what Misha put into it. He taught me everything I know and what's more he brought something fine to it, a professionalism it would never have had otherwise and I'm not the only person here who owes him something, respect if nothing else, and what's between him and me is our business."

Bella touched my shoulder and intervened. "The issue is not why Misha's blowing it but that he is blowing it, and your responsibility should be to the proper functioning of this troupe. He's creating tension and bad feeling. He's not reliable in the ring. He mucked up the racism skit the other night and it's getting dangerous. If he's drunk when he's spotting for you or . . ."

"Bella, I trust him with my life."

"Well, you can do that if you want, but you can't trust our lives to him. You're jeopardizing us because of your concern for his pride." She paused then added, "Think about it."

While we all thought about it, Bella slid her arm around me and I took little Spike in my lap.

"Can't we just carry him for a while?" I pleaded, rubbing my chin into Spike's curls. "If I can keep him off the booze before the shows . . ."

"We've been carrying him for months."

"Well, what then? Fire him? Like a factory worker?"

"Of course not, but he has to stay out of the ring entirely until he's pulled himself together."

"Yes, he can collect the garbage and sell balloons out the front. So good for the morale."

Glumly we all stared into the flames.

"Okay," I said at last, "I'll tell him."

"We'll all go. We care about him, too, you know."

"I think it would be easier if you didn't."

We continued to talk for a while, easing ourselves back into the spirit of camaraderie which held the group together. When no one was paying any attention, I slipped out of the tent.

Misha was still on the bed, partially concealed by a marbling of cigarette smoke. I began to undress, feeling his eyes on me, the demand in them. My muscles were sore from the day's lifting and I resented the fact that I would have to work out early in the morning and Misha would be too hung over to help test the rigging. All I wanted was sleep. I pushed the resentment away by vigorously brushing my teeth, then turned to give him my full attention.

"You know what went on in there."

"*Oui.*"

"So"—I went to him and took one of his warm hands in my frozen ones—"what do you want to do?"

There was no answer and no expression on his face. Then, moving his head on the pillow to stare at the candle, he muttered, "Since how long we have been together?"

"I don't know. Four years, isn't it? Five?"

He allowed a long, significant pause in which he closed his eyes and inhaled deeply on his cigarette. "Do you know in so much time you have never said 'I love you.' "

I retracted my hand impatiently. "Of course I do. I share my whole life with you."

His laugh was a soft, humorless rattle. "Go on, see if you can say, 'Misha, I love you.' "

I felt my face go hot and stood up quickly to hide my confusion. "I won't play that game. It's childish. You know what I feel for you."

"Then make love to me. Now. Give yourself to me just once as if you really wanted me." He gripped my wrist but I flung him off, retreating to the other end of the truck.

"Don't do that to me," I hissed.

When I looked at him, collapsed on the bed like a deflated doll, not caring about the problems he was causing the rest of us and grinning at the ceiling like a halfwit, I wanted to beat him and shout that I was tired of his relentless, cloying weight dragging me down.

"I don't know what you want from me. Everything was fine until that accursed film."

"No it was not."

"Of course it was. What do you mean?"

"I mean . . . I mean," he repeated, leaning forward and chopping the bed with the side of his hand, "that I have always been in love with you and you have never been in love with me. I mean that I want a real life with you, children, a real home. How long we are going to live like this?" He opened his arms and swiveled his head to indicate the poverty of the truck. "What happen in a few years when your body no longer . . ."

But at these words, the temper for which I was infamous and of which I was so ashamed deafened me to anything further he had to say. I grabbed the vodka bottle and flung it outside. Shouting unkind things, I slammed the door and went to sleep at Bella's. When Spike crawled under my blankets at dawn, rousing me from a two-hour sleep, I hugged her delicious little body to mine and wiped the wetness from my eyes with the corner of her flannelette pajamas.

"Shh, don't wake Mummy," I whispered, bundling her up in the blanket. "We're going to play with Misha." I slung her onto my hip, crept into my truck and laid her on one side of him while I snaked my way along the other. He cuddled us close, smiling blearily, then rubbed his morning whiskers first on Spike, who squealed with delight, and then me.

"Mish, I've been thinking."

"*Ah, bon.* You are very clever when you think."

"Maybe I'm not the right person for you but this is the way I am and you and Georgie are the only people in the world I think I'd die for."

"But we like you better alive." He rolled me on top of him and began to remonstrate that it was all his fault but I interrupted him.

"No, wait. You're not happy with the circus any more. You're thirty-five years old. A healthy retirement age. Well then, this money I have, what to do with it? I buy a farm that's what. And you can work it, you know, pluck the chickens and all that, and travel with us whenever you want then there'll always be a place for us to return to. But I don't want to retire yet. I'm in my prime. So we wouldn't spend all our time together, only most of it."

He protested, as I knew he would, but it was half-hearted and I could sense the relief and rising hope in him. When we returned from the tour, an extravagant party was held in his honor during which everyone was suitably emotional. He left the circus to dedicate himself to my welfare full time. He still toured with me occasionally, working on the acts, smiling proprietorially after each performance, keeping a clippings file of reviews and interviews. He gave up drinking and I learned to be kind and to take my rages elsewhere.

I bought a sprawling old house in the mountains but the longest time I could bear to live in it was three weeks. I did try. I made jams. I even plucked chooks. But the domesticity hemmed me in. The idea of sending a root down anywhere made me quiver with claustrophobia. I preferred my truck, strangers' spare bedrooms and my hole in the wall at Georgia's. The word "home" had a funereal ring to it. Gloom, doom, home.

"At last you have a real home," he had said, flourishing the deeds aloft and already immersed in fantasies of house improvement and duck ponds. As I watched him transform, I felt the kind of sorrowing joy a mother must feel as she sees a crippled child take his first steps. Misha dug gardens and exposed roof beams. He was happy.

He suggested marriage, an idea I rejected scornfully. He wanted a child, I did not. I did not want lovers, he did. I accepted because, as he said, I was the only one he really loved. And if I felt a twinge of resentment when I arrived unexpectedly to find a woman there, I soon put it out of my mind because surely I owed him a home after all he'd given up for me. And how could I deny him the companionship of others when I was so seldom there? He was family and he loved me. For that feat of endurance I owed him everything. We were the envy of all our friends. "The heterosexual hope of the world," Georgia once proclaimed, albeit ironically. Yes, the relationship was perfect and I had everything I wanted. Everyone said so.

20
The White Feather

When the butcher bird called a halt to Olly's story, Lucy hoped that it might also summon Laura into the pale, uneasy light of the drawing room. But her aunt did not return. The thought that the white feather might have banished the old ghost forever filled Lucy with grief. For now, although she could not imagine what the feather might divulge, she understood that it was a sign marking out one of those immutable choices which give a life its shape. It signified pain.

That night Lucy woke from a nightmare, ranting as usual, filling Olly with nervous dread. He would not admit it but he missed having the old tartar around. He soothed his raving granddaughter as best he could, by continuing his story.

"Did Sharada/Charlotte dream?" shouted Lucy, interrupting him unexpectedly, and thumping her pillow from which a mephitic odor of sweat and mold flew up. She flashed those disconcerting eyes at his puckered nose and the poised feather, as if daring him to tell her an uncomfortable truth.

"Why, certainly," he said. "As soon as she understood that there was no home for her anywhere on this earth, she dreamed her last dream and decided to die.

"She was setting out along a path certain that her mother would meet her at the other end. The path was through barren country— mountainous and scattered with boulders. A desert of rock, with not a stick of vegetation or a flutter of life anywhere. There were bandits close behind her and she knew she must leave the path, but felt no fear.

"She came to a rapid, or waterfall, which cut its way through bare

222

rock. The water was very muddy, as if the river were in flood. She jumped into the rapid and was carried away from the bandits, thinking, all the time, that she might die. She skimmed along the surface of the water, noticing shards of broken glass sticking out of the banks. At the end of the waterfall, in a still pool, she felt exultant that she had succeeded. Naked, she looked into the pool and saw, with annoyance, that it was pink with blood. Then she saw that a piece of glass had punctured an artery in her leg. It did not hurt, but she could not remember what to do, other than stanch the wound with her hand. But she was a long way from the path, and it was impossible now for her mother or anyone to find her. She was lost and she could not move.

"Soon after this dream, McTavish gathered his sons around Sharada to witness her death. They saw a shrunken woman propped up in bed, black hair falling around a face turned away from all of them. And heard her final words—'Go, go eat air.'

"Sharada was pruned from the family tree, and the tracks of the journey from her origin covered over as if they had never existed. Her stigma was erased, her books burned and her bed reinhabited by a second wife who produced six more McTavishes all inheriting from their father the competitive, jealous streak which would pollute the whole line.

"When Sharada's oldest son returned from Cambridge, he married a well-bred horsey type, a Huntington, who produced Laura, two brothers and five sisters. Most of these sisters, fed on coldness and pride, could not submit to a man and remained virgins."

"How very wise of them," interrupted Lucy sourly, but when she saw the scowl of disapproval on her grandfather's face, and noticed Laura reappearing from the kitchen, as if drawn to Lucy's bitterness like a fly to dung, she smiled inwardly and said no more.

"The two brothers, weakened by the domination of the women, took to drink and dwindled the family fortunes on wild parties and bad business deals. Laura was encouraged to marry a wealthy landowner, but true to her contrary nature, she fell in love with a doctor. Battles raged in the family, which only strengthened her determination. It was during the First World War and the young doctor, being of the liberal persuasion, refused to enlist, saying that it was time Australia resisted British domination. Laura bullied, bribed and blackmailed him. She said that her father's connections would ensure

223

that he would be kept out of battle. Her lover argued that it was a matter of conscience; she countered with a refusal to marry him unless he went to war. The father called him a cowardly blaggard and threatened to disinherit Laura.

"But she did truly love the young doctor, as much as that woman is capable of, and so she devised a plan.

"He was to attend a dinner with the family—an austere and formal affair, at which many pointed references were made to Bolsheviks and the Tsar, to Britain and glory, to moral bravery and physical cowardice. The young doctor remained polite and carefully avoided entering discussions.

"When the main meal was served, he lifted the silver warmer from his plate and the whole company fell silent. There, instead of roast pork, was a single white feather, placed on the dish by Laura herself."

"Stop it," breathed Lucy, for she saw that Laura's fists were pressed into her chest and tears were streaming down her face.

"The young man wiped his lips with the napkin, stood up silently and left. Laura ran after him in a panic but he refused to speak to her. When she heard later that he had indeed joined the army, she was delirious with happiness. He was killed at Passchendaele."

Laura sank down as if all the air in her body had been released with one blow. "I'll never forgive them, never. They could have protected him but they wanted him dead. I took lover after lover to shame them, but my heart had closed up. They gave me Binjigul to get rid of me. And my brother's son. My little black lamb. Your father deserted me like you. You left me here to die alone."

Lucy placed her hands over her ears, her grandfather placed his hands over his mouth, Laura placed her hands over her eyes. And there they remained, tied together by silence, waiting for the butcher bird to cut them free with his call, as sharp as glass.

21
Grounded

The plane droned darkly through a slipstream seven miles above the Timor Sea. I was too tired to sleep and too miserable to concentrate on the letter I was writing. I was flying home from the International Circus Festival in Monte Carlo, where I had just given my final performance, thus concluding an aerial career in order to reside on earth. The Performing Arts Board had offered me a position, respectability, influence and fat paychecks. Yet when I imagined sitting in conferences, fighting with petty bureaucrats, standing on podiums to discuss the direction-of-the-arts-in-this-country, I felt as if I had just missed the web and there was no safety net in sight.

The very success of Circus Caelestis had brought about its demise. Visiting acts were brought in and resentment festered between new groups and old hands. Many members wanted to stick with what was safely successful, sacrificing the spirit of risk and innovation which had been at the heart of our work. Under the pressure of competing visions, the collective had fractured and a hierarchical structure had taken its place. The intimacy and élan of the original circus disappeared. I decided to leave, and keep my memories intact.

And where was Mikhail now that I needed him? Now that I had made one of the most painful decisions of my life largely to please him? When he mentioned, in passing, that he would not accompany me to Monte Carlo, I was so shocked that I had to leave the room.

"But whyever not?" I demanded crossly when I came striding back in. "What's the matter with you?"

He came to sit at my feet, placing his head, lapdog style, on my knees. "You will not admit it, but you are exhausted by the life you lead. And so am I. It's time to rest. And there are things to do on the house so it will be ready for you when you come back."

Put like that, his reasoning was difficult to argue with, but I had, saying that I had no intention of resting as I would have plenty of time for that when I was dead.

"But I want you to come," I said at last. He kissed the top of my head, and muttered something about artistic temperament. I left him digging in the garden. As I watched his back bent over the fork, I understood, with an unpleasant jolt, that I had never really known him. He existed in my mind as a comfortable, background presence. Mikhail the yes-man.

I had not told Georgia I was coming home, wanting to surprise her. I paid the taxi driver, bounded up to the front door and banged. Annie opened it.

"Lucy," she bellowed.

"Annie," I yelled, and we squeezed the breath out of each other, faces stretched to extremity, tears pricking. "God Almighty look at you, you're as beautiful as the day." She had been away during my last visit and when last seen had been a gawky teenager. Now she was a sleek, healthy, glowing young woman. "You're not a policewoman, are you?" I teased.

She thumped me good-naturedly. "That was always a lousy joke. Well I've turned out all right despite the lot of you."

"Yes, you're quite right, it was a lousy joke." We grinned at each other with mutual approval. "Come now, help me with this stuff and tell me everything, I want to know absolutely everything."

Yes, Archie had recovered from the nervous breakdown, was now respectable and selling his paintings for obscene sums. Billy Byrd was working with an Aboriginal Land Council in the Kimberleys. The big burly man from Vietnam was dead—overdose. We did not mention Hydraulic's suicide.

Yes, Annie was still studying, only a year to go. But then she wasn't sure. "Jobs aren't so easy to get these days, we can't afford to muck about as much as you did." I agreed that our lot had been luckier.

"Spoiled," she added.

"Hmm," I said.

"You have to think about the future," she said.

"Must be difficult trying to imagine one," I said. "Thank God I'm not in my twenties now."

"Oh, I don't know," she countered. "It's really just a matter of buckling down and saving some money and getting on with things. Anyway, Wayne is buying some land in the country so when the inevitable happens, we'll have a fighting chance."

I looked at her aghast. "Annie, what are you saying?"

"Please, Lucy, don't start. I get enough of it from Mum. It is inevitable and all the peace marches and disarmament parties aren't going to prevent it."

"This is very cynical stuff," I felt forced to say. "You have to proceed as if it were not inevitable, surely, and try to do something about it."

"Maybe. But as far as I can see you're all bloody neurotic, and you've handed the mess you've made of things on to us. And of course I'm concerned but I'm not going to sit around and whine about it. What changes did all your angst-ridden discussions make?"

"Many, many changes, you don't know what it was like before, you have more opportunities now, as a woman . . ." I checked myself. I did not like the tone in my voice any more than Annie did.

"Anyway, who is this Wayne? Can't you get him to change his name?"

She pursed her lips, studied the wall for a moment and said softly, but with a certain old defiance, "I'm going to marry him."

My tea went down the wrong way. I coughed and spluttered as Annie clapped me on the back.

"God, you're just like Mum," she laughed. "So predictable. You know, I used to sit and listen to you two go on about men, you were hardly even conscious I was there, and I'd think, all men aren't bad, they can't possibly all be bad."

"But surely we didn't say they were all bad, did we?" I said, weakly.

"That was the message. And honestly, I can't see that Mum's any happier with her female lovers than she was with her male ones. I think it nearly killed her when she and Lilly split up."

I wasn't drinking tea so I couldn't splutter. Who the hell was Lilly? Annie went blithely on. "I just don't want to be like that, Lucy. I want to have my feet on the ground. I want to know what's going to happen from one day to the next. I know you all think I'm hopelessly conservative."

"No, Annie," I said, getting up to put my arms around her, "I don't.

227

I think you're normal." I stopped myself before saying, "But do you have to get married?"

"I always admired you, you know. The way you got out and made something of your life. But I don't have your talent or your courage so I just have to do it in my own way." I closed my eyes and was about to say that courage had nothing to do with it, but she went on. "I'm not even terribly bright."

"What nonsense," I said angrily, aware that she was pleased to have got this rise out of me.

"Georgia can't bear it when I say things like that either, but it's true. You see she can't bear the thought of not having a brilliant child."

"Oh, Annie that's unfair." I wanted to tell her that she was narrowing her life simply to punish her mother, but when have such statements ever done any good? Like the rest of us, she would have to learn by her mistakes. I changed the subject.

"If you wanted to travel for a while, I could get you a ticket, and I know plenty of people you could stay with. If you're so sure the world's about to disintegrate, why not go and see it before it does."

"If you're going to throw your money around, I'd rather you put some toward the farm. Anyway, I don't want your money. I can do it on my own." There was the old Annie, struggling along mulishly with her picnic basket. But just as I smiled with recognition, she changed abruptly, becoming friendly and indulgent, light and funny. It was as if, having stated her boundaries, she could afford to relax.

She spoke of her mother with genuine affection and mimicked her perfectly. We roared with conspiratorial laughter and I wondered what it cost her, this about-face forgiveness. She had an inner toughness, a sharp perception of people, and no doubt she would let go of Wayne and move out into the world when she was ready. She had no intention of popping out babies and she was not on heroin. What more could one ask for these days?

As soon as Georgia came home we opened the suitcase of presents, and in the midst of the uproar, Wayne arrived. I restrained myself, and my friend became uncharacteristically decorous. Wayne kissed Annie on the cheek.

"Make us a cup of tea, will you babe," she said. He did. Then she ordered him to get something out of the car. When he came back with it, she smiled at him warmly from where she sat, put her arm around his waist, leaned her head against him and said, "Ta." Georgia and I communicated with our eyes.

"Well, well," said mine.

"Extraordinary isn't it?" said hers.

Annie encouraged him to talk about the farm, interrupting him to elaborate or contradict. She then stood up and said, "Come on, Wayne, let's leave the old boilers to it, they'll be changing the world till dawn." Wayne stood obediently, said goodbye to Georgia respectfully, shook my hand and followed Annie out. When we heard the door bang, we looked at each other and collapsed with laughter.

"She controls him utterly," said Georgia with a look of wonderment. Then her face puckered into lines of worry. "What am I to do? She's going to bury herself away with that lunkhead and I know she's only doing it to take revenge. Oh God, he's so polite." She screwed her face up and clenched her fists in the air. "As if I'm already in the nursing home with my teeth beside the bed."

"But he's kind to her. What more do you want? Besides, maybe she's happy."

"She is happy. But she's happy because she doesn't understand. She says things like 'feminism is irrelevant, women have got what they want now.'" Georgia gave a snort of incredulity. "How did we manage it?"

I took advantage of the pause which followed to scrutinize my friend. She was in her forties, her full-flowered prime, but she looked haggard. Puffy sacks had formed under her eyes and the two frown lines which had given her face its inquiring intensity were now deep furrows, indicating only anxiety. Her hands shook as she broke matches in the ashtray. I folded my arms on the table, rested my head on them and stared at her. She continued fiddling with the matches, and would not look up. "Why didn't you tell me about Lilly?" I asked, leaning back and pouring more tea.

Her eyes slid all over the table like slippery eels, then she opened them wide at me. "I don't know really. You weren't here . . ."

She gave me a long look and behind it I saw an old resentment. I concentrated on the teacup, hurt and surprised at the dissonance between us. One of the unchallenged assumptions in our friendship was that her life was harder than mine. She was tied down, I was free. She was ignored, I was famous. She was a coper, I was irresponsible. I had Mikhail, she had nobody. And I was never around when she needed me. It may all have been true, but I disliked being made to feel guilty.

The excitement of seeing her again was doused by that envious look and a long-buried disquiet began to smolder in its place. Georgia was the still point from which all my journeys radiated, and returned. Without her, without the idea of her, my life would fly into pieces. I thought, with alarm, that maybe this time our paths had diverged too widely for us to be able to comfort each other as we had always done.

"I had a dream about you when Lilly and I broke up. I was outside a large house, at night, looking in through a window. You and Misha were sitting at a long table with friends, all couples, candlelight, lots of luxury. I knocked at the window and you turned to look, but you didn't see me."

"But it's not like that," I burst out, surprising both of us. "It was never like that. Mikhail and I stay together because we never properly fell in love. I risk everything in my work, I've based it on risk, because I wanted my life to be as important as death, but in my private life, my inner life, I'm a fraud, I've risked nothing." I felt a lump rise in my throat and suppressed it.

Georgia blinked at me in astonishment, then reached across, pushed my cheeks into a smile and pulled a sad clown face so that moisture leaked out of my eyes while I giggled.

"Aren't you and Mish getting on?"

"Of course we're getting on and I don't know what's the matter. He's good to me. He's so damn good to me I want to hack his liver out. No, Misha's not the problem, it's me. It's as if I'm waiting for something to happen, as if I've come to a full stop. I run and run, but inside I'm stuck, Georgie. I feel stale and stagnant and I'm terrified by it." This was as much a revelation to me as it was to her. I gave a little ironic laugh. "I'm just no good at intimacy, it's not one of my talents."

We smiled at each other, remembering when I had said those same words to her long ago, when she first made love to a woman.

In the old days, we had sat so often at this very kitchen table wishing we were dykes. How much easier it would make things, we had said. Our most painful experiences had been with men, the sex would undoubtedly be better, why waste our energies training emotional retards, we had said. But when Georgie took the leap, I was secretly scandalized, jealous and confused.

230

A tension had been building between us because she had been spending less time confiding in me and more time cultivating a woman called Joyce whom I did not much like. I came down to breakfast one morning to find Georgie all dressed up.

"You look nice," I said brightly. "Got something special on to-day?"

Ordinarily I might have said, "What have you got all that crud on for? You look like a cake," but that morning something stopped me.

Instead of making some self-deprecating response her eyes dropped expressively and she colored. "Nothing special. Joyce is here by the way." She looked everywhere but at me. My stomach lurched and I almost let go of my cup. I buried myself in the paper and read the headlines without understanding what they said. In the terrible silence, I searched for any words to cover my recognition of the fact that our friendship, once so safely sexless, was no longer so. I cleared my throat.

"What?"

"Nothing."

"Oh, I thought you said something."

"No. No."

They left, but the day was ruined. I could not concentrate on anything. Whenever I thought about Georgia and the unspeakable Joyce I would have to fling open the balcony doors in order to breathe.

The following weeks did nothing to alleviate the tension or to lighten the silences. We began avoiding each other, then, like elastic stretched to its limit, we would twang back and collide with each other, knot ourselves into feverish, animated talk which was undone by the inevitable silences.

Was this the same Georgia who had taught me how to use a contraceptive cap because she was predicting, ahead of time, that the pill was a killer? Who had sat with me in the bathroom and told me not to be so squeamish, and then bumped her head on the gas heater because she laughed so hard when the cap, slippery with jelly, kept shooting all over the room like a greasy little UFO? I wanted that Georgia back, the safe, comradely, mothery one. Not this blushing carnivore.

And all this dressing up like an aging blonde. She looked lovely just as she was, her sleeves rolled up showing those strong brown arms . . . I threw open the balcony doors.

"Enough's enough," Georgia announced when the wrongness between us became unbearable. She was always more courageous than I. "You make me feel predatory," was how she began. Thumping my powder-puff paw, sniffing the air for danger and paralyzed under the spotlight of her gaze, I assured her that I did not think she was predatory.

"Well, good," she said in a starched voice. "I have no intention of playing the seductress so there is simply no reason for you to avoid me like this. God knows it's difficult enough with lesbian women, but you're not only a confirmed heterosexual, you're my closest friend and I would never jeopardize that."

"Exactly," I said, swallowing hard.

We talked for half an hour (oddly the silences did not diminish in length or pregnancy) and agreed that everything was now Cleared Up. We could go Back to Normal. There was no need for me to Feel Threatened. She had even laughed, dismissively, at the idea that we could ever be lovers. Then she patted me on the cheek and left, whistling, for work. "Well, of course," I thought, staring peevishly into the mirror at my crumpled morning face, "why would she find *me* attractive?" But the desire to be thought attractive was obliterated by rage. Who was Georgia to tell me I was so hopelessly heterosexual? And that pat on the cheek. It was more like the biff of a tiger's paw. Did she think I was an idiot that I couldn't pick up conflicting signals? Confirmed het? Too right I was. Lesbianism was a maladjustment. Infantilism. I, on the other hand, had been adjusted just right and I intended to stay that way.

I flew through the day buoyed up by resolution and a sense of injustice, planning exactly what I would say that evening. I cooked dinner, then found myself dressing too carefully—creeping infantilism. I tore off my finery in disgust and went downstairs to wait. Georgia was late.

As I sat fidgeting in the armchair, absentmindedly polishing off the wine and crushing out cigarettes as if they were scorpions, I found that the speech I was preparing kept changing, and rather than confuse myself I took up a book. *Women and Madness.* Chapter 7: Lesbianism. "All women are lesbians except those who don't know it . . . until women see in each other the possibility of a primary commitment which includes sexual love they will be denying themselves the love and value they readily accord to men, thus affirming their second class status."

I slammed the book shut. I paced. I chain-smoked. I didn't go around saying they were sick because they poked around in each other's bodies, did I? I opened a bottle of port.

"They have every right in the world to indulge in whatever perversion they want, as long as they leave me alone," I addressed the walls.

"Who?" said Georgia, standing in the doorway, clutching her briefcase and yawning.

"You, that's who," I barked, pointing a shaky finger at her. "And bloody Joyce whatsername." I brushed past her and stomped upstairs to my room, leaving her temporarily stunned. I flattened myself against the wall. Thump thump on the stairs. Thump thump in my chest. She peeped in the door holding out two glasses of wine.

"Please go away."

"No I won't go away. It's just as confusing for me, you know."

"I don't want to talk about it."

"Oh no, you don't," she said, coming in, "it's too easy for you to run. It's what you've always done when something frightens you. But this is me and I'm not out to get you."

"Oh, aren't you?" I thundered, unable to hold back the solar flare of my anger, which reached out and ignited hers.

"That's right, play victim. Gets you out of every spot, doesn't it."

"I won't listen to this," I said coldly and strode to the door. She blocked it, her face white and her mouth trembling.

"You gutless wonder, you haven't got the courage to admit your jealousy or to stay and sort it out . . ."

The leash snapped on my trapped beast. I flung both glasses across the room.

"Damn you, you think I don't feel the knives you stick in my ribs and the little sugar-coated controlling mechanisms you're so clever at. You turn me into Little Lucy so you can continue being in charge, so let's not kid ourselves that I'm the only one seeking safety around here. 'You're so beautiful and talented,' you say, as if it were a crime, as if it were a personal insult to you."

I stopped, breathless, and grinned, in the same way that a cat will suddenly clean itself in the middle of a fight. Quickly, I gathered up a few things and left the house, muttering as I hurried blindly down the street, "So much for the superior moral quality of female love."

We had patched it up, of course, and remembering the incident now, we leaned back in our chairs guffawing at those past, unrecognizable selves. All the warmth returned and we hugged each other across the table.

"Well at least you can't accuse me of running any more. Now when something frightens me I enter a state of total paralysis."

When the laughter had eased I stood up quickly, postponing any further discussion of my failures in the field of love.

"Anyway, never mind all that. I found some broken capillaries in my thigh the other day and almost had heart failure. Where are the starring roles for aerialists with broken capillaries, I ask you? Look." I hoisted my skirt and displayed my thigh. "See that? What good is my fame going to do me when these little blighters start taking over?"

Georgia frowned at my thigh, opened her glasses case and balanced the specs on the end of her nose. She leaned forward, peering over the top of them at my turned leg, then removed them thoughtfully, like a doctor about to give a professional opinion.

"Horsepucky," she said, moving out from behind the table like a general and raising her skirt. She poked fiercely at a slightly dimpled bottom.

I stood back, gasping. "Are you kidding. Navratilova would kill for a bum like that. What about ... this." I twisted my arm out and showed her the skin crinkling around my elbow. "Beat that," I said smugly.

She took me by the hand and marched me out to the mirror. "Regard," she said as we stared into it. "Wrinkles," she proclaimed.

"What do you call this, then?" I imitated a capuchin monkey.

"I call it a baby's bottom in the shape of a face."

"You do need glasses." We put our arms around each other's shoulders, leaned our heads together and heaved sighs at the mirror.

"At least we've got each other."

"Yeah."

"Let's have some champagne."

22
Enter the Hero

After a week of slumping over the kitchen table with Georgia, sipping tea and unstitching each other's lives, I agreed with some relief to go to another city to join a radio panel discussing the direction-of-the-arts-in-this-country. It would release me, temporarily, from the glut of muddy soul-searching. When I rang Mikhail to tell him I'd be home after it was all over, he wanted to know which hotel I'd be staying in.

"I don't know yet," I lied, "I'll ring you." I so seldom deceived him that as I slowly replaced the receiver I felt as if I'd committed a crime.

I slept in the hotel room for a whole day, so that by the time I arrived at a party held in my honor, all my vitality had returned and my companion of so many years had faded to the background of my consciousness where he belonged.

But the fluttery anticipation I had felt left me as I surveyed the glamorous people—the famous and the not so famous, slyly eyeing each other, poised to crawl or dismiss, craning to see who had come into the room, judging their social value. The gaiety dripped off me, as if I were a wax doll held too close to a fire.

I propped my back against a wall and held my drink in front of me like a shield. For an hour, acquaintances had come to me ready to be entertained, but had left disappointed, driven off by my monosyllabic answers. I swallowed the spritzer in one gulp and escaped to the kitchen where a nebula of people were clustered around someone in the opposite corner. He was tall, thin and conventionally dressed, and he looked as out of place as an eagle among peacocks. Sandy hair had receded like a king tide, leaving behind an expanse of forehead. A beak of nose twisted slightly sideways and a thin line of mouth tipped

235

up at the corners into incongruous dimples. His was not a pretty face, but it was alive with intelligence. The lustrous eyes brimmed with it. He was American and he had ears like Wally.

His audience raised brows at one another, indicating appreciation of a superior wit and at the same time a certain malice, as if they might turn on him the moment he ceased to be funny. I watched him with critical intolerance then understood that what I disliked was seeing my own behavior performed by someone else. Behind the wall of chatter and the eagerness to entertain lay a shy and frightened man. It was as though my sympathy were a tentacle which reached out and touched him, for he looked up, startled, stared straight into my face and paused in the middle of a sentence. Our glances married, there was a flash of pure recognition followed by involuntary smiles. But his audience turned to look at me, catching me in a moment of exposure. I frosted over my smile, hid myself behind my eyes, and turned my attention elsewhere.

From then on, I was conscious of his glance flickering in my direction. When I looked again, he was showing off like a child in a playground saying, "Watch me, watch me." There was something so arrogant in it, and at the same time, ingenuous, that I could not help liking him, just a little.

The wearisome inanities of party talk flowed over me as I edged my way through the kitchen, nodding here, smiling there, loathing everyone and longing to be left alone. On the back stairs, I breathed in the soggy night air gratefully. I could not tell the day, or the month, but somewhere, in the turmoil of the last two years, I had lost my direction, my certitude and my bravery. I remembered, with a kind of anguished longing, that first leap into the void, and all those other moments in my life when I had summoned my courage and felt a quickening of spirit; when a second person inside me stepped in and gave directions, like a guardian angel. But where was she now? And where could I leap? Only when I performed did I escape the seductions of the future and the revulsions of the past. Consequently I had channeled all my passion into my work, leaving no time in which I might mourn whatever it was that was missing from the rest of my life. But *what* was missing?

The door creaked open behind me. An American voice, smooth as warmed honey, said, "I hate parties, too. Can we commiserate?"

My body language was loud and discouraging. Undaunted by my

impatient sigh, he folded his tall frame like a deck chair and lowered himself down—a suitful of bones. "Am I interrupting deep thoughts?" he inquired, after an uneasy silence.

Politeness won over surliness and I granted him an amused, forgiving little sound. "Yes, you are as a matter of fact. But maybe that's a good thing."

"Ah, those sorts of deep thoughts."

We smiled down at our drinks but as I was still irritated by his presence I said no more.

"I saw your film," he began. "You're a very fine actress."

"Oh, please," I said, with more vehemence than I had intended. The anger in my response surprised him and I could sense him changing conversational gears.

"I guess no one lets you forget it."

"No one lets me forget it because what they're responding to is my celebrity not my talent. It's an appalling film, I was awful in it and I hate the whole damn business and, besides that, I am a performer not an actress."

He put down his drink and silently searched my face. When he spoke again, his expression was full of concern. "Yes, I can see how someone like you could be damaged by ... It's made you suspicious . . ." He paused, and then a note of incredulity crept into his voice. "But you *were* good. Don't you know that?"

The cheek of this man, referring to me as "someone like you." He knew nothing whatever about me. But when I looked at him, his face was so warm and kind that my indignation melted.

"If you close everyone out because a few of them want to rub up against your fame, then you close out the good guys as well."

"That's a terribly trite thing to say," I remarked, but without nastiness. He laughed and said that he supposed it was.

"Anyway, your telling me that you're a good guy doesn't necessarily make you a good guy, does it? You followed me out here because you'd seen my face on the screen, not because of the integrity of my soul."

"I followed you out here because I wanted to escape the bimbos in the kitchen." We grinned at each other, then he added, "And because of your singularity."

There was a long silence until both of us said "so" at the same moment.

"So," I said, "who are you?"

"My name's Zac Appelfeld. I'm here for a conference and I go back to New York in two weeks. People tend to think I'm extrovert and overconfident but really I'm Jell-O." He gave me a look which indicated that I might not believe what he was about to reveal.

"And I'm a theoretical physicist."

I didn't believe him. "I see, tell me, then, theoretical physicist, what is the nature of reality?"

"Gee, let's see now." His dimples deepened and he cleared his throat. "Rabelais said, 'Everything is for the best in the best of all possible worlds,' right?" I gave an assenting nod, though in truth I could not remember who had said it. "As a physicist I seek the mathematical meaning of that best of all possible worlds—the one, unique reality in which all nature's mysteries are unraveled, all fundamental numbers are calculable and all interactions unified. And yet this entire picture must be formed within the weird quantum world where deterministic principles succumb to probability, where things that are impossible in the classical world become not only possible but give rise to our very existence." He glanced across at me to see if I were following him so far.

"Go on," I said.

"So reality is only incompletely describable, that is in terms of probabilities and these probabilities are reduced once you make a measurement."

I blinked rapidly at him, imitating a dense but willing student.

"For example," he continued, "you don't know a tree has fallen in the forest until you've witnessed it. In fact there is no reality of any trees falling until you've gone into the forest. Once you observe how many trees have fallen, it's a deterministic reality, but that measurement has reduced the array of further possibilities."

"Ah yes, the old tree-in-the-forest conundrum. In other words the world dwells in a partially real state until an act of observation brings some of it into full existence? The world is real only when looked at?"

His smile broadened. "I wouldn't say that exactly, but there are those who theorize that each act of observation, besides making our world 'more real' as you put it, creates alternative universes alongside our own."

"You mean they are clinically insane."

He laughed. "Well even Einstein said that quantum mechanics

reminded him of the system of delusions of an exceedingly intelligent paranoiac."

"He doubted the ultimate validity of it all his life, didn't he? Couldn't bear to think of God as a gambler. What's that phrase?— 'Subtle is the Lord, but not malicious.' " There was a slight pause until I added, "So you really are a physicist."

"Either that or an exceedingly intelligent paranoiac." He watched me now with a different kind of curiosity and I understood precisely what his silence meant.

"You think circus people can't read, Professor?" I said in my driest, most mocking voice. But he was not in the least disconcerted and only continued to observe me in that discomforting way.

"What a prickly and touchy person you are. I bet everyone's frightened of you." He began to brush my shoulders with his fingertips.

"What are you doing?"

"Getting rid of the chips. It's a wonder you can stand up under the weight of them all." I swiveled away from him and did not smile.

"Okay. I admit when I came out here I wasn't expecting to have a conversation about Einstein. A guy in there asked me what I did and when I told him, he wanted to know if we'd found the sixth dimension yet and if so could he go there."

I scowled at him for a moment longer, then cracked into laughter.

We talked until our bones ached with cramp and cold, peeling away layers of conversation, becoming more and more personal, laughing helplessly at each other's jokes like children, both of us opening up with excitement. We marveled at our uncanny ability to finish each other's sentences. There was something disquieting about it, this entangling of thoughts, as if we had a previous knowledge of each other. And later, when I reviewed the minutiae of that first encounter, I would wonder why I had not been more astounded at the instantaneous familiarity, the easy sympathy of souls.

He described his life and I imagined it all vividly. I saw the intimate disorder of his apartment—papers scattered on the floor, a fireplace, a lovely old green lamp on the desk where he worked, a soft snow falling outside the windows. I was sitting by that fire as he talked, watching him at his desk, as if I had always belonged there.

My heart went out to the little boy who spent years in a basement playing with his ham radio, tyrannized by a psychotic father and adored by a powerless mother. I wondered how much pain lay concealed under the buoyancy and the brilliance, and why the stresses of such a childhood did not create more visible fracturing in the adult.

I found myself thinking, "I can't remember warming to anyone so quickly. But I could never make love to him. No, decidedly not." With that realization came relief, so that when our hands reached out to pick up the wineglass and touched, and both of us pulled them quickly away and went silent I did not know what to make of the sensation that made me gulp like a schoolgirl. He had been sitting very close to me, peering into my face from a few inches away. I moved back a fraction and talked about interesting topics like American foreign policy and why the U.K. was disintegrating.

When we eventually went back inside, only stragglers were left, sagging blearily over armchairs, their finery twisted and creased. The room smelled of stale butts, booze and bitchiness. I was tired and cold. When I turned to look at Zac, the man I saw was a stranger, a fact which the night and his mellifluous voice had concealed. When he insisted on taking me home in a taxi, he was conscious of, even pleased by, the knowing smirks around the room. Of course, men like him needed to be seen with pretty women, in the same way that they needed to have fast cars. The more he fussed over me, the more vexed I became. I did not want to go with him and was angry at myself for my infernal inability to give a simple "no."

We were silent on the drive home, and I could feel him anxiously willing me to acknowledge him. When we stopped he asked urgently if I would show him around the next day.

"I'm seeing a friend," I snapped, with my hand on the door, then thought, "Why are you being so mean? You liked him an hour ago. He doesn't know anyone here and he's lonely. He's only asking to spend a couple of hours with you."

"But maybe in the morning."

As soon as I went into the hotel, I felt on edge. There was something overbearing in his determination. Yes, that was what I did not like, the assumption in it. "My God," I thought, "I'm being pursued by this brain on stilts. He'll try to maneuver his way into my body tomorrow and I'll have to fend him off." I resolved to ring him in the morning to cancel our date.

He arrived at seven a.m.

"Did I wake you? I've been awake all night. I thought it was late. I'm sorry. Really." But the look on his face was not apologetic, it was

240

gleeful and guileless. He dripped water on the carpet and shivered. What could I do but laugh with him, march him into the bathroom and insist that he take a hot shower. Sheets of rain doused the windows while I made coffee and listened to him sing off key. Who was this person? I handed a blanket through the door, draped his clothes on the heating and wondered what could possibly have made me feel anxious about him the night before—even his underpants were those of a touchingly harmless man.

When he came out swaddled and steaming, the cozy familiarity returned. The white noise of rain and the dull gray light from the streaming windows cocooned us in the hotel room just as the darkened porch had done the night before. We were so engrossed in each other that when breakfast was brought in I jumped up as if caught stealing. Zac scurried around looking for a tip but could not get his arm out of the blanket without risking exposure. At last he managed to wave a dollar bill at the waiter, who had turned away, saving Zac from the shadow of a smirk. I felt myself blush for the first time in a decade. I wanted to dissociate myself from him, and at the same time, protect him.

It caused me acute discomfort, this ambivalence. Annoyed one minute, captivated the next. His intensity made me nervous, as if he were constantly stepping across some invisible barricade. In order to regain control, I would go cold and retreat. But his absolute attention to me did not waver.

"Why do you keep disappearing?"

"Do I? I'm sorry. I'm not really conscious of it."

"You can disappear if you want. But I'd kinda like to know where you go."

"It's not a very interesting place," I said, laughing it off. But he continued to look straight into my eyes in a way that was both challenging and gentle.

"All right," I thought, "I have to take risks in my private life, why not with him. He's leaving in two weeks and I wouldn't care if I never saw him again."

"It's just that I'm rather confused by the . . . by the . . ." I could not say, "by the way you make me feel exposed."

"By the attraction?" said Zac, eagerly.

"Oh dear," I thought, "he thinks I'm attracted to him. How funny."

"Yes, kind of." I looked for the light of victory in his eyes which would allow me to despise him, but there was none. "I like you," I said, smiling.

"Good. You got taste."

"So," I said, jumping up and rubbing my hands together, "what do you want to see?"

"I don't wanna see rain. We got rain in New York."

"Well, I don't know. Have you been to the gallery?"

"We got them in New York, too."

"All right," I said, laughing, "what do you want to do?"

He considered for a moment. "We could . . . celebrate liking each other over champagne."

"Hey, I know what you haven't got in New York. I'm going to take you out bush."

"Out bush? You mean snakes and green stuff?"

"You'll love it. Trust me."

"It's raining." There was a hint of desperation in his voice.

"It's stopped raining."

"Out bush, huh." He did not sound convinced.

By the time we reached the forest, all my nervousness had eased. This was where I belonged and I showed it to him as if I were displaying priceless jewels. Above all, I wanted him to see it as I saw it, to feel what I felt.

"Look," I said, diving into undergrowth. "Flannel flowers." But Zac was not looking at the flannel flowers, he was looking at me and there was a peculiar little smile on his face, the kind of smile one reserves for a favorite child, and it made me turn away from him quickly and bite my lip. To cover up the quivery feeling, I showed off abominably by climbing a tree, walking along a narrow branch and somersaulting to the ground.

Later, we sat by a pool. Ordinarily, I would have ripped off my clothes and swum but, as I already felt naked, I merely dangled my feet in the water and tried to think of something to say. His interest in me was like a physical contact, like hands dropping lightly onto my shoulders, and the way he stared at me, as if the words I spoke were only of secondary importance to what lay hidden behind them, threatened my carefully reinforced defenses.

"Your face keeps changing, you know that? Sometimes it's almost

242

ugly. Only the truly beautiful can do that." I looked away from him and did not comment.

"Sunny one minute, turbulent the next. You're a very complex person."

"So they tell me." I laughed nervously and again there was a silence.

"Why are you so sad?" The question was so unexpected and the solicitude in his voice so disarming that I could only stare at him, fighting down inexplicable tears. His hand was lying near mine and the urge to hold it was, I knew, as great as his to grip mine. But we did not touch.

"The most vulnerable people always have the best acts."

"Yes," I said quietly, and got up to leave.

That night I had dinner with Hiro, a theater director whose real talent lay in the field of gossip. Over the brandy, he said, "And who was that American you seduced last night?"

"He drove me home from a party, Hiro. Hardly seduction."

He pursed his lips and blinked coyly. "Well it's all over town. And I must say, darling, he doesn't really look like your type. Still opposites attract, eh?"

I almost struck him, but realized that if I were to show anger, it would only feed the rumors. When I returned to the hotel, I lay down to sleep but was soon back on my feet. I walked the hotel room all night, going over every phrase Zac had spoken. "Did he really say that? What did he mean when he said that? Why did I tell him that? I've never told anybody that. I do like his jokes. And what a pleasure it is not to have to slow my pace. He understands everything I say instantly, sometimes before I've said it. When we talk it's like being in a race we're both winning. But he is most definitely not my type and I'm not remotely physically attracted to him so . . . why am I pacing the floor of this bloody hotel room at three in the morning? Maybe he won't ring tomorrow. Good, that would solve everything." But the thought that he might not ring in the morning did not feel good at all. When the phone rang at eight a.m. I pounced on it and said, "You're late."

He arrived at twenty past eight and this time demanded champagne with breakfast.

"Why not," I said and thought, "Ordinarily this would be a ploy to get me into bed, but he's not so crass. I like champagne and I like him and if he does make a lunge for me, I shall smile kindly and say no."

243

My room was high up and as I looked out over the city, I felt a sudden elation. No one in the world knew I was locked in this tower. I was completely secure and completely free in my anonymity. I held the gently sizzling glass up to my ear, then rolled its coldness on my cheek.

I don't know how it happened. One minute we were racing along in a delightful matching of wits, the next, fingers touched, words stopped and we were both staring down helplessly at two entwined hands.

In some ways it felt quite natural, as if we had been married for twenty years, but the event was also detached from reality. The real me was observing, with wry amusement, my shadow self being led so meekly to the inevitable.

"Do what you like," said the observer. "It will be good for you, a little change. He's leaving soon. No one will know."

Waves, however, did not crash into cliffs. The camera did not cut to erupting volcanoes.

"Oh, what a mistake," I thought. I was used to Mikhail's physical beauty and sexual confidence. Zac possessed neither.

"You do not care a fig for him," said the observer, "therefore take charge, leap in the deep end. You will never have to see him again."

I abandoned myself to the experiment.

With Misha, I had always felt myself to be the accompaniment to his solo. A flawless solo, admittedly, but not mine. Now I sang my own song, Zac's lascivious whispering acting as counterpoint. Finally, I rolled on my stomach and as I came, the keening in my left ear went softer and higher. "Now," I thought, as the last sighs, moans and shudders floated and sank, "I must rise up out of this well of pure pleasure and face his look of fear and contempt. Just as well I don't care a fig for him."

But when I rolled back and took him in my slippery arms, I was not protected against the power of that most erogenous zone of all, the eyes. What I saw, in the watery, softened orbs of Zac, was neither fear nor contempt, it was something I had never seen before—my own beauty.

Waves crashed onto cliffs, the camera cut to erupting volcanoes and I drowned in the deep end of Zac Appelfeld without a second thought. "This time I'm really going," I said, hours later, outside the door. But we were so drunk with the success of our lovemaking that we found ourselves back inside, clutching, laughing and eventually falling on the bed.

At last we managed to disengage. I swung down the busy street with the dazed look of a born-again Christian. People looked infinitely beautiful to me. I wanted to know and love them all. My own body felt voluptuous. It was milky and smooth, soft, warm and lovable. The soft cotton of my shirt stirred as I walked, caressing skin. My body had emerged, all velvety and new, from another broken cocoon.

23
Out of My Country and Myself I Go

I sat amidst the ruins of the hotel bed, staring at my hand poised above the phone. It drew back, reached out again, and refused to lift the receiver. Kicking the sheet away, I marched into the bathroom muttering, "He's always having affairs. Anyway it's your house, bought with your money." But the distracted-looking woman in the mirror did not seem convinced. I left her and went to inspect the refrigerator. One of the few compensations for no longer being an aerialist was that I could drink as much alcohol as I liked. Swilling down a miniature bottle of gin, I quickly picked up the phone and dialed.

"*Allo.*"

"Misha, I'm having an affair."

Long-distance static crackled into my ear. I saw him subside into the old, overstuffed armchair beside the phone and watched the tiny motions of his face—a wince, some rapid blinking then that infuriating mildness descending like a fog. I saw his eyes drop to his left hand fiddling with the frayed tapestry of the chair. I felt the warmth of the fire in its grate and smelled the tart, invigorating air of the mountains. I was no longer myself, I was Misha, sitting in an armchair, feeling panic.

"Mikhail, don't panic. He's going to be gone in ten days. Why don't you say something?"

"I'm not panicking."

"Good. Because there's absolutely nothing to panic about."

"You are the one who is panicking."

"I'm not panicking. I just wanted you to know, that's all."

He seemed to be having a conversation with himself. Eventually he let me hear some of it.

"You are having an affair. I have had affairs. Fair's fair." He sniggered at his own joke, and assured me he was not too upset.

I told him a little about Zac, being careful to leave out anything which might upset him.

"A physicist? With big ears? Sounds wonderful. And does he make love with great, ah, intellect?"

The conversation lingered briefly on the subject of love, moved on to trust, dwelt for a moment on how long I wanted him to stay at Georgia's so Max Applesmell and I could have the house to ourselves, and finally settled on Black Orpington chooks and exposed roof beams. When I hung up the phone, I sat hunched on the edge of the bed, biting my nails and wondering which of the three of us I had just betrayed.

It was the beginning of August, and the eastern side of the country was threatening to tip into the sea under a deluge of unseasonal rains. Rivers broke their banks and on the TV news, flocks of upside-down sheep floated past families waving from the roofs of their houses. Zac thought Australia a very strange country.

"You do have central heating up there in the hills. I mean everyone in the developed world has central heating, right?"

"Er . . . nope." Smiling broadly, I took one of his hands and inspected the buttermilk palm. "You'll have to chop wood, I'm afraid. But don't worry, everything else is terribly up to date. The dunny is a double seater and the red-backs are so friendly they pat you on the bottom when you sit down." Zac made frightened animal noises in the back of his throat.

"And you'll have to feed the chickens."

His hand lifted to his heart and his mouth opened. "I've never even *seen* a live chicken. Do they bite?"

"Only when they're angry but, hey, just let them take one piece of your flesh and they're as good as plucked."

The house wore a tattered coat of mist and drizzle, and looked more slovenly than usual. "Her looks have faded," I said, "but inside she's still lovely." We struggled up the pathway, slipping in the mud and giggling at each other, until Mikhail's two geese came charging out of the rhododendrons, hissing at Zac who dropped his suitcase and sprinted to the front door.

"Killer chickens," he said as he bolted the door and leaned against it. "And I thought you were exaggerating." But my convulsive laughter petered out into an awkward smile as I watched him slowly survey the large room we had entered.

One wall offered a stupendous view of the valley, but Zac was not interested in the view. He was interested in the other three walls which were covered by posters of Circus Caelestis, and photographs of Misha and me. The largest of these showed an intimate moment captured from the life of the Perfect Couple. My face opened joyously to the camera, I clutched an object to my chest, and Misha, his eyes shining with love and pride, was kissing my cheek. Underneath was a caption written in his hand. "*Ma Princess Eloignée.*"

"A temple to Louise," murmured Zac, as though to himself.

"It's really Mikhail who keeps all this junk," I said, as dismissively as I could. "Funny, isn't it. I've never really noticed it before."

He continued studying the image, and a critical note broke into his voice. "He's very good looking. In a generic sort of way."

Now he went to the lintel above the fireplace, picked up the object shown in the photo, and raised his brows at me questioningly.

"It's an award I got. Prix de la Dame du Cirque..." The ugly bronze horse was one of the few things I felt truly proud of, representing the acknowledgment by my peers of so much hard work and dedication, but now, seeing it in Zac's soft elegant hands, it seemed absurd and trivial. I followed him silently as he drifted through the rooms. I wanted the inspection to stop, because it was an assessment of my life with Mikhail. When it did, at last, stop, he stood staring out at the valley in sullen silence for a full minute until he said, "I hate him."

I laughed at first, but stopped when I saw the look on Zac's face. "You'd like him if you met him. Everyone likes him."

"I hate him and he hates me. You say he's not faithful to you?"

"Not sexually faithful, but then I've never asked him to be." He gave the photo one last contemptuous glance and turned his back on me.

"Well, I'm hardly being faithful to him," I burst out. But the man who turned to face me was not Zac. A ripple of malice passed across his face, then his lips set, the features tightened and his expression turned stony and punishing. It was as if he had disappeared inside a fortress and was arming himself against attack.

There was the child in the basement, protecting himself from abuse, angry, frightened and alone. In an attempt at palliation, I softened my voice and gingerly took hold of his little finger.

"It's against the rules for the lover to be jealous of the husband." But the gesture had the same effect as opening a jack-in-the-box.

"He's not your husband . . ." Choking back the end of the sentence, he stared at me, his cheeks quivering with emotion. I made myself not-think, not-hear, not-see, and went to boil the kettle.

Five minutes later I felt his hand rest lightly on the back of my neck. I turned and a little perplexed look passed between us, slowly dissolving into a smile that obliterated the drowned world outside and swept Misha's presence out of the house.

The gray, watery days washed around our ark. We saw no one, rang no one and wanted nothing but each other. All my previous lovers, and the warm, lusty lovemaking with Mikhail, counted for nothing. I had never experienced anything like this swallowing of my soul. Each night with him took me deeper into a syrupy, enervating swamp from which I would struggle to rise at daybreak, only to sink back into sensual ooze. Little by little I was losing myself in him and as the days passed, the fear of annihilation began to demand expression.

But my need to be alone, to reestablish my own boundaries, seemed to cause him physical pain. Consequently, I would sneak away to dash blindly beneath gaunt, bedraggled trees, until the pull of his intensity slackened and he seemed almost ordinary in my mind. How could I open my whole self to him, take him inside me like some long-lost, long longed-for part of myself, then, a few hours later, have to resist an urge to push him roughly away? When I returned, I would see the stricken look on his face and hate myself for my fickleness, but no amount of self-persuasion could control the swings.

One morning I watched as he crawled around on the floor of the darkened room, picking up coins which had dropped out of my handbag or my clothes. He looked so vulnerable and ridiculous with his naked bottom stuck in the air. He was making little exclamations of surprise and pleasure. Eventually, he crawled over to me with the change in his palm, counted out the money exactly and said, "Look, I've found two dollars and forty-two cents on the floor." There was Laura, stingily fingering her coin purse. He held his face up to me, and a sick feeling rolled up my legs and lodged in my stomach. How could he be so trusting? How could he leave himself so defenseless before another? I turned my face to the wall, to protect him from what he would read there. He crept up onto the bed.

"What's the matter?"

"Nothing." But I found myself thinking, "Thank God you're leaving soon, you're drowning me." Then he touched me, cautiously, took my hand and pressed the palm to his own. They matched. I looked into his face and thought, "How is it possible that I can love, so deeply, this man I hardly know?" I looked at the mouth, the nose, the fragile skin around the eyes, and could not imagine how I had not, at first, been in love with each of these things or seen how beautiful they were.

I placed my head in the hollow of his chest, kissed his toes, rubbed my cheek along the curve of his buttocks. We smothered each other in love, and in that fog of abandonment, I dimly became aware that Zac was slapping me.

Afterwards we curled into each other and slept, tangled together like two snakes, and I did not have to think about what had happened because the womblike security canceled out the violence that had gone before.

I woke with a start, to a feeling that I was in danger. Zac's luminous eyes were a few inches from my own. He was staring intently into my face. I thought, briefly, that I must get up quickly and scurry away into the dark. But he clutched at me, as if he could read my thoughts, as if he, too, was drowning. Something heaved in my chest. Tears came. He placed his hands over my face and whispered the three fatal words. Abracadabra. Open Sesame. "I love you."

The day before he was due to leave, Georgia paid us a visit. This had seemed a good idea when I'd arranged it a week before. Now my anxiety at having to fit these antithetical pieces of my life together manifested itself in obsessive cooking. Not one, but two chickens went under the axe. From a cornucopian oven spilled scalloped potatoes, spinach loaves, butterscotch pies, vanilla soufflés. Heavenly Hash Candies lay heaped on the benches. Predictably, no one was hungry. Zac did far too much nervous babbling, Georgia observed him with green, judgmental eyes, I hid in the kitchen clutching my stomach. For the first time in my life, I felt her presence as an intrusion.

After lunch, I escaped with Zac into the garden.

"Isn't she wonderful?" I said, nestling up close to him.

He smiled down at the soggy grass and said nothing.

"Well?"

He chuckled softly and squeezed my hand. "It's very endearing the way you turn your friends into giants. She's a very nice woman."

"Nice? Georgia?" I could only stand gaping at him.

His face took on a more serious expression. "It never ceases to amaze me that you don't perceive your own specialness. There are countless Georgias in the world, but there is no one like you." There it was again, the sensation of precariousness he could elicit, as if my center of gravity had shifted slightly. His faint praise had just damned my closest friend yet I restrained myself from commenting. He was staring moodily at the limestone cliffs tumbling into the abyss, pondering some precariousness of his own.

"Zac."

He seemed to be returning from far away. "I was just picturing you prowling around New York like a caged panther. How you'd hate it."

"Nonsense," I said, before the implication of his words had sunk in. "I love big cities."

He turned to face me with anxious eyes. I drew in my breath quickly, muttered something about the oven and scurried into the house. We drank our coffee in an atmosphere as glutinous as the butterscotch pie. Georgia began to make polite leaving noises.

"You only just got here," I protested but in my eyes she read, "Yes. Go. Quickly. Now." I walked her to the car, my heart banging wildly against my ribs. I opened the door for her, and watched her settle behind the wheel. She turned the ignition, peeped at me from over the top of her spectacles and said, "I'd watch that heart of yours if I were you."

On my way into the house I picked up some logs from the woodpile. Zac was sitting in the overstuffed armchair, his fingertips pressed together in front of his face. I busied myself with the fire.

"Louise, I love you."

I brushed tetchily at the front of my sweater. "Damn cobwebs."

"I want you to come back with me."

"The wood's so wet I'll never get this thing going."

"We worried about each other before we met."

"Shouldn't have let the coals die down."

On the morning of the last day he said, "Remember you told me about that crazy bird of yours, Darling, how she would let you take

251

her whole head in your hand and you said she was a fool for trusting you because you could have twisted her head off with your thumb? But she wasn't a fool because she knew you would never hurt her. She was wise enough to trust."

As he was packing to leave he said, "Something like this only happens once in a lifetime, if at all. It's a crime to throw away such a thing."

As he was getting into the truck, there were tears in his eyes as he said, "Did it all mean so little to you?"

When he took one last look at me before going through passport control, his face was expressionless. In the curious stillness of my mind there was only one thought—"Thank God you're leaving. You're drowning me. I have to reach dry land." All the way back to Georgia's I was conscious of a faint queasiness, and of my hands gripping the wheel too tightly. Georgia let me sob for five minutes before asking me what was wrong.

In the week that followed the spasms of desire were so painful they took my breath away and the oscillations between euphoria and despair became wilder and wider with each passing day. I had thought I could control the whole event, lock it safely away as soon as he left, but neither Georgia nor Mikhail could assuage the loneliness and longing he had left behind. Not a minute would pass in which I forgot to miss his infinitely precious face, his bones, the hollow in his chest, his laughter, the warmth of his voice.

"I dreamed him up, Georgie."

"Yes."

"I'd been preparing myself for a grand passion, and when I was ripe, he appeared. It could have been anybody. But I wasn't expecting this aftermath."

"No."

"It was only as passionate as it was because I knew he was going. I couldn't sustain intensity like that. I stay with Mikhail precisely because he gives me plenty of room. I don't even remember my mother, but now I'm dreaming about her all the time. Why this *ache*?"

Georgia released a stream of air through her nose.

"You know, I watched you two in the garden, strolling along, immersed in each other. You were like two lost waifs. And I thought, 'If he stays they would have to learn how to mother each other.' " I did not understand what she was getting at, but when I pressed her she seemed to have changed her mind about something. "Listen," she said, "you did the right thing and once the pangs wear off, which they will, believe me, you'll come out of this a new person. You'll have felt all that passion without having to pay too high a price."

"But *when?*" We both laughed and I blew my nose.

On the tenth day of torment, a letter arrived from Zac. I read it, threw it in the bin, retrieved it, and reread it a hundred times. He had included a fragment of a poem.

> "But one man loved the pilgrim soul in you,
> And loved the sorrows of your changing face."

That night I got very drunk. I made a phone call which I instantly regretted. I left a message on Zac's answering machine saying, "It's Louise. If you still . . ." before slamming the receiver down.

My conversation with Georgia the next day was interrupted by Mikhail coming down to breakfast. He saw that I had been crying and gave me a hug. "*Tu n'as pas l'air bien,*" he said and I noticed a glance pass between them. I got up to make him some eggs. I had been inundating him with kindness to make up for the coldness of my response to him.

I had tried to explain it to myself as I lay night after night rigid as a bone beside him, unable to sleep, my stomach churning, praying that he would not try to touch me, telling myself that what had been unleashed with Zac would eventually be transferred to Mikhail.

So far the attempts at transference had only acted like aversion therapy. Mikhail would move away, patient, and I would beg forgiveness, ask for time. I told him cautiously that perhaps I really had fallen in love with Zac, but he had looked at me with his kind brown eyes, smiled and shaken his head.

"What are we to do with you? You take these things too seriously." He intimated that I must learn to have affairs lightly, as Zac obviously did, as he himself did. He said he did not mind that I was going through a sexual withdrawal. He would wait; he loved me. I could not admit to him what I was too afraid to admit to myself—it was not the sex that connected me so deeply to Zac, but rather the depth of connection to him, the improbable, fatalistic matching was what had made the sex so all-consuming. I was in love with the soul of Zac Appelfeld and no other soul would do.

Mikhail wolfed down his eggs. Faintly I could hear Georgia teasing him while I daydreamed of a darkened room, of hands spread over my face. I heard the doorbell. I heard Georgia come back saying there was a telegram for me. I knew what it would say and that I was about to hurt Mikhail as I had never done before. Everything was very still and calm. I opened the envelope. The message said, "Marry me."

The paper fluttered to the floor. Mikhail picked it up. The furniture looked distorted and I thought, "I must transfer the deeds to him before I go." Mikhail stopped chuckling. He was staring at my face.

"You can't," he whispered. Georgia was reading. She glanced at Mikhail and reached out to him tentatively before leaving the room.

Mikhail wept. He smashed things. He left for his home in the mountains. At last I had made him angry. When Georgia returned I was still sitting at the table, immobile.

She said, "Lucy, you mustn't do this, it's too crazy."

"I am doing it."

"You play a game with your life in your work, but to do the same thing with your . . . You're giving up everything . . ."

"I'm gaining the one thing that matters."

She told me an Aboriginal myth about the origins of marriage. A man sees a woman and wants her. He dresses himself up in beautiful rainbows and she loves him. But she loves her country—her identity and independence—more, and will not go with him. The man spears her through the leg, crippling her, and carries her back to his country. I distanced myself from Georgia then, thinking her a very bitter woman.

She said, "You've known him two weeks."

"I've known him all my life."

A few days later she drove me to the airport. I held her for a long moment. "Promise me you'll always be here."

"I'll always be here."

I was on my way to Zachary Samuel Appelfeld, whose being towered over other beings like a cathedral over slums, whose faint, peppery odor could make me dizzy with wanting when I buried my trusting nose in his armpit, whose whispered wickednesses could make me slither with craving, whose life would interpenetrate my own, whose love was the destruction of solitude, who was, at last, the One, who knew me, saw me, opened me throat to pelvis, and saw that my flummery was good and who, all those decades ago in Binjigul, had knelt before me while I sat on the toilet, taken my child's hand in his and begged me to marry him.

Zac. My lover, my life, my home.

24
Eros and Thanatos

A dismal melancholy had descended on the residents of Binjigul homestead, and a burden of mist obscured Mount Misery from view as if a giant's cauldron were steaming away on its peak. Lucy was the first to rise. She stood in front of her great aunt, touched her shyly on the shoulder and asked the old lady to forgive her. But Laura flinched away scowling and Lucy, instead of tripping outside as she usually did at this hour, flounced up to the attic, muttering rudely about the virulent diseases which afflicted her family tree, particularly two dead branches of it.

When she had gone, Laura turned her glaring attention to the old Jew as if plundering inside her head for some words of animosity she could unleash against him, but they seemed to have been washed out with her tears. He drew his neck down into his collar and beat a timely retreat to the kitchen, leaving Laura to grumble to herself that tears weakened a woman and so did love and if she had not loved this impossible child who was, typically, sulking in the attic, she would not have been lonely in death.

Olly was wishing that he'd never mentioned the wretched white feather and thinking that if only these two women weren't so contrary they would see that he was upset and miserable and would do something to make it easier for him to say he was sorry. Women were meant to be good at that sort of thing. A man was not immune to a woman's tears after all, even the tears of a dried-up old spinster like Laura. He sat at the long table in crotchety silence, occasionally taking out his bad temper on the blowies he clouted with a rolled-up seed catalog, but which continued to buzz unconcernedly, as if to say,

"You are an impotent old ghost incapable of hurting a fly." He spat out the word "impotent" several times, like poisonous pips.

Perhaps these two might have remained fixed in their misery forever, had an infernal wailing and banging not erupted from the top of the house, as if Beelzebub himself had landed on the roof to escort them both to hell. They almost collided at the foot of the attic stairs, but both reeled back like sprinters on the edge of a cliff. "After you," said Olly, adjusting his waistcoat with trembling fingers and making sure that the crisp handkerchief in his pocket was arranged correctly. Laura lifted her nose, gave him a withering look and swept up the stairs. They hesitated outside the door, then stooped to the keyhole.

"Come in, come in," cried Lucy, flinging open the door, causing Laura to clutch at her heart and Olly to let out an odd little gurgling noise.

Lucy was in the full bloom of lunacy. She had draped herself with a glittering black gown over which she had thrown a cape lined in flaming satin. On her head was a feather fascinator, set at a jaunty angle, its net dangling over one eye. Truly she looked like a witch, with her mad black hair and her furious eyebrow. She was holding a rake and laughing malignantly. With the grandiloquent gesture of a queen she beckoned them to her before falling back into a chair, causing puffs of dust to fly up from the stuffing.

"Sit," she shrieked, thumping the floor with her rake.

The imperious command affected Laura like an extra turn on an overwound clock. "Ho," she bellowed, "wicked, monstrous child. You summon me here but where were you when I was dying? Where were you when those crows of relatives came, picking over my things, insulting me, drinking my sherry? But I paid them all back. And you. And you."

"Why yes, you did," said Lucy, frowning a little and putting her fingers to her lips as if discovering the answer to some perplexing question. "Yes indeed. You, a self-professed atheist leaving everything to the church. A clear enough message from the dead. But it did not hurt me. It confirmed what I already knew—that you hated me." Lucy cocked her head to one side and studied her aunt, whose chin began to quiver in a most pitiful way. Two big tears rolled along the deep furrows beside her nose and she sank down onto a sack of barley straw. Olly snapped the handkerchief from his pocket and gallantly passed it to the old lady who blew her nose vigorously into it and

handed it back. Taking it between thumb and finger as if it were a dead rat, he dropped it surreptitiously to the floor beside him.

"Love," mused Lucy, and there was a faraway smile on her face. "I've known love." She nodded her head at nothing particular, then as if she were returning from a great distance, brought her attention back to the ghosts.

"It's true that when you died, Laura, I did not grieve. I simply went on believing that you were still here, snoozing in your squatter's chair, waiting for the prodigal niece to return. That is how I thought of you when you were alive, and I continued to think of you that way when you were dead. In other words, you died for me long before your physical death and if I grieved for the loss of you it was when I left Binjigul as a child."

Lucy's words trailed away and she began rocking slowly from side to side, staring vacantly at the jungle pressing against the attic window. She detached the fascinator from her hair and placed it tenderly in her lap, smoothing it down as if it were a damaged hen. A look of utter fatigue came over her.

"But when my darling died . . ."

Suddenly, she bounded out of her throne, raised a finger to her lips as if she were about to reveal a vitally important, possibly even dangerous secret, turned her head around then, satisfied that they were alone in the attic, whispered, "Don't let anyone tell you there's no such thing as perfect love."

The stare she fixed on her ancestors was so intense that Olly's mouth fell open and his neck disappeared inside his collar. Laura eyed the black fascinator which her niece was now plucking viciously.

"He haunts me," continued Lucy, ripping out feathers and flinging them on the floor. "He is there wherever I turn, whatever I do, and all I know is that he's gone and what happened cannot have happened."

The ghosts cast a sidelong glance at each other.

"You see," she went on, pacing back and forth in front of them, "we were more than, better than ourselves when we were together."

"True love," said Olly, nodding his head sagely and managing to indicate that he was the only other person in the attic who possessed an intimate knowledge of that precious commodity. Laura muttered "Silly old fool" under her breath and tried not to look at the almost denuded hat.

The attic creaked with heat but Lucy shivered a little—the skin along her arms puckering into gooseflesh which she rubbed vigorously away. She stared at the window for a while then settled herself in her chair.

"Please note," she announced at last, "that you are a captive audience and I will thank you not to interrupt my story with your fatuous and utterly irrelevant comments."

The whole house settled into a listening silence and an eerie quiet fell over the forest surrounding it. The only sound was the ticking of the wall clock, like a finger tapping at the door. When she was quite sure that she had her ancestors' absolute if grudging attention, Lucy drew a long, theatrical breath, and began.

"My heart was beating so hard I could barely breathe. I came through the doors and there he was, and I have to say it was something of a shock. His ears seemed larger than I remembered and his nose twistier." She smiled to herself. "But his eyes were the same, those eyes I had loved all my life. When we embraced and I looked back to his face, the ears had shrunk down to proper size and his nose was just right. We couldn't let go of each other." She wrapped her arms around herself, her face alight with the trusting happiness of a child. . . . The driver watched the two lovers in the back of his taxi as it swooped across the Triborough Bridge toward Manhattan. The man, gesticulating toward the skyline with one arm, holding her to him with the other, as if he wanted to isolate her from everyone except himself, shield her from the world which flashed past them as unreal and harmless as a movie. The woman, fitting snugly inside that protecting arm, casting small joyful glances up at him, or exclaiming over some sight he pointed out. And in the eyes of the taxi driver was the curious mix of envy, irritability and hope that people in love evoke in the embittered and lonely . . .

But here Lucy paused and the light seemed to drain out of her. "I'd imagined it so often. I had lived in it, I knew every inch of it, so that when he opened the door . . ." Her nose wrinkled involuntarily as she described the inexorably modern loft, white, polished and bleak, and a painting, complete with broken plates, sullying one of the walls. "It had no . . . soul," she went on. "But what really mattered was that there were no nooks where I might secrete myself away. The one bedroom was enclosed only by bookshelves and even the books looked desolate." She lifted her restless blue eyes to them again. "There was no place for me in it."

As Lucy seemed to require a response, Laura, after a pause, said, "Sounds perfectly odious."

"Oh, why do you always misunderstand?" Lucy glowered at her aunt and tried to explain. "I had doubted many things in the previous weeks, but never that I knew Zac as well as my own self. I had risked everything on that belief. I had just exploded bombs under the rest of my life. I had no other life. And now this barren, loveless place . . . He was suddenly a stranger to me, and it was as if the floor had disappeared from under my feet.

"Oh, it was mean of me, mean," she went on, ripping the ticking from the now bald fascinator. "I tried to say how wonderful it was but he could see through my pretenses. I'll never forget the expression on his face then. Wounded, then wooden and cold. I have never known anyone as touchy, or as tender, or as easily hurt as Zac."

Laura shuffled in her chair impatiently, showing that she already disapproved of Lucy's choice of a husband but her niece pretended not to notice.

"There was the frightened child again, cowering inside his fortress, trusting nobody, not even me. And as soon as I recognized it, all my disappointment vanished. I began to imagine what I could do with the place—Turkish rugs, lovely old lamps, comfortable chairs. How lucky he was that I had come into his life because I would loosen him up and open him out and he wouldn't have to live in that ice palace any more . . ."

"And wipe his bottom, I suppose," grumbled Laura, unable to restrain herself any longer. But receiving such a threatening glare from Olly, and no response at all from Lucy, she clamped her lips shut and folded her arms as if she were being interrogated and had decided not to say another word.

"I noticed a green door behind the kitchen. I should have paid more attention to the fact that his lips had disappeared again, but we had just been dancing around the kitchen together and he'd been singing out of tune and kissing me, so I bullied the keys from him and unlocked the door to his den . . ."

Much to the ghosts' surprise, Lucy suddenly hid her face behind her arms as if a specter had risen up before her, and Olly, overcoming what was obviously a deep revulsion, stroked her matted hair. She took deep breaths to steady herself. After two or three swallows she had regained her composure enough to go on.

"*The room had no windows. A bare light bulb hung from the ceiling. Gray dust-covered books and papers scattered over a desk and a stereo. Chalk equations were scribbled on the side of an old cupboard with a broken leg which leaned into the corner. The room smelled musty and unclean as if someone very old and ill had been living in it. I stood there dumbfounded and when I reached out to him, I could feel his body trembling under my hand. He was ashamed of that room and I had forced him to display it as if it were some hidden deformity.*" *Laura gave another harrumph and again Lucy refused to notice.*

"*That night I could not sleep. I saw myself floating in the darkness, my hair spread over his shoulder, curled into him, our faces close.*" *She hesitated as if waiting for the right words.* "*But I did not recognize myself. I got up and went to the window. It was dark, neon lights cast candy stripes around the room, and when I looked through the blinds, I could see a pale green moon rising behind the skyline.*" *Here her voice lowered to a whisper.* "*I might have been on Mars.*

"*I stood there for an hour, trying to visualize Georgia, astonished at the intensity of the dislocation I felt. I was falling out of sight of myself.*" *She went silent.*

"*Well,*" *prompted Laura.*

Lucy turned her head toward her aunt but did not quite look at her. "*When I made love with him . . . the size of the need that man aroused in me, the sense that he could make me do anything . . . there were no boundaries, anything was permissible between us.*"

Olly blushed and searched for cat hairs on his suit. Laura studied the freckles on the back of her hands. Lucy chewed at the inside of her lip then turned a panic-stricken face to her relatives.

"*I delivered my whole self up to him and what that required was absolute, primal trust. But what if he should die, what if he should leave me, what if he was not who I thought he was . . .*" *Lucy stood up and began to pace the floor.*

"*I shook him awake.*

"*'I'm so frightened Zac, tell me it's all right for God's sake, I don't understand what's happening.' His face was right next to mine. He touched my hair, rubbed it between his fingers, marveling at it. He kissed me softly, so lovingly. 'It doesn't really worry you does it?'*

261

" 'Doesn't it you?'

" 'No, because it's under control. But if it frightens you we'll stop.'

"I wanted to say, 'yes, stop, no more.' But his gentleness, his concern, made me feel foolish suddenly, as if I had overreacted. He wrapped himself around me and said I was everything he'd ever wanted, we could do anything we wanted together and it was safe because of the love." All the anxiety left Lucy's face and her voice was soft as velvet. "I melted into him, Laura, feeling happier than I would ever have thought possible." In the silence which followed, Lucy gave a crooked little smile to the walls and remained unaware of the unspoken words being exchanged between the ghosts. She was so absorbed in her reverie that she might have been watching a film projected onto those walls. The changing expressions on her face responded to various scenes, and by the time she drew herself away from the flickering images of the past, the smile she fixed on Olly was impish enough to make his eyes shift warily.

"We spent three weeks in bed. We ate in bed, read in bed, laughed in bed and learned each other in bed. Zac even worked on his papers in bed. When we did manage to extricate ourselves to buy food or a video, we stuck to each other like winkles and soon, unable to resist the magnetism of the bed, hurried home to it." Her smile broadened at Olly's growing discomfort. "Best of all we cracked jokes in bed. Wouldn't you say, Olly, that one of the most erotic things in the world is jokes in bed after lights out?" Without waiting for a reply she continued.

"On the third day the phone rang. Zac twinkled at me and said, 'Yes mother dear, she's right beside me and we're in bed and no you can't meet her yet I want her to myself.' My mouth had gone dry and it was all made more embarrassing because I had to push Zac away." Lucy glittered evilly at her grandfather. "And here was his mother, saying how happy she was and how she was dying to meet me and Zac had told her such wonderful things about me and she could tell from my voice that he hadn't exaggerated. Then she started to discuss the wedding plans and asked whether I was going to wear white. I said no and she said I must meet the Rabbi . . ."

"Rabbi?" gasped Laura.

"Rabbi!" cooed Olly, and a look of gloating satisfaction replaced the disapproval on his face.

"Rabbi," confirmed Lucy airily. "As I said to Zac, when I hung up *the phone, I didn't care whether we were married by a Rabbi or a Southern Baptist because I didn't believe in marriage and I was only doing it because of passports and work permits but Zac smiled slyly.*

" 'What do you think you're grinning at?' I said.

" 'You might be able to fool yourself, but you can't fool me. You'll tell all your friends that you're doing it for pragmatic reasons, but I know you, you want it as much as I do, flowers and all.'

"So, there was another deeply embedded belief about myself fluttering out the window like torn paper. I hated it when he got things right." Laura was now hissing incoherently under her breath—something about marriageable doormats and independence. Lucy turned to face her and said, with unexpected seriousness, "I knew you would hate the idea of my marrying. And Zac a Jew, at that. You would have said I was reverting to type or something equally acerbic and unkind." Laura opened her mouth to deny the charges but Lucy shook her head at her and went relentlessly on. "You would have considered his mother a 'frightful fool' and Zac a 'milksop.' You would have been beastly and rude to everyone. But I tell you, Laura, I would have given anything to have had you with me that day. I took out the pearls you gave me on the night of my first dance, do you remember? Creamy moons. Something old. All I had left of you. And I sent you a silent wish. 'Watch out for me Laura, I may need you, old dragon.' "

"Well, the old dragon was dead," said Laura tartly, "and she didn't receive the message." She sat down on the sack, back rigid, hands gripping her elbows as if they might flap away. The next words she uttered came out of her mouth as easily as extracted teeth. "But I'm glad you had the pearls." Lucy touched her lightly on the knee and continued with her narrative.

. . . Zac's mother continued to ring the blissful couple every few days but otherwise they were left completely alone. It was Lucy's opinion that the reverberations from their passion could be felt for miles around, creating a kind of impenetrable force field. She knew that soon enough the real world would impinge upon them and for the time being she was grateful for the opportunity to immerse herself in Zac. But when it was time for him to return to the Institute, and for her to discover what lay outside the apartment, neither of them found the adjustment easy . . .

"He'd say, 'We've really got to get out of bed today.'

263

"I'd say, 'Let's get up now then.'

"He'd say, 'So you don't really like it in bed? The flame has died?'

"I'd say, 'Of course not.' Then later, he would blame me because we hadn't got out of bed. And I did quite want to get out of bed by then because the smell of sperm, sweat, pheromones and old farts impregnating the bedclothes, our hair, our skin, the very air, was beginning to oppress."

This was too much for Olly, who began to make popping sounds. He stood up and declared that if his granddaughter said one more word about ... that, he would be forced to leave the room. Lucy leaned back in her chair.

"Sex," she said.

The old man shot up, stalked to the door, closed it firmly behind him and furtively put his ear to the keyhole. His granddaughter tiptoed over, bent down and shouted "sex" into the keyhole, before yanking open the door and dragging him back inside by the lapel of his beautiful suit. The two heartless women did not even try to stifle their evil laughter, but Lucy promised she would say no more about "that" and would tell him, instead, about the wedding. Mollified, but still an ugly shade of red, he rearranged himself fastidiously on the wooden chest.

... Lucy and Zac were married on September 6 in a synagogue. It was a clear autumn day with a wind blowing. There were thirty guests, none of whom Lucy knew. The rituals were strange to her, and it all felt a little disorienting, but Zac's hand was warm and it anchored her down and she was happy. After the ceremony they spilled onto the street, where confetti was swept up by the wind like colored snow. She wore a blue dress, the same color as her eyes. She felt as if her chest might explode, releasing a swarm of butterflies or singing birds. On a whim, she tossed her bouquet and a winning smile toward a woman called Vivienne, a colleague of Zac's who, Lucy noted, had been staring at her from time to time—"I was already on the lookout for women friends," she said. The pearls slipped from Lucy's neck; Zac trod on them, crushing them to moon dust; Vivienne caught the flowers ...

"My pearls," moaned Laura.

"An ill omen," said Olly, showing the whites of his eyes.

Lucy made a dismissive sign indicating that she did not believe in ill omens.

. . . The wedding party was in Rachel's apartment. Zac would not leave Lucy's side and this need to be in constant physical contact with her, as if she were some precious object which someone might steal from him, both pleased and embarrassed her. If she managed to detach herself from him for a moment, she would notice his eyes anxiously searching her out, and within seconds, he would be at her side, interrupting any conversation which might be developing between herself and a guest. She was also aware that others noticed his possessiveness. Glances were exchanged and it seemed to Lucy that there was something unkind in the wry amusement behind those glances. But these were his closest friends, people who cared about him, so she reasoned that her instinct to protect him was absurd . . .

"Naturally, all I wanted was to make a good impression but that very desire made me shy. I was so different from them. I did not know how to begin to explain myself. At one point I was asked about the Circus. Twenty pairs of eyes were fixed on me and what do you think happened? My first real experience of stage fright. I stammered and fumbled and Zac picked up my hand and somehow this gesture only made me feel more ridiculous. Luckily, Rachel, that's his mother, spirited me away to the kitchen. As soon as she closed the door she took my arm and said breathlessly, 'I've never seen him so happy.' It was as if this were an enormous relief to her. My eyes must have blinked with surprise, for she pulled back a fraction and added, with a coy smile, that she was delighted he had found someone so charming and original. 'Oh we'll be such good friends.' I was so absurdly grateful for those words of warmth that I hugged her impulsively."

"And?" said Laura, when Lucy's thoughtful silence had gone on too long.

"They never touched each other, don't you think that's odd?"

"Yes," said Olly.

"Not particularly," said Laura in that way of hers which always made Lucy smile.

"Well, I thought it was odd. And when I hugged her I knew instantly that I'd transgressed. I suppose part of what I'd wanted from Zac was a . . . family. A real one." She paused then added, in a softer voice, "A mother." The ghosts refused to look at each other. "But of course to Rachel I was only something which made Zac happy or unhappy. I had no other value.

"The night before the wedding I'd dreamed that all three of us were

265

in bed together and Rachel was my mother, not Zac's. I wanted her to approve of him and then they liked each other so much that I felt abandoned. We all placed garlands of flowers around each other's necks. The smell of the flowers was cloying, like funeral wreaths, and I could not breathe for the thick, rich stench and the weight of the wreath bearing me down . . . Zac woke me up by telling me he'd just been dreaming that I'd placed flowers around his neck . . . So there I was in the kitchen with his mother and when he came in looking for me a moment later, the feeling of the dream came back, because Rachel was so relieved to see him." Lucy tossed her hair away from her face, an I-don't-care gesture which did not conceal her hurt.

The ghosts learned that for the following two weeks, she saw no one but Zac. Husband and wife loved each other so intensely that parting each morning took an hour. Often he would call her from the office to tell her that he could not do physics because he was missing her. Or he might come home unexpectedly, filled with anxiety that something might have happened to her. Their hunger for each other astonished and delighted them. She would wait impatiently for the sound of his key in the lock, hearing a hundred keys turn before the real one brought him into the apartment. At night there was laughter and love; during the day she bought flowers and delicacies and thought of him, postponing the moment when she must take on the world outside their Shangri-La. In short she was adored, and Zac opened that portion of her heart which had been closed since childhood, as easily as a well-greased door.

One evening he came home a little later than usual. She had been going to the window every thirty seconds and when he came in at seven p.m. she jumped into his arms and covered him with kisses.

Lucy was now on her feet, delivering her story with Shakespearean gusto. "He said, 'Control yourself, Mrs. Appelfeld, we have guests for dinner.'

" 'Why didn't you tell me?' I cried. 'I've got to buy food, prepare a meal. Who's coming? How many?' and I charged around trying to find something to wear which did not smell of sex. Five guests at least for dinner and one of them was Vivienne. I bounded out of the apartment and flew down the street like a witch on a broom. I knew it would be difficult at first, entering Zac's world. I had never been on chatty terms with scientists, after all. But I'd read enough books on contemporary physics to give way to something like religious awe.

266

The questions it posed about the fundamental nature of reality scratched at my mind as Schrödinger's cat might, or might not, have done at the walls of its imaginary box. Zac's friends would be serious, solid people, not the arty neurotics I was used to. Tonight was my chance to inveigle my way into their hearts and be welcomed into their world. Tonight I would make a confidante of Vivienne." Lucy seemed to have forgotten the ghosts were there, as if the apartment and the streets of New York were now more present to her than the attic.

"There was no time to prepare a gourmet meal, so I bought fish, vegetables, cheeses and fruit. Would it do? Did it matter? My hands trembled as I stuffed the fish. Zac was working in his den. I searched, panic-stricken, for the right pots and pans. I gazed, flummoxed, at the computerized oven and gulped wine.

"Then I stopped short. So what if it were a horrible meal. Who was I, that I had suddenly, and willingly, taken on the role of hausfrau? And why was Zac in the den instead of helping me in the kitchen?" Lucy placed her hands on her hips and stared fiercely at the walls.

"I took another long and satisfying draught. By the time Vivienne arrived, I was tipsy. She was so flawless that if I'd laid a hand on her it would have slipped off. And there was I in tights and one of Zac's old jumpers. Lord I felt a frump, but I smiled from ear to ear and shook her hand enthusiastically." Here Lucy jerked her arm up and down as if she were pumping water from a well, and grinned like a village idiot. *"She said a polite hello and turned to talk to Zac."* Lucy smacked a hand to her forehead, bent forward from the waist and took a couple of steps. *"I went back to the kitchen, listening to the way they chuckled so easily together. I wished I hadn't had the wine, because now the oven was incomprehensible. Would the fish be overcooked if I put it on now? I heard the others come in and went out to greet them. A fur coat had arrived—not mink but something wild and rare. Ten guests! Was I Jesus that I could make the fish go round? They were all wearing suits, even the women. I went back to the kitchen and skolled another glass."* Lucy tossed invisible liquid down her throat and crossed her eyes. *"I chucked the green stuff into the bubbling pot and went to sit with them."* She plonked herself back in the chair. *"They were talking about perturbation theory and the infinite root of unity; Busonic parts and ghost insertion factors; path integers and asymptotic out-bases. They were talking to each other. I went back to the kitchen.*

"*The broccoli was overcooked; the fish, pink on the inside. I emptied the broccoli into the sink, scalding myself in the process. I whacked the oven up to such a high temperature that the outside of the fish turned to charcoal. I said 'Fuck it' several times and finished off the bottle of wine. When Zac called, asking if I wanted help, I said no and meant yes.*

"*I brought out the tasteless meal and placed it before them. I swallowed a full glass of wine while Vivienne sipped at her Perrier and looked at me in a way that made me feel I had offended her. However, I was determined to put all judgmental thoughts aside and show how much I liked them and welcomed them but my silences fell in all the wrong places and I laughed when no one else did. I searched for some doorway in the conversation through which I might enter. From one end of the table I heard something like, 'The p-adic gamma function is first defined on the integers by something similar to this n factorial except there's a problem when one of the divisors divides P so in fact the p-adic analogue of this is . . .' I swung my head to my end of the table and heard Zac say to Vivienne, 'Incidentally, did you see what that asshole Epstein wrote the other day? What a second-rate fool that guy is. You've no idea . . .'*

"'*Who?' I interrupted. My dinner guests suddenly became aware of my existence.*

"'*A colleague of mine. You'll meet him when you come to the Institute.' Zac turned his attention back to his friends and went on to explain not only the asshole Epstein's lack of vision, but the same failing in a host of other scientists of his acquaintance, bringing out the words 'you've no idea' as if instructing minors on the horrors of drug addiction. Vivienne assented profusely to everything he said. Zac, she intimated, was a genius surrounded by fools.*

"*There was a malicious glee developing among them all, a kind of schadenfreude, as they pulled to pieces half a dozen physicists and half a dozen wives. I had not seen this side of Zac before—the bombastic, self-promoting tone, the pettiness. He was not only participating in the vindictiveness, he was leading it and I could not fit this unaccountable flaw with the man I had a million reasons for loving. I tried to catch his eye but to the new Zac I was invisible. I fixed a noncommittal smile into place and tuned in to the underneath of things. What I heard was that none of them trusted each other. Theirs was a world of Byzantine intrigue and professional competition. All social interac-*

tions were about performance and this was regarded as necessary. Any attempt to shorten the distance between them would be seen as inappropriate. If it were true that these were Zac's closest friends, it meant that he had never known friendship, but that thought made me pity him—a contemptible emotion which I did not want to feel for my darling. I decided I must be wrong about our guests. This was, after all, an alien culture to which I must adapt.

"I took another swig of wine and lapsed into a fantasy in which Georgia comes striding through the door like a Virago and sweeps me into her arms and we both say terribly clever things in loud voices so that everyone at the table suddenly recognizes how witty and attractive I am even if I don't know what a Busonic part is. Then Georgia and the guests disappear but just as Zac and I start making love, I heard Vivienne say, 'Zachary tells me you're something of an actress.' Before I'd recovered from the insult, Zac chipped in with, 'She's a very fine actress but she doesn't believe it.'

" 'I'm a performer not an . . .' But they were paying no attention.

" 'I didn't see the one you mentioned,' she addressed him, 'but some of these Australian films are surprisingly good. Tell me'—she turned her bland perfection to me—'is Australia as . . . backward as I imagine?' From the other end of the table I heard the words 'and perhaps in these four theories will be an ultrametric structure that's relevant . . .' I was having trouble focusing. I wondered what would happen if I broke a bottle over her head, but all I said was, 'Depends how mowerful your impagination is.' There was a faint shadowing of her brow followed by a cool smile. 'I guess I have the sense that they lack reverence for . . . things intellectual?'

"Indignation and alcohol unleashed my inner demon. It leapt at Vivienne's throat. 'Yes Australians shoot physicists on sight but at least they lack that particular brand of ignorance and provincialism that goes with thinking you exist at the center of the world. Isn't it odd,' I said, leaning forward and sending my neighbor's plate skidding across the table with my elbow, 'that a truck driver from Illinois will have a sense of power, simply because he is American. When Americans travel, they are always shocked at how deeply they are despised. Hey, I'll tell you a very funny story,' I went on, collapsing into uncontrolled mirth. But Zac interrupted my very funny story by suggesting it was time for coffee. I remained more or less mute for the rest of the evening.

"When the last guest had gone, I closed the door and slid down it. Zac was observing me from his position at the head of the table.

" 'Well well well,' he said, 'I must say I hadn't predicted jealousy in you.' I could only stare at him with my mouth open. 'It was silly of you to have made it so obvious in front of her. There's absolutely nothing to be jealous about.' He wore that ironic, I-know-you-better-than-you-know-yourself expression which, when he was right about me, I liked a lot. Now it left me speechless.

" 'But I'm not jealous, I tell you.'

" 'Noooo. Of course you're not.' He smirked. There was a long silence in which a lot was going on.

" 'But she didn't like me. She was rude to me and has been since the moment she met me.'

" 'Vivienne's incapable of disliking anyone.'

" 'But . . .'

" 'Oh, let's forget it. I'd kinda hoped you might make an effort. She is my closest ally y'know.'

"He got up and disappeared behind the bookcase. I stayed where I was, listening to him undressing. Was he right? Had I projected some anxiety of my own onto her? Could I have misread a situation so badly? Why in hell's name had I been stupid enough to get drunk. It always made me aggressive.

"By the time I crawled in next to him he was asleep, his back turned to me. I lay awake for hours, obsessively reliving the events of the evening, searching out my mistakes like a gorilla furrowing through fur for parasites. But no matter what fresh interpretation I gave those events, I always came back to the same points. His friends had been impenetrable; Vivienne, whom I had so wanted to like, had been nasty, and Zac had ignored me in their presence. I went to sleep and dreamed about drowning.

"During the night I woke to find him staring at me. Something moved behind his eyes like a quick, dark shape darting behind trees. I did not want to see what I had seen there. I canceled it out.

"When I woke, the other side of the bed was cold and empty. Music was coming from the den. He emerged an hour later, locked the door behind him, put the key in his pocket and without saying a word, prepared to leave.

" 'Hey,' I said, smiling in what I hoped was a mystified and appealing way, 'what's going on?'

270

"He turned and on his face was a look of such remoteness that I felt it like a punch, winding me. 'I'm going to work, that's what's going on.' He added that as it was so obvious that I neither enjoyed his company nor the company of his friends, no doubt I would be grateful to see the apartment empty. With that, he left.

"The anger I felt during that interminable day was held in check by a stronger feeling of bafflement. I must have missed some explanatory clue. The punishment did not fit the crime. If the facts do not fit, one must search for a new hypothesis. I cooked an evening meal and waited.

"When he returned, he took off his coat and went straight to his den without a word. I watched him from my seat at the table.

" 'Two can play this game,' I thought, and threw on his coat to go out. But no sooner had I reached the door than I changed my mind. The music curled around me like tentacles, holding me back, sucking me in. I paced the flat aware that the music was a message: 'I am here but you cannot have me.' I did not understand why this was happening. I wanted an explanation, a fight if necessary, anything but mystery.

" 'You think this childish trick will work with me?' I shouted, hammering on the door. 'When does the punishment stop, for God's sake?' The volume went higher. I kicked the door and left the apartment.

"But the punishment did not stop that night, or the next day. 'I don't know why you are doing this,' I began, the minute he arrived home late at night. 'What have I done? You're acting like a four-year-old.'

"Zac's response was measured and cool. 'I? Doing something to you? What an interesting reversal. I would have thought your behavior toward Vivienne had little to do with me. I would have thought that you might have a little respect for my work, the peace I need for my work, but no you bang on the door . . . When I told Vivienne that, she was appalled.'

"The injustice of the accusations came like a series of unexpected blows. And the use of Vivienne as a weapon was such a betrayal, not of me so much as my idea of Zac, that I rounded on him. 'How dare you say that to me? You're behaving like a school bully and I don't take to being bullied, I fight back.' With the word 'back' I poked a rigid finger into the hollow of his chest."

271

Lucy looked up from a contemplation of her shaking hands and her eyes opened wide.

"His whole head suddenly suffused with blood. He crumpled into a chair as if shot in the stomach. A violent struggle was going on inside him and I did not know how to understand it or even how to reach it, but it shocked and frightened me out of my own anger.

"I went to him and took his hand; it lay in my own like a dead fish. He blinked a couple of times and jerked his head as if coming out of a trance. Tentatively, I touched his stony face and he continued looking at me in a peculiar way until I led him into the darkness of the bedroom. I undressed him and held him until he stopped trembling." *Lucy was now biting furiously at her thumbnail and her growing distress alarmed the ghosts.*

"Later we made love with such tenderness . . . such tenderness. We were quiet for a long time afterwards, lying in each other's arms. I wanted to find some way to begin to talk about what had happened but words wouldn't come. At last he said, 'It was a mistake.'

" 'I know Zac, it's all right . . .' " *Lucy slowly bent over and sat back on the chair as if she no longer had the strength to stand on her feet. Tears welled in her eyes but she was reliving that night so intensely she was unaware of them. The next words came out of her in a hoarse whisper.* " 'The marriage was a mistake. It's over. I don't love you. I thought I did but it was a mistake. I'll stay with Rachel until you've arranged things. Don't feel you have to leave straight-away.' "

"Dear Lord," breathed Laura but Lucy did not hear her. She continued holding her belly and rocking back and forward, her eyes staring into nothing.

"He had just made love to me, his sperm was inside me, his words did not make sense. I lay on my back on the bed and he sat beside me. He held me as if I were some stranger he had found dying on a battlefield. I had been opened from throat to pelvis, my viscera were on display, warm and wet all over the covers." *Lucy covered her face with her hands as if it displayed something privately shameful.* "My begging went on hour after hour."

She dragged her hands away from her head and stared at them. The ghosts, whose horrified stares remained fixed on that white, stricken face, seemed incapable of speech.

"My hands had stiffened, I could not use my fingers. As long as I did *not move I could endure the pain. I must have slept, because I was drowning in brown water, the bubbles popping to the surface, but the pain woke me up as I was running, my feet sucked down into mud."*

At this point Lucy experienced a relapse. Her story degenerated into incoherence. She continually repeated that she had gone through an initiation and was no longer the same woman, that something had been broken inside her and she could hear it rattling around at night, that she was the Aboriginal woman who had been crippled, who had left her country and entered Zac's. She pointed out the split that had opened down the front of her body and was amazed that the ghosts could not see it. It took them some time to calm her down and to piece together what had happened.

... By the third day Lucy could move around and take care of basic self-maintenance, but she was ill. She blanked out the nights with pills. When she had packed her things and arranged the plane trip home, she half woke one afternoon from a soggy sleep ...

"Someone was holding my hand. It was large, cool and safe, like a father's hand. When I woke again, Zac was sobbing beside me. He said he had been mad and that he had never stopped loving me; that I had no reason to forgive him but in leaving me he had understood that he could not live without me; that he had never loved anyone so intensely and it had frightened him. He said that what he wanted more than anything on earth was the love we had, all of it, and now he was really ready for it. He said he needed me so much it hurt."

"You went back to him?" breathed Laura.

"Oh yes."

Laura opened her mouth several times before she could manage the words, "But why?"

Lucy frowned in perplexity at her aunt as if she had just asked the silliest question in the world.

"Because when he held me the pain went away. He was the only one who could close the wound."

Laura stared down in consternation at the sniveling creature in the chair.

"Where was your pride?" she said in a wondering voice.

The younger woman seemed to have shrunk, and there was a twisted half-smile on her face as she murmured her reply.

"The disemboweled have no pride."

25
The Labyrinth

Dusk was gathering around the house, sucking light from the rooms. Lucy walked to and fro between the window and the chair, lost in thought, her chin sunk in her hand.

"Certainly I was a cripple. It was as if I had survived a terrible fall. I leaned on Zac, but my maddening preoccupation with his abandonment of me left me in a state of perpetual fear—that he would leave me again.

"Oh he was kind and good, so solicitous, worried about me. God knows how many bunches of flowers he bought. But sometimes I caught him looking at me as if I were offal. He would hurriedly paste a smile over that look, and disappear into his den, but whenever it happened, the grief and humiliation would return, as they always did, like a blade, reopening the wound."

"Pah," *spat Laura.*

She rolled her eyes, crossed one leg over the other and let out an impatient puff of air. "All this grief over one man. I don't know what possessed you to choose someone so neurotic."

"Well I'll tell you then." *Lucy clutched the arms of her chair and leaned forward to dazzle her aunt with a blaze of evangelical zeal.*

"Because he was the handsomest, funniest, most brilliant, most tragic, most needy, most complicated and most loving person I have ever known. Because when we were happy we were the happiest couple on earth. Because we could read each other's thoughts and finish each other's dreams. Because I loved him more than I can tell you and to lose him would be to lose the self that was brought into being only . . . with . . . him . . ."

When the crying had stopped and Lucy had blown her nose several times into Olly's now saturated handkerchief, she hiccuped once or twice and continued.

"*The night of my birthday, he was watching me dress in front of the mirror. 'You're much too thin,' he said. I was by then skeletal, but I grinned back at him, knowing that he loved my thinness, loved every crevice, curve, angle and atom of me. We were going to hear Menuhin play and I was dressing myself up for a celebration. We were utterly besotted with each other and the bliss had gone on, uninterrupted, for a month—long enough for some semblance of stability to return. He came to stand beside me. We pulled faces at each other, leaned our heads together, stared at the loving couple in the mirror, embarrassed almost at the mutual adoration displayed there. He moved his hand into the moist warmth between my legs and said, 'Think of the child we could produce.' I replied that I did, often.*

"*'Wait,' he yelped, startling me so much that I dropped the mascara. He bounded outside, bumping his shoulder and ordering me not to move. Our giggles echoed each other as he fumbled through drawers in the kitchen. He came back with a pair of scissors and before I could stop him he had cut off a chunk of my hair. 'I'm going to keep this next to me forever,' he said, 'in memory of the night we decided to have our baby. And if you ever for one second doubt that I love you more than anything on this earth I'll show you this lock of hair, I'll wave it under your nose.' "*

Lucy's face crumpled up with such misery that even Laura stretched out a hand toward her. "*Whenever things were blackest between us, I would remember that lock of hair.*

"*The auditorium was packed. I let him guide me through the torrent of humanity, my hand curled safe and sweaty into his. We took our seats and when the lights dimmed, we groped for each other in the dark like teenagers.*

"*The music started up—the Brahms Violin Concerto in D Major. I felt my skin go clammy. By the second movement, I had to double over. Zac grabbed at me and whispered, 'What's the matter? Darling, are you all right?' I did not know what was happening to me. The vision of my mother sawing away on her violin had appeared vividly in my mind's eye and with it came a pain as intense as the pain I had felt when Zac left me. He bundled me into a taxi and we went home.*

"*I lay back on the bed fighting for breath. My hands had gone stiff with shock. Zac raced to call a doctor but by the time he came, the fit, or whatever it was, had passed, leaving me weak and wretched. I hid my alarm from Zac and took the sleeping pills he offered. I could hear their voices murmuring, susurrating, becoming more and more distant. I was sinking down gratefully into brown water.*

"In the morning when I woke, he was sitting on a chair opposite the bed, scrutinizing me.

" 'What was that all about?' I was still feeling shaky and the look on his face was unpleasant, as if I had failed him.

" 'I don't know. It doesn't matter, does it? I'm all right now.'

"He was as stern as a headmaster. 'I don't know what to do, I really don't. You terrified me last night. Rachel and I think you should . . . see someone.'

"He got up from the chair, hesitated as if he were going to say more, and left the room. I could not stop myself calling to him. He came back, sat on the bed and patted my hand. But I could feel that all he wanted to do was escape. I was like a leech, bleeding him dry. I rolled my head into the pillow so he would not see the tears."

The ghosts learned that from this point on, Lucy's decline was dramatic. The unnameable dread which infected her manifested itself in nightmares and insomnia. Her loneliness, isolation, and dependence began to shrivel her soul . . .

"I continued to walk the streets, looking for a job, setting my sights ever lower, wondering if I could do some busking without Zac finding out. What he did not know and what I could not bring myself to tell him was that I was running out of money. It's not that he was mean," she hastened to assure the ghosts, *"it's just that he was . . . anxious about money. If I had to buy things for the apartment, he would take a few notes from his wallet as if we were peeling off his own skin. It made me feel like a prostitute . . ."* Lucy looked down at her folded hands. *"In the end I could not bear to take his money because he reminded me so much of you, Laura."*

"Ha, stingy was he?" cut in Olly, but Laura told him to shut up and Lucy had to interrupt her story to pacify them both.

"Then a circus came to New York for a season before traveling north. They must have thought I was crazy. The first day I walked into their tent, I burst into tears. Such good people they were. They sensed I was in trouble, but I could not talk to them because there was

no way I could explain my life to them. I knew they would give me some sort of job, stagehand if nothing else. But best of all I could use their rigging. I went every day and worked till I bled. The calluses had gone from my hands and wrists; it was like starting all over again. I took Zac to meet them and to watch me practice. For the first time he could see . . . who I really was." Lucy paused and tears brimmed in her eyes. She fought them down and continued. "He didn't say anything, of course, but I could tell they bored him.

"I practiced with Jesse and Karen. Beautiful young fliers. One dark day I brought Jesse back to the apartment for lunch. He was my first guest and I was nervous of bringing him into a home which did not feel like my own. It seemed to go well enough, Zac went out of his way to be charming. But three nights later, as we lay in bed reading, he suddenly slammed his papers down and said, 'Sometimes I feel you know me better than anyone on earth, and then I understand that you don't know me at all.' With that he got up and went to his den. 'But what are you talking about?' I said, following him. He turned to me with a look so cold, so faraway, that I felt a familiar paralysis steal into my bones.

" 'That you should even have to ask . . .' The door shut behind him. Didn't he understand that the hurt from these accusations accumulated like poison in the heart? But I must have done something to bring it on. I sifted through the last couple of days for a clue.

" 'Zac, you idiot,' I yelled, banging on his door. 'I didn't even like him.' I lied because it was simpler. The door opened. Sweat gleamed over his upper lip. 'He's just a kid, for heaven's sake. I'm not even remotely attracted to him.'

" 'Well he was attracted to you. He was practically salivating down the front of your shirt. Anyway, he's so brainless I'm surprised you find anything to talk to him about.' "

Lucy shook her head. "He was jealous of my past, my future, my success. I had once shown him my portfolio and as he went through it I could feel his agitation. I knew that at any moment he would tease me about something and it would hurt. He lifted his head, smiled dryly and said, 'You should add to this that you're a graduate in melancholy.'

"One would think that my ability to predict his jibes would inure me to their sting. If anything, it made them worse, like waiting for an

injection. And his attempts at making me jealous worked in the same skewed way. He might say, 'There's a very pretty woman coming to interview me today.' A fist would form in my stomach.

" 'Oh that's nice.'

" 'She's very pretty.'

" 'Lucky you.'

" 'I think she's a little bit attracted to me.'

" 'Well that's because you're an attractive man.'

" 'You can't fool me with that cool stuff—you're jealous.'

"And I would smile uneasily while he danced around, knowing that my face betrayed me. It was not that I thought he was interested in another woman, but the fact that he needed to construct these illusory romances made me feel off balance." Laura threw her hands up in the air and even Olly raised his eyebrows.

"The next day, I was twirling on the web, and the thought came to me that it would be so much easier just to let go. I stopped breathing, or rather the air stopped breathing me." Lucy's voice wavered. "I came down and rested, but when I tried to climb again, the terror was waiting for me at the foot of the rope. And when I went to sleep that night, it was waiting for me in my dreams."

. . . Lucy could no longer fly and into that emptiness seeped a corrosive despair. Even leaving the apartment required an act of courage but she forced herself to creep out each day and wander the streets aimlessly, her will casting a watery glow on everything, but refusing to focus. The books she read left no trace, her consciousness closing behind the words like ice behind a knife. She rang Georgia occasionally, simply to hear a familiar voice, but the phone calls contained mostly silences. Soon the letters from Australia stopped arriving.

When Lucy searched inside herself for something to depend on, there was nothing—no ambition, no identity, no self-respect. She spent most of her time standing by windows of rooms containing nothing of hers, staring down at streets full of strangers. She was so anonymous that she began to yearn for the history she had obliterated, for there to exist, somewhere, the emblems of her childhood— a lock of baby hair pressed in a yellow envelope, a photograph, a musical box. But no one had held her past close to them. She was without a beginning. And she, too, had thrown away these proofs of continuity, confident of her ability to construct a new self each day with greasepaint and costumes . . .

"And what about your husband," interrupted Laura, "didn't he help you?"

"Of course he did, but how much help could he be expected to give?" Lucy sank her head into her chest. "I could feel him distancing himself, every day a little further. And the more I needed him the more he backed away. I remember one morning he woke me up by licking water away from my face.

" 'That's the third morning in a row you've been crying in your sleep. What the hell's the matter with you? You used to be funny in the mornings, remember?' Groggy and thick with depression, I turned to him and slipped my arms up under his own. My wrists were burning where he . . ." Lucy stopped herself in time and turned her head away in shame.

"Oh, Lucy," said Laura softly. "How could you think so little of yourself?" There was a new tenderness in the old lady's voice so that Lucy, who had previously dismissed any wisdom or understanding from her aunt, gazed at her as she might once have gazed at Georgia. She took a deep breath.

"Ever since he left me that first time, an unwholesome thought crept into my head. It is because I let him do this to me that he loves me. If I did not let him do this to me, he would leave me. So that what originally had been sexually liberating became a kind of prison. And I could not bear that new self. What she thought and what she did were inconceivable, given the person I thought I was."

The attic was as silent as a confessional for several minutes.

"I lied to him by saying it was just a dream and he moved away as if I had said something offensive. He wanted to know why I wouldn't talk to him. 'Because,' said a voice in my head, 'whenever I tell you I'm unhappy you cut me off and I can't take it any more.' I nestled closer into the warmth of him, wanting to stay buried in him forever. It was the only place I felt safe. I told him it was just a vague depression and that it would pass.

" 'There must be something behind it.'

" 'I'm tired that's all. I didn't get to sleep till six.'

"He sighed. 'What was it this time?'

" 'Nothing.'

"He moved completely away now, impatient. 'These acts of vandalism you perpetrate on yourself. I don't know where all your self-hatred comes from. Really, you must see a psychiatrist.'

" 'Yes, and who would pay for it, Zac? You?'

"We faced each other across the bed like dogs with their hackles up. He said he was sorry he had opened his mouth and got dressed for work. I heard him in the kitchen, then the door closing behind him. I rang Georgia but she wasn't home. I took a slug of whiskey. It helped me to sleep. I crawled back into bed and dreamed that Zac was a red rosebush, bending over me. A prickly stem went down my throat, right down in my stomach so that I could not scream. The stem turned into his hairy arm . . ."

"But didn't you have any friends to turn to?" inquired Olly.

"There were Zac's friends, of course, but I have never felt so lonely in my life as when I was surrounded by them. All they ever showed of themselves, or expected to see in others, was surface. There was no real intimacy, they could not afford it. Every time I had to be with them, I would prepare what I would say, how I would be, because what I was was incomprehensible to them. But the moment they looked at me, I would see the dislike in their eyes, and I would forget my lines. Then I could think of nothing to say, and I would sit through dinners, my face frozen into the nervous smile of the terminally shy, imagining what they said about us behind our backs, knowing that afterwards I would have to face Zac's exasperation. He simply could not understand my fear and if I tried to explain it to him, he assumed I was criticizing his life and he would disappear inside his den." Lucy leaned toward the ghosts, opening her hands toward them.

"What his world came to show, like a mirror, was the failure of personal faith. There was no security of heart or mind and everything I had believed in, all the guiding principles of my life, were nothing but illusion." She got up, wandered to the window, wrapped her arms around herself and leaned her forehead against the glass. "Esse percipi," she whispered and gave a little shudder.

"One night after a conference, a few of his colleagues came back to the apartment for drinks. I moved from group to group, smiling politely, saying nothing but yes and no. I went to the toilet to escape and on my way passed a gathering in the corner. I heard one of them say, 'Lie down with tightrope walkers . . .' before he saw me and stopped. I kept the smile on and did not allow myself to understand

280

until I had locked the bathroom door. 'And catch fleas.' The words hung on me like spit. I went back outside and joined Zac's group. At last I could prove to him that I was not imagining things, that I was not mad. I only wanted them all to go away, so I could talk to my husband, so I was not listening to what they said. Then I became aware that they were looking at me.

" 'I said, what did you think of it, Louise?'

" 'I'm sorry.'

" 'The play. I was wondering what an actress thought of it.'

" 'I'm not an actress, I'm a . . .' I don't know why I did it. It was as if my second self, the fearless one, stepped in and took over.

" 'I'm not an actress, I'm a wife.'

"Zac laughed but his fury was understood by everyone present. I excused myself and went to the bedroom, where I crouched behind the bookcase, wanting to bite out my tongue, listening to Zac's too-loud chatter. Within the hour, they had all left. I sat on the bed, biting my nails, preparing myself for Zac's disappearance. But he came in and sat next to me, his head sunk between his knees.

" 'How long must I go on paying,' he began quietly. 'I don't know what more I can do. You need help Louise.' He lifted his ravaged face toward me. 'I don't know how to convince you that I love you, that my friends love you.'

"I let out a crazed hoot of laughter. Oh I was mad then, yes, I felt myself to be mad and it was a liberation.

" 'You despise me,' I said. 'Do you think I don't know? Do you think I can't see what lies behind your eyes?'

"His reasonableness burst and all the anger and resentment he felt toward me came pouring out.

" 'It's extraordinary to me that you pick one of the most important days in my career to display your sickness to everyone, and all you can do now is cry in that aggressive, punitive way of yours. You're destroying me with your madness. Yes, you're mad, do you know that. You're deranged, violent, hideous.' He got up and turned at the door. 'You don't know how to love. You don't know what it means. I get more sweetness and understanding from Vivienne than I ever have from you. You should hear what she says about you behind your back. All of them. Rachel made me swear I'd ditch you, did you know that?' "

At this point, Lucy staggered and dropped to her knees. Olly caught

*her and lowered her to the floor. Deep black caverns had formed
around her eyes and her hands fluttered at her side like moths.*

*"Mad or bad? A moral or medical judgment? The shadows had
chased me all my life until they caught me up . . ." The two ghosts
conferred in whispers. Lucy heard shreds of things—"looking after
her . . . eaten for days . . . her mother . . ."*

"My mother? Is she here?"

*"No child. Get up now. We'll help you downstairs. It's time to see
the garden of delights."*

*A full moon had arisen and clouds, as whispy as tulle, were draped
between the stars. Mist swirled around Mount Misery and from its
base, a silver path led across the sea. Lucy was escorted like an invalid
around the glowing garden, Olly claiming her left elbow, Laura her
right. She took the fruits they offered, managing to swallow small
mouthfuls. The tin plate on the back porch contained scorched meat
which she could not touch. Afterwards, they led her to the large room
and lay her down on her nest of quilts. Olly tucked her in and Laura
placed a cool, dry hand on her forehead. Lucy clasped that hand in her
own and curled it against her chest. So closely did the two women
now resemble each other that they might well have been mistaken for
mother and daughter.*

*"When you died, Laura, I did not grieve. I simply went on believing
that you were here, waiting for me. I lost you when I lost Binjigul. But
when Georgia died . . . When Georgia died I could not afford to
grieve. If I let myself feel her loss, I knew I would go under.*

*"I had been thinking about her when the call came through. Zac
was sitting across the room, at the table. He asked who was on the
phone.*

*" 'Georgia's daughter, Annie.' He grunted with disapproval. 'What
did she want,' he said. I didn't know how to answer. The words were
too small, or too big. To say that she had rung to tell me her mother
was dead would have made Zac look like a fool. As if I were playing a
nasty trick on him. I said nothing but sat very still in my chair,
wondering what to do next. I decided that I would sit in that chair to
eternity if need be. After a while he looked up from his papers. I could
feel his eyes on me, cautious, puzzled.*

" 'Louisa? What is it?'

*" 'She rang to tell me her mother's dead.' I turned toward the
window. We sat there like stuffed dolls for several minutes, my elbow*

resting on the arm of the chair, my gaze fixed on the blackness outside, my hand supporting my chin. Zac at the table, watching me across the expanse of parquet floor.

" 'Car accident. The most ignoble of deaths, isn't it? Banal.' *I heard him coming toward me. Felt him place his arms around me. But it was as if I had not been touched.*

"When *he realized that I was not going to fall apart, or cry, or even talk about it, he said,* 'It isn't natural this . . . coldness.'

" 'Isn't it? People die. Billions of them. All the time.' *He stared at me as if I were deformed. I stared back, expressionless.*

"For *the remainder of that year there was no joy but there was hardly any pain at all. I spent most of my time by the window, Zac spent most of his in the den. He was happy. He said,* 'Looks like we're gonna make it after all, Mrs. Appelfeld. Had our ups and downs haven't we? But now it's the real thing.'

" 'Yes, the real thing,' *I agreed. The stillness was neither lonely nor dispiriting because I was waiting, for what I couldn't say. When it came, it was not at all what I expected. I had gone to spend the night with Rachel who had the flu. But when she fell asleep, I felt a sudden compulsion to go home.*

"I *let myself into the apartment. It was quiet enough for me to be aware of the ticking of the bedroom clock. I was about to turn on the switch, when I noticed a shaft of light coming from the open door of the den. Zac had always been so careful to lock himself in there. Since that first day I had never, in the whole year of my marriage, been allowed to enter his holy shrine and had given up being curious about it.*

"I *waited for a moment, debating whether or not to let him know I was there. I had the curious sensation that something infectious was emanating from that room. I tiptoed over and stood watching him for a full minute.*

"He *was crouched on the floor naked, lost in concentration, fiddling around with a mass of papers on the floor. He had the furtive air of a jungle beast who, having sniffed the air for danger, was now drinking at a stream.*

"He *jerked up, sensing my presence. He shuffled the papers together hastily, turned to me, shook his head quickly and smiled.* 'You gave me a fright.' *I couldn't speak.* 'What are you staring at?' *He laughed—a flat, ugly sound. He came over to me, pulled me roughly* inside the door, turned me around to face the wall, lifted my dress and pushed himself against me. He clutched at my hair and pulled it, saying, 'This is what you like, isn't it. I know what you like.' I struggled against him until he let me go.

" 'No, Zac, it's not what I like.' I went to the bedroom.

"Later, he came and nestled into me. I thought he might be crying, but I wasn't sure. I dreamed.

"There was a war going on. I was on the telephone to Georgia and I said, 'I am in danger.'

" 'Go along the path,' she said, 'and I will meet you at the other end.' The path wound through barren desert—mountainous and scattered with gigantic boulders. There was not a stick of vegetation or a flutter of life anywhere. There were soldiers close behind me and I knew I must abandon the path. I was not afraid.

"I came to a waterfall, which cut its way through bare red rock. The water was muddy, the river was in flood. I jumped into the rapid and let it carry me away from the soldiers and as I did so, I wondered if I would die. But I seemed to skim along the surface of the water as if it were a tremendous slippery dip. I noticed, in the narrow gorges, shards of broken glass sticking out of the sheer rock walls.

"At the bottom of the waterfall, I lay in a still pool, exultant that I had succeeded. I was naked and when I looked down I saw that the pool was pink with blood. I was annoyed at this inconvenience. Then I saw that a piece of glass had punctured an artery in my leg. It did not hurt but I could not remember what to do other than stanch the flow with my hand. But I could not move because if I did the blood would drain out of me. I was in the middle of nowhere and a long way from the path. Georgia would never find me. I was utterly lost.

"I woke saying to myself, 'You will die in this place if you do not remember how to heal your own wound.'

"I peered closely at Zac. He was asleep. I watched him for a long time then, careful not to make any noise, dressed and went out.

"It was snowing lightly. Occasionally a vehicle shattered the low humming noise of a city dreaming in its sleep, or groups of chattering people came toward me. I steered a course away from them, never slackening my pace, not resting for a moment. Now and then a lone figure emerged from the shadows then fell away behind. I remembered the day I ran along these streets buoyed up by hope, looking for food to buy for our first guests. I was not that same person. I was her *shadow self and we haunted each other. I fancied we might meet each other there in the dark. Here and there the wind rattled shopfronts and billboards or whipped black things into corners. The snow got heavier and more violent as I hurried down the length of Manhattan until I found myself somewhere on the Lower East Side near the water.*

"I had not been here before, I was sure of it, though I thought I had explored every inch of the city. I did not recognize the buildings, one tenement looked like another. The snow whirled and stormed around me. I heard footsteps behind me but when I turned there was no one. I hailed a lone cab but it plunged past, drenching me with freezing water.

"I was seized by a sudden panic and headed in a different direction. But I was trapped by unknown streets and did not know which direction to take. The snow made everywhere the same. I began to run. I was no longer in New York but in some phantasmagoric city conjured up from the past. The buildings took on medieval forms, shadowy as dreams.

"I stopped short, listening to my own breath ripping out of my lungs and knew, with the certainty of revelation, what I had done. This was the labyrinth, the disorientation of my own life made manifest. I had delivered myself into it willingly, knowing with some part of myself that solving it was the only chance I had for transformation.

"I stole the key to the den. I had a copy cut. I waited. Zac had to go on a lecture tour.

" 'I can cancel it, you know. I'm worried about you. You don't look well. Yes, I think I'll cancel it.' I made him go.

"When the time came, he had turned at the door looking scared. Perhaps he knew. I waited for the sound of the lift, and then I stood at the window, watching him get into the taxi. He glanced up at me once, hesitated, then was gone.

"I went to the door of his den. It creaked a little on its hinge. I noticed that one of the screws was missing on the doorknob. It shook a little under my hand. I switched on the light and went to the center of the room. I turned slowly in full circle. There was no hurry. I felt cold.

"By the time I found the key to the locked cupboard I was calm because I knew I had reached the end. In the cupboard was a box full of paper. I took out the box and spread the contents on the floor.

"Underneath a stack of unopened mail from Australia were publicity photos of me which Zac must have stolen from my portfolio. He had drawn cuts and bruises on my face. There were old reviews and articles pasted onto cardboard with curses written beneath. There were fantasies of the future, in which I kill myself, in which I die in childbirth, in which I am found mutilated in a Harlem parking lot.

"At the bottom of the box was the tuft of my own black hair."

26
Milk

Lucy lay staring up at the molded arabesques of the ceiling. In her right hand she clasped Laura's fingers; in her left, Olly's, curling them sweatily into her chest and occasionally giving them a convulsive squeeze—a signal that some poisonous memory had stung her. Yet even when her face contorted into one of these momentary grimaces, the ghosts noted with satisfaction that the background expression was a little more peaceful, as if a benedictory hand had smoothed the skin.

"Laura, I love you, and Olly too," she murmured as her eyes went milky and she drifted into a gentle sleep. Laura whispered, "It is not you trapped in that room, it is he," then quietly closed the shutters.

The cat curled up by the nape of Lucy's neck purring away any bad dreams, the ghosts yawned and nodded off, the wall clock ticked as steady as a heartbeat, slowly moving its hands together in supplication—twelve o'clock. Steenie's ears twitched. One basilisk eye opened, then the other, and the hair along its back began to bristle. His yowl lifted Lucy straight out of her nest. At the sound of two men giggling, the inhabitants of the house bounded toward each other and stood motionless together holding their breaths. Laura, never wishing to admit to faintheartedness, was the first to break the silence.

"What's that noise?"

Lucy clapped her hand over Laura's mouth. Outside, a voice said, "A haunted house, man, can you believe it? I'm sure I heard someone talking just then, didn't you?"

The light painted tiger stripes across Lucy's face as she stooped in front of the shutters, swept her eyes right and left along the veranda and said, in a high, quavering tremolo, "What are we going to do?" When the front stairs creaked under the weight of cautious footsteps, she shrank back into Olly's arms.

For the first time in history, Laura Olivia Huntington McTavish and Mordecai—Oliver Weber—Mead looked at each other without hostility. She raised her eyebrows, he nodded in understanding.

"Aaooo," sang Laura, softly.

"Eeaaa," answered Olly. Steenie added a hiss. The footsteps hesitated.

"Hey, Jimmy, you hear something?"

"Nah, cool it, you're giving me the creeps. Will you stop holding on to my shirt."

"I could've sworn I heard something. Must be the Sumatran hash. Really heavy stuff."

"Oooo," said Laura.

"OOOO," echoed Olly, forming himself into sinuous smoke, which threaded through a gap in the slats.

"What's that?"

"What?"

"That."

"Smoke."

"Smoke?"

There was a short silence. Jimmy cleared his throat. "Is anyone in there?" A shutter banged. "For crying out loud, man, will you let go my shirt. It's just the wind." After a significant pause the first voice pointed out that there wasn't any wind.

At these words, a breeze from nowhere began to rustle at things, making dry, sinister noises like the scrapings of insect wings. The air darkened. Purple clouds billowed out from Mount Misery, rolled across the jungle and settled on the world like a lid.

Lucy watched the two men through her peephole. They were clutching each other's shirts and trying to speak, but although their mouths formed words, no sound vibrated the air. A ball of Saint Elmo's fire swept down the veranda toward them, then whooshed off into the garden. They tore into the forest, where the wind cut a swath for them.

Moored by its vines, the house creaked and tossed in the gale like an old ship. Lucy waved her arms in the air and cheered as trees corkscrewed down into the ground, leaving a frenzy of leaves. A dimple, *zigzagging through the rain-lashed hills, showed the intruders' passage down to the sea. Black fruit bats followed the dimple like gnats.*

When the ghosts returned they could barely contain their jubilation.

"Impotent, eh?" yelled Olly, puffing out his chest and shaking his fist at the walls which bellowed in and out as if the rooms themselves were laughing. When Laura called for victory celebrations the shutters banged like clapping hands.

Lucy sat with her ancestors at the kitchen table opening one after another of the old bottles of beer Laura had kept in the cupboard for horse colic, proclaiming that it was the best bit of theater she'd ever seen and joining in with the most riotous laughter Binjigul homestead had ever heard, and which brought it to life in the most wonderful way, so that the limpid light from many candelabra shot prisms through crystal, and Sharada's Persian rugs radiated their original rich warmth, and the orchids cascading from silver vases were reflected in polished cedar surfaces. Oliver hiccuped and clapped Laura on the back.

"I must say, the disappearing trees were a stroke of genius."

"You didn't do too badly yourself, old boy," said Laura, horse teeth bared drunkenly at him. Lucy noticed that, while they had not actually imbibed any alcohol themselves, they had somehow absorbed her own inebriated state.

She listened to them indulging in mutual flattery and exhuming the stories of their youth. They were positively flirting with each other and taking no notice of her at all. They swallowed each other's reminiscences in great greedy gulps, as if they'd been starved, guffawed at each other's jokes, and once, Laura, her eyes streaming tears of laughter, dropped her head onto Olly's shoulder, where it disappeared inside his suit.

Lucy drifted into a reverie of her own. Shreds of things she remembered. Going into her parents' bedroom in the early morning and snuggling down between them. The itching dust smell and the crystalline call of magpies. She had come in because she was frightened of the geckos, scuttling upside down on the ceiling above her bed.

"Never mind the geckos," her father had said, "they only eat the spiders and the flies."

He had gone away to make a pile of toast with Vegemite, peanut paste and marmalade, because it was Sunday. He brought it in on a tray, with tea in an enamel pot. Then he stood at the window, gazing at the dry plain, brooding because the rains hadn't come. Her mother had sneaked up behind him and undone the string on his pajama trousers so that they fell to his ankles. That was what had brought the memories back, the rare sound of laughter, which had relieved her then, as it did now. She must have been very young.

In quick succession, different memories assailed her. The sounds of raised voices, sobs, seeping through the walls. "I'll kill you, you bloody woman." Her father coming to her bed in the middle of the night, telling her gruffly to go and sleep with her mother. Days in that furnace of a kitchen, watching her mother ironing, sweating, working, then stopping suddenly to stare blankly through the windows at the far distant hills.

Little things. The tink of cutlery at a silent meal. Her father's stock whip, the yapping of a dog, churning up dust in its rut. Her mother's veined hand, always busy, twitching nervously even as it held Lucy's. Patterns of broken lino on the kitchen floor, her mother on her knees, scrubbing, then placing her hand on the small of her back.

She remembered squealing with delight and fear as she rode on her father's shoulders. Seeing him kick a dog six feet in the air, while her mother pulled her away and told her not to be afraid. A Billy Graham meeting in a sports stadium. The prickly discomfort of a best dress, hair itching under a hat. Her mother beside her, standing up saying, "I want to be saved." A fight afterwards, in the car. Her mother laughing wildly, saying that God had appeared to her, would protect her. A packet of boiled lollies and being sick in the backseat.

Her grandmother grasping her with her crooked hooks, telling Lucy that her daddy didn't love her mummy and was cruel to her. How she hated that woman, with the pure hatred of a child who knows everything and knows nothing.

A musical box for Christmas, and her mother kissing her all over, breathing, "my only sunshine," between the kisses. The same woman, roaming through dingy, impoverished rooms, silent, as if submerged, picking up objects, staring at them, putting them down, weeping silently. Sometimes she did not see or hear Lucy, but looked straight through her. At other times, she sprang like a cat, and slapped.

Lucy felt a sharp pain in her chest which made her gasp. Olly and Laura were bending over her, staring intently into her face.

"She's remembering."

290

"She's pale as a ghost."

"Lucy? Darling?"

"Here child, don't be sad, I've brought you the musical box."

Olly pulled her up and together they waltzed solemnly around the kitchen and out into the large room.

"You'll never know, dear, how much I love you, please don't take my sunshine away." Now Laura was whirling her slowly around saying, "We have to remember everything, Lucy dear, otherwise . . ." The musical box turned out its melody, the ceiling went into spin and in the revolving roar of the cyclone Lucy could hear the faint strains of violins and french horns, kettle drums and spoons playing nursery rhymes then lullabies growing louder and wilder until they drowned the notes of the musical box. She twirled giddily, caught in a vortex of sound which resolved at last into the full passion of the final movement of Brahms's Violin Concerto in D Major, a cacophony loud enough to wake the dead.

As she spun she saw a blur of ghosts, hundreds it seemed, in period costumes, pushing and shoving, sitting on tables, floating cross-legged in the air, squabbling, giggling, some hugging each other, others attacking Laura or Olly for telling preposterous lies. Some argued about history, and Lucy caught snatches as she turned. "People against landscape. Men against women. British against Irish. Protestant against Catholic. Old immigrant against new. Lies and silences. Hidden wars. Refined cruelty of the British. She's as much responsible for our stories as we are for hers. Limbo, oblivion, loss." Sharada lowered her book long enough to say, "Jao, jao, hava khao," at her husband with the side-whiskers and bright blue eyes, who slunk backwards into shadow, just as a pockmarked man swigged sherry guiltily and shoved an ashtray into his pocket. A sweet-looking woman in a long calico dress and apron lifted her shoulders as if to say, "Strange isn't it," while the rest crowded around Lucy, prodding her like a zoo specimen, each claiming an ear, nose, or a laugh; a weakness, a strength, or a dream. And here and there in the maelstrom of faces, eyes blue as morning glories stared at her or a single black eyebrow alighted like a bat on various branches of the family tree.

Above this hullabaloo the wind rattled the roof, smashed the hippies' huts to smithereens and shot a blade of straw through a rustic sign in the middle of the town, where the residents prayed for salvation from the plastic bunting which strangled the Kentucky Fried

Chicken shop so tightly that it burst, and for protection against the sheets of corrugated iron flying through the streets like avenging angels, ready to decapitate anyone who got in the way. The ocean roared, dumping dolphins and a debris of aluminum boats a hundred yards into the forest, while the bats in the abandoned railway tunnel kept their secret safe against the bolt of lightning which blasted the peak of Mount Misery, and an almighty thunderclap silenced the clamorous confusion of the ghosts and heralded the entry into their midst of a wizened, naked, toothless Aboriginal woman, holding a glowing ember of wood.

The ghosts stepped back in consternation, forming a whispering wall around her. Words and phrases detached themselves from the wall—"got no business," "as the day she was born," "the ace of spades." The old woman paid them no attention but muttered something in her incomprehensible tongue, crowed with laughter, and smashed a chair with her flat, horny foot. Then she gathered up some old letters and, using the embers she carried with her, built a fire in the middle of the room, eased herself down beside it, groaning pleasurably, shuffling her friable old bones into a comfortable position, legs to one side. All eyes turned to Lucy's great great grandfather, Robert McTavish, who was leaning forward on the balls of his feet, mouth agape, arms flung back, his eyes staring wildly at the specter before him.

"I . . . I . . . she's . . ."

"Well spit it out, man," said Laura crossly, "what in the Lord's name is she doing here?"

"She was my son's wet nurse. She's saying she has a claim to Lucy through milk." A collective gasp of dismay went up from all the ghosts except Sharada. Laughter exploded from her like corellas from a river gum. She tossed her book into the air and as its pages came fluttering down, Lucy saw a white beach along which galloped men on horseback. She heard the thudding of hooves, a crackle of shots, black figures running toward the green wall of jungle, only to be wheeled around like herded beasts. They formed tangled groups, and fell, pumping bright blood over the sand. Horses whinnied and reared. Sprays of sand flew into the air around their lunging legs. One young girl with a baby was picked up by McTavish, picked up by the hair belt around her waist and flung across the front of the saddle. The baby fell to the ground.

The vision dimmed. As the old woman chanted to herself and painted her breasts with ocher, the ghosts dissolved, one by one, their outcries fading into silence. Laura and Olly were the last to go. They stood together at the french windows.

"We have to remember everything, Lucy dear, otherwise we are condemned to repeat . . ." Then they too were banished by the light of the fire. Lucy sat opposite the old woman, and gazed as though hypnotized, into the pale blue flames. The figure of another ghost, her back turned toward them, slowly formed out of the deeper shadows in the hallway. Her brown hair was plastered to her back. Water dripped from her body onto the floor at her feet. There was something fastened around her neck.

"Mother?" said Lucy, softly, but the only response was a spasm of shivering. Lucy took a fringed silk shawl from the back of a chair and gently, timidly, placed it around her mother's shoulders. Slowly, the head began to turn.

It was late afternoon. Outside the suffocated house, rain fell in thick slanting sheets, but the cyclone was now well out to sea, carrying the wreckage of the town with it. The wind had wrenched armfuls of foliage away from the wave of jungle poised above the house, leaving large tattered holes. In one of these holes stood a cascade of human hair supported by two legs clad in green trousers which ended in enormous feet. From the side of the hair poked two battish ears which were turned in the direction of the house like radar dishes. Two large eyes did not blink, but stared intently at the french windows. In his hands, he held a dish of Lilly-pilly and candlenuts.

The scream sent wet parrots flapping out of the mango tree, but the Yeti did not flinch. The noise went on and on because Lucy could not take her eyes away from her mother's face—blackened, green and swollen, one eye distended and a web of broken blood vessels covering it like a net and in all of Lucy's dreams she had never dreamed such a face. She remembered now the smell of burning scones, and the sight of her mother's body gleaming with sweat, playing her violin, unaware of the little girl peeing on the floor with fright because she knew that something big and terrible was happening. And when her mother did turn, she stared right through the child, and the child offered her a glass of water, because she could not think what else to do, and the mother had stared at the water, and at the child, then taken the water and thrown it in the child's face hissing,

"It's not enough, it's not enough."

Laughing crazily, she grabbed the child, pulling her arm almost out of its socket and raced with her down to the dam, until the taste of copper was in the child's mouth and she knew that whatever terrible thing was about to happen, it was her doing. The mother had shaken the little girl and told her to stand and watch. She ran to the flat boat that was tied to the jetty. She picked up a rock from the side of the dam and having put the rock in the boat and taken the rope from the jetty, pushed herself out to the middle of the dam and tied the rock around her neck with the rope, and all the child could say was "Please Mummy, don't Mummy," but her mother did not hear her or perhaps did not care because now she was staring at the rusty water, her neck weighed down with a stone. And then she jumped.

All the little girl saw was bubbles popping to the surface and all she felt was the sick feeling of warm mud between her toes, a split forming down the front of her body, and her hands going stiff. She stood in the mud until the water became still and closed, and then she turned and ran all the way back to the house because there was nowhere else to run, but she wanted to run forever, as far as she could from what she had caused, just as now Lucy ran and crashed through the undergrowth, oblivious to her falls and her shrieks and the taste of copper in her mouth until she tripped and lay semiconscious in the mud with the rain pelting down on her and no strength left to run. She was oblivious to whatever picked her up and ran with her, carrying her along the forgotten paths of Mount Misery until they reached a railway tunnel where he laid her down on a bed of jungle litter, wiped her dry with blankets, salted the leeches from her skin, lit the hurricane lamp and waited.

When she first regained consciousness, she was aware only of a dark, velvety enclosure, like curtains stirring. Later, when she woke again, she twisted her head clockwise on the bed. Fruit bats, furniture and pile upon pile of damp-rippled books. By the time her head reached the position of nine o'clock, she knew where she was and which ghost would be waiting for her.

27
Absolution

Wally Gajic considered himself a very fortunate man. His had not, perhaps, been an enviable life if it were to be seen only from the outside looking in—a parricide at the age of fourteen, and a prisoner of the jungle ever since. But as no one had looked in or, indeed, knew of his existence until now, there seemed little point in speculating on what an external perspective might reveal. Perhaps he was the answer to the old conundrum—"If a tree falls in a forest and no one is there to observe it, can it be said to have fallen?" Well, no one had observed Wally for nearly three decades. Lucy's reentry into his life might have proved that he existed, had she not spent the last few phases of the moon conversing with ghosts, thereby undermining her credibility as a reliable witness.

The year of suffering after the murder of his father had almost killed Wally. He had hidden in the deepest folds of Mount Misery, barely surviving, tormented by a ghost, and ill with the fear of being discovered by the outside world which would surely order his hanging. He was, he supposed, deranged during that time, but if so his madness had saved him. His mind had been far too scrambled for the idea of suicide to have crossed it successfully.

Yes, he was a supremely lucky man, even though he had never tasted French cuisine or been transported by car, bus, train or plane. He had not walked through the streets of a metropolis, except in his dreams, nor had his eyes ever searched beneath the surface of a living painting or his diaphanous ears heard Bach played in a cathedral. He had never fully made love to a member of his species, and in all the time he had been living in the jungle, he could count the conversations he had had with others of his kind on the fingers of one hand.

When that first difficult year ended, he was sane enough to suffer grief and loneliness. He felt he would go mad again if he could not hear a human voice. In the dead of night, he committed his second crime by stealing into Mrs. Rawlinson's shop and taking a radio and her entire supply of batteries. When the radio failed, he entered a long period of boredom and unhappiness. Years passed. The third crime. A newsstand opened in Binjigul. He relieved the shop of all its printed material. He read everything, cover to cover, yet when he had learned enough about the world to know it would take him back without punishing him, he began to fall in love with his own fate and to see his jungle prison as a monastery of leaves.

His only act of vandalism on the world around him, which remained oblivious to his existence, was to steal knowledge from it. He emptied libraries and bookshops from every town within a radius of fifty miles, believing that knowledge and poetry were now as important to his life as food. He learned to discriminate.

He studied the world for fifteen years, knew all the great philosophies and theologies from the Aborigines to the Greeks, from the Enlightenment thinkers to Foucault. He pored over Kant and Kierkegaard, Spinoza and Marx; knew whole passages from the classics off by heart; recited poetry to the moon like a wolf. He disinterred the buried voices of women and read between the lines. He studied physics and chemistry, languages and history. He grappled with the question of man's place in the universe and he followed the map of the history of ideas, taking many pleasant detours of his own along the way.

But more wonderful to him than all this knowledge was a skill he had developed during the time he spent alone in reverie. He had learned to catch the tail of his own thoughts, and to follow them until they dissolved into new thoughts, which themselves sprouted tails so that his itching curiosity was soothed only for the time it took to complete one oscillation of a butterfly's wing, before being enticed on. These meditations were a source of continual delight to him, moving as they did from question to answer to question, a puzzle solved only to reveal a deeper, more tantalizing enigma. He traveled the length, breadth and depth of sidereal space as easily as he entered the improbable world of the microscopic, and all without moving from his campfire. He could remain transfixed for hours by the shape of a single leaf—its form representing the divine mystery of order at work on chaos. And if one single leaf could saturate his mind with wonder, the multifarious forest offered such unlimited possibilities that he did not need to search beyond its boundaries for meaning. In short, he was at home within himself, his soul comfortably seated during its journey to becoming.

"Beautiful," said Lucy in a small voice. He watched her turning the sculpture around in the air with one hand and stroking the white possum absentmindedly with the other. She was so frail it was painful to look at her as she lowered the anguished likeness of herself, sunk her head down into her chest and began, again, to cry. "How lucky human beings are," thought Wally. The other broken forest creatures he mended could do no more than squeak in protest at their pain and fear. But tears were a gift of kindness to humankind, relief for the heart. He did not try to comfort her. That was not what she wanted.

The jungle cast its watery green twilight around them and spoke with a myriad chirrings, chatterings, rustlings, warblings. The abandoned railway tunnel opened its black mouth behind them, yawning through its beard of green. An orange fire fluttered between them like a tattered flag. And all around, in nooks and crannies, on tree stumps and in the lichenous crevices of rocks, sat hundreds of sculptures of Lucy; Lucy pulling a boy down from a flagpole; Lucy galloping along with the boy behind her; Lucy and the boy tangled together on a bed of jungle litter. Lucy the child, the girl, the woman, the crone. Lucy laughing, sleeping, flying—all of them staring in at the two figures sprawled beside the fire, one white and blue, like a fragment of fallen sky, the other brown and green, like a clod of living earth.

"Ghosts are invisible," said Wally, whittling away at silky wood, and raising his voice to be heard above the din, "because they live inside our heads. Try cleaning them out, though, that's when they kick up a fuss." Lucy lay on her stomach, her face cupped in her hands, watching the precise and fastidious movements of the possum as it rotated a fruit in its delicate hands and nibbled.

"White possums are supposed to be extinct."

"Take my old man, for instance. It took me a year to lay his ghost."

Lucy rolled over on her back and closed her eyes.

"I wonder if its brothers and sisters survived the cyclone."

"Up on the mountain that night, do you remember, I ran away from you because I thought his ghost would get you too."

The specter which had terrorized Wally was of the most malignant kind. It had tempted him to kill Lucy, so that no one would ever find out where he was hiding. But Wally had run away with the ghost chasing him, up to the very summit of Mount Misery. He had heard Lucy calling to him, out there in the night, and had shivered and sobbed, knowing that he must never see her again, because he was a murderer of everything he loved.

"I told myself at first that I hadn't meant to kill him. But his ghost made me see that wasn't true. I must've plunged the knife in five, six times. There were gashes all over him, and the knife sticking out of his heart. I don't know why it happened just then, and not at some other time. God knows, he'd bashed me just as badly before. But that time? I don't know. I had the knife in my hand, and it seemed the most natural thing to do.

"He haunted me for a year, always just behind my back, pointing the finger at me until I couldn't stand it any more. I took the hunting knife you gave me, planted it in the ground, and got myself all lined up so when I fell on it, it'd hit the vital spot. I could hear him laughing behind me. Then, I don't know why, I just turned round and stared at him, and pointed my finger back at him. He looked real sad all of a sudden. Just a sad old man with a knife sticking out of his chest. I felt sorry for him, but I didn't feel frightened any more. He left me in peace after that, never came back."

"I know, but I can't go back into that house."

"Not yet," thought Wally, and held the figurine away from him, turning his head on one side and then on the other, pursing his lips and frowning. He liked this one. In the haggard, wasted face he had created lay the suggestion of strength. He smiled to himself.

It had taken him some time to convince her he was alive, or rather that he believed himself to be alive, which, he admitted, was not the same thing. When she first spoke to him, he had to take the spoon away from her mouth, and lean close to catch her words. "Is this the meal of fellowship—*agape*? Are you my brother?" He smiled and nodded. He had spoon-fed her for days, then carved her two walking sticks so she could totter around on her own. He asked for nothing from her and looked after her as he would any damaged creature he happened to find.

"You knew I'd come back, didn't you? You've been waiting."

Wally took a while to answer. "Yes. But then, you knew I was here too. You called to me from the veranda that first night."

"Why didn't you come out?"

"Because it wasn't time."

Time, since that conversation, was notched only by the appearance of new statues, by the development of muscles over Lucy's bones, by the growth of calluses on her vine-swinging hands, and by the cyclical extinguishing of green twilight by damp dark. She relearned the habits of the jungle. She hunted, gathered and ingested it. Her pulse began to throb in time with its pulse. Her body regained its vigor, and if her mind lagged a little behind, hampered in its progress by sudden squawls, it was nevertheless heading away from the storm. Imperceptibly, the sculptures changed and she waited impatiently now to see each new one as it came to life in Wally's hands.

On the morning he stopped making them, nothing was said. He handed her a pair of trousers and a neatly folded shirt. She washed herself in the creek and dressed. They walked together to the edge of the forest, where it rose in a wave around the house. He touched her lightly on the shoulder, then seated himself behind a fringe of leaves.

She walked to the gate, gazed at the horizon, where a fat, red sun was about to disappear into darkness, then slowly crept up the stairs.

He waited in the gathering dusk, and on into the night, until Orion had completed his solemn circuit of the sky, until the butcher bird landed on the veranda rail and rinsed the world with its song, until the figure of Lucy emerged from the darkness of the house, paused at the gate, lifted her arm toward him in silent valediction, then turned and walked away.

He waited until the first sinews of smoke snaked through the shutters as the flames of a ceremonial fire crawled across photographs and furniture, curtains and letters, licking and cleaning with hot blue tongues the useless vestiges of something that had irrevocably ceased to exist. The smile on his face then might just as easily have been a trick of the sun dappling a wall of green, and the face itself an indistinct shadow glimpsed, half seen—an illusion of twilight and leaves.